TO KISS A KNIGHT

Wrapping her arms around his neck, Victoria stood on tiptoe and touched her lips to his cheek. Gareth let out a breath he had not realized he had been holding. She was teasing him, getting even for his rough treatment of her.

His arms came up and he gripped her waist convulsively. Victoria took his face in both her hands and pulled his head down. "Now, sweetie pie. I want you to pay attention. This is how a woman—a woman who does not belong to any man—kisses."

Her mouth found his. Her open mouth. She used her tongue to trace the line of his tightly closed lips. Her teeth nipped his bottom lip. His lips parted. Victoria immediately took full advantage of his small surrender.

Victoria felt his arousal. She ought to stop kissing him. Now. She had only meant to teach him not to use her to test his antiquated ideals of feminine virtue. But with her lips touching his, she was finding it difficult to keep thoughts of lessons and tests in her head. *Her* knight, the knight she had dreamed about was kissing her back. Slowly. Endlessly . . .

Books by Linda Kay

TO TAME A ROGUE

TO CHARM A KNIGHT

Published by Zebra Books

TO CHARM A
KNIGHT

Linda Kay

ZEBRA BOOKS
Kensington Publishing Corp.
http://www.zebrabooks.com

To Freddie and Marsha Anderson,
for being there

One

Victoria Desmond did not believe in premonitions of disaster. If she had, one glance at her boss would have had her crawling under the nearest desk. H. Walter Harrington IV was staring at the painting of Castle Avondel on the wall opposite his desk. He looked like a little boy staring at his first Christmas tree, all wide-eyed wonder and heart-pounding anticipation.

Rolling her eyes, Victoria took one step closer to H. Walter's desk. She knew what put that look on his face, and it wasn't twinkling lights and shiny ornaments. Nope. Walter got glassy-eyed over other things. Chain mail. Broadswords. Longbows. Tournaments. Knights. Castles.

H. Walter was a medieval junky.

Two years ago, his addiction had led him to purchase the ruined castle at whose image he was gazing. Walter had enthusiastically set out to restore the pile of rubble to its former thirteenth-century glory. He had failed, but not for lack of trying. He had hired the best engineers, the most competent contractors, the acknowledged experts in castle-building and restoration.

Castle Avondel resisted every effort made to repair it. Stones refused to sit on top of one another. Mortar crumbled into dust as soon as it dried—which wasn't very soon, since Avondel was shrouded in a perpetual

damp, gray mist. The mist might have explained why
equipment rusted, but the rust occurred overnight. And
the fog did not explain why workmen came down with
mysterious maladies, illnesses that disappeared as soon
as they were removed from the site. The list of catas-
trophes had gone on and on. The best that could be
said about the effort was that no one had died.

Eight months ago, Walter had called a halt to the
renovations. Victoria had hoped his obsession with
Castle Avondel was over, but from the way he was
fixated on the painting, she had a strong suspicion that
she had been wrong about that.

Stifling a groan, she advanced another step closer.

Victoria had been counting on a lengthy respite from
all things medieval. She needed it, and Walter should
be giving his addiction a rest. He had just had his annual fix. Once a year, he sponsored a Medieval Fair
for the citizens of Seattle, and this year's fair had ended
only yesterday. Based on past behavior, she expected
him to be more or less normal for twelve months, until
the next fair rolled around.

Of course, planning for the next fair would begin in
a few weeks, but Walter did not take an active interest
in the event until it was almost ready for the public.
Then he had an unfortunate habit of demanding last-
minute changes that cost time and money—his money,
other people's time.

Positioning herself between Walter and the painting,
she waited until his gaze focused on her. "You
buzzed?"

His blue eyes cleared, and Walter drew his eyebrows
together in the piercing scowl he believed terrorized
his employees. In conferences around the water cooler,
said employees agreed that the scowl was not unlike
a teddy bear's frown: cute, not scary. But they didn't
want to hurt H. Walter's feelings, so they all swallowed

their grins and faked quaking in their boots whenever he directed the scowl at them.

All except Victoria. She glowered back.

On this occasion, prudence dictated that she let Walter win the battle of the frowns. Victoria smoothed her brow and looked at him expectantly.

Walter nodded. "Yes. I did ring for you. I want you to cancel my appointments—"

"For today or tomorrow?" she asked, pen poised over her notepad.

"For the next three weeks. When are you going to allow me to finish—"

"A sentence without interrupting? When you learn to talk faster," Victoria drawled, letting words drift lazily from her mouth as if she had all the time in the world. "Wait a minute—did you say for the next *three weeks?* Are you nuts? Why?"

Shoving a hand through his stylishly cut blond hair, Walter breathed out a long-suffering sigh. "I pay you to—"

"Do your bidding." She bowed her head in mock deference. "Yes, oh lord and master. I know that's what you think, but what you really pay me for is to keep you in line."

"I am not a child, Victoria. I am a grown man, and if I want to step over the line—"

"You are a man with more money than two-thirds of the countries in the United Nations. That, plus your unfortunate tendency to behave as if you were an absolute monarch, means no one ever says no to you. Except me. For which service you pay me big bucks. To tell you no when you need to hear it."

Walter narrowed his eyes. "If I paid you less, would you say yes more often?"

"Oh, no, you don't. Try to cut my salary, and I'll

file a complaint with the EEOC. Now, what is this nut stuff about canceling your appointments?"

"I'm going to visit Castle Avondel."

"Boys and their toys," she muttered under her breath. Out loud she said, "Haven't you had enough of the Middle Ages? The fair ended only yesterday and you visited your castle a few months ago."

"Eight months ago. I'm going back."

"What for? Can't you accept that you made a bad bargain? That broken-down castle is never going to look like it did in the thirteenth century."

"Yes, it will. Curse or not, there is a way to restore Castle Avondel." Walter's blue eyes gleamed with fanatic fervor.

"There is no curse. The castle is old. Very, very old. Extre-e-e-emely old. Too old to fix."

Walter's mouth dropped open, then snapped shut. He scowled at her. "How can you say there is no curse? You're the one who found out about Aethelwyn's amulet."

"The amulet is a myth." Not for the first time, Victoria wished she hadn't come across the small, illuminated manuscript while surfing auction sites on the Net. She'd been looking for a Christmas present for Walter—it was never easy finding an appropriate and affordable gift for her billionaire boss—and a medieval tome that mentioned Castle Avondel had seemed perfect. "The monk who wrote the story of the fall of Avondel had a vivid imagination. He certainly was not an eyewitness; the book dates more than a hundred years after the castle was besieged."

"The amulet is not a myth. Some of the antiquities dealers I spoke with had heard of it. And that old crone we met at the Darkvale Inn knew all about it. She's the one who told us about the Saxon princess Aethelwyn and Sir Gareth, the Norman knight who—"

Victoria waved her pencil under his nose. "Walter. The story she told you is the plot of half the medieval romances ever written. The old woman told you what you wanted to hear."

"She told the truth." Walter gaped at her. "What do you know about medieval romances? I thought you hated all things medieval."

"Hate is too strong a word. I am indifferent to the Middle Ages."

"Then why are you reading medieval romances?"

"For sheer entertainment. I certainly am smart enough not to believe the fantasy. I mean, really. A conquering knight, a rough, tough Norman warrior, brought to his knees by love for a Saxon maid? A magic talisman that ensures 'happy ever after' will really last forever? Puhleeze. A fantasy is exactly what the old lady at the inn was telling you."

H. Walter stuck out his dimpled chin. "I know when people are lying to me. She told the truth."

Victoria shrugged. "So, she believed the story. That doesn't make it true. Face it. If the amulet ever did exist, which I doubt, it disintegrated into dust centuries ago. It hasn't turned up anywhere, even though you let it be known you would pay a fortune for it. Suppose you did get your hands on the amulet, what makes you think an old hunk of quartz would solve the problem of restoring Avondel? Why don't you give up on that ruin of a castle and spend your money on something useful?"

Walter shot a fulminating look her way. "I spend most of my money on useful things. Half the successful dot-com businesses from Seattle to the Silicon Valley got started with my venture capital. Plus, I give millions to charity. If I want to indulge my hobby with a few pennies here and there, I'm entitled."

"Pennies? Get real. I work up the budget for the

Medieval Fair you so generously sponsor every year. And I know exactly how many pennies that pile of rubble you call a castle has cost you."

"My pennies. I can spend them any way I want to." Walter clenched his square jaw. "We're going to Avondel. Cancel my appointments."

After working for the man for five years, Victoria knew H. Walter well enough to realize that he was not going to back down on this. The man had a stubborn streak that would do an Eastern potentate proud. "Oh, all right." She stalked toward the door, then turned back. "Wait one minute. Did you say 'we'? Why do I have to go? I should stay here and soothe all the people whose appointments I am going to cancel."

Shaking his head hard enough to ruffle his expensively styled blond locks, Walter said, "You're going because you are my personal assistant. This trip is personal. I need your assistance. And you are not soothing, not by a long shot. As a matter of fact, you are the prickliest broad I know. Mrs. Bradley can take care of telling people we will be out of pocket for a few weeks."

Victoria grumbled for a few more minutes, just so Walter wouldn't think he could get away with that 'broad' business unscathed. She would die before she let Walter know, but she did not absolutely hate the idea of a quick trip to England. She would never tell Walter that, any more than she would admit her own mild obsession with certain things medieval.

Walter would laugh his designer socks off if he knew that she, Victoria Elizabeth Desmond, thoroughly modern and rabidly independent, fantasized about being a helpless damsel locked away in a tower, waiting to be rescued by a handsome and noble knight.

In shining armor.

On a white horse.

The whole romantic scenario had filled her dreams for years, even before she came to work for Mr. Middle Ages himself. And not only her dreams. Lately, even in the daytime, wide awake, Victoria found herself fantasizing about a chivalrous knight rescuing her from her hectic life and taking her away to his remote and peaceful castle. She felt her cheeks grow warm. Talk about guilty pleasures . . .

But while Victoria enjoyed the fantasy, she was smart enough to recognize it for what it was. A dream. Not reality. Women who believed the fantasy was real were doomed to disappointment. There had never been men like King Arthur, or Galahad, or Lancelot, and there never would be. Romantic illusions, every one of them.

Victoria had learned at an early age that men were not to be depended upon, the day she had watched her father walk out the door never to return. The lesson had been reinforced by two—count them, two—failed romances, in both of which she had been the one dumped, not the one dumping. Victoria had thrown in the towel. No more real romance for her. Romance novels and the occasional erotic dream would do her just fine.

Victoria continued grousing with renewed vigor about having to make the trip. When she figured she'd complained long enough to make her point, she gave in. "Oh, all right. I'll make the reservations. What day do you want to fly?"

"I've already made our travel arrangements. We're leaving tomorrow morning."

"Tomorrow? You expect me to be ready to leave the country tomorrow morning? I have responsibilities, you know. People who need me. I can't just drop everything."

"Yes. You can. Tell Aunt Crystal to get a life."

"H. Walter! How can you be so unfeeling? She's my family." Victoria wouldn't let anyone else criticize her only living relative, especially someone who had no living relatives. "Aunt Crystal's divorce is barely final. I can't just up and leave her with no notice."

"Your mother died three years ago. Where was Crystal then, when you needed help? As I recall, you were the one who took care of your mother, with little or no help from your mother's sister. Crystal let you get along without her then. It's past time for you to return the favor. She can do without you."

"For three whole weeks?"

"For the rest of her life. After three divorces, Crystal should be a pro at getting over it and getting on with her life. Without your help. You do not have to take care of her."

Victoria tapped her pencil on her steno pad. "But I do have to take care of you."

"Exactly right. Blood may be thicker than water, but money trumps them both. I pay you to take care of me." He gave her a crafty look she had seen many times before. In her mind, Walter's primary flaw was that he thought everyone and everything could be bought. "I'll give you a bonus. To make up for any slight inconvenience."

"Fine. It had better be a big one. Are you sure you couldn't postpone the trip for a day or two?"

"Not a chance. Thistlewaite—the travel agent—was very clear on that point. Tomorrow morning or never." He glanced at the clock on his desk. "It's early yet. You can go home now and make whatever arrangements you need to make. Don't worry about packing for a three-week trip. We can buy anything you need once we're there." He reached for a Post-it Note and scribbled on it, then handed it to her. "Meet me at this address at seven o'clock."

She took the note without looking at it. "Seven? In the morning? You never travel before noon."

"This time I do. Thistlewaite, the agent, was most insistent."

"What kind of a name is Thistlewaite? And what kind of travel agency dictates the time of travel? Give me their number. I'll call them and postpone the—"

Walter shook his head. "No. No delays. We leave for Castle Avondel tomorrow."

"Walter—"

He held up a hand. "Not another word. We are going to Avondel tomorrow."

At six o'clock the next morning, Victoria climbed into a taxi and sleepily gave the driver the address Walter had scrawled on the Post-it Note. Between packing and listening to Crystal complain, she had gotten very little sleep. She couldn't blame her aunt for being upset—Crystal relied on her.

Victoria was never sure how she had become the one her mother and aunt depended on. She knew when: soon after her father had deserted her and her mother. Victoria had been nine. Her mother, helpless with grief and shock, had not been able to cope with being a single parent. Crystal, her mother's older sister, had tried to lend a hand on the few occasions when she wasn't looking for a man or getting rid of one, but most of the burden had fallen on Victoria.

Over the years, Victoria had gradually reversed roles with her mother, becoming the responsible adult while her mother remained a charming but helpless child. By the time Victoria reached eighteen, she had become the recognized matriarch of her small family.

Victoria knew it was past time for Crystal to take more responsibility for her life. She resolved annually to limit her assistance to the really important things, but she never managed to keep her resolution. Walter pointed out her failure every time he caught her doing something he considered trivial for her aunt. And she had promised herself to stop handling every little problem for Crystal, starting very soon.

But not this soon.

Crystal needed her right now; she always turned to Victoria when she was between husbands. After each divorce, Victoria had encouraged her aunt to learn to take care of herself. Crystal never listened. She claimed she needed a man to take care of her. Crystal really believed there were knights in shining armor, ready, able, and willing to solve all her problems. She just had to find the right one. Crystal had the old-fashioned idea that a woman needed a man, a man able to care for her in every way, but especially in a financial way. Her aunt called herself a practical romantic. Her motto was, "It's as easy to love a rich man . . ."

This time it might be different. After four failed marriages, and four generous divorce settlements, Crystal might be more receptive to the idea of becoming self-sufficient. If she had a few more weeks, Victoria was positive she could wean her aunt away from her dependence on the male of the species. But she couldn't do it long-distance.

To add insult to injury, Crystal hadn't even objected to the trip all that much. Once she was sure Victoria had scheduled her appointments with her therapist and her divorce lawyer, her aunt had wished her a pleasant trip. A very pleasant trip. With a sly wink, and a nudge of the elbow, Crystal made it clear a trip to England with Walter could be the chance they had been waiting for. She had the silly idea that H. Walter and Victoria made the perfect couple, and that all Victoria had to do to set them both up for life was to marry him.

Victoria had tried telling her aunt that a romance between her and Hiram Walter Harrington IV was about as likely as winning the lottery, but Crystal still had hopes. High hopes. She could not believe that any woman would be immune to Walter's charm, his blue-eyed blond good looks, the cute dimple in his chin, or the staggering balance in his bank account.

As for Walter, he could not do better than Victoria, Crystal loyally insisted. Oh, he might find someone more beautiful, but looks weren't everything. Tact made Crystal add that of course there was nothing *wrong* with the way Victoria looked, but she might consider going blond, or at the very least, adding some red highlights. Brown hair was so . . . ordinary. And hazel eyes were so . . . unpredictable. Sometimes green, sometimes light brown, on occasion cat-eye gold. Still, according to Crystal, she was pretty enough. Looks aside, Walter would never find anyone smarter, more loyal, or more dependable. No doubt about it, Victoria would make Walter a perfect wife.

Not in this lifetime, thought Victoria. She could see Walter's attractive qualities, but there was not the slightest spark of attraction between them. Never had been, not even when they first met. Never would be, now that they had been together for five years. Each was much too aware of the other's faults. Walter thought she was too prickly and too picky.

She knew he was too rich ever to trust a woman, even the woman he would eventually marry. Unless Walter happened to meet someone who had more than fifty billion dollars in her Gucci purse, he would never believe any female could love him for himself and not his bank account.

The cab pulled up in front of a storefront in Pioneer Square. The sign over the door read, ANY TIME, ANY PLACE. Trust Walter to find a travel agent they had never used before. Victoria got out of the cab and looked up and down the street. No limousine or airport bus was in sight. How were they going to get to the airport? She almost asked the cabbie to wait, but thought better of it. H. Walter might think he could make travel plans all by himself, but it would be just like him to overlook transportation to SeaTac. Her boss was not what anyone would call a detail man.

Handing over the fare and a generous tip, Victoria got out of the cab. The driver deposited her one piece of luggage on the sidewalk and drove away. Victoria extended the handle and rolled her suitcase to the door of the shop.

It really would be too bad if they missed their flight. The trip might have to be postponed for a day or two, long enough for her to coax Crystal into at least thinking about going it alone for awhile. And Walter would think twice before attempting to make his own travel plans again. That thought had her grinning as she walked in the door of the shop.

Her grin faded the instant she got a look at her boss. H. Walter was dressed in the costume he had worn at the Medieval Fair: a dark-blue tunic lavishly embroidered with silver thread, and silver-gray tights. Walter came forward and took the suitcase from her hand. "Right on time. Didn't I tell you, Tobias? Victoria is always punctual."

Victoria tore her gaze away from Walter long enough to look at the man behind the counter, a middle-aged man with a cherubic face and a ginger mustache. He was dressed in a hooded cloak covered with stars and moons, a medieval costume that did not match his Victorian whiskers. She recognized that cloak. She had seen Walter talking to a man wearing it, or one just like it, at the fair. A wizard's cloak, she had thought at the time, and quite a good replica at that.

The man shoved the hood off his head and beamed at her. "Being on time is a virtue. Time lost is never found."

"Right." Victoria let her gaze slide around the shop. It looked like a travel agency. Colorful brochures were arranged on the counter, which also held a computer and a telephone. Posters hung from the walls. But something was not right. The tiny hairs on the back of her neck were standing at attention.

Warily, Victoria eyed her boss. "What are you dressed for? Won't the other passengers find your costume odd?"

"There are no other passengers. Only you and I."

"You chartered a flight?" She should have anticipated that. Without her to watch his bottom line, Walter always spent money like water.

He tugged on his collar. "You might say that."

"The crew—"

"There is no crew. Only Tobias here. He's the man who will take us to Avondel."

The man smiled and bowed. "How do you do? Tobias Thistlewaite, at your service. My time is your time."

"Hello. Are you the travel agent?" When the funny little man nodded, she said, "How are we getting to the airport? I didn't see a limo or a bus."

"No need. Merlin's stone will take us to our destination." Tobias waved his hand at a hunk of granite in the corner of the shop.

Sure she had missed something important, Victoria directed her next question to Walter. "Is there a helicopter pad on the roof?"

"No." Walter took her by the arm. "You had better change. Your clothes are in the top chest." He pointed to a stack of carved wooden chests piled in the corner underneath a poster of the Acropolis.

A brand-new Acropolis, she noted as she got closer. Too bewildered to dwell on that oddity, Victoria knelt down and opened the chest. It was filled with garments she recognized—costumes she had worn during the past few Medieval Fairs. She looked over her shoulder. "What is going on? Why do we have to dress in costume?"

"So we will blend in, of course," said Walter, not quite meeting her gaze.

"Oh. Of course. Have you been experimenting with drugs?"

"No." He looked right at her and grinned his most charmingly boyish grin. "With something much more exciting. Time travel."

Victoria's eyebrows shot up. Walter might spend his money foolishly at times, but he was too smart to be taken in by such an obvious scam. "Ah. Time travel. I should have known." She looked at the posters again. All of the ancient monuments pictured in the posters appeared bright-shiny-new, including one of a medieval castle.

Walter would not have fallen for fake photographs, would he? Fingering a yellow silk tunic, Victoria looked over her shoulder at Walter. "How much did Tobias here charge for this trip?"

"Not much, considering. Only a million."

Dropping the tunic, Victoria stood up and turned to face him. "One million *dollars?*"

"Two million in all. One million apiece."

"Y-you gave this c-con man two m-million dollars?" Disbelief had her stuttering.

"That's round-trip, you understand. A bargain when you think about it. And Tobias is not a con man. He's a wizard."

"Oh. A wizard." She glanced at the travel agent, who winked at her. "That makes all the difference, doesn't it? But Walter, if it's all right with you I would just as soon stay here. And now."

"Victoria, I am shocked. It never occurred to me that you wouldn't jump at this chance. Where is your sense of adventure?"

"The same place as my sense that this is a scam."

"It is not a scam, Victoria. But if you really don't want to go—"

"I *really* don't want to go. And neither do you. Get your money back, Walter. Before it's too late."

"No refunds," said Tobias. "Too late, anyway. Time to go."

A sudden lurch threw Victoria against H. Walter's chest. "What was that? Earthquake?"

"No. We're on our way." The so-called wizard seemed very sure of that.

Walter hugged her close. "Hold on to your hat, Victoria."

"I'm not wearing a hat." Another lurch. "What is going on?"

"We're going to Castle Avondel. In the year twelve seventy-four."

"Perhaps you should sit down, Miss Desmond," said the travel agent. "The journey may be a trifle rough from time to time. Clear-air turbulence, you know."

Walter held out a chair and Victoria sat down at the Sheraton table in front of the window. She glanced out the window, expecting to see Pioneer Square. She saw nothing but black. Turning her gaze away from the window, she looked at Walter. He was holding on to the back of another chair, grinning broadly. "Isn't this great?"

"No. I think I'm going to be sick."

"Nonsense." Walter leaned across the table and patted her on the shoulder. "You're never sick. You'll be fine."

"H. Walter, you distinctly said time travel. I want an explanation. Now." She slapped her hands on the table.

Tobias answered. "It is a simple concept, Miss Desmond. Instead of traveling from here to there, we're going from now to then. Look." The wizard swept his arm in an arc.

Victoria's eyes widened in shock as she realized the shop was disintegrating around her. At least, the computer had disappeared, the clock on the wall had faded away, and the Sheraton table was melting beneath her palms. "We're going to die," she croaked.

"No, no. Absolutely not." Walter reached across the rough-hewn wooden table that replaced the Sheraton and took one of her hands in both of his. "Tobias assures me that time travel is perfectly safe."

"Walter?" She whimpered his name. Victoria bit her tongue. She never whimpered. Only weaklings whimpered. But she felt weak. Weak and helpless.

And, costume or not, the man seated across from her was no knight in shining armor. She could not count on Walter to save her. He was the man who had gotten her into this . . . whatever was happening.

"I know it's fantastic, but time travel is simple once you know how it's done." Walter paused for dramatic effect. "Magic."

"M-magic?"

"Exactly. Magic. Tobias explained the whole thing to me. Once upon a time magic was much more common than it is today. It turns out that the practice of magic increases or declines in direct relationship to the number of people who believe in it. Naturally, there isn't much magic around today since in the twenty-first century the vast majority of people over the age of seven don't believe in magic at all."

"Present company excepted," Victoria muttered, convinced that her boss had lost his mind.

Walter ignored her and continued with his explanation. "When we get back to the thirteenth century, there will be lots of magic, since most people then believed in it. Aethelwyn's amulet is a good example: the lords of Avondel believed a magic talisman protected the castle and its inhabitants, so it did."

"Magic. H. Walter? Have you gone stark-raving mad?"

"I never felt saner in my life. Let me finish. Tobias was born in the nineteenth century, in the same year as Queen Victoria. He inherited Merlin's stone from his parents, but didn't divine the use of it for several years. Once he mastered the secret of the stone, he used it as the cornerstone of his travel agency, and here we are."

Tobias cleared his throat. "I'm not a very good wizard, you see. It took me almost fifty years to discover how to use Merlin's stone. The nineteenth century was the Age of Reason, if you will recall. People were more enamored of science than magic. It had a debilitating effect on the practice of wizardry."

Victoria looked from Tobias to Walter and back. They were both serious about this magic business. "How did you two find each other?"

"I read about Mr. Harrington in the *Wall Street Journal*. The article mentioned his affinity for the Middle Ages and included an estimate of his net worth. He seemed a perfect candidate for time travel. Not many can afford my fees, you see."

"At a million a pop, I can understand that. H. Walter—"

"Tobias here caught up with me on the last day of

the fair. He told me about his time travel agency, and I booked a trip to Castle Avondel in the year twelve seventy-four—before the siege. We will arrive in time to save the castle from the marauding Scots."

"How? Did you pack an Uzi or two?"

Shaking his head impatiently, Walter said, "We have no need for advanced weaponry. All we have to do is make sure nothing happens to Aethelwyn's amulet."

"The amulet?"

"Of course. The amulet protected the castle and the curtilage. I told Tobias here the monk's story, and he agrees with me that the amulet was a magic talisman that kept the castle and its inhabitants invincible. Once it was gone, of course the castle fell. It follows logically that if the amulet stays put, the siege will fail."

"Logic? Walter. Time travel isn't logical. Magic isn't logical. How can you rely on logic to save Castle Avondel? I'm telling you, we need assault weapons." Her voice squeaked alarmingly.

"I have my sword."

She managed a feeble glower. "Oh. That makes me feel ever so much better."

"Good."

"I was being sarcastic."

"I know."

"I'm scared, Walter."

"I know." Walter squeezed her hand. "Don't worry, Victoria. Everything's going to be all right."

Two

The castle, lands, and forest of Avondel were cursed.

Thomas, sixteen years old and squire to Gareth of Avondel, kicked his horse and urged it forward through the brambles and undergrowth, following his lord deeper into the forest. The packhorse, tethered to his saddle by a long rope, trailed behind. Thomas would not have followed anyone but his liege lord to a bewitched castle. Gareth had taken him under his protection when he had been a scrawny youth of twelve, orphaned and alone in a foreign land. Thomas would follow Lord Gareth of Avondel anywhere, even into the depths of hell.

Which might be exactly where their journey would take them.

Everyone they had met on the way to Gareth's childhood home had reminded them of the curse on Avondel, some in loud, angry voices, others in horrified whispers. The closer they got to the ruined and deserted castle, the more Thomas believed in the grisly stories they had been told. The forest surrounding Lord Gareth's castle was dark and forbidding.

And silent.

Unnaturally so. There should have been birds singing, deer munching on the underbrush, hunters seeking game, but nothing dwelled in the forest of Avondel: not bird, or beast, or man. The abbess of Northumber, a holy woman and worthy of belief, had told them about the silent forest and the barren fields beyond. She told Gareth that no bird or beast, wild or tame, lived in the forest, that only noxious weeds grew in the once productive fields. The abbess said the cottages of the villeins and freemen were vacant and in disrepair. She had done her best to dissuade Gareth from returning to Avondel. Revenge was better left to God, she said.

Gareth had thanked the abbess for her hospitality and asked for her prayers. But he had not heeded her advice. They continued on their way.

Gareth intended to end the curse.

Thomas was not completely convinced that a knight, even a knight as bold and brave as Gareth, could triumph over a curse. But he understood why Gareth must try. The castle, fields, and forest of Avondel were his heritage, stolen from him years ago. Gareth meant to reclaim his estate and to avenge its loss. Lord Ranulf would finally pay for murdering the lord and lady of Avondel.

If Ranulf of Darkvale were the only one Gareth had to face, Thomas would have no doubts about who would be victorious. He had been by Gareth's side in many battles, and he had never seen him lose a fight against mortal men.

But whatever or whoever had cursed Avondel was not mortal. Only wizards and sorcerers wielded the kind of black magic that had doomed Avondel. And a very powerful wizard or sorcerer would have been needed to overcome the magic of the amulet.

The path widened enough for Thomas to come alongside Gareth. "Tell me again about Aethelwyn's amulet."

Gareth raised a quizzical eyebrow but complied. "Aethelwyn was a Saxon lady. Her father called himself a king, but his subjects were too few and too unskilled in the ways of war to save the kingdom of Avondel. They were defeated in battle by Gareth of Normandy."

"Your ancestor," said Thomas. "The one you were named after."

"Aye."

"He besieged the Saxon castle—"

"There was no castle then, and no curtain wall or moat. Only a wooden tower for a keep, protected by ditches and earthen ramparts faced with timbers. The first Gareth built the castle at Avondel after he defeated the Saxon lord."

"And after he married the Lady Aethelwyn, daughter of the Saxon king," said Thomas.

"Aye." Gareth reached over and ruffled Thomas's hair. "You know the story better than I do."

"I like to hear you tell it. It makes the time pass." And Gareth's voice, rich and deep, conquered the eerie silence. Thomas stirred uneasily at the sudden quiet and prodded Gareth to continue the tale. "What happened between Aethelwyn and Gareth?"

"She refused his suit at first, even though her father gave his consent. Aethelwyn said, with logic on her side, consent gained by force was no consent at all. But she was only a maid, and she could not hold out against Avondel's conqueror for long. Gareth meant to marry her, no matter how she felt about it."

Thomas nodded. "He had to marry her, to secure his claim to her father's lands."

"Either marry her, or kill her and her father. When she refused him for the second time, Gareth the First drew his dagger and threatened to cut her throat. Aethelwyn bared her neck, swearing she would curse him and his through the ages if he dared to murder her. She refused him once again, vowing to marry only a man she loved, who loved her in return. Princess Aethelwyn's courage and her passion captivated him, and he sheathed his knife."

"The fair maiden bested the warrior."

"His own desires defeated him. The Norman knight was weary of killing. He longed for a peaceful life surrounded by a loving family and loyal knights and villeins. Being clever as well as strong, the first Gareth set about to get what he wanted without shedding any more blood. When his threats failed to intimidate Aethelwyn, Gareth changed tactics. He used soft words and tender caresses to win her over. Women prefer gentle wooing, Thomas. Remember that."

Thomas nodded. "But Aethelwyn won his heart as well." Gareth often left out that part of the story. Thomas thought it was because Gareth was embarrassed that his Norman ancestor had been conquered by love.

"So the story goes. The Saxon lady charmed the Norman knight even as he seduced her. Gareth fell deeply in love with Aethelwyn. Only when she was sure of his love did Aethelwyn agree to marry him. By all accounts it was a happy union, blessed with five children."

"Three boys and two girls," said Thomas, who did know the story by heart.

"Aye. Gareth gave his wife the amulet on the occasion of the birth of their first son. In return, Aethelwyn infused the stone with magic—magic which she vowed would protect Avondel and its people for as long as the amulet remained in the castle. And so it did, until Aethelwyn's gift disappeared. Then a neighbor became an enemy and attacked Avondel. The castle fell and the curse began."

Thomas blinked moisture from his eyes. The romantic story never failed to touch his heart. Brave knight, beautiful maiden, magic amulet. The tale had everything, including an evil villain and an unsolved mystery. He sighed loudly. "I vow, the story is sadder each time I hear it."

"The story is not finished. Not yet. Not until Ranulf of Darkvale pays for his crime. And he will pay. I swear it."

With that vow, Gareth urged his mount forward along the narrow, overgrown path through the forest, eager to end his journey. Castle Avondel should be visible soon. The forest had not grown so close to the castle in his youth, but he had not seen his childhood home in more than ten years. Gareth had left Avondel when he was eight years old, to be educated and trained as a knight by Baron Edmond, his father's liege lord. He had been Thomas's age when he last visited Avondel.

Gareth had not been present two years later when Ranulf had besieged the castle, murdered his parents, and kidnapped his sister. He had not learned of the fall of Avondel until several months after the siege. When his old nurse had found him at Baron Edmund's keep and told the story of the conquest, Gareth had sought redress with a young man's passionate belief in justice. He had petitioned King Henry for permission to challenge Ranulf for his crimes, and for Castle Avondel to be restored to him and his sister.

King Henry had summarily denied his petition.

Lord Ranulf of Darkvale was a supporter and friend of the king, as well as a seasoned knight. In an age when might equated with right, that made Ranulf a force to be reckoned with. Gareth had not understood that when he was eighteen. Rashly, he had taken matters into his own hands, meeting Ranulf at the king's tournament. He had been defeated soundly by the older, more experienced knight, and, for defying his king, Gareth had been banished from the kingdom by King Henry. At Ranulf's insistence, the king had forbidden Gareth a last visit Avondel before being exiled.

Gareth had learned two important lessons from the fall of Avondel and his reckless attempt to punish Ranulf: one, a wise man sought the favor of his king; and two, a successful man planned before he acted.

Knowing he had no hope of regaining Henry's favor, Gareth had cast about for another way to end his exile. It had not taken him long to find it. Henry had a son, a son who would be king someday. With a calculating eye on the future, Gareth had set out to befriend the future king, and he had succeeded. He had offered his sword to Prince Edward when the heir arrived in France to join Louis IX on a crusade to the Holy Land. He had fought by Edward's side in Egypt and Syria.

When Prince Edward became king, Gareth had been rewarded for his loyal service. King Edward I had restored his birthright to him.

A ruined and deserted castle.

As important to Gareth as the fief of Avondel was the king's unspoken permission to seek revenge against Ranulf. King Edward preferred that his lords settle their differences peacefully and save their swords for enemies of the crown, but he understood Gareth's need for revenge. Gareth knew full well that "unspoken" meant if he failed, the king could and would deny any knowledge and all responsibility for Gareth's acts.

He did not intend to fail.

Gareth broke through the final barrier of undergrowth onto the plain, racing ahead of his squire. There. The gray stone walls of Castle Avondel were visible rising out of the mist on the river that curved in front of it, forming a natural moat.

His heart swelled, whether from pride or sorrow he could not tell. There was still much he did not understand about the fall of Avondel and the curse that had settled on the castle built by his ancestors.

Vague memories from his childhood disturbed him, making him question the story of Avondel's magical shield. Gareth sometimes dreamed dreams that left him with the impression that sorrow had come to Avondel before the loss of the amulet. He brushed aside his discontent. Confusing memories and strange dreams were not enough to alter his plan for revenge.

Thomas caught up with him and halted his steed and the packhorse he was leading. "God's teeth. The castle looks undamaged."

Gareth stood in his stirrups and peered into the fog. "The damage must be hidden by the mist. I was told by my old nurse that the square tower was undermined. A wall collapsed, and Ranulf and his knights gained entry and overwhelmed the garrison."

"Why did Ranulf attack? Is it not true that he had been a friend to Lord William?"

"Aye. Ranulf had been neighbor and friend to my father for many years." Gareth shook his head. "I do not know what caused Ranulf to change. Greed, perhaps. Or jealousy. In those days, Darkvale was not so prosperous a place as Avondel."

They reached the broken tower. Bringing his horse to a standstill, Gareth said, "When I rebuild, this tower will be round like the others, with no blind spots to give shelter to attackers." He urged his destrier forward across the drawbridge and into the bailey.

Thomas followed. The clip-clop of the horses' hooves was the only sound reverberating through the gloom. When the horses were halted, the quiet settled around them like a blanket of sorrow. Gareth and Thomas dismounted. Thomas saw to the horses while

Gareth forced open the double doors that led through a wide hallway to the castle's great hall.

Gareth entered, stopping at the entrance to the hall. The long tables still stood, but the wooden benches were overturned, some whole, others little more than splinters. The twin chairs in which his father and mother had sat at the head table were missing altogether. Tattered banners hung limply from the cold stone walls, banners that Gareth remembered fluttering gaily in the soft breezes that had caressed Avondel in his youth. The rushes and sweet herbs that had covered the floor had long since turned to dust.

As had all who had fallen there.

Nothing remained but silence and shadow.

Gareth walked into the room, his footsteps making the first sound heard in the castle for ten long years. Castle Avondel had stood empty since the day his parents died.

Thomas followed him into the hall. His eyes grew wide at the sight of the decaying relics of a time long past. "Ranulf has much to answer for," he whispered. "Think of the ghosts that lurk in the dark corners of the hall. The lord of Darkvale is responsible for them all."

Gareth nodded, his face grim. "The defeat of Castle Avondel brought him no joy. This castle was once a happy place, Thomas, and the surrounding valley was prosperous, with fields yielding bountiful harvests. Herds of plump sheep grazed in the meadows, and the cottages of the villeins were filled with laughter. With the loss of the amulet, all that changed. But I have vowed that Avondel will be as it was before the siege."

"Once Lord Gareth and Lady Elwyna reside within these walls, all will be well," said Thomas.

"More than our presence is needed. We will not end the curse until the amulet is restored to its rightful place. 'Twas magic that guarded Avondel and made its people invincible and its lands prosperous."

"The talisman has been missing for ten years and more. How will you find Aethelwyn's charm?" asked Thomas.

"We will seek out all who were present during the siege and question them closely. Someone will know what happened to Aethelwyn's amulet."

"Perhaps Ranulf stole it."

"Nay. Ranulf took advantage of the theft, but if he had possessed the amulet his victory would have been rewarded," said Gareth.

"No wealth, either. If he besieged the castle so that he could claim the rents and services of Avondel's villeins, he failed. Mayhap Ranulf did steal the amulet to ensure his victory, not knowing that the magic only works for the lord of Avondel."

"Ranulf could have claimed that title if he had married my sister." Elwyna. Gareth felt the familiar mix of emotions her memory always evoked: guilt, sorrow, anger. Guilt because he had not been present to save her, sorrow for all she must have suffered during the years they had been apart, and anger at the lord who kept her hostage. "King Henry made her Ranulf's ward, but she is not his wife."

Gareth had learned that much from the abbess of Northumber Abbey. The abbess was an infrequent visitor at Darkvale, but she had seen Elwyna there at Christmas. His sister had served as handmaiden to the abbess. She also supervised the kitchens at Darkvale, and saw to the comfort of its lord and his guests. "A servant. Ranulf has made Elwyna his servant."

"He could have killed her," Thomas pointed out.

"Aye."

"Why did he spare her, do you think?" Thomas asked.

"She was only a child of eleven when the siege took place. He may have intended to marry her to secure his claim to Avondel. But when the villeins fled and the lands became barren, he lost interest in Avondel and, it appears, in Elwyna."

"The abbess said Ranulf has never married. Why not, do you suppose?" asked Thomas.

"Mayhap he has not met an heiress with dowry rich enough for him."

"Mayhap he has never found a woman to love," sighed his squire.

Gareth's eyebrow went up. Thomas was at an age when he saw romantic possibilities everywhere—even, it seemed, in the black heart of the lord of Darkvale. "Ranulf is not waiting for love, but for wealth and power. See how Elwyna lost her ability to charm him as soon as Avondel lost its magic protection."

"When will you challenge Ranulf?"

"In my own time. First we must find the amulet and rescue Elwyna."

His squire shot him a doubtful look. "How do you plan to accomplish that? There are only two of us."

"We must use cunning. For my plan to succeed, we must travel incognito and in disguise."

Gareth had thought long and hard about how to rescue Elwyna and destroy Ranulf. He knew he could not hope to storm the castle at Darkvale with only Thomas at his side. Darkvale was heavily fortified and manned by a garrison of experienced knights. Even if he had a force capable of taking the castle, Gareth dared not mount an overt attack, not as long as his sister was a prisoner within the walls of Ranulf's keep.

Subterfuge was the only way. He would gain entry to Darkvale in disguise and seek out those who might have knowledge of the amulet. Once the talisman was in his possession, he would enter the castle at Darkvale and snatch Elwyna from under Ranulf's nose. When his sister was safe, he would challenge Ranulf. This time he would win. Might *and* right were on his side.

Gareth intended to play the part of a poor and unsuccessful knight, late returned from battle against the Saracens. The way he might have returned had he not saved Prince Edward from an assassin's attempt and won his undying gratitude and friendship. His presence at Darkvale would not be questioned once he entered the tourney sponsored each year by Ranulf.

"We will rest here for the night, and start for Darkvale tomorrow morning. The spring festival will be in progress. Our arrival, among all those arriving for the fair and tournament, will not be noticed. I will enter at least one joust, and win. It is Ranulf's practice to invite the victors to dine with him at his castle."

"And once you are inside the castle you will find your sister and rescue her."

"No. I cannot take Elwyna away until I have the amulet. If Elwyna disappears from his keep, Ranulf will know that I am responsible. He will search for us throughout his fiefdom. We would have no chance at finding the amulet with Ranulf's men nipping at our heels."

"Will you speak to your sister? Tell her who you are?"

"If I can do so without arousing Ranulf's suspicions. Or hers. It is possible that Elwyna has given her loyalty to Ranulf. She might betray me in that case."

"He killed her mother and father. She cannot have given her allegiance to Ranulf."

"She was only a child. She may not understand what happened during the siege. I do not know what she may have had to do to survive these ten years. I will not seek her out. Not this time. This time I want only to see Ranulf."

"You will need another name to complete your disguise. What shall I call you?"

Gareth thought for a moment. "Perceval. I shall be Sir Perceval."

"Perceval? King Arthur's perfectly pure and innocent knight?" Thomas snickered.

The corners of Gareth's lips curved slightly. "Who better to rescue a fair maiden and seek a magic talisman? But this Perceval shall not be pure or innocent. He will be rough, unchivalrous, and . . . dirty."

"Dirty?" Thomas winced. "I hate dirt."

Gareth grinned at him. His squire was fastidious to a fault, bathing at every opportunity. As did he, preferring cleanliness to filth. "It is the perfect disguise. I will dress in worn and dirty clothes. Unbathed and unshaven. I would have people turn from me in disgust."

"All people? Even women?" His squire's mouth fell open in surprise. Thomas often boasted that Gareth, with his sea green eyes and night black hair, drew women to him like clover drew honeybees.

"Especially women. This is not the time for dalliance." Warming to his subject, Gareth continued planning his disguise. "Gareth is known for the keen edge on his sword and the shine on his armor. Sir Perceval's sword will be stained, and his armor will be rusted and dented."

"Dented?" Thomas looked as if he could not believe what he was hearing. *"Rusted?"*

"Rusted. We will leave it out tonight; the mist will take care of that part of my disguise. Come, let us begin." Gareth left the great hall and strode purposefully toward the stack of baggage Thomas had taken from the packhorse. He reached for one of the bundles and opened it. "Get my hauberk. Scar and dent it as much as you like. I will start with this." Gareth took his newest tunic from the sack and let it fall onto the ground. He walked on it.

"Not the black velvet," moaned Thomas.

Gareth eyed his squire, and continued grinding dirt into the tunic. " 'Tis a small sacrifice. Get on with the armor."

Thomas gave the suit of chain mail a whack with Gareth's broadsword. "This may not be necessary. Ranulf has not seen you since you were my age. He would not recognize you now that you are a man."

"I cannot risk it. The abbess said some of the freemen and villeins from Avondel settled in Darkvale. The miller and the blacksmith also gave their services to Ranulf after the fall of Avondel. They might recognize me. I am sure the blacksmith would. I spent hours at his forge when I visited Avondel, learning about swords and armor. And Ranulf has spies everywhere, even at court. He knows I vowed to avenge my family. And by now he knows that Gareth of Avondel has returned to England. He may even know that King Edward has restored my estates to me."

"Ranulf will be waiting for you."

"Yes. All the more reason to keep him guessing about when and where I will appear. This disguise will allow me to decide when to reveal my return. Ranulf will not suspect that I am the rough and ragged Sir Perceval, nor will the men and women of Avondel, those who followed him to Darkvale."

"Changing your appearance and name may hide your true identity, but questioning people about the amulet will surely raise suspicions."

Pausing in his destruction of his wardrobe, Gareth smiled grimly. "You have hit upon the weakness in my plan. Too much interest in the amulet may very well bring us to Ranulf's attention before I am ready to make myself known."

"Then how . . . ?"

"We will have to be careful, pretend only to have a stranger's mild curiosity about a local legend. We will use our ears more than our mouths."

Thomas nodded, and gave the armor another whack. "There will be troubadours at the fair. They are always eager to tell a tale."

"Any minstrel performing at Darkvale will make Ranulf the hero of the affair. We cannot rely on songs and legends. No, we must find those who have first-hand knowledge of the siege."

"Some of them may still be loyal to your father's memory. You could reveal yourself to them and learn more, mayhap."

"We will not have much time to test their loyalty. The fair lasts only a week, and after it ends we will have no excuse to tarry in Darkvale."

Thomas gave the armor another whack. "If we must be discreet, and we won't have much time, how . . . ?"

"How will I succeed? By the will of my ancestors and by the grace of God."

When the ruin of Gareth's armor and wardrobe had been completed to his satisfaction, he ordered Thomas to repack their baggage. Gareth built a small fire in one corner of the huge fireplace in the great hall and roasted the two hares he and Thomas had killed earlier in the day.

After eating, Gareth laid his cloak on the dusty floor of the great hall. "Rest now, Thomas. We leave for Darkvale at dawn."

Thomas spread a blanket on the floor and laid himself down. "I cannot sleep. My mind is full of myths and legends. And ghosts. You must tell me a story, Lord Gareth. I would hear your plans for the castle and lands of Avondel once you have returned the amulet to its rightful place."

"I have not thought that far ahead."

Thomas snorted. "You plan everything well in advance. 'Tis the secret of your success. Share your plans with me, if you please. To take my mind off this haunted place."

"If the castle is haunted, the ghosts are friends of mine. My mother and father. The knights who defended the castle."

Shuddering, Thomas drew his cloak closer about him. "Not of mine. They do not want me here."

"Nonsense. You are my squire. You are welcome in my family's home."

"Tell me what you plan. Please."

Gareth stared at the stars visible through the arched windows and spoke his plans aloud. "Very well. As I said, I plan to restore Avondel to its former glory. The fields will be tilled and planted; sheep and cattle will breed and multiply. This hall will ring again with the sounds of joy and prosperity."

"You will become a farmer."

Gareth knew that Thomas longed for the success a man could earn with his sword. Part of him shared his squire's love of travel and adventure. But the time had come to put that wandering way of life aside. Gareth was ready to settle down. "I will be content to be a farmer."

"You will need a wife."

"Aye." His heart beat a little faster. This part of his plan was not so well thought out. Gareth only knew that he hoped to find a woman like his mother. His father had been blessed with a virtuous woman, a woman who pledged her heart and body to her lord and never betrayed her marriage vows. From what Gareth had seen in his travels, such women were rare.

Poets and minstrels sang of a different kind of woman, almost always a married woman. Sometimes their songs were of an unapproachable and pure lady, loved only in the imagination of her suitors. More often they told of earthly love, in which the woman betrayed her lord and took another knight to her bed. Had not Guinevere betrayed King Arthur? With her as an example, many ladies played at love, not caring a fig about their marriage vows.

If not for the example the lady Juliana had provided, he would not have believed faithful wives existed. But since his mother had given him proof that there were such women, Gareth did not intend to settle for less.

The problem would be in finding her.

"Where will you find her?" asked Thomas, echoing his thoughts.

"Under the oak tree on the village green. In the forest glen by the cool, green pool. In the meadow, riding on a butterfly's wing." His romantic words made Gareth smile to himself. Being within the walls of Avondel was having a strange effect on him. But it was too soon for the warrior to lay down his sword and turn poet. The last battle had not yet been fought.

"You do not have a plan for seeking a bride?" Thomas sounded incredulous. Gareth always emphasized the importance of planning when instructing his squire.

"I do not know where or when I will find my future wife. Finding a bride is not as easy as planning a campaign. But I have faith that when I need her most, she will appear."

"How will you recognize her?"

"By her soft words and gentle touch. She will be wise, courteous, and humble."

"And beautiful."

"Hmmm," Gareth said, closing his eyes.

"With silken blond tresses and large, blue eyes," said Thomas, his voice slurred with sleep. "You always choose women with light hair." Thomas yawned.

"Always. Go to sleep."

Even after Thomas began to snore gently, Gareth could not sleep. Within the walls of Avondel ghosts of yesterday and dreams of tomorrow collided and kept him awake. He could not avenge the past or create the future without Aethelwyn's amulet.

He had to find the magic talisman.

Three

"We're here." Walter's voice was hushed. He was standing in front of the shop window, gazing through the glass.

Rising on tiptoe to peer over his shoulder, Victoria could see nothing. Fog swirled outside, obscuring the view. "Here? Here where?"

"Castle Avondel." Walter picked her up and whirled her around. "We made it!" He dropped Victoria onto the bench and grabbed Tobias by the hand. Shaking the wizard's hand vigorously, Walter beamed his million-dollar smile. "You did it! You really did it! Not that I ever had a doubt, but still . . . you did it. Victoria, do you believe it? Here we are!"

"Where are we?" Victoria repeated, turning to stare out the window again. "I can't see anything."

"I saw the castle wall." Walter was grinning like a fool. "You know it's always misty around the castle."

Victoria started to rise, but a queer dizziness made her sit back down. "Would someone please answer me? What just happened?"

"We traveled through time and space in the blink of an eye. That's what happened. If that's not worth a few million dollars, I don't know what is. Come on, Victoria, get up. You can't sit around all day. Let's go, kiddo." Hefting a chest, Walter headed out the door.

Tobias followed him out the door carrying another wooden chest.

The light-headedness seemed to have passed, so Victoria got up from the bench. Her knees were shaking. She grabbed the edge of the table to steady herself. Something very strange had just happened, no doubt about that. With her own eyes she had seen objects disappear, furniture metamorphosize from old to new to old again. But time travel? Magic? Not likely. Not at all likely. "I suppose I should have asked when we are, not where."

"Twelve seventy-four," said Tobias, reentering the shop. "As agreed."

Victoria shook her head. "No. This can't be twelve seventy-four. I don't believe in time travel. Or magic. This is not happening to me. Take me back to Pioneer Square. Right now."

Walter came through the door of the agency. Together he and Tobias lifted one of the two remaining chests. "Get your chest, Victoria. And grab your suitcase. Tobias will be leaving soon." They took the chest out the door.

Sitting down again, Victoria waited. When the two men reentered the shop, she wrapped her arms around her middle and refused to look at Walter. "I'm not staying here." She angled her head toward the travel agent. "I'm going with him."

Tobias chuckled. "Not possible. I have an appointment in Paris, during the Terror. French aristocrats avoiding the guillotine are some of my best customers." He picked up the last chest, the one with her costumes in it, and pushed it out the door. Reentering the shop, he said, "You would not like that time."

Linda Kay

"I don't like *this* time." She eyed him suspiciously. "If it really is twelve seventy-four."

"Oh, it is. Right time, right place. Be on your way." He took her hand and pulled her from the bench, then gently but firmly pushed her toward the exit.

Victoria had just enough time to grab her purse and suitcase before being shoved out the door. "Well. That was rude." She reached for the doorknob, intending to tell Tobias Thistlewaite, time-travel agent, a thing or two about customer relations. The knob melted in her hand.

"Oh! Did you see that? The travel agency melted."

"Interesting," said Walter, squinting his eyes. "Damn fog. Can't see a thing. Leave the baggage here. Let's explore."

"I'm not moving a step. Not until you explain what just happened." She sat down on one of the wooden chests and tried not to think about the way her stomach was behaving.

"You know what happened, Victoria. We traveled from Seattle to Avondel, from two thousand one to twelve seventy-four."

"Sure we did. How?"

"Magic. I told you that, too, in detail."

Victoria opened her mouth, intending to point out a few salient facts. Such as, that there was no such thing as magic. That wizards did not exist. That time travel was impossible.

No words came out of her mouth. She had felt the shop shudder and creak as it flew through time and space. She had seen it disappear into the fog. When the mist parted briefly, she could see the stone wall of the castle in front of her. "Magic." Her stomach rolled over.

"Magic." Walter grinned at her. "Who would have thought? Here we are, in the bailey of Castle Avondel.

We'll introduce ourselves to the lord and lady of Avondel, and tell them to keep the amulet well guarded. The siege will fail. The castle will be saved, and we'll have time for a little sight-seeing. Maybe pick up a few souvenirs. I brought money—that chest is filled with gold."

"Sight-seeing? Souvenirs? You make this sound like a vacation trip to Disney World."

"It's not so different. But the best part is, when we return to the future, my castle will be repairable."

"Sure, just your average thirteenth-century fixer-upper," muttered Victoria, trying to clear the fog from her brain. She hadn't quite managed to wrap her mind around the concept of time travel, even though she had just lived through the trip, and her confusion was interfering with her ability to focus. One of Walter's words penetrated the buzzing in her head. "Siege? You planned for us to be here during the siege?"

"Of course. I told you that, too. Weren't you listening to me?"

Holding her head, Victoria ignored the question. She hadn't been listening to much of anything except the frantic beat of her heart during their journey through time and space. "You don't know when the siege was."

"Sure I do. The book said May, twelve seventy-four. This is April. Monday, April second, twelve seventy-four, to be exact. As it turns out, the calendar in this year is exactly the same as two thousand one. We will be returning to Seattle on Saturday, April twenty-first."

"Walter! The date of the siege had to be a guess on Brother Martin's part. The book was written a century after the fact. And weren't there changes in the calendar?"

That wiped the grin from Walter's face. For the first time since they had left Seattle, he looked unsure of himself. "Julian to Gregorian? I hadn't thought about that." His worried look faded away. "But Tobias must have. Time is his business, after all."

"Some business. Did it ever occur to you that this particular time is dangerous? We could get killed."

"Killed?" Walter appeared shocked by the idea. But then, Walter thought his wealth made him invincible. "Not a chance. No way. Once the amulet is secure, the castle will be unconquerable. No one is going to die. Not us, nor any of the castle's inhabitants. Victoria, you know I never would place you in danger."

"Not intentionally. I know that. But H. Walter, this trip is not exactly a walk in the park. You should have given me a choice."

"I suppose so. But it never occurred to me that you wouldn't want to take this trip. Anyone would jump at a chance to travel through time."

"Not me."

"Now, Victoria. If I had told you I had arranged a trip to the past and asked you if you wanted to come with me, you never would have believed me. Or if you had, you would have nagged me to death trying to talk me out of it. I didn't have time for that. But there's no reason for you to worry. Nothing bad is going to happen while we're here."

"Nothing bad? What about being trapped in a castle without food and water? Dodging boulders hurled over the wall with those . . . giant slingshot thingies."

"Trebuchets, not slingshots. The siege will be short-lived and unsuccessful, thanks to us."

"On the off chance you're wrong, I hope you packed a Kevlar vest for me."

"Victoria, my dear. Your lack of trust wounds me to the core. I promise you, we will be perfectly safe."

"Oh, yeah? How are you going to explain us to the locals?"

Walter's brows drew together in a puzzled frown. "Explain? Explain what, exactly?"

"Where we're from, for starters. You're not going to tell them Seattle, are you?"

"What's wrong with Seattle?" Walter jutted out his dimpled chin and glared at her.

"You dummy. It doesn't exist yet."

"Oh. Right. No problem. We'll tell them we're from the West."

"The West? Isn't that a little vague? And what about how we got here? We show up with no visible means of transportation, and people are bound to wonder. You can't tell them about the time-travel agency."

"Yes, I can, if I have to. Remember, people in this age believe in magic."

"People in this age burn witches at the stake. People in this age have torture chambers instead of media rooms. People in this age——"

"Stop. No one is going to be burned at the stake or tortured. You worry too much. I tell you, everything is going to be all right." He paused, eying her from head to toe. "But just to be on the safe side, maybe you'd better change clothes. Ladies in this century don't show so much leg. And do something about your hair. It looks too . . ."

"Twenty-first century? Duh. That's my time, and I want to go back to it." Victoria bit her bottom lip to keep it from pooching out in a childish pout. Now she was whining. She *never* whined. But she'd never been tossed back seven or eight centuries in time before. She had a perfect right to be upset. "I want to go home, Walter. Today."

Walter turned his back on her, avoiding dealing with her demand. "The fog seems to be thinning. This is definitely the bailey of the castle. That was the specific destination I asked for. As far as I can tell, that is precisely where Tobias dropped us off."

Giving up on trying to make Walter think about what he'd done, Victoria peered through the fog, which seemed as thick as ever to her, trying to see something besides cold stone walls. She shivered, although it wasn't any colder here than it had been in Seattle. Still, the atmosphere was . . . doleful. Sad. She had never felt such palpable sorrow. Victoria could feel tears pooling in her eyes. Either she was reacting to the atmosphere, or she was on the verge of turning into a pouting, whining crybaby. Blinking fiercely, she asked Walter, "Have you noticed anything odd?"

"Of course I have. Time travel is odd. Tobias is odd."

"Not that. Listen."

Walter tilted his head to one side. "I don't hear anything."

"That's my point. Neither do I. Don't you think that's strange? Shouldn't there be some noise? Cows mooing, chickens clucking, that sort of thing. And why aren't there any people around? Where is everyone?"

"They must be inside the castle. Perhaps it's dinner time. Trenchers. We'll eat off of trenchers. In the great hall of Castle Avondel. Come on, Tory." He grabbed her by the hand, grinning gleefully.

Victoria held back, reluctant to come face to face with the castle's inhabitants. Walter might think they could waltz in, give a few orders about the amulet, and then go on about their business. She wasn't so confident. Questions were bound to arise, questions for which they had no believable answers. Gesturing toward the pile of wooden chests, she asked, "What are we going to do with our luggage?"

"Leave it for now. No one's going to bother it."

"What about the gold? Should that be left lying about?"

That stopped him. He let go of her hand and walked back to the pile of baggage. Muttering something under his breath, Walter opened one of the chests, filled to the brim with gold coins, and took out a generous handful. He handed the coins to Victoria. "Here, take these. We might need a little walking-around money. The rest of the gold will be perfectly safe where it is. Tobias cast a spell on the chest so no one can open it but me."

Shoving the coins into her shoulder bag, she asked, "Did Tobias teach you a spell to get us home? Do we click our heels together and repeat—"

" 'There's no place like home'? No. A spell isn't necessary to get us back to Seattle. Thistlewaite will come for us in three weeks."

"Three weeks? We're going to be out of our time for three weeks? That's too much time, Walter. Aunt Crystal is going to think it's strange if I don't call her. She will worry about me."

"I took care of that. I left instructions for Mrs. Bradley to call her. She will explain to Crystal that you and I will be incommunicado until further notice."

"Oh, great. We're off together alone and out of the loop? Aunt Crystal will be sure we're holed up in some kind of romantic hideaway having a torrid affair."

"Good. Then she won't worry about you."

"Okay, so you took care of Aunt Crystal. Did you think to ask for an interpreter? This may be England, but have you ever tried to read Chaucer's Canterbury Tales in Middle English?"

Walter grinned smugly. "That's taken care of, too. Tobias assured me we would understand every word. And we'll speak the language like natives."

Victoria was impressed in spite of herself. "To think I ever doubted you were a detail man."

"These details are more important than most. Like your clothes. Change."

"Oh, all right." She opened her chest and pulled out the yellow tunic and the forest green gown that went under it. "Turn around, Walter." Victoria changed quickly, then folded her suit and blouse neatly and put them in the chest. "All right. I'm decent."

"Your hair? You look more like a page than a lady."

Shaking her layered, shoulder-length hair, Victoria said, "There's nothing I can do about that. I can't suddenly grow silken tresses to my waist."

"I guess not. I should have told you to get a wig, or some extensions. I know. Tuck your hair up in one of those hair nets. I saw a couple in your chest."

With a sigh, Victoria rummaged around in the chest until she found the gold-mesh snood. Tucking her hair into the net, she said, "If you had told me to get a wig, you would have had to tell me why, and I would have seen to it that you were committed to the nearest mental hospital." Victoria smiled a purposefully insincere smile at him, then picked up her purse and slid the strap over her shoulder.

"You're keeping your purse?"

"Yes. What else would I carry the gold in? This outfit doesn't have pockets. I wanted pockets, but you said they were not historically accurate."

"You need a leather pouch, like mine."

"My purse *is* a leather pouch."

"It's not right for this time."

"Neither am I." She clutched her handbag to her breast. "I'm keeping my purse, Walter."

"Now, Victoria—"

A sudden gust of wind moved the fog around, revealing a pair of huge wooden doors. "This must be the entrance," said Walter. He knocked on the door.

The sound reverberated, then faded away. He hit the door again, louder this time. They waited, but no one answered the summons. Giving the door a push, Walter managed to open it an inch or two. "Door's stuck. Give me a hand here."

Victoria placed both palms on the door and shoved. Inch by inch the door creaked open, until there was an opening big enough for Walter to enter. He stuck his head in first. "Hello! Anyone home?"

No one answered. Walter squeezed through the partially opened door, dragging Victoria along behind him. As she crossed the threshold, she dug in her heels. "You go on. I would just as soon wait in the yard."

He did not release her. "Not the yard. The bailey. It looks like no one is home. That's strange. Come on." He headed down the hallway, stopping in front of another pair of double doors. "This is the doorway to the Great Hall." He pushed the doors open and entered.

Victoria followed him. "There is no one here. Maybe they took a trip to the future. Perhaps they wanted to attend H. Walter Harrington's famous Medieval Fair."

"Sarcasm does not become you, Victoria. This is serious. The only reason for the castle to be deserted is . . ." He trailed off, staring into space.

"Yes? What? Walter, look at me. Why is the castle empty? Where are the people?"

Walter met her gaze. "Uh. Don't be upset, okay? I'm sure everything will be all right."

"I sense a 'but' coming on."

"But . . . I think that the siege has already happened."

Victoria gave him a blank stare. "The siege has happened?"

"It's the only explanation. Look around. The over-turned benches, the tattered banners . . . the empti-ness."

She looked around. Victoria hadn't paid much atten-tion to their surroundings before, being too occupied with berating Walter. "Dusty, too," she whispered. "This is creepy, Walter. Where is everyone?"

"No one is here, and no one has been here for some time. Well? Aren't you going to say I told you so?"

"I told you so," Victoria said, her voice shrill. Words were not enough. She made a fist and punched Walter on the shoulder. "Now look what you've gotten us into. We're stuck in a deserted castle miles from anywhere, centuries from when we should be. What are we going to do?"

Walter backed away from her. "I could be wrong. There may be someone around."

"You're right about that." Victoria pointed to the floor. "Look. Footprints." She whispered the words.

"Probably some kind of animal."

"I don't think so. There *are* people here."

"Helloooo!" Walter shouted.

Victoria punched him again. "Walter! Shut up. They might hear you."

Rubbing his shoulder, Walter scowled at her. "I want them to hear us."

"Why? They could be dangerous. If the siege has happened, they may be the . . . the besiegers."

"Nonsense." Walter started up the stone stairs, care-ful not to step on the footprints in the dust. "I'll find them. They can tell us when the siege happened. But it must have been some time ago—several months at least."

"Why?"

"No bodies. No blood."

"Eeuuw. I don't like this, Walter. Not one bit." Victoria hissed the words.

"Come on, Victoria. We're not outnumbered here. There are only two sets of footprints. Let's find them."

They searched the castle from dungeon to towers—four of them—and found nothing and no one. Walter did discover a gaping hole in the bottom of the square tower on the south corner of the castle. "I recognize this hole in the wall. It's the one we couldn't patch, no matter what kind of mortar we used. No doubt about it. The siege has happened."

Victoria opened her purse and pulled out her cell phone. "What is Thistlewaite's number? I'll call and have him pick us up early."

"We can't call him. Your phone won't work in this century. We can't go home until Thistlewaite comes back for us."

"You're telling me we're stuck here for three more weeks? Without food or water?"

"There is water. You're forgetting that well we found. And there's bound to be a cistern or two on the roof. This is a great castle, Victoria. Well built, plenty of rooms. Modern plumbing, for this century. I'm glad I bought it."

"I'm not. Lord knows what microbes lurk in that well. Did you remember to pack antibiotics?"

"No one is going to get sick." Walter eyed her purse. "And you always travel with a medicine cabinet in your bag."

"I take it that's a no." She advanced on Walter. "I suppose if we are very, very lucky, and if we boil before we drink, we may not get sick from drinking polluted water. But one of us may get killed. Soon. And it won't be me."

Walter backed away from her, hands raised, palms

out. "Calm down, Victoria. We'll be fine. We'll take a few things and walk to the nearest village."

"Which is where, exactly?"

"You should know that. It's where we stayed during the renovations."

"Attempted renovations." Victoria nodded. "Okay. I know where we stayed. At the inn at Darkvale. That's thirty miles from here. On modern roads. I don't see any pavement, Walter. And the inn where we stayed wasn't built until the sixteenth century. Darkvale may not even be there."

"Darkvale is there. Professor Arnold said the castle at Darkvale coexisted with Avondel; he was using it as a guide for the restoration. And there will be an inn, too. The inn we stayed in replaced one built on the same site around twelve fifty. I read about it on the back of the menu in the inn's restaurant."

"Wait just one minute, Walter. I remember something else. Brother Martin's manuscript said Ranulf of Darkvale was the one who laid siege to Avondel. We'll be going from the frying pan to the fire."

"No, we won't. I'm sure the monk was wrong about that. It was the Scots who besieged Avondel. King Henry the Third exonerated Lord Ranulf. The only thing Ranulf did wrong was to arrive too late to relieve the garrison at Avondel. If he had, the siege might have failed, amulet or no amulet. Going to Darkvale will be perfectly safe."

Victoria grabbed his sleeve. "If the siege happened a few months ago, where are the besiegers? Shouldn't they still be here?"

"Why would you think that? There's no reason for them to hang around."

"No? They sacked the castle, carried off their plunder, and just left it vacant? Why?"

"The curse. The book said the fields became barren,

the livestock sickened and died, and the villeins left the land. No reason to hang around under those circumstances."

"Those things take time," said Victoria.

"Not if magic is involved. It could have happened overnight. Now that I think about it, maybe the monk was wrong about the complete destruction of Avondel and its inhabitants. I always thought Brother Martin exaggerated when he said Ranulf spared no one, not woman or child, and that he and his knights rode through the castle in blood up to the knees of their horses."

"I certainly hope he exaggerated," said Victoria, swallowing to keep from gagging.

"There may be survivors at Darkvale. One of them may know where the amulet is. Let's get going."

"How are we going to get there? We can't call a taxi."

"Walk."

"Walk? Thirty miles?"

"I'm sure we won't have to walk the whole way. We're bound to run across someone with a horse or a cart we can borrow. Or we'll hitch a ride with a farmer going to market."

"I am not lugging those wooden chests thirty miles."

"No. We'll pack what we need in your suitcase, and leave the rest here. It has wheels, doesn't it?"

"Yes. But won't a Samsonite suitcase raise a few eyebrows? It has zippers. And plastic handles. Magic or not, I really don't think it's a good idea to advertise that we're from the future."

"Oh. Right. Okay. We'll make bundles and carry those."

"Bundles. Like hobos?" Victoria asked.

"Exactly. You get what we'll need, and I'll look for a couple of sticks."

"What will we need? Which chest has the AK Forty-sevens?"

"I didn't bring any modern weapons, only my sword. Get a few changes of clothes out of the chests. That should do for now. We can always buy more in Darkvale."

Victoria remembered that she had her Swiss Army knife in her purse. Not much of a weapon, but better than nothing. She had medicine, too: antihistamines, Band-Aids, and antibiotic cream. And aspirin, luckily. She could already feel the beginning of a headache in her left temple. And she was almost sure she had a Snickers lurking in the bottom of her bag. That cheered her up. Chocolate always made life more bearable. "How long do you think it will take us to get to Darkvale?"

"I run five miles every morning in less than an hour. I know you are opposed to vigorous exercise, but I'm sure you can walk a mile in fifteen minutes."

Victoria widened her eyes. "In your dreams. I stroll, I don't run. People who run miss *seeing* the roses, much less smelling them."

"Okay. Twenty minutes. That's three miles an hour, so thirty miles will take us ten hours. Or so. That doesn't factor in rest stops. Since we're getting a late start, we'll have to spend at least one night on the road. It may get cold when the sun goes down. Take a cloak."

Shuddering, Victoria pulled out a gray wool cloak lined in yellow silk and spread it on the ground. Walk three miles an hour? Not her idea of a good time. Aimless physical activity—walking or running around in circles, sit-ups, push-ups, or jumping jacks—made no sense to her. If she moved, Victoria wanted it to be for a reason. On the other hand, getting far away from the haunted castle as soon as possible was a very good reason.

And since walking seemed to be the only available

means of transportation, she would walk. Victoria began piling clothes on top of the cloak. "What about food? Did you bring anything to eat?"

"No. We'll find something."

"Where? What?"

"I don't know. Nuts and berries."

"Nuts and berries? Isn't it too late for the former and too early for the latter? If it really is April, that is."

"Maybe. Never mind. If we're lucky, we'll meet a farmer going to market who will give us a bite to eat and a lift to the inn. Have you got everything you need? I'm going to take the chests and put them inside the lady chapel." He pointed to a smallish stone structure built against the curtain wall.

"No, but what I need isn't in those chests." Victoria finished wrapping the clothes she had chosen in the cloak and tied it into a bundle.

Walter hauled the last chest inside the chapel, then pushed the door closed again. He tied his bundle to one of the sticks he had found and handed the other one to Victoria.

"I don't know you at all, Walter. Not at all. I never knew you to rely on luck, much less magic. All these years I thought you were a hardheaded businessman. Oh, you had that quirk about the Middle Ages, but it never seemed to interfere with your ability to make a buck. Who knew you'd go bonkers over this castle?"

"I've made enough bucks." Walter's eyes glazed over. "I want . . . adventure . . . romance . . . things money can't buy. If that makes me bonkers, so be it."

"What do you mean, things money can't buy? We're not talking the sun in the morning and the moon at night here, Walter. This adventure isn't free. You paid two million dollars for this trip."

"That was just to get us here. What happens next is up to us. Come on, Victoria. Aren't you the least bit excited about the possibilities? We're in a different time, a time when men had to be brave and resourceful to survive."

"Oh, I'm excited, all right. Hungry and terrified, too. It obviously escaped your attention, Walter, but this was not a good time for women."

"Terrified? Come on, Victoria. Nothing frightens you. You're the bravest woman I know. And how can you say this isn't a good time for women? It's the age of chivalry. Women are placed on pedestals and worshiped from afar."

"If some man is going to worship me, I would just as soon he did it up close and personal—as long as he was a twenty-first-century man who knew how to take no for an answer. But, on pedestals or not, women in the Middle Ages were chattel. Things. *Subservient* things. I don't do subservient very well."

"Tell me about it," Walter muttered.

"So don't try to convince me this is a safe time for me, H. Walter Harrington the Fourth. For your information, being in this place, in this time scares the peewaddleysquat out of me."

"There is nothing for you to be afraid of. No one is going to hurt you. Men protect women in this time. The chivalric code requires them to do that, and more. Remember your Tennyson?

> *"To ride abroad redressing human wrongs,*
> *To speak no slander, no, nor listen to it,*
> *To honor his own word as if his God's,*
> *To lead sweet lives in purest chastity,*
> *To love one maiden only, cleave to her*
> *And worship her by years of noble deeds . . ."*

quoted Walter.

"Yeah, right. Somehow I don't think a thirteenth-century knight will have read *Idylls of the King*. Even if Tennyson was not taking poetic license, and all knights truly are honorable men, which I doubt, there are plenty of other things to fear. Like pestilence and plague."

"The black plague won't happen for another fifty or sixty years. Besides, your immunizations are up to date. I checked with the company doctor before we left. Are you all packed? Here's your stick."

Victoria tied her bundle to the stick and dropped an awkward curtsy. "Lead on, my lord and master."

"Lord and master?"

"I'm practicing submissiveness. Something tells me it's a skill I'm going to need to survive.

Four

The castle at Darkvale sat on the side of a hill at the end of a broad valley. Built of stone as black as its lord's heart was purported to be, the castle had stood unconquered for a century or more without the aid of magic. The lords of Darkvale relied on strength and cunning to maintain their power over the lands and people of their valley. Unlike Avondel, Darkvale had no need of magic.

The latest of their line, Lord Ranulf, sat at the head table in the great hall of his castle. A feast was in progress for the noble visitors to the tournament and fair licensed by the late King Henry III. Several powerful barons and their ladies graced his table, as well as a few of the knights who had come for the tournament. Ranulf had also invited the wealthier of the merchants who had brought items—spices, silks, and furs—to sell at the market held in conjunction with the fair.

King Edward had not sent a representative. Frowning, Ranulf of Darkvale reached for his goblet of ale and drank deeply.

The slight had not gone unnoticed by those present. A trip to London to pledge his allegiance to the new king was past due, but Ranulf hesitated to leave

Darkvale until the matter of Avondel was settled. At least it would be over soon. Word had reached him that Gareth of Avondel had returned to England.

Avondel.

That cursed place haunted him still. He might have managed to forget the past if Elwyna had not provided him with a constant reminder. He should have sent her away long ago. Several lords had made it clear they would consider marriage if he would provide her an adequate dowry, something well within his means. Elwyna insisted she did not want to marry. She wanted to enter the convent at Northumber. The abbess also would expect a generous dowry.

If gold were the only cost, Ranulf could have rid himself of his ward long ago. Her presence was both a curse and a blessing, and Ranulf knew he could not lose the bitter without relinquishing the sweet. If Elwyna left Darkvale, the last light would go out of his life. With her dark hair and soft gray eyes, Elwyna looked exactly like her mother. He had lost his lovely Juliana. He could not lose Elwyna.

Ranulf frowned. Whether or not Elwyna remained at Darkvale might not be within his sole power to determine much longer. Gareth surely intended to rescue his sister, as well as avenge his parents' deaths. The lord of Avondel would seek his revenge soon. Ranulf had half-expected him to appear at the tournament, but Gareth had not taken part in the jousting. Perhaps the boy had learned patience. A sardonic smile curving his lips, Ranulf reminded himself that ten years had passed since he and Gareth had met on the jousting field. He should not think of him as a boy.

Gareth would be a man now, a dangerous man.

Ten years ago, when they met at King Henry's tournament, the boy knight had relied on the justness of his cause. Luckily for Ranulf, Gareth had not yet possessed the skill or the experience to defeat him. By now, after ten years of battles in France, Syria, and Egypt, Gareth would have both. And he had the new king's favor, too, it seemed.

Ranulf drank deeply again.

Balen, a troubadour who sometimes spied for Ranulf, approached him from behind and whispered in his ear. "There are strangers arrived at the inn. A man and a woman."

Shrugging, Ranulf did not bother to raise a brow. "Come to the fair."

"They arrived only today." Balen paused. Bringing his mouth closer to Ranulf's ear, he whispered, "My lord, they say they came from Castle Avondel."

"Avondel!" Ranulf sat up straighter and motioned the troubadour closer. He did not notice that the unkempt knight on his left also attended to Balen's whispers. The knight had won the last joust of the tournament, crudely but effectively, earning a place at the head table. His talents seemed limited to jousting. The man had no conversation and, after a few questions, Ranulf had ignored him. The knight—Perceval was his name—had spent the evening drinking and eating, his discourse limited to grunts and loud belches.

"They seek Aethelwyn's amulet," said Balen. "The man offers a gold coin to anyone who will bring him information about the talisman, a chest of gold to the man who brings him the Saxon amulet."

"So." Ranulf leaned back in his chair and closed his eyes. He felt a sudden throbbing behind his right eye. "Gareth has returned. I expected that."

"No. This man is blond and has blue eyes. You said Gareth had dark hair and green eyes."

"Yes." Ranulf opened his eyes and focused on Balen. "Take some men and bring the stranger to me. Alive."

"The woman?"

"Bring her, too." As soon as Balen left to carry out his orders, Ranulf picked up his goblet and brought it to his lips. Two strangers in the village openly questioning everyone they met about the amulet . . .

Ranulf set the goblet down, the wine untasted.

Victoria sat on the massive bed, rubbing her bare feet. Walter sprawled in the only chair next to the window in the room at the Darkvale Inn. The room was not that different from the one she had occupied during the failed renovations at Avondel. The massive bed, the heavy beams in the low ceiling, the stone fireplace appeared much the same. A large chest stood in the corner where an armoire had been placed in the twenty-first-century version of the room. Walter had unpacked their bundles, folded their clothes neatly, and stored them in the chest.

Naturally, the room lacked electricity and there was no adjoining bath with toilet and hot and cold running water. That would have been enough to ruin her day, but lack of modern amenities was far from the biggest problem they faced.

"Ten years, Walter," she pointed out again. She knew she was rubbing it in, but he deserved it. Taking her on a trip through time with no advance warning, no opportunity to beg off—what had he been thinking? "We are ten years too late to save your blasted castle. No one here knows what happened to Aethelwyn's amulet."

"I don't see how that monk could have been off by ten years. How could he have written the siege took place in twelve seventy-four when it happened in twelve sixty-four?"

"Maybe his quill slipped. Brother Martin wasn't

wrong about everything, don't forget. He was right about Ranulf. It was the lord of Darkvale, and not the Scots, who besieged Avondel."

"If he knew who, he should have known when. Why didn't he?"

"I told you the date might not be right."

"Not until we were already here." Walter continued staring out the window.

"If you had bothered to tell me about this stupid trip in advance, I might have told you in time for you to do something about it. I hope you've learned a lesson, Walter. It's not nice to trick people into going on trips through time."

Walter favored her with one of his teddy-bear scowls. "I promise it will never happen again. But as long as we're here, we might as well make the best of it and find the amulet."

"How? So far, no one you've asked has known anything that we didn't already know. Aethelwyn's amulet is magic, it protected Avondel, and it disappeared around the time of the siege. Which happened ten years ago. I think we should buy some supplies, go back to Avondel, and wait for Tobias."

"Not yet. It's too soon to give up. We've only spoken to a few people about the amulet. Besides, looking for it will give us something to do while we wait for our ride home. We're going to be here for a couple of more weeks."

"Home." Victoria sighed.

"Don't do that."

"What?"

"Sigh mournfully. Like you really miss Seattle and Aunt Crystal."

"I do miss them." She sighed again. Mournfully.

"Ha. You're doing that to make me feel guilty."

"Is it working?"

"No. You should be grateful to me for taking you on the trip of a lifetime. Not to mention getting you away from your aunt. It will do Crystal good to stand on her own two feet for a change. There is absolutely no reason for you to miss her."

"Well, I do. Maybe not as much as I miss taxicabs and toilet paper, but I miss my aunt Crystal. And I'm going to have to do a lot of explaining when we get home. After being gone for weeks on a romantic getaway with you, she'll expect us to be engaged at the very least."

"Forget Aunt Crystal. Who cares what she thinks? As for you, some women would think a trip to the thirteenth century was romantic. Knights in armor riding to the rescue of fair maidens, and all that."

Victoria snorted. "Knights are men, Walter. The fact that they wear armor does not change that. I seriously doubt that they waste a lot of their time rescuing fair maidens. Even if they do, since I'm neither fair nor a maiden, I fail to share your enthusiasm for this particular time in history."

"You shouldn't be so hard on my sex, Victoria. A couple of unfortunate experiences, and you've written off the entire male gender. Some of us aren't so bad. And you should not listen to Crystal."

"What is that supposed to mean?"

"Crystal tells you you're not pretty because she's jealous. I think she must have a magic mirror in her closet, and when she asks who is the fairest of them all, it says you."

"Crystal is my aunt, not my wicked stepmother. She has no reason to be jealous of me."

"Oh, no? I beg to differ. Crystal has always traded on her looks. Now that she's reached an age where her beauty is fading, she builds herself up by tearing you down. You shouldn't let her do it."

"I never knew you were into pop psychology," said Victoria.

"Understanding people is the secret to my success. For example, I understand that, although you do not believe any male past or present possesses the knightly virtues, you refuse to settle for anything less than a man who is honest, courageous, and loyal. Picky. That's what you are."

"If you're so understanding, why didn't you know I would hate the thirteenth century?"

Walter threw up his hands. "Because I'm a selfish jerk, that's why. Now look what you've done. You've managed to put me in a bad mood."

"Don't blame me for your mood. You're sulking because we got here late and missed the jousting."

Walter responded with a scowl.

"That's better," said Victoria. "I like to see you scowl." On the trip to Darkvale, Walter had kept a hearty smile plastered on his face to keep her spirits up.

She appreciated the effort, but she needed more than Walter's determined good cheer to put her at ease. Being stuck in a different time, a dangerous time, was scary. Victoria thought of herself as a competent, intelligent woman, able to deal with all sorts of problems. However, her intelligence and abilities, more than good enough to deal with twenty-first-century problems, could very well prove useless in this day and time. Scary.

Victoria was not used to being afraid. She did not care for the feeling.

Even Walter, the perennial optimist, had lost some of his buoyant self-confidence. By the time they had arrived in Darkvale—three days after leaving Avondel—the fair was on its last day. When he found that out, his smile had faded to be replaced by the stoic expression of a martyr. Looking at it from his point of view, she supposed he had reason to pout. Walter had missed all of the tournament and most of the fair. The majority of the knights who had attended the tournament had left as soon as the jousting was over, and the merchants and peddlers were packing up their unsold wares and dismantling their stalls.

"At least we got a room. If we had arrived a day earlier, we would have had to sleep in the stable." Victoria continued massaging her arches. She should have worn her Reeboks, no matter what Walter had said about "blending in."

"If you had walked faster, we would have gotten here in time to see a real medieval fair."

"I don't power walk, Walter. I told you that. You were overly optimistic about how long it would take to get here. You failed to factor in poor roads, *no* roads, and all the time we wasted looking for nuts and berries. And it's not my fault that we couldn't hitch a ride until yesterday. Stop sulking. There are a few knights still around. Why don't you go hang out with them in the bar?"

"Tavern," Walter corrected. "The knights and barons are all at the castle tonight. Some sort of celebration to honor the knights who won their jousts at the tournament. We should have gotten an invitation. You should have seen to that."

"Me?"

"You. It's your job, remember? You are my personal assistant."

"Oh, yes. How could I forget? My job is what got me in this mess. But wangling invites from a thirteenth-century castle owner with the unlikely name of Ranulf is not in my position description. Besides, no one here knows or cares that the great and powerful H. Walter Harrington the Fourth is in town."

"Now, Victoria, don't—"

Hoofbeats sounded loudly. "What is that racket?" Slipping on her shoes, Victoria went to the window and looked out.

The street below, if the rutted dirt track could be called a street, was lit by moonlight. She could make out four men, three wearing chain mail. Knights in shining armor—the moonlight glinted on the chain mail. They were large—larger than Walter, who was six feet tall and built like a tight end. Any one of these guys could have played in the Seahawks' defensive line. With swords strapped to their sides, they looked more like hoodlums than romantic heroes. Victoria sighed again.

"Now what are you moaning about?" Walter got up and joined her at the window. "Oh. Knights." He sat back down.

"Yes. Knights. Complete with shining armor. Not to mention wicked-looking swords and daggers. To think that modern women still dream about men like them. Canned thugs." If she ever got back to her own time, Victoria planned to give her subconscious a stern lecture on the subject matter of her erotic dreams. No more knights.

Walter was outraged. "How can you say that? They are not thugs. They are heroes who embody the ideals of chivalry: honor, courage, loyalty."

"Uh-huh." She watched as three men dismounted and entered the inn. The fourth man, who was not wearing armor, remained with the horses. Victoria turned away from the window. "I guess they weren't invited to the castle tonight, either. They must be the losers. Go talk to them, why don't you? I'm tired of your grousing."

She walked back to the bed and flopped down on the feather mattress.

Loud footsteps sounded on the stairs, and the door to their room burst open. The three men she had seen on the street pushed their way into the room, swords drawn.

Walter jumped out of the chair. "Hey! What do you think your doing? This is a private room."

One of the men put the edge of his sword against Walter's throat. "Lord Ranulf of Darkvale commands your presence. Come." The man grabbed Walter by the arm.

Pulling his arm free, Walter said, "There is no need to use force. I am perfectly willing to go with you. I expected an invitation to his feast." He walked through the open door, followed closely by two of their uninvited visitors. "Don't wait up for me, Victoria. I may be out late."

The remaining knight approached Victoria. "You. Come with me."

Victoria scooted on her rump until her back was against the headboard of the bed. "I don't think so. I'm not much on parties."

The man grabbed her by the arm.

"Let me go! Walter, tell this protector of femininity to release me."

Walter did not respond. She could hear him and his escort clattering down the stairs. Where were those men taking him? Wherever it was, she was sure she did not want to go there. Victoria clawed and scratched at the hand gripping her upper arm, without any noticeable effect on the man pulling her off the bed.

Her captor drew a dagger and held it to her breast. Victoria stopped struggling. "Well, as long as you put it that way——" The knight silenced her with a jerk, making her stumble and fall to her knees. "Hey! Not so rough!"

He grabbed her by her hair and forced her to her feet. Prodded by the dagger, Victoria hurried down the stairs. They joined the others in front of the inn. All were mounted, including Walter, who sat on a horse looking perplexed. The fourth man, the one not wearing armor, sat on his mount and held the reins of another horse. Her knight pushed her toward the riderless horse.

"Walter? What's going on?"

"As far as I can tell, Ranulf of Darkvale wishes us to join him at the castle."

"I figured that much out for myself. Why?"

"I'm not sure. But I'm sure there is nothing to worry about."

"Are you, really? I'm not so—"

The man escorting Victoria tossed her onto his saddle, ending her conversation with Walter. Mounting behind her, he spurred the horse, and they galloped into the darkness.

Bouncing up and down, Victoria clutched the wooden pommel and tried not to think about what Ranulf of Darkvale had in store for them. The evening had not started out well. Her knees were bruised from hitting the floor; her scalp tingled from the hair-pulling she'd received. And her feet still hurt.

If she knew her Middle Ages, things were bound to get worse.

After a bruising ride, they arrived at a castle made appropriately menacing by the blackness of its walls and turrets. Flags with a silver lion centered on a black background flew from the battlements. Crossing a drawbridge over a moat filled with oily black water, they entered the bailey. They dismounted, and the three knights hurried them inside the castle. A feast was in progress in the great hall.

Walter was obviously entranced by the sights and

sounds filling the torch-lit chamber. He looked from side to side as the knights herded them forward along the wall. Victoria had to admit there was an impressive collection of people and things to look at and listen to.

Tapestries hung from the stone walls above dark-paneled wainscoting. A huge fire burned in the room-sized fireplace. Three long tables covered in white cloths were arranged in a U shape. Seated at the tables were richly dressed men and women, none of whom appeared to be the slightest bit interested in the new arrivals. Minstrels wandered about the room strumming lutelike instruments.

Victoria noticed the smells. Acrid smoke from the torches. Roasted meat. Pungent ale. Body odor. The large hall was crowded with people. Most of them had not bathed recently. Or maybe they had, but were suffering from deodorant deprivation. There were dogs rooting in the rushes, searching for discarded bones and scraps. Victoria detected another unpleasant odor. The dogs were not castle-broken. Wrinkling her nose, she tried to pull free of her guard's grasp.

He tightened his hold on her arm painfully.

"Lighten up, will you? I'm going to have bruises."

Their captors pushed them toward the head table. Victoria focused on the man seated in the place of honor. He must be Ranulf. He was a handsome man, scholarly in appearance, although his size almost matched that of his goons-in-armor. She guessed his age to be forty or so. Gray tinted his temples and colored his short beard. He said something to the man next to him. The man stood, leaving the seat on Ranulf's left vacant. The ornate chair on his right was not occupied. Where was the lady of the keep? Locked in a tower, awaiting her lord and master's bidding, no doubt. Victoria swallowed a hysterical giggle.

Ranulf motioned his minions to bring Walter and her closer to him.

The knight escorting Walter shoved him into the vacated chair next to Ranulf. Victoria was pushed to her knees again, between and slightly behind Walter and their host. The man who had been seated in Walter's place moved to stand in back of her. He swayed a little and put his hand on her shoulder to steady himself. She shrugged, trying to move out of his grip. The man obviously had drunk too much ale. He reeked of it.

Walter recovered his aplomb and inclined his head. "My lord. Ranulf, I believe? Thank you for inviting us—"

"Who are you?"

"H. Walter Harrington the Fourth. This is Victoria Desmond, my personal—"

"You came from Avondel."

"Most recently, yes. Before that—"

"You seek Aethelwyn's Amulet."

Walter nodded. "Yes, we—"

"For Gareth of Avondel."

The man behind her leaned closer, tightening his grip on her shoulder. Victoria shrugged again, this time managing to dislodge his hand. She pinched her nose with her thumb and forefinger. "Not so close, buster," she hissed. "You stink."

"Gareth? Aethelwyn's consort?" asked Walter, obviously confused. "He has been dead for a couple of hundred years, hasn't he?"

"Not that Gareth," said Ranulf, with an impatient wave of his hand. "His descendant, the current Gareth of Avondel."

Frowning, Walter shook his head slowly. "No. I am not acquainted with the gentleman."

"Then what is your interest in the talisman?"

Victoria held her breath. If Walter started talking about wizards and time travel they were doomed.

After only a short pause, Walter answered. "I am a scholar, interested in myths and legends. And magic. The legend of Aethelwyn and her Norman knight intrigues me. Moreover, the amulet is said to possess magical powers." Walter sat back in his chair and smiled ingratiatingly at Ranulf.

Victoria took a cautious breath. She should not have worried. Walter was in his element when negotiating with a tough opponent. From the little she knew about him, Ranulf of Darkvale fell into that category. This was the man who had besieged Walter's castle, whose men had murdered all its inhabitants and laid waste to Avondel's fields and forests.

Ranulf stared at Walter, his blue eyes unreadable. "As it happens, Walter of Harrington, I want to find the talisman as well. And I have more right to it than a stranger."

Walter leaned forward in the chair. "How is your claim greater than mine? I am willing to pay well for the amulet."

Squeezing her eyes shut, Victoria began to pray. Walter also had a competitive streak a mile wide. They were going to die.

"You offer a chest of gold, I believe?" Ranulf asked, his tone mild.

Victoria opened her eyes a slit. Maybe Walter hadn't gone too far, after all.

"Yes. What do you offer?"

Ranulf picked up a knife and ran his fingertip across the blade. Looking at Walter, he smiled a cold, calculated smile. "Your life."

"My life?" Walter drew his brows together in his don't-mess-with-me scowl. "Now see here, my good man, I am not accustomed to being threatened. I am an honest businessman—scholar. I have offered to pay for information leading to the discovery of the amulet. If you wish to compete with me on those terms—"

Ranulf paid no attention to Walter's fierce expression, or his words. He signaled the men who had brought them to the castle. "Take him to the tower."

Pushing Victoria and the smelly knight aside, the three men took hold of Walter and dragged him from his chair. "Victoria, don't worry about me. Everything will be all—" Walter disappeared up a stone staircase before he could finish.

Victoria got to her feet to follow Walter. The smelly knight moved closer, apparently intending to reclaim his chair, and blocked her way. Turning back to Ranulf, she asked, "What are you going to do with H. Walter?" Her voice shook. She told herself it was anger, not fear, that had her voice quaking and her knees trembling. She could handle being on her own in a strange and violent age. She had no choice. Her life and Walter's depended on it. "You better not hurt him; he's a very important man."

Ranulf turned his gaze on her. "You. His leman. Let it be known that I am holding your master for ransom."

"Ransom? Are you out of your mind?" Victoria bit her lip. Now was not the time to call her host crazy. "What I mean to say is, no one will pay a ransom for Walter. No one knows him in this time—I mean place. Except me."

Ranulf turned his cold gray gaze on her. "Then you will pay the ransom I demand. I want the amulet. When you have it, bring it to me, and I will release your master. Now go. I must attend to my guests."

Victoria had had more than enough of being pushed, pulled, and bossed around. Terrified she might be, but she was far from cowed. She stepped forward. Her bruised knees were wobbling, but her eyes were blazing. At least, she hoped they were. "Listen to me, Mr. Ranulf of Darkvale. In the first place, Walter is not my master, and I am not his lemon, or whatever you called me. I am his personal assistant. In the second place, I have no idea how to find the amulet. In the third place, even if I begin looking this minute, there is no guarantee I'll be able to find it in time to—"

Ranulf held up a hand. "Stop your ranting, shrew. You *will* find the amulet. Soon. If you do not . . . what did you call him? Walter. Walter will die."

Sucking in a breath, Victoria said, "That is not fair. Walter hasn't done anything to you. If he found the amulet, he did not plan to keep it. He was going to return it to where it belongs."

Ranulf sat back in his chair, a grim smile on his face. "I thought as much. He seeks the amulet for Gareth."

"Whoever. My point is, Walter is not a thief. So death is a little extreme, don't you think? And I'm sure if he had a choice, Walter would be more than happy to forget all about Avondel and the amulet. There are other legends to investigate, after all. Why don't you let us go? We'll be on our way and out of your hair in no time at all."

Ranulf moved his hand in a gesture of dismissal. "I have told you that you may go. Walter remains."

"Go?" Victoria looked around, her eyes wild. "Where am I supposed to go?"

"To find the amulet." Ranulf picked up his goblet and drank. He obviously thought the conversation was over.

"But—"

The smelly man standing behind her put his hand on the small of her back. His touch shocked her silent.

Leaning closer, he whispered in her ear. "Go now, before Ranulf changes his mind and locks you in the tower along with your lord. Wait for me outside the castle, on the road to the village."

Victoria looked over her shoulder. The man was not drunk, after all. His words had not been slurred, and she could see intelligence gleaming in his green eyes. Who was he?

She asked the question out loud. "Who are you?"

"Later. Go now. I will join you soon." He gave her a gentle push in the direction of the exit, then resumed his seat next to Ranulf.

Victoria walked slowly toward the massive doorway where she and Walter had entered together only minutes ago. Her feet moved at a snail's pace, but her mind was racing. What was happening to Walter? She had a vision of him chained to a wall in a dank, rat-infested cell. Victoria shuddered. What was she going to do? Where should she go? Who was the knight who had told her to wait for him? Should she wait for him or not?

Taking deep breaths, Victoria tried to calm down and think clearly. She would not do Walter any good at all in her present befuddled state of mind. As she reached the door to the outside, two men in livery opened it for her. She stepped outside into the court-yard—the bailey. Victoria paused only for a second before hurrying as fast as her sore knees would allow over the drawbridge.

"Why should I wait for him? I don't know who he is or what he wants with me. Probably nothing good."

Continuing to mutter to herself, Victoria walked to-ward the village. She had to calm down and make a plan. Walter was depending on her. Stopping, she looked back at Darkvale. Five towers reached skyward from its dark, forbidding walls. She didn't even know which one held her boss. Her friend. She might have been a little peeved at Walter for taking them on this crazy trip, but she did not want him to die.

Victoria bit back a sob. Tears were not going to help. Even if she did need a good cry, she didn't have time to indulge herself. She had to find the amulet and ransom Walter.

And she had less than three weeks in which to do it.

Five

Gareth slumped in his chair and watched as the woman slowly made her way out of the hall. With her brown hair, hazel eyes, and unremarkable features, he had thought her plain until she had lashed out at Ranulf for his treatment of her lord. Then her eyes had sparkled like molten gold, and her passion had transformed her features into a fierce kind of beauty. He almost envied Walter of Harrington his paramour.

Gareth might find her beguiling, but, as he had told Thomas, this was not the time for dalliance. He needed the woman—Walter had called her Victoria—for more practical reasons. Victoria was the missing piece that made his plan complete. She would provide a reason for him to ask questions about the last days of Castle Avondel, the siege, and the lost amulet.

He had to follow Victoria and offer himself as her champion, and he had to do it quickly. A survey of those seated at the head table did not reveal any immediate competitors. The conversation between the two late arrivals and Ranulf had been conducted quietly for the most part, except for Victoria's outburst. It appeared that the other knights at the head table had paid scant attention to the drama unfolding under their noses, being more interested in the varied and exotic dishes being placed before them.

Even so, Gareth could not hope to keep the quest to himself for long. Sooner or later one of the other knights would hear of Walter's offer of a chest of gold. Ranulf would surely send one or more of his men to assist the woman once he had given the matter more thought. The lord of Darkvale had reacted to the strangers seeking the amulet impulsively, taking the man hostage and sending the maid on her way. Once he had given the matter some thought, Ranulf would realize that the woman could not succeed on her own.

As Victoria reached the exit and disappeared from view, Gareth put those thoughts aside. He would deal with any competition when it arose. First things first. He had to get away from Ranulf.

Clutching his stomach, Gareth moaned loudly.

Ranulf glanced at him. "Are you ill?"

Nodding weakly, Gareth groaned again. "Stomach . . . aches. I must purge."

Recoiling in disgust, Ranulf ordered, "Take yourself from my table. Now."

"Yes, sire." Gareth rose, staggered a few steps until he was sure no one was paying him any attention, then hurried from the great hall. Once outside, he scanned the bailey. Several armed men were standing about looking bored. No woman. She had not waited.

Gareth spotted Thomas leaning against a wall, close to a group of guards. "Thomas!"

His squire pushed away from the wall and strolled to meet him. "Sir Perceval. Is the banquet over so soon?"

"It is for me. Did you see a woman leave the castle? She wore a yellow tunic over a dark green gown."

Shaking his head, Thomas chuckled. "Is she blond? Did you find your future wife at your enemy's table?"

"Nay. This particular woman is another man's mistress, and her hair is brown. We must find her. Ranulf has ordered her to find Aethelwyn's amulet, and I intend to assist her in her quest. Where are the horses?"

"Tethered outside the castle walls. There was no room in the stables. Ranulf ordered a maid to find the amulet? Why would he—?"

"Later." Gareth strode across the drawbridge. Thomas followed, then led the way to the clump of trees where their horses waited.

As soon as they were mounted, Thomas asked, "Now, if you please, tell me everything that happened at the banquet. Did Ranulf recognize you?"

"Nay. I have changed much since we last met—from a stripling to a man. When Ranulf attempted to engage me in conversation, I made my manner crude and disagreeable. After a while, he turned from me in disgust and paid me no mind. Once Balen, Ranulf's pet minstrel, appeared and whispered in his lord's ear, Ranulf took no notice of me at all."

"What did the minstrel tell him?"

"That a man and woman were seeking Aethelwyn's amulet. Balen said they had come from Avondel. Ranulf bade his knights bring them to him."

"This is the woman we are looking for?" asked Thomas.

"Yes. Ranulf holds her lord hostage. The ransom he demands for the man's release is the amulet."

"Why was her lord seeking the amulet?"

"He told Ranulf he is a scholar interested in legends, myths, and magic. For that reason he seeks the magic stone."

"Did you believe him?"

"Nay. Nor did Ranulf. Ranulf thinks the man and his mistress are looking for the amulet for Gareth of Avondel. And so she shall be, but she must not know that. Take care how you address me in her presence, and do not let on that we have our own reason to find the amulet. Once it is found, she will want to take it to Ranulf to ransom her master. I plan to return the amulet to Avondel."

"You want Ranulf to meet you there, at Avondel."

"Aye. He will die where he shed my father's blood. And my mother's. It is more than fitting that Ranulf's blood should sweeten the barren fields of Avalon."

"Did you see Elwyna?" asked Thomas.

"No. She was not present in the great hall, and I had no opportunity to seek her out."

"I spoke to the guards, asking them about the lady of the castle. They said Ranulf does not have a wife, but that his ward Elwyna acts as lady of the keep. Ranulf treats her as a daughter, they said, and he indulges her love of learning. She rebuffs all suitors, preferring to spend time with tutors and books. Ranulf does not complain. One of the men overheard Ranulf tell her he would never force her to marry against her will."

Gareth was silent. Thomas's words gave him pause. He wanted to believe that Elwyna had not been mistreated, but if that were true it would mean Ranulf was not the complete villain he had always imagined him to be. "If his guards are to be believed, Ranulf's kind treatment of Elwyna must grow out of guilt for his crimes against her family."

"If he feels guilt, mayhap he feels remorse as well," said Thomas. "A priest would say that remorse should be rewarded with forgiveness."

"Ranulf may seek forgiveness from God. He will not get it from me." His squire might be ready to avoid bloodshed—Thomas had always been a bit queasy when it came to battle—but vengeance demanded it. No matter how kind Ranulf might be toward Elwyna,

Gareth could not forget that he **was a thief** and a murderer.

Thomas had more questions. "Why does Ranulf seek the amulet now? He has had years to discover its whereabouts."

"Perhaps because he anticipates my return to Avondel. He knows I will look for the talisman. He may intend to use it as bait to draw me out. Or he may want it simply because he knows I do." Gareth slowed his horse to a walk. "Where is she? We should have caught up with the woman by now."

"She would have heard the sound of hoofbeats," said Thomas. "She may be hiding."

"You must be right." Gareth dismounted and began walking back down the road, leading his horse. "Look closely. Her pale yellow tunic should be visible in the moonlight."

They progressed slowly, walking softly and stopping every few steps to listen for the sound of breathing.

"I thought I heard something . . . there," whispered Thomas, pointing to a bush close to the road.

In a loud voice, Gareth said, "Nothing human made the noise you heard. 'Twas a bear, mayhap, or a wolf."

The bush began to quake. Throwing the reins of his horse to Thomas, Gareth moved quickly and pulled Victoria from behind the shrubbery. She struggled, and he let her go. "You wound me, my lady. You did not wait for me."

She fairly quivered with outrage. "You tricked me. There isn't a bear in the bushes."

"No. But there are other dangers for a woman alone. You should have done as I asked."

"It sounded more like an order than a request to me. I'm not very good at following orders, especially from men I don't know. For all I know, you are the greatest danger around." She walked away from him. Slowly. She was limping.

Gareth fell in step beside her. "I mean you no harm, lady. To the contrary, I intend to help you. You will need assistance in your search for the amulet."

"No, I won't. If you want something done right, do it yourself. That's my motto, and that's what I intend to do."

"You cannot do this alone. Look at you. You are limping—"

"My knees are a little sore, that's all. Walking will work out the stiffness. I do not need help. Go away."

"And you are going the wrong way."

She stopped in her tracks. "What?"

"The village of Darkvale is that way." He indicated the direction opposite from the way she was walking.

"Oh." She turned around and began retracing her steps. "So what? I got turned around. That doesn't prove I need your help. I would have figured out I was going the wrong way once the castle came into view. Anyone could make a mistake like that; there aren't any street signs, and it's dark out here."

Gareth refrained from pointing out that although it was night, it was not completely dark. The moon and stars shone brightly, illuminating the road. The woman was disoriented, babbling. Obviously, she had not recovered from the shock of seeing her lord and master imprisoned and threatened with death. "You did intend to go to the village, did you not? To the inn?"

"Yes."

"I will escort you." He held out his hand.

She did not take it. "Why did you follow me? What do you want?"

The woman did not trust him. That annoyed Gareth more than it should have done, but he hid his irritation. In a mild tone, he said, "My lady. I am a knight. When a knight encounters a lady in need of help, or any damsel in distress, he must aid her. All honor lies in such deeds."

"Yeah. Right. Honor. I don't suppose Walter's chest of gold has anything to do with it?"

"Gold?" said Thomas, his ears pricking up. "What gold?"

"Her lord offers a chest of gold to anyone who brings him the amulet. 'Twas his generosity which brought him to Ranulf's attention. My lady, may I present my squire, Thomas? Thomas, this is Lady Victoria. I am Sir Perceval."

"My name is Victoria Desmond. You may call me Ms. Desmond. We are not on a first-name basis." She tripped on a pebble. "Great, just great. I can't even walk without falling all over myself. How am I going to rescue Walter?" She sniffled.

"You are not going to cry, are you?" Thomas sounded horrified.

She shook her head. "Me? Cry? Don't be silly. I never cry. Not that I don't have plenty of reasons to cry. I'm tired and lost and my knees hurt and I'm being harassed by two . . . men. Walter is locked in a tower and I have to find the amulet and save him and there isn't much time before—" Her voice broke.

"Walter is your master?" asked Thomas.

"Yes," said Gareth. "Walter of Harrington."

Victoria stopped walking. "Excuse me. Let us get one thing straight here. Walter is not my master. He is my boss."

"Boss?" asked Thomas.

"I work for him."

"Work?" Thomas scratched his head. "You do him service?"

"Yes. For which he pays me handsomely."

"You owe him loyalty?" asked the squire.

"I owe Walter a day's work for a day's pay."

"Then he is your master," said Thomas, smug satisfaction in his tone.

Victoria threw up her hands. "Fine. Whatever you say. Walter is my master. He would be pleased to know that. How far do you think it is to the village?"

Gareth answered. "Not far. Two or three miles."

"Miles?" She stopped again, and he thought he saw her bottom lip tremble. "Of course. I should have known it would be miles."

She never cried? Gareth could see moisture gleaming in her eyes. He felt a surge of protectiveness for her. He did not welcome the feeling. This woman, Sir Walter of Harrington's leman, could be nothing but a means to an end for him. "Will you allow us to escort you to the inn? On horseback?"

Her shoulders slumped. "Oh, what the heck. It beats walking. All right."

Gareth placed his hands on her waist, intending to lift her onto his horse.

She immediately pushed his hands away. "Wait. I want to ride with Thomas."

"Why?"

"He looks cleaner. He must smell better." She smiled tremulously at Thomas. "Will you give me a ride?"

Snickering, his squire dismounted. Thomas had refused to give up bathing, pointing out that he did not need a disguise. "It would be my pleasure, Lady Victoria."

"Do not try your courtesan tricks on this boy, Victoria. I will carry you to the village." Lifting her onto the saddle, Gareth mounted behind her. She held herself stiffly away from him, but her bottom nestled between his thighs.

"Courtesan. You called me a courtesan. Isn't that a fancy word for whore?"

"I did not call you a whore. You are Walter's leman."

"Leman? That's what Ranulf called me. Is that another word for prostitute?"

"Mistress. You said you perform services for Walter. For which he pays you. There is no shame in that," Gareth said soothingly.

She poked him in the ribs with her elbow. "Not that kind of service, you oaf. I am his personal assistant, not his mistress. And I am not ashamed. I have absolutely no reason to be ashamed."

"Pardon me, my lady. I did not mean to insult you. Forgive me." Hell's teeth, but the woman was prickly, and he could not afford to offend her.

"Oh, all right," she said, her tone grudging. "I suppose it was a natural assumption on your part. Women today don't have many career choices, do they? Wife or mistress, that's about it, right?"

"Or nun," said Thomas.

"Wife, mistress, or nun. Good grief," she muttered.

With a sigh, she slumped against him, her head coming to rest on his upper arm. Her eyelids fluttered shut. To his mortification and Thomas's amusement, she began breathing through her mouth.

Victoria was riding on a white horse with an honest-to-God knight. Not one in shining armor, true, but nevertheless . . . Some women—maybe most women—would be thrilled. Victoria told herself she wasn't. But the feel of the knight's chest against her back was solid and comforting. And riding on horseback, while it would never be her favorite method of transportation, was better than walking miles back to the inn. She relaxed slowly, her eyes drifting shut.

Her eyes popped open almost immediately. How did she know that was where they were going?

"Percy, you had better be taking me to the inn. If you have any other destination in mind, I object. Strongly."

"I am taking you to the inn at Darkvale." He sounded irritated. "I told you that. You have no reason to doubt me."

"Oh, no? Why not?"

"I am a knight."

She straightened her spine. "Well, let me tell you a thing or two. The fact that you are a knight does not reassure me, not at all. Three knights kidnapped me earlier today. And another knight—Ranulf is a knight, isn't he?—is holding Walter prisoner and threatening to kill him."

Gareth pulled her back against his chest. "I am not that kind of knight."

"That's what they all say," she grumbled.

"I mean you no harm. I want only to help you."

"Really? Why? What's in it for you?"

"Chivalry dictates my actions."

"Uh-huh." Recognizing several landmarks reassured Victoria that they were in fact returning to the village. She allowed herself to lean her back against the knight's broad chest again.

When they arrived at the inn, Victoria wiggled off the horse before the presumptuous man could assist her. Her abused knees almost didn't hold her upright, but she managed to stand. Turning to the still-mounted knight, she said, "Thanks for the ride, Percy. Good night." She hobbled through the courtyard and entered the inn.

Perceval caught up with her at the bottom of the stairs to the second floor. He took her by the arm and asked, "Which is your room?"

"There is no need for you to escort me to my room."
She tried in vain to pull her arm free. His grip was
firm, but not bruising.

"Innkeeper! Which room is this lady's?"

Clement, the proprietor, appeared in the doorway
leading to the stables. "First on your left at the top of
the stairs. Who are you? Where is her lord?"

"Sir Walter is at Darkvale Keep, a guest of Lord
Ranulf. I am Sir Perceval, and this is my squire,
Thomas." Taking a lit candle from a table next to the
door, the knight indicated the stairway with a sweep
of his arm and said, "After you, my lady."

Victoria detected a note of sarcasm in his voice. "I
am a lady. I'll thank you not to forget it. In case the
code of chivalry does not cover the point, for your
information, ladies do not take strange gentlemen to
their rooms."

"We will not be strangers for long." Placing his
hand on the small of her back, he urged her forward.

"That's what I'm afraid of," Victoria muttered under
her breath.

"Up the stairs, woman."

Victoria climbed the stairs. "Oh. I got demoted from
lady to woman. That's interesting. I suppose knights
only have to practice chivalry on ladies. Well, I'm not
going to put up with any—"

"Quiet." Perceval moved in front of her and opened
the door to the room she had shared so briefly with
Walter.

The room was dark, and the single candle only made
the shadows in the room more pronounced. Victoria
held back. "I'm not going in there with you. It's dark."

Perceval entered the room, leaving her hovering in
the doorway. He found the candles on the fireplace
mantel and lit them with the candle he had brought

from downstairs. He turned back to Victoria. "Come in, my *lady.*"

Victoria had nowhere else to go. She felt a lump forming in her throat. Swallowing hard, she took a step inside the room. This was no time to lose her nerve. She could deal with one pesky knight. She had to. H. Walter needed her. She was the only one who could save him.

To do that, she had to find the amulet. But how? She didn't know what the talisman looked like, or where to start. The thing had been missing for ten years or more. It could be anywhere. Victoria swallowed again and rubbed her forehead. If she were not so tired, if her knees didn't ache, if she were alone, she might be able to come up with a plan.

But she was not alone. Perceval was making himself right at home, and she couldn't seem to muster the energy or the attitude necessary to get rid of him. He had turned his attention to the small fireplace, and within minutes, he had a fire blazing.

Victoria shivered and moved another step closer to the warmth. She hadn't realized she was chilled until she saw the flames. Spring nights were downright cold in this part of the world. Maybe because global warming was centuries in the future.

The future.

She whimpered, "I want to go home."

"Where is your home?" asked Perceval.

She hadn't realized she had said the words out loud. "Seattle." Victoria didn't care what Percy made of that answer, she wasn't up to concocting a believable lie.

"Where is that?"

"West of here." She waved her hand toward the window.

"You are pointing to the north. Come closer to the

fire. You are shivering. Ranulf's men should not have taken you away without your cloak."

"They were in a hurry." She moved closer and held her hands in front of her. "Thank you for the fire. Good night, Percy. I'm tired, and I want to go to bed."

"Not yet. We have much to discuss."

"No, we don't." Drawing herself up to her full five feet, four inches, Victoria turned to face him. In the tone she used to bring junior executives in line, she said, "Sir Perceval, you have given me a ride home. You have escorted me to my room. You have lit the fire. By your actions, you have demonstrated that you are indeed a chivalrous and honorable knight, as you claimed. But I have no further need of your assistance at this time. Please leave. I want to be alone."

"It is not safe for you to be alone."

"Tell me about it." Being alone with the scruffy knight did not make her feel safe. Not at all. The time for talk was over. Mustering her last bit of energy, Victoria bent her bruised knees, raised her hands in a defensive gesture and said, "Eeeeyaah!"

She succeeded in startling him. His eyes widened in shock. "Are you sick?" He took a step in her direction.

Victoria held her ground, and her pose. "Percy—Sir Perceval—I'm warning you. If you come any closer, I will have to hurt you."

"You cannot hurt me, little one."

"I may be little, but I'm tough. I took a self-defense course." She didn't feel it necessary to tell him that it had been six years since she took the course, which had lasted all of four hours.

Before she had time to put her meager knowledge to use, Perceval picked her up by the elbows and moved her to one side. Stepping around her, he sat in the chair. He pointed to the bed. "Sit," he told her, in exactly the tone a man might use with his dog.

"I will not sit. Go. Away. Now."

He didn't move.

Perceval had not responded to polite requests, he had not quailed in the face of her pathetic attempt at violence, and he did not take orders. She was running out of strategies here.

Without much hope of success, Victoria decided to appeal to his nobler nature, assuming he had one. "If you are truly a knight, a man of honor, a defender of . . . damsels, you would respect my wishes."

Perceval smiled at her. "I am truly a knight. But I am not leaving your side until the amulet is found. Sit, and we will discuss what is to be done next."

"There is nothing to discuss. Finding the amulet is my business, not yours. I will do whatever needs to be done to rescue Walter."

"Maidens do not rescue lords."

He said it with complete assurance. Forgetting that even the notion of equality of the sexes was centuries in the future, Victoria bristled. She stuck her chin out. "This maiden will."

"No. You are weak and helpless. You need me."

"I do not need you. And I am not helpless, you macho male chauvinist—"

"Yes, you are."

"No. I'm not. But even if I did need help, I wouldn't need yours. You don't even look like a knight. Where's your shiny armor?"

"It would not be proper to attend a feast in armor."

"The men who kidnapped Walter and me wore armor."

"They are Ranulf's men, part of the garrison guarding his castle. It was right that they should be dressed for battle."

"Do you even have any armor?" She looked him over, taking in his scruffy, unshaved face and his dusty velvet tunic. "If you do, I bet it's rusty."

His cheeks reddened. "I *am* a knight, Victoria."

"Oh, yeah?" she blustered. "How many dragons have you slain? Ball park."

"Two." The knight spoke the word solemnly, but she thought the corners of his mouth twitched. "What is this park you speak of?"

"Never mind that. Maybe you are a knight. But I'm no damsel in distress. I can take care of myself."

He gave her a look that told her he did not believe her. "You need me. I will be your champion." He rose from the chair and knelt before her. Taking both her hands in his, he looked up at her, his expression solemn. "I swear on my honor as a knight to protect you and aid you in your quest for Aethelwyn's amulet."

She had a man at her feet swearing to take care of her. Suddenly light-headed, Victoria tugged her hands free. "I don't want a champion." Her protest sighed out of her, lacking any semblance of conviction.

The knight rose to his feet. Towering above her, he said, "The matter is settled. I have sworn a sacred oath to assist you in your search."

"That was very sweet of you, I'm sure, but I did not ask for your assistance. I don't want you to help me. What part of 'no' don't you understand?"

"Your protests begin to annoy me. I have vowed to help you, and I will. You must accept that. Now, tell me why you seek Aethelwyn's amulet."

Victoria took a step backward, coming up against the bed. Perceval's green eyes glittered menacingly, and his brows were drawn together in a ferocious frown. His clothes were dirty, he hadn't bathed in weeks, and he could out-scowl Walter any day of the week. And he had obviously lost patience with her.

She had dreamed of him.

This was the knight who had haunted her dreams for years. Victoria shook herself. That could not be true. She would never dream of a knight like him. Never. A scruffy, stubborn knight without armor? She would not have known his kind existed. He was not the sort of knight immortalized by poets and romantics, not by a long shot. This rough specimen, smeared in dirt and smelling . . . male could not have been the subject of a romantic fantasy. Her subconscious could not be so stupid as to dream about someone like Perceval: dark, dangerous, masculine, and all too real.

Rattled, Victoria said the first thing that popped into her head. "Are you growing a beard, or did you forget to shave this morning?" She felt a sudden and surprising tug of attraction. The damn dirty knight was *sexy*.

And he didn't smell so bad when she was downwind of him.

"Victoria, do you accept me as your champion?"

Her unexpected and unwanted reaction to him tied her tongue in knots. "Y-yes," she managed, through clenched teeth.

"Then tell me why you seek the amulet."

"You know why. Ranulf wants the amulet in exchange for W-Walter."

"Ranulf had you and Walter brought to Darkvale Keep because you were looking for the amulet. Why?"

"I am not looking for it. Walter is."

Sighing, Perceval resumed his seat. "And why does Walter want the amulet?"

She took a deep breath, trying to get control of her wayward thoughts. And her powers of speech. She was not used to being intimidated by a man, even a large man. But she had to remember this was the thirteenth century, and Perceval was a man of his time. A time when men really were in charge. As she had pointed out to Walter, this was not a good time for women. Attempting a nonchalant shrug, she said, "No special reason."

When he merely looked at her, she blurted, "I mean it. A whim, a passing fancy, an impulse. That's all."

"A man does not offer a chest of gold on a whim." Perceval looked around the room. "Where is the chest of gold? We must secure it from thieves. Your lord was foolish to have mentioned it."

"Not that foolish. The gold is not here."

"Where?"

"Never mind that. It exists and it is in a safe place. Walter has more money than is good for him. He thinks he can buy anything and anyone. It makes him reckless sometimes."

Silence. The knight merely stared at her. Victoria found his stare unnerving. She found everything unnerving and overwhelming. Walter was imprisoned, her scraped knees burned, her head swam, and she couldn't get rid of one lousy knight. Victoria wanted desperately to be alone. She needed time to think about what to do next, time to tend to her wounds, and time to rest.

Victoria was not up to dealing with a knight, especially this knight, in her present exhausted condition. But it was obvious that he was going to sit there and stare at her until he found out what he wanted to know. She would have to tell him enough of the truth to satisfy his curiosity. "Well. If you must know, Walter has the idea that Avondel belongs to him."

Perceval's scowl deepened. "It does not."

"No. Of course it doesn't." Not stopping to wonder how Perceval knew that, she added, "Not yet, anyway."

"What?"

"Never mind. I know Avondel does not belong to Walter. I'm not sure whom it does belongs to. Ranulf, I guess. But he obviously doesn't want it. I don't know why anyone would want it, come to think of it. The place is deserted, and it's falling apart. That's to be expected, I suppose. You know how quickly property deteriorates when no one lives—"

"Victoria, why does Walter seek the amulet?"

She made a circle with her forefinger next to her temple.

Mimicking the gesture, Perceval raised an inquiring brow. "What does that mean?"

"He's crazy. Nuts. Out of his mind. Insane."

"Ahh. Your lord is mad."

"Exactly." Loyalty to Walter made her add, *"Mad* may be a trifle harsh. *Eccentric* is a better description. But now that you know about his delusion—that he owns Avondel—you must see he is no threat to anyone. I'll rescue Walter, with or without the amulet, and I'll take him home, away from Darkvale and Avondel. He won't bother Ranulf, or you, any longer."

Perceval got out of the chair. "You cannot rescue Walter, not without the amulet."

"Yes, I can. Maybe. If I have to. Why do *you* want the amulet? You and what's-his-name? Thomas?"

"Only to aid a damsel in distress."

When she raised an eyebrow in disbelief, he added, "I have heard the story of the Saxon lady and the Norman knight. It is a pretty legend, worthy of a quest."

"Are you working for Gareth?"

He showed surprise for the second time that night. "Gareth. What do you know of him?"

"Ranulf mentioned him. He thought Walter might be looking for the amulet for someone named Gareth. Not the Gareth who married Aethelwyn, another Gareth. Do you know who he is?"

"Nay. I do not work for this Gareth. Enough talk. It is time for rest. We begin our quest tomorrow." He bowed. "Good night, my lady. Rest well."

He left, closing the door behind him. Victoria rushed to the door, intending to lock it. The key was gone. She tried the door, but it would not open.

The scruffy knight had locked her in.

Six

After checking to make sure the door was locked, Gareth put the key in the pouch hanging from his belt. Leaning his back against the locked door, he crossed his arms across his chest. He could feel his heart beating as if he had just engaged in battle. A battle he had not won. He was in retreat, running from a woman, a woman who belonged to another man. If he had stayed with Victoria a heartbeat longer, he would not have left until morning.

Victoria was not a beauty when her features were in repose. But that was seldom. When anger or sorrow or glee animated her face, her countenance was most pleasing to the eyes. When she opened her mouth to bargain, to cajole, to wheedle, her voice held not the shrill sound of the shrew but the charming tones of a seductress. Her large brown eyes had flashed gold sparks at him from beneath winglike brows when he angered her. And whenever he had gotten close to her, her pert nose had twitched, as if she smelled something foul. Him. He had not bathed in four days.

Even so, there had been a moment, when her eyes had widened and she had ceased speaking, that Gareth knew she had forgotten his bad odor. She had felt the same pull he felt. It had left her speechless. For a least a moment or two.

It was then he had discovered that her mouth fascinated him. When she had closed her mouth, she had given him time to admire her bowed upper lip as it rested on her full bottom lip. Then, as he had stared at her mouth, a pink tongue had darted out and given a quick lick, wetting her lips. Garth had felt a sudden tautness in his groin, an urgent need to touch those lips with his.

And so he had fled.

What had he said to Thomas? That he would find his lady love in a bower seated on a butterfly's wing? Some such poetic nonsense. He was certain he had said nothing about finding her in another man's bed.

Gareth shook his head to clear it. The small amount of ale he had consumed at the feast must have been more potent than usual. Strong drink and the months that had gone by since last he was with a woman explained his unexpected and unwanted desire for Walter's leman. It was lust, nothing else, which had unnerved him and sent him hastily from her room. Victoria was not the sort of woman he envisioned sitting beside him in the great hall at Avondel. Only a virtuous woman would sit in the chair once occupied by his mother.

Gareth forced himself to walk slowly down the stairs to the tavern room below. He could imagine what his squire would say if he ran down the stairs like a scared rabbit.

Thomas was talking to the innkeeper.

"I have secured a room for us this night, Sir Perceval," said Thomas when he caught sight of Gareth.

The innkeeper bowed to Gareth. "Sir Knight. Your presence honors my humble inn. I saw your joust yesterday. Your skill with the lance is formidable."

Gareth lowered his head in acknowledgment of the compliment. "Thank you, innkeeper. We would have graced your inn sooner, but the rooms were all taken before today."

"I have rooms aplenty now that most of those who came for the fair have departed."

"Who fills your rooms the rest of the year?" Gareth asked.

"Pilgrims, wandering knights, merchants, and peddlers. And while the rooms are sometimes empty, the tavern rarely is."

Gareth engaged the innkeeper in conversation a while longer, then said, "I am for bed. It has been a long day."

As soon as they were out of earshot of the innkeeper, Thomas said, "A long day, but a day when fortune smiled on you. You have found a way to openly seek for the talisman."

Gareth opened the door to their room, noting that it was next door to the room occupied by Victoria. He motioned Thomas to enter. "Aye. Luck is with us."

"So, the lady agreed to accept you as her champion."

"Aye. She did." Gareth smiled. Grudgingly, but Victoria had accepted him. For the time being. He had no doubt she would try to wriggle out of their agreement. Gareth found himself looking forward to holding her to it. Virtuous or not, he found a verbal joust with Victoria as exhilarating as tilting with lances.

"Why do they seek the amulet? Did she say?" asked Thomas.

"Her lord believes that Avondel is his."

"That cannot be!"

"Nay. And the lady admitted as much. Next she told me her lord has lost his wits."

"Do you believe her?"

"Not a word. However, why they seek the talisman is of no great moment. 'Tis enough that we have joined in the search, with Ranulf's blessing."

"Lord Gareth—"

Gareth held up a hand to silence him. "You must call me Perceval, even when we are alone. We do not know who may be listening."

"I beg pardon. Sir Perceval, do you find this woman . . . odd?"

He found Victoria intriguing, infuriating, and damnably attractive, but he would not tell Thomas that. Gareth temporized. "In what way?"

"She uses words I have never heard. 'Boss.' What is a boss? Or a personal assistant? Why does she deny that she is her lord's mistress? Did she say from whence she and her lord came?"

"See At El, or some such foreign name. She said it is west of here, but the name sounds Eastern. And the lady does not have a good sense of direction."

"Mayhap her lord is a Saracen wizard. A wizard would seek a magic talisman, would he not?"

"I find it hard to believe that Walter of Harrington is a wizard. If he is, he is not a very good one. He allowed Ranulf to capture him without a struggle. What did you learn from the innkeeper?"

"Sir Walter and his lady arrived at the inn shortly before noon today. They came on foot. Clement talked to them while they ate. Walter asked about the amulet right away and told all present in the tavern that he would give a gold piece to anyone who had information about its whereabouts. He set a stack of gold coins on the table to prove he spoke the truth. The innkeeper earned one piece of gold by telling him the names of those in the village who came to Darkvale from Avondel after the curse took hold."

"Did he repeat those names to you?"

"Yes. John the miller, Matthew the blacksmith, and Matilda the brewer. Also several of the villeins, but he was not sure which ones. He said that those he mentioned will know who the others are."

"Matthew," muttered Gareth, scratching his beard. "Unshaven or not, he may recognize me."

"Will he tell Ranulf who you are?"

"Nay, I do not think so. But I cannot be sure. We will speak to him last. Mayhap we will learn what we need to know without talking to him. Now, it is time for sleep."

"There is only one bed."

Gareth raised a brow. "Aye. We have shared close quarters before."

"Yes, but on those occasions you had bathed." Thomas snickered. "I suppose I can breathe through my mouth as the lady did."

Grinning, Gareth cuffed Thomas lightly on the ear. "Are you saying I stink?"

"I am. You should have seen the look on your face when she asked to ride with me. 'Twas priceless. You are not accustomed to ladies holding their noses and refusing to ride with you." Thomas narrowed his eyes. "How did you overcome the lady's aversion to you? Did you woo her with soft words and gentle caresses?"

"I did not woo her at all. I do not seek this lady's good opinion, or her caresses. She is only a means to an end. Now, Thomas, for the sake of your nose, you may sleep alone. I am going to keep watch outside the lady's door."

"Do you think that someone may try to harm her?"

"Her lord showed the village a stack of gold coins. Someone may be tempted to see if he left any gold coins behind."

* * *

Bright sunlight pouring through the window woke Victoria. Blinking, she sat up in bed and stretched. This century had one good thing going for it—no alarm clocks. Considering what she had been through the day before, she had slept remarkably well. No dreams had disturbed her, at least none that she remembered. Pushing back the covers, Victoria pulled up her nightshirt and looked at her scraped and bruised knees. Moving her legs experimentally, she discovered that they worked well enough.

Her mind was clear, another product of a good night's rest. Hugging her knees to her chest, Victoria began to think. Before she and Walter had been so ruthlessly summoned to Ranulf's castle, they had engaged in a long and interesting discussion with their host, Clement, the innkeeper. He had told them that several of the village's inhabitants had formerly resided at Avondel. He had told Walter their occupations and where they lived. After she and Walter had retired to their room, she had written the information in the small notebook she carried in her purse.

Clement himself had arrived in Darkvale only five years earlier, after marrying the widow who owned the inn. Therefore, he had not been able to give them any firsthand information about the siege and its aftermath. Eunice, his wife, had told him the story of Aethelwyn's amulet, of course, but Clement had never heard so much as a rumor about the talisman's present whereabouts. He opined that Eunice might be able to tell them more about Avondel's last days—her sister had worked in the kitchens there—but the two women were on a pilgrimage to Canterbury and would not return for several weeks.

Victoria had to talk to the former Avondel residents, and she had to do it soon. That much was clear. She and Walter had left Seattle on Monday, April 2. By her count, after three days on the road, and one night in Darkvale, it was now April 6. She had a little more than two weeks to find the amulet, rescue Walter, and return to Avondel in time to meet Tobias on April 21.

"Time to get moving," she said. Victoria started to get out of bed, then remembered that her knight had locked her in.

Not *her* knight. Where had that come from? She did not want or need a knight. And no matter what her confused mind had tried to tell her last night, she had never, ever dreamed silly, romantic dreams about a knight like Sir Perceval. Never. Percy was much too real to play the male lead in her romantic fantasies.

Jumping out of bed, Victoria went to the door of her room, prepared to beat on it until someone released her. Before pounding, she tried twisting the knob. It turned. Victoria jerked the door open and almost tripped over the body stretched in front of her door.

"Thomas? What are you doing?"

The young man leaped to his feet, rubbing the sleep from his eyes with the heels of his hands. "Guarding your door. Gar—Sir Perceval thought you might have unwanted visitors."

"So Percy ordered you to spend the night on the floor outside my door?"

"Not the whole night. He took the first watch."

Oh, my. The knight had been outside her room while she slept. Perceval had promised to protect her, and he had actually followed through and kept his promise. Victoria squelched the warm and fuzzy feeling spreading through her. She was giving Perceval entirely too much credit. So he had kept one lousy promise, so what? He had more or less forced himself on her, protector-wise. And he had locked her in her room. She looked around. "Where is he?"

"Who?" Thomas was looking at her bare feet. And

Linda Kay

her bare ankles. And her bruised knees, visible beneath the short hem of her nightshirt.

Victoria backed into her room. She could hear a replay of Walter's voice telling her that women in the middle ages did not show so much leg. The nightshirt was not true to the period, there having been no need for nightwear at Walter's Medieval Fair. Using the door as a shield, she poked her head out and asked, "Sir Perceval. Where is he?"

The squire's gaze moved to her face. "Sleeping. The innkeeper gave us a room next to yours."

"Oh. Well, no one is going to bother me this morning. Would you go downstairs and ask the innkeeper to send hot water to my room? Lots of hot water. I want to bathe. Oh, and you might ask them to send hot water to Perceval's room, too."

"Yes, my lady. Right away." Thomas hurried to the stairs, almost tripping over his feet as he hastened to do her bidding.

Well. A knight who kept his promises, and a squire who hurried to do her bidding. Things were definitely looking up this morning. Victoria retreated into the room, made up the bed, and chose a chemise, dress, and overtunic from the chest and laid them out on the chair. They were badly wrinkled, but there was nothing she could do about that. No irons. Victoria grinned. Another good thing about this day and age.

When a knock sounded on the door, she hastily wrapped her cloak about her and opened it. Servants brought in buckets of hot water and a large barrel-shaped container, which they filled with the water. They also brought linen cloths and a bar of rose-scented soap. After they left, she eyed the steaming barrel. "Better and better. Who needs a hot shower?"

Stripping off her nightshirt, Victoria climbed into the barrel, bending her knees so that the water came over her shoulders. She soaped herself vigorously all over and even managed to wash her hair. She stayed in the barrel until the water cooled, then clambered out. She dried herself with the linen towels and brushed her hair until it was only slightly damp.

While she dressed, Victoria considered what to do next. Whatever she did, she wanted to do it herself, without the help of Perceval or anyone else. But much as she hated to admit it, that probably was not the way to go. She needed help, and she could not risk Walter's life by refusing aid when it was offered. She toyed briefly with the idea of advertising for a replacement for Perceval—someone local might prove more useful—but decided she did not have time to waste on what would probably prove to be a futile effort.

Perceval had named himself her champion, and even though they had only just met, Victoria felt she knew him well enough to guess that he would not easily relinquish the title.

Cracking open the door, Victoria peered into the hall. No one was there. Good. She was not ready to face the knight just yet. She needed time to come up with a way to convince him that, while he was bigger and stronger, she was going to be in charge. Not so rough as Ranulf's knights, Sir Perceval had nevertheless managed to have everything his own way. That had to stop. Victoria was not about to work with a man who could not take orders from a woman, no matter what century she happened to find herself in.

When she arrived downstairs, the tables in the tavern were all empty. The other guests, the ones who had come for the fair, must have departed. Taking a seat on a bench, Victoria greeted the innkeeper. "Good morning, Clement. What is on the menu this morning?"

"Porridge. Bread and cheese. Roast mutton."

"Porridge will do. And"—she almost asked for coffee—"something to drink."

"Ale or wine?"

She shuddered. "Too early for that. Just bring me water, please." Then she remembered the age she was in. "Hot water, that is. Boil it, please."

Clement gave her a strange look, but went to fetch her meal. When he returned, he placed it before her, including a steaming mug of water. "Your lord did not return from the castle last night."

"No, he did not. Walter is going to remain at the castle as Ranulf's guest for a few days."

"You intend to stay here alone? Without your lord?" Clement frowned a disapproving frown.

"Yes, I do. Is there a problem with that?"

"She is not alone, innkeeper. Victoria is under my protection now," said Perceval, standing at the bottom of the stairs.

Clement nodded his head. "Then there is no problem. Except that of payment."

"Walter paid you for the room," Victoria reminded him. "A week in advance."

"Innkeeper?" Perceval walked into the room and sat down on the bench opposite Victoria. "Is that true?"

" 'Tis true. I had forgotten. Will you break your fast, Sir Knight?"

"Aye. I left Ranulf's table last night before eating my fill. Bring me a joint of mutton and a mug of ale."

Clement scurried from the room, leaving Victoria alone with Perceval. She sniffed delicately. Nothing offensive reached her nostrils. He must have bathed. But he hadn't shaved. His face was still darkened with several days' growth of beard. Even though he was seated, he seemed to tower over her. With his square jaw set and his brows drawn together, he looked menacing and determined.

Very determined. Stubborn, even. She had been right. She was not going to get rid of him. Victoria had never run up against such an immovable object before. This knight had appointed himself her guardian, and nothing she could do or say was going to change that.

Nibbling on a crust of bread, she thought long and hard about her—about *the* knight seated opposite her. Did she really need him? Perceval could not storm Darkvale keep all by himself. What purpose did it serve to have a large and difficult-to-control knight following her around? He had said he would aid and protect her, but, myths of King Arthur and his Round Table notwithstanding, the males she had met so far did not seem to be all that restrained by courtesy or custom. They, Perceval included, had no qualms about using their superior strength to get what they wanted. Victoria had to face the fact that in this age, she was weak.

But not helpless. Never that.

She had a brain and it was time to use it.

All right. She had a knight, whether she wanted one or not. At least, this one was clean now. More or less. She narrowed her eyes and studied him. What she had to do next was figure out how to control him. Perceval could make a vow a minute from now until next Thursday, and she wouldn't believe he had her best interests at heart. "Sir Perceval? Why did you offer to help me find Aethelwyn's amulet?"

" 'Tis my duty as a knight."

"Why? You don't know Walter."

"I know you. You want to save him, and I am your champion."

"Percy, you're avoiding the question here. Why did you appoint yourself my champion? What's in it for you?"

He gave her a blank look. "I do not understand the question."

"If you don't want the amulet for some reason of your own, what do you want for helping me find it? Walter's gold?"

"I want nothing from you or from Sir Walter. I told you. Chivalry demands that I aid those in need."

"Uh-huh. Okay. If you don't want to tell me, I guess I can't make you." She ate a spoonful of porridge.

"Victoria, I would have you believe me."

"Then, Percy, you will have to tell me a believable story." He scowled at her. "You *will* believe me."

She grinned at him. "You do that really well."

The scowl faded, replaced by a puzzled look. "What?"

"Scowl fiercely. Walter tries, but he can't quite make it work. He ends up looking like a teddy bear with indigestion."

"Teddy bear? Indigestion?"

Clement appeared with Perceval's breakfast, saving Victoria from having to explain. The innkeeper placed half a round loaf of bread on the table and topped it with a huge hunk of roasted meat. He plunked a mug down.

Perceval took a wicked-looking knife from his belt and began slicing meat from the roasted joint. Victoria swallowed another spoonful of porridge and watched him as he ate. Unfortunately, he was as large as she had remembered him being. She had hoped that in her confused and frightened state of mind, she had exaggerated his size. Even more disturbing, Perceval's green eyes were filled with intelligence. A stupid man would have been so much easier to control. Or get rid of.

Well, she might as well start as she meant to go on.

Victoria took a last bite of porridge and stood. "Good day, Perceval. Enjoy your breakfast."

"Where are you going?"

"I am going to talk to some of the people who came here from Avondel after the siege."

He nodded. "Aye. That is the plan we agreed on last night. Sit down, Victoria, and wait for me to finish eating."

Victoria sank down on the bench. "We need to get a few things straight, Percy. One, I do not take orders from you. Two, you will take orders from me. Three, I will decide whom to talk to and when—"

"Whom will you talk to first?"

"I thought I would start with the blacksmith."

"Nay."

"Nay? Percy, pay attention. You do not say 'nay' to me. This is my quest, and I will—"

"Lady Victoria. I agree that this quest is yours. But I am your champion. I will decide how to proceed."

Victoria blew a stray wisp of hair out of her eyes. "And why do you get to make the decisions? Because you are a man?"

"Aye."

"Your sex does not make you smarter."

"Mayhap not. But my size and my sword will persuade the villagers to talk to us."

"You plan to intimidate people into telling us about the amulet?"

"If need be. The people you wish to interrogate may not be eager to recall painful times."

"Oh. I hadn't thought about that. You may be right."

He nodded. "I am right. We will visit the brewer first. Her house is a short walk from here."

"Her? The brewer is a woman?"

"Aye. She is called Matilda. Most brewers are women. Is it not the same in See At El?"

"No. So women do have another career choice. That's encouraging. Although I suppose it's only because brewing is something like cooking."

Clement appeared with a bowl of steaming water for them to wash their hands. As soon as that was done, Perceval rose and held out a hand. She took it, and he pulled her to her feet.

He kept her hand in his as they strolled through the village, which consisted of the inn and a scattered group of thatched cottages. Victoria glanced over her shoulder. "Percy," she hissed. "Someone is following us."

"Aye. 'Tis Balen, the minstrel."

"I thought I recognized him. He came with the knights who took Walter and me to the castle. Why is he following us?"

"Balen is one of Ranulf's spies. Thomas spotted him this morning, outside the inn. It seems he was waiting for us."

"I don't understand. We are doing what Ranulf told us to do. Why would Ranulf send someone to spy on me?"

"Ranulf may want to assure himself that you are obeying his command and looking for the amulet. If you were faithless, you might decide to keep the gold and leave Walter to his fate."

"I don't like being spied on. I think we should try to lose him." Victoria tugged her hand free and began walking faster.

Perceval caught up with her and took her by the arm. "Balen will learn nothing more than necessary to satisfy Ranulf. Today he will learn that we are talking to some of those who came here from Avondel."

"Why did they come here, do you suppose? I mean, Ranulf had just killed their lord and lady and sacked the castle. It seems to me they would have hated him, yet they came to Darkvale to serve him."

"They had no choice. Avondel was cursed." Perceval sounded grim. Before she could comment, he said, "This is the brewer's house."

Matilda answered her door at Perceval's first knock. "Good day, madam. We would speak with you."

The brewer looked him up and down, then shifted her gaze to Victoria. "Very well. Come in." She stood aside and let them enter.

Perceval introduced himself and Victoria. Matilda motioned for them to sit on a rough wooden bench in front of the fireplace. She sat opposite them on a squat barrel.

The house was not large and seemed to consist of one room. Several large cauldrons stood against the far wall, and baskets filled with grain—Victoria thought she recognized barley—were set about. She sniffed. "Is that malt?"

"Aye," said Matilda. "Are you wanting to learn the brewer's art?"

"No, thank you. I am looking for Aethelwyn's amulet."

Matilda stroked her chin and stared at Victoria. "Are you, now? You have waited long enough. The talisman has been lost for years. But you have come to the wrong place. I know not where it may be."

Perceval spoke. "We did not expect that you would. Lord Ranulf bade this woman find the amulet. He holds her lord hostage until she produces the amulet as ransom. We intend to talk to all those who were present at Avondel when the castle fell to Ranulf."

A curious look flashed in Matilda's eyes, but she did not ask any questions. "The last time I saw the amulet was at the Easter feast that year. Lady Juliana wore the jewel every feast day."

"Juliana was William's wife." Victoria remembered that Ranulf had mentioned the names of the lord and lady of Avondel.

"Aye. They had two children, Gareth and Elwyna."

"Children? I did not know there were children. How old were they? What happened to them? Were they all killed?" Brother Martin's account of the siege at Avondel had not mentioned children. But Ranulf had accused Walter of working for someone named Gareth—Gareth must be the son.

"Lady Juliana and Lord William died. Lady Elwyna lives at Darkvale Keep, ward of my liege lord. I believe she was ten or eleven when Ranulf brought her here."

"What about the son?" asked Victoria. "The second Gareth?"

"He was not at Avondel when Ranulf came. He had not been there for years."

"Where was he?" Victoria asked.

"Gone to his father's liege lord to be trained as a knight. We heard later that he went to France to serve in the French king's crusade."

"And he has never returned to Avondel?"

"That I do not know. No one goes to Avondel from here. No one has seen him here, although word has reached us that he is in England once more. Lord Ranulf has said that anyone who gives him aid and comfort will be punished."

"Thank you for your help. Come, Victoria, we must go."

"Wait. Matilda, do you know of any other villagers who came to Darkvale from Avondel?"

Matilda rattled off several names and told them where each of the villeins had their cottages.

Victoria thanked her, and followed Perceval out of the cottage. "Well. There were children, and one of them is right here. We need to talk to Elwyna. Was she at the feast? Which one do you suppose she was? And Gareth, the missing son. Ranulf thought we were working for him, Walter and I. Where do you suppose he is now?"

"We are not going to Ranulf's castle to speak with Elwyna."

"Oh, Percy. There you go again, making decisions. The least you could do is consult with me first. Why aren't we going to talk to her?"

"She will know nothing useful."

"How did you arrive at that conclusion?"

"Anything she knows, Ranulf knows. He does not know the whereabouts of the amulet. It follows that Elwyna does not know either.

"I see your point. It is unlikely that she knows where the thing is. But that doesn't mean she might not know something useful. Maybe some little detail that will point us toward the amulet."

"We are not going to the castle."

The set of his jaw convinced Victoria not to press the issue. Perceval had the same stubborn look Walter got when she pushed him too far. "I suppose we may as well talk to the other people in the village first. Let's go see the blacksmith."

"Nay. We will talk to the people Matilda mentioned first. They all live in the village or close by. The mill is outside the village, several miles from here."

Victoria refrained from pointing out that the blacksmith's shop, while not in the village proper, was close enough to walk to. "Choose your battles, Victoria," she muttered to herself.

Subservience was hard.

Seven

H. Walter Harrington IV lay on his back on a bed the size of a small country. Walter turned his head and stared at the small patch of blue sky visible through the narrow slit that passed for a window in his tower prison. Ranulf's men had tossed him into the room the night before and left him there without food or water. They had not completely ignored his body's needs, however. A chamber pot had been provided.

Operating on his guiding principle that everyone has a price, he had offered them gold to let him go. They had obliged him by relieving him of his leather pouch of gold coins, but they had locked him in the tower anyway. He had told them he had more gold, a chest full of it, for the man who would help him escape. No one rose to the bait. Not that he could blame them.

Ranulf and his men were operating on another principle: the old "bird in the hand" rationale. A hostage in the tower was worth more than a chest of gold in the bush. Ranulf would probably demand the gold in addition to the amulet before releasing him. The lord of Darkvale struck Walter as someone ready and willing to take whatever he wanted.

Walter stirred himself, rising from his unmade bed for the second time that day. He had wasted the morning alternating between feeling sorry for himself and worrying about Victoria. It was time to examine his prison more closely.

The ceiling was high over his head, fifteen feet or more. The room was round. After pacing it off, he estimated the radius to be twenty feet. There was a fireplace in the wall opposite the window, but no wood or coal with which to light a fire. Not that he needed one now that the sun had come up, but he would have welcomed a fire during the night. His host had not provided sheets or blankets for the bed.

A chair and table were placed under the lone window, which was shuttered but unglazed. The window was too narrow for him to squeeze through, but at least it gave him something to look at besides the black stone walls. His view was limited and consisted mostly of trees. By craning his neck and squinting, he could just make out a gleam of water—he could see a sliver of the moat surrounding the castle.

Moving away from the window, Walter began carefully examining each section of wall, paying special attention to the fireplace. He did not find what he was looking for: a secret passageway. "Damn," he muttered. "Every castle needs a secret passageway."

It made sense that any castle builder worth his salt would not put one where prisoners were kept, he supposed. It looked like the only way out of the room was the heavy wooden door, which was barred from the outside.

No visible means of escape.

Sprawling in the chair, Walter propped his feet on the table. Victoria was his only hope. It would serve him right if she left him to his fate. He hadn't asked her if she wanted to be whisked out of her time, a little oversight she had fussed about every step of their journey from Avondel to Darkvale. No matter how entranced he had been by the thought of time travel, he should have anticipated the possibility of danger.

Walter had read enough history to know the thirteenth century was a perilous time, but he had grown accustomed to the sanitized version of the Middle Ages represented at his annual fair. At his tournaments, the lances had rubber tips, the swords had dull edges, and no one ever found themselves prisoners.

Things were different in the thirteenth century. Whatever the number of "pretend" jousts and sword fights he had participated in over the years, Walter had not been prepared to deal with real knights with real swords. Ranulf's men had captured him and Victoria without so much as a struggle. Walter scowled in disgust.

No doubt about it, he had landed himself and Victoria in an awful mess. His naive trust in Brother Martin's manuscript had been misplaced. The amulet he had thought to secure so easily had been missing for at least ten years. The passage of time made Victoria's task that much more daunting. He knew she would do her best to find the amulet and save him, but he had to face facts. She might not succeed.

Walter knew it was politically incorrect of him, but he couldn't help cringing at the thought that he, a man, was locked in a tower waiting to be rescued by a *girl*.

He closed his eyes in shame. He was a wuss, not a knight, pretend or otherwise. He had never been a warrior of any kind. In the twenty-first century there had not been any real need for him to know how to defend himself and those he cared about. That was the sort of thing he paid others to do. He had to face it: he had gotten used to the security immense wealth provided.

On the other hand, he doubted even the most well trained security maven would have anticipated his ending up a prisoner in a medieval castle, without a penny to his name. Leaning back in the chair, Walter opened his eyes and gazed at the scrap of blue sky. As a voyage of self-discovery, this trip might prove very interesting. He would have to survive by using his wits, not his checkbook.

He might as well start now—there was nothing else to do. Walter leaned back in the chair, folded his arms across his chest, and concentrated on *thinking* a way out of his predicament. He had to get out of this cell, at the very least. There must be people in Ranulf's keep—servants, soldiers—who had been around ten years ago. If he could talk to them, he might learn something useful. He had to convince Ranulf to give him the run of the castle. That should be doable—hostages were quite often treated as honored guests. Walter seriously doubted that Richard the Lionhearted had been kept in a cell when he was held hostage by Emperor Henry VI.

Walter looked around his room again. As prisons went, this one wasn't bad. He should be grateful that Ranulf hadn't locked him in a damp, rat-infested dungeon. His room was clean, the bed had been comfortable—

A knock sounded on the door.

Walter called out, "Come in."

The door opened, and a knight appeared, sword in hand. A young woman followed the guard into the room carrying a heavily laden tray. Walter gazed at her appreciatively. She was the prettiest sight he had seen in days. Midnight black hair fell in soft waves to her waist. Her large eyes were the gray of the turtle dove, veiled with lashes the color of her hair.

"Good morning. I bring you food and drink."

Rising quickly from his chair, Walter took the tray from the woman's hand. "Allow me."

She curtsied. "Thank you, my lord."

For the first time, Walter noticed that the tray he

held contained bread, cheese, and a small roasted fowl of some kind. A mug of ale completed the repast. His mouth watered as the aromas reached his nose, but he postponed falling on the food like a hungry animal. He set the tray on the table and bowed to the woman.

She spoke to the guard. "You may leave us, Ulrich. I would talk with our guest."

"As you wish, my lady. I will wait for you outside." The guard left the room, closing the door behind him. Walter heard the bar falling into place.

Guest? Walter bowed again, encouraged. Guest was exactly the position he intended to claim and to exploit. "What do you want to talk about, beautiful lady?"

She shook her head and pointed to the tray. "Later. Please eat first. You must be hungry. I was not told of your presence until late this morning, so I did not see to it that you were fed last night."

"Not a problem. Missing one meal will hardly kill me. I do regret not meeting you sooner, however. It is very kind of you to bring me food and drink. But I cannot sit while you stand. Please take the chair. I'll move the table closer to the bed and eat there."

"Very well."

Walter held the chair until the woman was seated, then moved the table. Seating himself on the bed, he said, "My name is Walter, by the way. And you are?"

"Elwyna."

"That's a pretty name." After making short work of the bread and cheese, he contented himself with nibbling on the bird's wing between sips of ale. "This is very good. I feel able to converse with you now that I've eaten enough to take the edge off. What shall we discuss?"

"The amulet."

Walter grinned. He admired directness. "Ah. Of course. What about it?"

"You are prisoner because you asked about Aethelwyn's amulet. Why are you searching for it?"

"As I told Lord Ranulf, I am interested in legends and myths. The legend of the amulet interests me."

She drew her brows together in an adorable frown. "Why? Legends will not feed hunger. Myths do not quench thirst. And the people of Darkvale do very well without magic."

"As it happens, I am wealthy enough to provide food and drink for myself and my employees—my vassals. I travel the world seeking knowledge. And adventure. I have seen Avondel and heard the story of the Norman knight and the Saxon lady who built it. Now the castle is empty, the surrounding lands barren, the forest forbidding. Yet, I am told, it was a happy place until the loss of the amulet. I found it amusing to look for the magic talisman."

"And if you find it? Do you intend to claim Avondel for yourself?"

"No. I have no present need for a castle. I only want to solve the puzzle of the amulet's disappearance and see Avondel restored to its former glory."

"The amulet alone will not accomplish that. Avondel must have a lord, knights to guard the castle, villeins and freemen to work the land and tend the sheep."

"Well, yes, but you have to start somewhere. Once the amulet is restored, the rest will follow. Or so the legend goes."

Elwyna rose gracefully from the chair and began strolling around the room. "You truly did not intend to keep the amulet for yourself, assuming you found it?"

"No. I planned to return Aethelwyn's amulet to its rightful owner, Lord Ranulf."

She stopped in front of him. "That would please my lord as he has decided he wants the amulet, but Ranulf is not the heir to Avondel."

"No? I thought he laid siege to the castle and killed—disposed of all the inhabitants."

"Not all were killed. Very few, in fact. After the . . . siege and its aftermath, many of the people of Avondel followed Ranulf to Darkvale."

"Why would they do that? Because Avondel no longer had magic to guard it?"

She shrugged. "That was part of it, I suppose. The loss of the amulet meant that Avondel was cursed. And they needed a lord, since theirs was dead. At that time, Ranulf needed people. Many of Darkvale's inhabitants had succumbed to fever the winter before. Some—a very few—of the Avondel survivors wanted to wait for the heir to return, I believe, but they were overruled."

"Heir? What heir?" Walter asked, dumbfounded.

"The son of the lord and lady of Avondel. He was not present at the time of the siege. He had left Avondel years before for his knight's training, and he rarely visited Avondel."

"There is a son? A knight? Brother Martin's history of Avondel did not mention a son. Who is he?"

"Lord Gareth of Avondel," said Elwyna. "Who is Brother Martin?"

Walter stood and walked to the window. "Brother Martin is a monk who wrote a book about Avondel. His book is how I learned about the castle, the siege, and the amulet."

Elwyna frowned again. "I remember a friar. . . . That is, I remember being told that there was a friar present at Avondel before Ranulf came. I did not know he had written about Avondel."

Walter said, "Brother Martin was not at Avondel." He could not tell her that the monk had not been born until a century after the siege.

"I suppose this Brother Martin could have heard the story from the friar, but then he ought to have known about Gareth and . . . others." Elwyna chewed on her bottom lip, obviously puzzled.

"Maybe the monk got the story third- or fourth-hand. Actually, I have learned that Brother Martin's account was defective in several respects. Now that I think about it, though, I have heard the name Gareth before. Ranulf mentioned him last night. He thought I was working for Gareth. Where has the lord of Avondel—Gareth would be the lord, wouldn't he?—been all these years?"

Elwyna's gray eyes darkened to a smoky color. "No one knows. He never returned to Avondel after the siege."

"Ranulf must think the heir has come back, since he assumed I was working for him. Does Ranulf expect this Gareth to come here seeking revenge?"

"I do not know if Gareth will come to Darkvale. I cannot guess what is in his heart. But it is rumored that he has returned to England after many years abroad."

Walter snapped his fingers. "Gareth has come back. I'm sure of it. The footprints—"

"What? What footprints?"

"At the castle at Avondel. When Victoria and I arrived, the castle was deserted, but there were footprints in the dust. It is possible that they were made by this Gareth."

Elwyna's hand went to her throat. "You were at Avondel? When?"

"Several days ago." Sensing Elwyna's discomfort, Walter said, "Probably not the heir, after all. More likely the footprints were made by tourists. Like Victoria and me."

"Tourists?"

"Travelers. There were two sets of footprints, but no other sign that anyone else had been there recently."

"Why were you at Avondel?"

"We had hoped to save the castle and its inhabitants, but we were too late. Too late by a decade, as it turned out."

"I do not understand."

"No, I don't suppose you do. Some things are hard to explain. Do you believe in magic, Elwyna? The magic of the amulet, for example?"

She avoided answering the question. "I believe Ranulf wants the amulet. Will your lady be able to find it, do you think?"

"My lady? Oh. You mean Victoria. She is not my lady. She's my personal assistant."

Elwyna drew her brows together, obviously confused. "I do not know what that means. Is she your . . . mistress?"

Walter snorted. "Hardly. She wouldn't have me. Victoria works for me."

"Oh. She is a servant."

"In a way, but don't let her hear you call her a servant. She is my employee. I am her boss. At least, Victoria allows me to think I am the boss."

"Boss? I do not know that term. You are her lord?"

"Employer. I employ Victoria as my personal assistant. She does things for me, for which I pay her a salary." At Elwyna's still-blank look, he added, "I give her money in exchange for her services."

"She presides over your hall? As I do for my lord Ranulf?"

Walter gave up trying to explain twenty-first-century labor-management relationships. "Yes."

"Is she clever? Will she be able to find the amulet?"

"Victoria is very clever. If the amulet exists, she will find it. I have complete faith in her."

Elwyna appeared dubious. "But she is a woman alone. She will have to find someone to help her. A knight, perhaps."

"Possibly. Generally speaking, Victoria prefers not to delegate." Walter was certain Victoria would not choose a knight to help her. She had called them "canned thugs." "She likes to do things herself."

"But she is a woman," Elwyna repeated. "A woman is soft and weak, not suited for quests or adventures."

"Who told you that? A woman can do anything she sets her mind to, and she can do it well. Victoria is a strong and independent female, for which I am extremely grateful. If anyone can save me, she will."

"I can see that you really believe that. My lord Ranulf must have agreed with you, since he bade her find the amulet."

"Is Lord Ranulf your father?" Surely he was too old to be her husband. On the other hand, lords in the Middle Ages favored young wives. Walter suddenly felt an intense interest in Elwyna's status. He did not want her to be married.

"No. I am his ward. My father is dead. My mother, too."

"I am sorry. When were you orphaned?"

"A long time ago. King Henry named Ranulf my guardian when I was eleven."

"Does he treat you well?"

"Well enough. I do not wish you ill, but I hope your Victoria does not find the amulet."

"Why?"

"Because the legend of the amulet grows stronger every year. Ranulf says the legend is false, that the amulet never protected Avondel. I believe he fears many of his subjects will return to Avondel if the amulet is found and Gareth returns to claim his inheritance."

"What will Ranulf do with the amulet?"

"I believe he intends to destroy it."

"Can magic be destroyed?"

She shrugged. "I do not know if the amulet is magic

or myth. I know that Aethelwyn's legend has brought unhappiness to many people."

"Unhappiness? I thought Avondel was a happy place."

"Not for everyone within its walls." She paused, a faraway look in her eyes. After a moment, she focused her gaze clearly on him. "Or so I have been told. Are you finished with your food?"

"Yes. Thank you."

Elwyna picked up the tray. "Good day to you."

"Wait. Don't go. Stay and talk with me a while. I would hear more of Avondel."

"I cannot stay. I have other duties. But I will visit you again when I can. And I will see to it that you have fresh linens for your bed and clean clothes for your body."

"Thank you. I hope you find time to visit me again, and soon. Until then, I don't suppose you could find a book or two for me to read? It would help pass the time."

"I will try." Elwyna knocked on the door. The guard opened it, allowed her to exit, then closed and barred the door.

Walter found himself alone again. At least he now had something new to think about. Ranulf said he did not believe in the legend, and yet he wanted the amulet found. Why? If the amulet was not magic, its return to Avondel would make no difference in the scheme of things. Even if the heir had returned, an old piece of magicless jewelry would not help this second Gareth make the castle strong and its lands productive again.

If Ranulf was lying, and he did believe in the amulet's power, why had he waited for ten years to look for it?

Something did not add up.

No matter what Ranulf believed, the story of the magic talisman had to be true. After traveling through time,

Walter was a firm believer in magic. And what but the loss of the charmed amulet could explain Castle Avondel's resistance to twenty-first-century technology? Something was preventing his castle from being restored. It had to be the loss of Aethelwyn's amulet.

Walter walked to the window and stared out at the scrap of landscape visible to him. Where was Victoria now? What was she doing? By now, she would have decided on a course of action. She had probably begun taking steps toward her goal. Victoria would find the amulet if she could; Walter was certain of that.

But what if she couldn't? There was only a limited amount of time available for the search, after all. Barely two weeks remained before he and Victoria had to meet Tobias at Avondel. As Tobias might have said, time was of the essence. Instead of waiting around for Victoria to rescue him, he had better start doing what he could to save himself. Walter looked around his prison. The first thing he had to do was get out of this cell.

If he had another chance to talk to Ranulf, he might be able to convince him that they should work together to find Aethelwyn's amulet. Walter groaned and hit his forehead with the heel of his hand. He ought to have thought of that sooner. He could have asked Elwyna to arrange an audience with Ranulf. But he had been so dazzled by her beauty, and so interested in what she had told him about Avondel, he had forgotten all about his plan to gain the run of the castle.

Walter strode to the door of his prison and pounded loudly. No one had responded to his knocking before, and no one responded now. Ranulf must not be worried that his prisoner would escape. He had not posted a guard outside the door.

Not that a guard was needed, with no visible means of escape and no way to communicate with the outside world. He would have to wait for Elwyna to return.

* * *

Elwyna left the tower cell and slowly made her way to Ranulf's chamber. Her guardian would be waiting for her report, and she wanted to marshal her thoughts before meeting him. Her thoughts had been chaotic for days, ever since word had reached Darkvale that Gareth had returned to England a favorite of the new king, Edward.

Her brother. The last time she had seen him, she had been nine, much too young for a swaggering knight-in-training to bother with. But on his last visit home, Gareth had spent hours in her company. He had taken her fishing, told her stories of Baron Edmond's keep and the wonders he had seen in his travels with the baron. When he left, Gareth had promised to visit again very soon.

He had never come back.

When Ranulf had asked her to question his hostage, he told her only that the man was seeking Aethelwyn's amulet, probably for Gareth. He had not told her that Walter had visited Avondel.

Elwyna's snail-like progress slowed even more. Avondel. She had not seen her childhood home since Ranulf carried her away that awful day—the day she had witnessed the deaths of her mother and father. Elwyna grimaced. She would not think of that. When they had arrived at Darkvale, Ranulf told her never to think of that day again, to remember her mother as she had been before. . . .

Elwyna had tried to obey, but sometimes the memories came upon her so quickly she could not avoid them. Once, she had asked Ranulf to take her back to Avondel. She wanted to see if the place was better than her dreams, or worse than her nightmares. He had refused. Since then, Elwyna had focused on the present, immersing herself in her studies, which were interrupted only occasionally by a visit from a would-be suitor. She was fortunate indeed that Ranulf allowed her to decide whether to accept or reject such suits.

Walter of Harrington's face appeared in her mind's eye. Handsome and educated, he was the sort of man she might choose to marry, if she were eager to be a bride. But a handsome face and pretty manners were not proof of kindness. Elwyna wanted most of all a gentle man. The men who visited Darkvale Keep from time to time were warriors or merchants, more interested in glory or gold than in catering to a silly female's dreams of tenderness.

Walter had been considerate of her, seeing to it that she was comfortable before beginning his meal. More impressively, he had talked to her as an equal, listening to her questions and answering them politely. He believed a woman could do anything she set her mind to. That was a novel thought.

Elwyna arrived outside Ranulf's chambers. The door was slightly open and she could hear that her guardian was not alone. The troubadour Balen was with him. She paused at the door and listened.

". . . do not need the woman. I can find the amulet for you. I would have done sooner had I known you wanted it."

"I did not know I wanted it until I heard others were looking for it." Elwyna could hear the amusement in Ranulf's voice, and smiled. She liked her guardian best on those rare occasions when he showed his sense of humor. "Now that I know I want the amulet, it is better that a stranger seek it out. If they know I want it, the people of Darkvale might think I plan to use it to save myself from Gareth's vengeance, or to thwart the rebirth of Avondel."

"Which is it?"

"Both." Now Ranulf's tone was grim, devoid of humor.

"Gareth may not return to Avondel. And those who followed you to Darkvale are loyal to you. They have forgotten Gareth."

"I do not fear Gareth. I defeated him once, and I will do so again if it becomes necessary. As to my followers, I prefer to avoid putting their loyalty to the test. I do not intend to rely solely on this woman to find the amulet. That is why I ordered you to follow her. Report. Tell me who she talked to."

"A knight aids her—Sir Perceval. He was at the banquet last night."

"I remember him. The promise of gold must have stirred him to action."

"This morning they spoke to the brewer."

"She is one of those who came from Avondel. They must plan to interrogate the others."

"Aye."

Elwyna knocked and pushed open the door.

Balen bowed and greeted her effusively. "Lady Elwyna, you are as lovely as ever. You must grant me an audience soon. I have composed a new ballad for you."

"Later, perhaps." Never, if she had her way. She did not like Balen. He was small of stature and cowardly, unsuited for knighthood. Balen sought to gain respect with flattery and charm, but he tried too hard. Elwyna found his compliments false and his charm too buttery to be sincere.

Ranulf dismissed the man. When they were alone, he motioned for her to sit. "Well? What have you learned?"

"I do not believe Walter conspires with my brother. He was not aware that the last lord and lady of Avondel had a son."

"He may be lying."

"I do not think so, not about that. His face is open and guileless except when he lies. Then he hides his eyes."

"What did he lie about?"

"When I asked him his reasons for seeking the amulet, he repeated what he told you last night. He said he was a scholar interested in legends. He did not meet my gaze when he told that tale."

"So." Ranulf folded his hands together and waited for her to continue.

"I am sure he seeks the amulet for his own reasons. But I do not know what they may be."

"Nor do I. But I would be surprised if they have anything to do with scholarship. Scholars do not usually have pouches filled with gold coins. Nor do they promise chests of gold to those who assist them in their studies."

"Walter of Harrington is not a scholar. You are right about that. However, he can read. He asked for books to pass the time. May I give him my books?" Elwyna asked.

"He grows bored already. Good. But do not give him books and do not visit him again today. We will learn nothing from him that way. Wait a day or two; then visit him again. Hours of solitude may loosen his tongue. Where is he from?"

"I do not know. I did not think to ask."

"What of the woman? Does he think she will be able to find the amulet?"

"Sir Walter says she is clever."

Ranulf smiled, showing his teeth. "For his sake, we may hope so."

Eight

By the end of the day, Victoria was thoroughly disgusted, dismayed, and almost discouraged. To top it all off, her feet hurt again. They had gone from house to house asking about the amulet. Not one soul they had talked to knew anything. She had the feeling that fear kept them from speaking freely, but she had no idea what they were afraid of. "Why won't they talk to us? What are they afraid of? Ranulf? That does not make sense, since he is the one who ordered us to find the thing."

"Mayhap they fear the curse that has settled on Avondel will follow them here to Darkvale if the amulet reappears." Taking her arm, Perceval guided her around a fresh pile of cow manure.

"I thought the curse was caused by the absence of the amulet. They must be afraid of what Balen will tell Ranulf. The little snoop made sure everyone we talked to saw him following us." Balen had disappeared for a few hours early in the afternoon, but he had not stayed away. Victoria did not have to look to know that the troubadour dogged their steps once more. He was so close behind, he might as well have joined them. Grumpily, Victoria hoped his feet hurt as much as hers.

The soft boots Balen wore could not provide any more arch support than her thin-soled slippers.

"I doubt anyone fears Balen," said Perceval. "Mayhap the villeins are not afraid, only reluctant to talk to strangers."

"I suppose it doesn't matter. I don't think any of them knew anything useful. To tell the truth, I'm beginning to wonder if anyone knows anything about the amulet. What if it wasn't lost, mislaid, or stolen? What if it just disappeared? Disintegrated? Went 'poof' and was gone? Maybe magic doesn't last forever. Nothing else does."

Releasing her arm, Perceval patted her on the shoulder. "Victoria, you cannot give up hope so soon. We have only been searching for one day. Some quests take years."

"That is a problem, a big problem. I don't have years." She sighed heavily. "But you're right, Percy. I shouldn't be so negative. We can't give up hope this early in the game. The blacksmith may know more."

"Or the miller," said Perceval.

His tone of voice let her know that he intended to visit the miller next, no matter what she said. She was too worn out to argue with him—especially since she had not won an argument with him yet. Not only did her knight not take orders from her, he persisted in bending her to his will. Was being saddled with a stubborn knight some kind of cosmic payback? Walter had told her repeatedly that she was too bossy, even for the twenty-first century. She supposed it was unreasonable for her to expect a thirteenth-century male to bow to her command.

Resentfully, Victoria watched Perceval out of the corner of her eye. He did not appear to be at all tired. He strode along the rough path as if he could walk for hours, while she had to stop every few feet to shake the pebbles out of her shoes.

Victoria could not match Percy's stamina or his strength. She couldn't order him about—well, she could snap out orders as much as she wanted, but not with the slightest hope that they would be followed. Perceval had decided in which order they would visit the villagers; he had taken the lead at every interview, and it appeared he had the next day's agenda all worked out.

Not once had he bothered to ask if she agreed with his decisions.

She was beginning to get seriously annoyed. There must be some way to handle Sir Perceval. What could she do? How did women in the Middle Ages get by? Women had survived this age, after all. Some women had flourished during the era. Eleanor of Aquitaine came to mind.

Eleanor had been a queen, though, which must have given her an advantage other women did not have. What about the women who were not queens? How did the average woman manage to coexist successfully with the men of this age? She should have asked Matilda. The brewer had seemed like a strong, independent woman. Even in this benighted age, the female sex must have something going for it. What was it?

Sex.

Victoria almost tripped. That could not be it. Women in this age could not possibly sleep around to get what they wanted. This was a time when men placed a ridiculously high value on a woman's innocence. They expected women to remain virgins until marriage—except for the ones they seduced and discarded, of course. A smart woman would not easily give up something men prized so highly. Victoria narrowed her eyes and considered. But a clever woman might use something short of actual surrender. Like feminine wiles. That had to be it. They must use feminine wiles to exercise some control over the men of this era.

She could do that.

What was she thinking? She could not, would not sink so low. Victoria was not about to use female trickery to charm her knight. Fawn and simper and pretend to be dumb? How demeaning. How degrading. She almost gagged at the very idea.

But it might work.

Perceval had shown on several occasions that he . . . liked her. He touched her every chance he got, for one thing—a hand on her elbow, her waist, the small of her back. All in the interest of steering her where he wanted her to go, but still . . . Victoria could tell he was attracted to her. For another thing, even though he was bossier than she ever thought about being, Perceval was trying very hard to help her find the amulet. It was conceivable that a little feminine persuasion might make him more tractable. Victoria swallowed her disgust. Whether she liked it or not, she had no choice. Walter was depending on her. She had to do it.

She had to charm her knight.

How hard could that be? Men were notoriously easy, after all. The difficult part would be to keep things from going too far. The damn, stubborn knight was even sexier now that he had bathed. She could handle that. Victoria had never been a pushover where men were concerned. Easy to get rid of, as demonstrated by her record of being dumped two consecutive times. But hard to get. As Walter had pointed out, she was picky. It would take more than sex appeal for Percy to get more from her than she intended to give. In this battle of the sexes, she intended to be the winner.

The fact that Perceval had no idea they were about to joust gave her an unfair advantage, an advantage she had no qualms about exploiting. All's fair in love, war, and quests for magic amulets.

They were approaching the inn. Victoria cleared her throat to get the knight's attention. When he glanced at her, Victoria gave him what she hoped was a seductive smile. "It will be good to get back to the inn. I'm hungry. Will you join me for dinner?"

His brows rose in surprise, and a gleam of masculine interest appeared in his eyes. "I will, thank you."

It couldn't be *this* easy. She had been grumbling and complaining all day because of his high-handed behavior. One smile, an invitation to dinner, and he forgot all that? Perhaps Percy was not as smart as she had thought he was.

Victoria smiled at him again, then simpered, "Good. We can discuss what to do next. Thank you for taking me to see the brewer and the others today. And thank you for watching over me last night. That was very considerate of you, sleeping outside my door to protect me from thieves or worse."

"I promised to keep you safe, Lady Victoria."

"I know you did. And you kept your promise. Some men don't, you know." She placed her hand on his forearm and favored him with an adoring look. "I am so very fortunate to have you as my champion."

Perceval opened the door for her. As she passed by him, he leaned in and whispered, "Shall we dine in your room or in the tavern?"

"In the t-tavern." Two smiles, and he wanted to be alone with her? In a room with a bed? Oh, this was *too* easy. And much too fast. She had to slow him down. "Thomas can join us." Victoria looked around. "Where is Thomas? I haven't seen him all day."

"He will be along. Thomas has been following Balen."

Victoria gave a startled laugh. "Has he really? I didn't see him."

"Thomas is better at it than Balen." Perceval steered Victoria to a table in the corner and signaled to Clement. The innkeeper gave the menu for the day—roast mutton or mutton stew—and went to fetch their order.

Perceval said, "Balen spent as much time looking over his shoulder today as he did watching us. It does not hurt to distract an enemy."

Sobering, Victoria said, "I've never had an enemy before. Neither has Walter. I wonder how he is. I wish I could see him."

"You must care a great deal for your lord."

"He is not my lord. He is my employer. But naturally I care for him. We've been together for five years."

"You are loyal to him."

"Of course I am."

"Good." Perceval nodded in satisfaction. "A lady should be loyal to her lord."

Clement placed a bowl of stew in front of her, and a round loaf of bread and what appeared to be a whole leg of lamb before Perceval.

"Where is the silver?" asked Victoria. "I need a spoon. And a napkin."

Clement nodded and returned with a spoon and two mugs of ale.

"Now, where were we?" she asked Perceval. "Oh, yes. A lady should be loyal, et cetera. I agree, as long as the lord is as loyal to his lady as he expects her to be to him. But Walter is not my lord. He is my boss."

"Hmmm," said Perceval, taking a dagger from his belt. He sliced a piece of mutton off the joint. "Boss. Is that not the same as a lord?"

"No. It is not the same. I work for him. That's all. You don't listen to me, Percy." Victoria winced. Her tone had bordered on peevish. This was not the time to get indignant.

"I am listening now," Percy said. "How is it that Walter took you as his . . . assistant and not his wife?"

"You sound like my Aunt Crystal. I am not Walter's wife because I do not want to be Walter's wife. And because he never has and never will ask me to marry him. There are no sparks."

"Sparks?"

"No chemistry. No attraction." At Perceval's continued blank look, she added, "There is no lust lost between us."

"Ahh. No lust." Perceval sliced another hunk of meat off the joint and took a healthy bite.

"Right." Victoria's gaze went to his mouth. His teeth were strong and white. She remembered Walter telling her that people in the Middle Ages did not suffer from dental decay until the use of sugar became widespread. Sugar had not become widely available until the seventeenth century. Victoria's eyes widened.

No sugar. No coffee or tea, either, or potatoes, or tomatoes. No chocolate. *No chocolate.* She *had* to get back to her own time. She could not survive in this age. No twenty-first-century woman could deal with men like Perceval *and* go without chocolate. She had to get busy and get Walter out of that castle so they could go home. *Think charming,* she told herself. Batting her eyes at Perceval, she asked, "How is it that a big, strong, handsome man like you is not married?"

"I do not have lands of my own."

"Is that necessary?"

"Aye. A man may not marry until he has the means to take care of a wife and family. For a knight, land and castle are the means. I will have them soon."

"And then you will look for a wife."

"I will look for a virtuous woman. When I find her, I will take her to wife."

"Virtuous? You mean a virgin?"

Nodding, he said, "A virgin, aye, but that is not all. I must be the first man she lies with, and the last."

"Are you a virgin?"

"Nay."

"Will your wife be your last lover?"

"Mayhap."

"Humph. The old double standard is alive and well in Darkvale."

"Double standard?"

"Different rules for men and women. Men may behave like rabbits, before and after marriage, but a woman must be pure before marriage, and virtuous after. That is not fair, Percy. Not fair at all."

" 'Tis necessary. How else will a man know that his heirs are the fruit of his seed?"

Squeezing her eyes shut, Victoria strained to keep her mouth shut. Nothing feminine or wily would come out if she opened it. How could he ask such a stupid, chauvinistic, *male* question? She began taking deep, calming breaths.

"Victoria? Are you all right?"

She did not answer him. Why would she be all right? She was in a strange place, with even stranger people. Her boss was locked in a tower and threatened with death. She had to find an amulet that had not been seen for ten years or more. The only person who had offered to help her was a stubborn, unenlightened, un-yielding, unshaven knight.

"Victoria?"

After taking one more deep breath, she opened her eyes, and she managed to flutter her lashes at him. "I'm all right." Reaching across the table, she took one of his large hands—the one not gripping the dagger—in both of hers. "Only because you're here to help me. I don't know what I would do without you, Percy. You're so big and strong, and I'm so weak and"—she gritted her teeth—"helpless. Can't we please talk to the blacksmith tomorrow?"

Perceval's gaze went to her hands holding his. "I thought we agreed that a lady ought to be true to her lord."

She dropped his hand. "Oh, good grief. This is not going to work. I cannot do this. Listen, Percy. We need to get a few things straight. I am not Walter's lady, woman, wife, or mistress. I am his personal assistant. I assist him. In his business. That's it. That's all. I do not sleep with him. Walter is not, I repeat, *not* my lord."

"What is Walter's business?"

Her mouth dropped open. She shut it. Why hadn't she thought before speaking? She could not explain venture capitalism to a medieval knight. Capitalism hadn't been thought of yet. She had to rein in her feminist sensibilities no matter how difficult that was proving to be. She could be charming. She *had* to be charming, for Walter's sake.

Victoria reached for Percy's hand again. She forced herself to smile winsomely at him. What had Walter told Ranulf last night? "He is a scholar. I help him with his research."

"You can read?"

"Of course I can read, you—" She bit her tongue in the nick of time. She had been about to call Perceval a dolt. Probably not the way to charm him. ". . . that is, can you?"

"Yes. Baron Edmund saw to it that I had a well-rounded education as well as the best training in swordsmanship and other skills."

She squeezed his hand. "I'm sure you have all the right stuff."

"Right stuff?" He turned her hand so that his hand covered hers.

Just like a man to want to be on top. Victoria strained to keep her lip from curling. "The proper qualifications. You are strong, wise, and noble. Exactly the kind of man I need to help me find the amulet." She made her voice low and husky. "Why can't we talk to the blacksmith?"

"We will. After we talk to the miller."

Victoria dropped his hand. So much for the efficacy of feminine wiles. She should have known they would not work. Not for her, anyway. "You are the most arrogant, stubborn, unyielding . . . male I have ever known. I insist we talk to the blacksmith tomorrow."

Clement reappeared with another mug of ale for Perceval. "The blacksmith is at Darkvale Keep today and tomorrow, shoeing horses for Lord Ranulf."

Perceval grinned at her. "Then we will speak with the miller tomorrow. But not until evening."

"Evening? Why? What are we going to do all day?"

"We are going to buy a palfrey for you. Did Walter leave you any gold?"

"Yes. A few coins." She patted her purse. "I have them here. Why do I need a horse?"

"Where is the chest of gold he promised? Does it exist?"

"Oh, yes. It exists. Walter wouldn't go anywhere without his own personal Fort Knox. About the horse—"

"What is Fort Knox?"

"A place where gold is stored. I don't really want a horse."

He squeezed her hand. "I understand. You prefer to ride with me. But if we have to travel long distances, we will travel faster if we each have our own mount."

"I suppose so." There were no taxis in this benighted age, after all. No trains, or planes, or buses, either. Victoria sighed. She was tired of beating her head against a stone wall, but for Walter's sake she gave it one more try. "But I won't need a horse until we leave Darkvale, and we won't leave here until we know where the amulet is. I don't think we can afford to spend a whole day horse hunting. We will talk to the miller first, horse shop after we're done with him."

Perceval shook his head. "The miller will not talk to us during the day. We would be taking him away from his duties. He will speak more freely at home, without the distractions at the mill."

After a moment, she nodded her head. "All right. That makes sense. But there isn't much time—that is, I want to get Walter out of Ranulf's clutches as soon as possible."

Victoria spent the next day learning how to ride the adorable donkey Perceval and Thomas had bought for her. The lessons were more complicated than they should have been because she was required to ride seated sideways on the beast. They had not been able to find a horse trained to be ridden by a lady. She didn't care. Victoria had taken one look into the donkey's liquid brown eyes and fallen in love.

Her mount was white and female and gorgeous. Victoria named her Hilary.

At dusk, she and Perceval set out for the miller's house. Perceval instructed Thomas to remain behind and distract Balen while they slipped away.

The miller's house was a long, low rectangle with a thatched roof. The exterior walls were timber framed and covered with something that looked like stucco. Victoria remembered Walter talking to the architect at

Avondel about wattle-and-daub construction. That must be what the stucco was: willow or oak wands covered in clay. Walter had planned to build replicas of thirteenth-century cottages once the castle was restored.

This cottage boasted several glazed windows and a chimney. Victoria supposed the miller must be well off. He did have a monopoly, after all. No one but him could grind grain into flour. Perceval knocked on the door, and the man of the house opened it.

"Good evening. I am Sir Perceval, and this is Lady Victoria. We have come to speak with the miller."

"I am the miller. John is my name. Come in."

The miller was dusty. All over. She ought to have expected that. The man worked in a closed environment all day, a place where flour filled the air. She shuddered to think what his lungs must look like.

Perceval spoke first. "Ranulf of Darkvale has set this woman a task. She must find Aethelwyn's amulet, or her lord will die. We were told that you were at Avondel during the siege."

The miller nodded. "I was there, but I know nothing of the amulet."

"Did many people die?" asked Victoria.

"Enough. The lord and lady died. Some of the castle guard. And a number of Ranulf's knights and archers."

"After the siege you came to Darkvale. Why?" Victoria asked.

The miller looked at Perceval before answering with a shrug. "There was nothing for us at Avondel."

Perceval spoke up. "Miller John, let us walk outside for a bit. Victoria, wait here."

"Now wait just one minute—" The miller and Perceval escaped before she could finish her thought. "Well," she muttered. "Did you see that? They just left."

"Men do not discuss important matters with women."

She should have let Perceval do the questioning, it seemed. "Why not?"

"Because they are afraid we will learn how silly they are."

"Oh." Victoria grinned at the woman. "What is your name?"

"Alice." Alice grinned back at her.

"How do you do, Alice? I'm Victoria. Were you at Avondel during the siege?"

"Yes. I would not call Ranulf's attack on Avondel a siege, however. It lasted only a day or two, and no one but the lord and lady died. Over the years, the men have embellished the story, you see, and made it bloodier than it was. Why do you seek the amulet?"

"Ranulf wants it. If I don't find it, he will kill my friend."

"He did not want it ten years ago," said Alice. "Nor has he wanted it since."

"So I have heard. I wonder why Ranulf didn't want it before now; don't you? I thought the thing was supposed to be magic. I was told the amulet protected Avondel and made it prosper."

Alice gave a snort. "If magic ever guarded Avondel, it had faded away before Ranulf appeared with his knights. Pigs and sheep sickened and died. Crops had failed for two years running. There was little grain to grind that last year, and without bread we all would have died a slow death of starvation."

"Hmmm. So the amulet lost its power before the siege. That's interesting. Did you ever see it?"

Alice nodded. "Many times. Lady Juliana wore it on holy days."

"What does it look like?"

"A green stone the size of the yolk of a hen's egg,

set in gold. Lady Juliana wore it around her neck, hanging from a gold chain."

"And when she was not wearing it, where was it kept?"

"I do not know. I suppose in a chest in the solar. But I did not live within the castle walls. The mill at Avondel was outside the curtain wall, as it is here in Darkvale."

"How is it that you and your husband came to Darkvale?"

"After the so-called siege, Ranulf invited all who agreed to pledge allegiance to him to remove to Darkvale. Many accepted, including my husband. Darkvale was in need of a miller. The mill here had stood idle for several months, since the last miller died."

"Do you regret the move? I mean, would you like to return to Avondel some day?"

"No. Lord Ranulf is a just lord. He does not demand more of us than we can comfortably give him. And he has a strong, well-trained guard to protect us from robbers and thieves."

"Wasn't the lord of Avondel a just man?"

Alice's lips thinned. "William of Avondel is dead. I will not speak ill of him."

"What about his wife? What was her name?"

Alice's features softened. "Juliana. She was a sweet thing, delicate and fine. Too good for that . . . She deserved better. . . ."

"Better than?"

"Dying so young." The door to the cottage opened. "Our men have returned."

"Oh, Perceval is not my—"

He interrupted her with a curt command. "We are leaving, Victoria. Now."

Victoria was whisked out of the cottage and placed

on her donkey almost before she had a chance to thank Alice. Perceval leaped into his saddle, took the reins of her donkey, and pulled her behind him, making the poor little animal strain to keep up with his horse. They were almost at the inn before he slowed down enough for her to attempt a conversation.

"Why are we in such a hurry? Did the miller have information about the amulet?"

"Nothing useful. The miller saw the amulet on feast days, when Lady Juliana wore it."

"Alice said the same thing. She did not know where the amulet was kept when Juliana wasn't wearing it."

"In a small silver box. The box was kept in a niche set into the wall of the solar."

"How do you know that? Surely the miller was never inside Juliana's bedroom."

Perceval responded with something that sounded like a growl.

"What is that supposed to mean? What's wrong with you? Why are you so grumpy?"

He ignored her questions. Perceval remained silent until they arrived at the inn. He dismounted. Handing the reins of his horse to the waiting groom, he stalked into the inn.

Victoria saw that Hilary was unsaddled and stabled, then followed Perceval inside. She found him in the tavern. "Alice didn't know anything about the amulet, but she hinted at something interesting about Juliana. She said—"

"I do not want to know what she said," snarled Perceval. "Go to your room."

She bristled. "I will not go to my room. Not until you tell me what has put you in such a bad mood. What did the miller—"

Perceval took her by the arm and hustled her up the

stairs and into her room. He closed the door behind him.

"Oh. You wanted to talk in private. Why didn't you say so? I'm not a mind reader, you know. Did John tell you that all was not well at Avondel for months, maybe years before Ranulf showed up? There were crop failures and sick animals, all sorts of calamities while the amulet was still on the premises. Doesn't that strike you as odd? Where did the magic go?"

Perceval advanced on her. "Would you betray your lord?"

The feral glint in his eyes made Victoria back away from him. "I don't have a lord to betray. What's gotten into you? What did the miller tell you?"

"He reminded me that women are not to be trusted. You smiled at me yesterday, Victoria. You took my hand in yours. I would see your smile again, and feel your touch."

"I don't feel like smiling. I want you to—"

Before she knew what he intended, Perceval had pulled her into his arms. "What do you think you're doing? Percy—"

He covered her mouth with his. Victoria went rigid. This was not good. Her hands were caught between their bodies. She tried to push him away, but he did not seem to notice. His mouth was ravenous, taking her breath away. She managed to twist her head away and gasped, "Perceval. Stop. I don't like this."

For a moment, she thought he hadn't heard her. His mouth had come to rest on her throat. She could feel his heart pounding, hear his harsh breathing. He seemed to be struggling to bring himself under control. "Percy?"

He loosened his hold on her, but kept his arms circled around her waist. Resting his forehead on the top of her head, he exhaled a ragged breath. "Forgive me. I should not have hurt you."

Perceval sounded as if he were the one in pain. Victoria, primed with righteous indignation, had been prepared to read him the riot act. But when she felt him shudder, phrases like "you big bully" and "you call this chivalrous?" no longer seemed necessary or appropriate. Her knight was suffering pain, some terrible emotional pain. Who would have thought? Sometimes even knights needed to be cuddled.

Instinctively, Victoria's arms went around his waist. She hugged him. "I'm all right, Percy. You didn't hurt me. You surprised me, that's all. What's wrong? What did the miller say?"

Nine

Gareth could not answer. He was not ready to share what John the miller had told him about his mother. He had to weigh his own memories of her against the vile rumors the miller had callously repeated.

John had said Juliana had been an unfaithful wife.

His mother, the woman he had idolized for all his life, the woman who had given him the model for his own future wife, had been an adulteress. Gareth did not want to believe it. But something about the accusation rang true. His own experiences with the female sex had taught him that women were devious and faithless. He had thought Juliana the exception, the virtuous woman whose price was above rubies. He had thought to find another like her, and when he did, to make that woman his wife.

But if Juliana had betrayed his father . . .

Gareth had pressed the miller for the origin of the ugly rumors, hoping against hope that the source would be obviously suspect and easily disproved. John said most of the talk had come from the servants in the castle. The women servants.

Women. They must have slandered Juliana because they were jealous of their beautiful, noble, and *virtuous* mistress. "They lied."

Victoria spoke. "Who lied? John? What did he lie about? Why would he lie?"

Gareth started. He had not realized that he had said the words aloud. Victoria had her arms around him. She was hugging him and rubbing him on the back; she was trying to comfort him, after his rough treatment of her. Something hard and cold in the middle of Gareth's chest began to melt and grow warm. Having someone comfort and console him was a rare experience.

The last woman who had offered such solace had been his mother. How could his sweet and loving mother have been his father's treacherous and deceitful wife? If Juliana had been false, then no woman was true.

Gareth stepped back, breaking Victoria's hold on him. "The miller sang Ranulf's praises. He had nothing good to say about Avondel or its lady. He said Juliana betrayed her lord. She took a lover."

"And that is what you think he lied about?"

"He believed he told the truth."

"Well. The miller's wife didn't have much good to say about Avondel, either. Times were not good there even before the siege. Before the amulet disappeared, even. What could—"

"And Juliana? What did the miller's wife have to say about her?" Gareth asked the question, not wanting to hear the answer but unable to stop himself.

"Alice said Juliana was a kind and gentle woman, and that she deserved better."

"Better than what?"

"She wouldn't say. Or rather, she said 'better than dying young,' but that wasn't what she meant to say. I think she was trying to tell me that Juliana was—"

"Unfaithful to her husband?"

"No. Alice did not say anything like that. From the

little she did say, I would hazard a guess that Juliana was a battered wife."

"Battered?" Gareth frowned. "That is a strange way to put it. She was murdered."

"I'm not talking about the siege, if there was a siege. There seems to be some confusion surrounding that, too. I was talking about before Juliana died. I think her husband may have abused her. What was his name? The lord of Avondel?"

"William," said Gareth.

"I think William beat his wife. Probably."

"The miller's wife said that?"

"Not in so many words. Alice refused to say anything about William, except to say she would not speak ill of him. But the look on her face when she said that made it obvious that she did not like him. She did like and admire Juliana, and she said Juliana deserved better. I think she meant better treatment from her husband."

Clenching his jaw, Gareth said, "And he deserved loyalty from her. She met another man at the ruins of the old Saxon keep whenever William was away. It was common knowledge, John said, although he could not name an eyewitness to her perfidy."

"Good for Juliana. I hope she found a little happiness."

"You believe a woman who cuckolds her lord deserves happiness?"

"Well, I don't think she should wallow in misery. If Juliana was unhappy in her marriage, why shouldn't she look for a little happiness elsewhere? She couldn't get a divorce, could she?"

"A lady must be faithful to her lord." Gareth repeated the words, although he had all but lost hope that they had ever been true for Juliana.

"And her lord should be faithful to her. But if her

lord is cruel to her, and she has no other recourse, no way to get out of the marriage, it is understandable that she might seek comfort in another man's arms," Victoria insisted.

Gareth could feel his anger building again. "Is it? Would you?"

Tilting up her chin, Victoria said, "The question does not arise, since, as I have repeatedly told you, I do not have a lord."

"The miller did not say William treated Juliana badly. And neither did Alice. You decided that." Gareth ought to have joined in Victoria's defense of his mother, but he could not. He believed she had betrayed his father. John the miller had no reason to lie. Neither did the servants who had seen his mother returning from assignations with her lover.

Had his father known? Gareth could only imagine the pain William must have suffered if he had discovered Juliana's perfidy. "Even if your guess is correct, and William did beat her, it would not excuse Juliana's sin of adultery."

"Maybe not, but nothing excuses a man beating a woman. Nothing."

"William did not beat Juliana."

Victoria blew a strand of hair away from her eyes. "Maybe, maybe not. Neither of us know the truth about William and Juliana, so there is no point in arguing about them. Why are they so important to you, anyway? You're getting awfully worked up over a pair of strangers."

"I am not worked up."

"Oh, really? You certainly looked worked up when you pulled me out of the miller's house. You didn't even give me a chance to thank Alice for her hospitality. Then you wouldn't talk to me all the way back to the inn. I don't get it. Why does the unfaithfulness—

alleged unfaithfulness—of a woman who has been dead for ten years get you so bent out of shape?"

"Bent? I am not bent. I stand straight and true. And a lady, especially a married lady, owes faithfulness and loyalty to her lord. His honor depends on her virtue."

"That's it? You get all pompous and prudish whenever you hear of a faithless—wait one second." Victoria narrowed her eyes and looked at him suspiciously. "You hear a story about a straying wife, and you drag me up here and kiss me? What was that about?" After another pause, her eyes widened. "I know. You were testing me. For some reason, you wanted to see if I would be faithful to Walter."

Gareth felt his cheeks grow warm. Taking his anger out on Victoria had not been his finest moment. Even though she had flirted with him over breakfast, she had not succumbed to his crude attempt at seduction. Victoria had remained true to her lord. "Aye, that was my purpose. I apologize again. I should not have attempted to seduce you. Walter is fortunate to have a woman like you."

"Oh, is he?" She advanced on him, the gold flecks in her eyes flashing ominously. "I guess that means I passed the test. You kissed me, and I didn't kiss you back."

"I am truly sorry, Victoria. You are a virtuous woman." Gareth retreated until the backs of his knees hit the side of the bed.

She stopped a hair's breadth away from him. Gazing up at him, she said, "Perhaps you should try again. That kiss came out of the blue. It's possible I was too surprised to kiss you back."

His brows shot up. "You want me to kiss you again?"

"Yes. No. I'll do it. You had your turn. This is my test." She leaned against him. "I am going to kiss you,

Percy. But I will give you time to get used to the idea first." Raising one hand, Victoria stroked his cheek. "Your beard looks scratchy, but it isn't. It's soft. But your jaw is hard."

Her fingertips followed the line of his jaw, then moved to the back of his neck. She curled her fingers into his hair. Gareth swallowed convulsively. "Victoria . . ."

"Hush. I'll get to it in a minute." She placed her hands on his shoulders, then ran them down his arms to his elbows and back. "Mmmm. Nice. I like a man with muscles."

Wrapping her arms around his neck, she stood on tiptoe and touched her lips to his cheek. Gareth let out a breath he had not realized he had been holding. She was teasing him, getting even for his rough treatment of her. There was nothing erotic about the soft touch of her lips on his cheek. . . .

She licked his cheek, then used her teeth to bite his jaw.

His arms came up and he gripped her waist convulsively. Victoria took his face in both her hands and pulled his head down. "Now, sweetie pie. I want you to pay attention. This is how a woman—a woman who does not belong to any man—kisses."

Her mouth found his. Her open mouth. She used her tongue to trace the line of his tightly closed lips. Her teeth nipped his bottom lip. His lips parted. Victoria immediately took full advantage of his small surrender. Her tongue slipped into his mouth, then out. Then in again. In, slowly. Out, even more slowly. The seductive rhythm she set inflamed his passion. Gareth could feel hot blood flowing to his groin, engorging his penis, making him hard.

Victoria felt his arousal. She ought to stop kissing him. Now. She had only meant to teach him not to use her to test his antiquated ideals of feminine virtue. But with her lips touching his, she was finding it difficult to keep thoughts of lessons and tests in her head. *Her* knight, the knight she had dreamed about was kissing her back. Slowly. Endlessly.

Not endlessly. There would be an end. And soon. Victoria felt panic clawing at her. *Time. Something about time.*

There was not enough of it.

She squelched that thought and kissed Gareth again. Slowly. There had to be time for this. This was the only time she would ever have with the man of her dreams. She had to make the best of it.

"Kisses are not enough," she gasped.

"More?" asked Perceval, his voice husky.

Opening her eyes a slit, she saw his green eyes staring at her. He looked dazed. She had done that to him. "Much more. I want everything." Greedily, she fitted her lips to his once again.

Victoria rubbed her belly against his crotch, glorying in his responsiveness. His readiness triggered a response in her. She could feel the dampness between her legs. Squirming, Victoria tried to get even closer to her knight. He obliged, wrapping his strong arms around her and pulling her closer, crushing her breasts against his chest. Someone was moaning. She thought it was her, but it might have been Percy. Maybe they were both moaning.

She wanted him naked. Victoria began clawing at his clothes, fumbling with the unfamiliar ties and cords. She succeeded in unlacing his tunic, and pushed it off his shoulders. Panting, she reached for the hem of his shirt, pushing it up over his head. Success. His chest was bare. Curling her fingers into the soft mat of hair, she lowered her head and found one male nipple with her tongue. She sucked.

Perceval groaned. "Victoria. What are you doing to me?"

She did not bother to answer. He knew very well what she was doing. He was helping, showing her how to loosen his braies and chausses. Her knees were melting. She couldn't stand up one more minute. Victoria pushed him and he fell backward onto the bed.

Gareth felt himself falling, but did not release Victoria. She sprawled on top of him. She had undressed him, and he meant to return the favor. He reached for her tunic, stripping it and her gown away. There was a sound of tearing; Victoria had ripped her chemise from neck to hem. She was naked. Quickly, he rolled over, tucking her beneath him.

"I wanted to be on top," she said.

"Not this time."

"Next time, then. I believe in equal—"

Perceval stopped her declaration of independence with another kiss. Victoria forgot all about talking when she felt his hands on her bare skin. He stroked her stomach, making Victoria arch her back.

Gareth pushed himself up on his elbows and gazed at her. Victoria's eyes were wide, her pupils dilated. Her breaths came in short gasps. His gaze slid lower, to her mouth, wet and swollen from their kisses. He leaned down and kissed her again. Once. Thoroughly. Then pulled his head up and looked again. Her breasts were round, full, tipped with roses.

He lowered his head again and captured one hard little rose pip in his mouth. He used his tongue and teeth to lave and nip, then drew her breast into his mouth and suckled. She bucked against him. Her hands were on his naked body at once, stroking, pinching, grasping.

Victoria wanted to touch him everywhere, all at the same time. She found she did not have enough hands, so she used her mouth, her legs, her entire body to caress, to fondle, to feel. "Touch me, Percy. Touch me everywhere. I want to feel your hands on me. And your mouth."

Gareth complied. He had never been with a woman so eager for him. He had never been undressed by a woman. The women he had known before Victoria had been coy, passive, allowing him to do what he wanted, but not asking—no, demanding—that he do what *they* wanted. Victoria insisted that he kiss and fondle, stroke and bite, give and take.

She was not a selfish lover. Victoria took his every caress and gave it back twofold. Hot for her, Gareth shoved his knee between her thighs.

Victoria parted her legs wide and sank her nails into his buttocks. "Now, my knight. Take me. Now."

He entered her. Her sheath was tight and hot and wet.

Perceval was inside her. Deep inside. Gasping a little, as her body adjusted to the sweet invasion, Victoria waited for him to withdraw and enter her again. And again. He remained still, unmoving. She opened her eyes and looked at him. "Perceval. Is anything wrong?" She moved her hips experimentally. Maybe he needed a little more encouragement.

It worked. Perceval withdrew, then thrust into her again. And again. And again. Hard. Fast. Hot.

Victoria shattered into a million shards of glittering sensation.

Moments or hours later, when the shining pieces had once again joined together, Victoria should have felt like herself again. Herself after wild, unexpected, and extraordinary sex, but herself.

She was not herself. She was someone else. She was a woman in love.

Victoria sat up and screamed.

Gareth's eyes opened. Victoria had screamed. Only once, but loudly. She was sitting next to him, the coverlet around her waist, her face buried in her hands.

"Victoria?" He reached for her breast, temptingly exposed.

She slapped his hand away. "I am Victoria Desmond. *Ms.* Victoria Desmond. I do not love you, Perceval. I barely know you. We only just met, and I do not believe in love at first sight. Or second sight. It has to be the time change. Jet lag. That's what it is. Centuries and centuries of jet lag."

Frowning, Gareth stared at her. She was babbling, using more words he did not understand. He had understood her when she said she did not love him. That should not have mattered, since he had not asked for her love, but he found her strong denial insulting. "Calm yourself," he said coldly. "You are no doubt feeling guilty for betraying Walter—"

She made a fist and hit him on the shoulder. "I did not betray anyone, you dolt. Do you really think I would do what I just did with you if Walter was my . . . my boyfriend?"

"You were not a virgin." Gareth had meant to state a fact. It came out like an accusation.

She hit him again. "Oh, and I suppose you were? What's that got to do with it?" She giggled. Her giggle had a touch of hysteria.

Grabbing both her hands in his, Gareth reined in his temper and tried to soothe her. "If Walter is not your lord, who is? Are you a widow, perhaps?"

"No, Percy. I am not a widow. The reason I am not a virgin is because you are not the first man I've been with." She had the audacity to look pleased about that.

Gareth forgot about trying to calm her down. His temper flared once more, and he was willing to give it free rein. Hot blood was still streaming through his veins, his heart was beating fast and hard, and he wanted Victoria again. And again.

A good fight was exactly what he needed to take his mind off his unseemly desire for the wanton who had taken him to her bed. "Who else?" he asked, his tone menacing.

Crossing her arms across her bare chest, she tilted her chin up. "I do not intend to discuss my sexual history with you. And, I might add, I am not at all interested in hearing about all the women you've gone to bed with. The past is not relevant." Her eyes widened. "Oh. My. God. How could I have forgotten? The past is *all* that is relevant. How to get out of it. Fast." She tried to free her hands, but he held on.

"What past do you speak of? Your past with Walter? Or the recent past we shared?"

"We are done sharing, Percy. Getting involved with a coworker is never a good idea. I can't think why I—never mind. It's over and done with. I am finished with you. I want you to go," she said, her voice imperious.

Gareth saw red. Victoria had seduced him, and now that she had had her way with him, she thought to cast him aside. The infuriating woman would have to think again. He would not be discarded like a worn-out boot. She might say she was finished with him, but he was far from finished with her. Pulling her hands above her head, he leaned over her. "No. I will not leave. I have not had enough of you. I want you again."

She looked at him as if he had just crawled from beneath a rock. A slimy rock. "You want to have sex *now?* In the middle of an argument? With a woman who absolutely, positively does not love you? A woman who was not a virgin when you—"

He put his hand over her mouth. "Stop your talking. I want to make love with you. Only you."

Narrowing her eyes, she glared at him. He was sure

she was going to refuse him, but instead . . . He felt
her lips curve into a grin under his hand. When he
took his hand away, she said, "Oh, what the heck. But
it's my turn to be on top."

Gareth threw back his head and laughed.

The next morning, Victoria woke first. Perceval was
sprawled next to her, and it took all her willpower to
keep from touching him. During the night she had
learned that Perceval was a very light sleeper. If she
touched him, he would waken immediately. His green
eyes would go all smoky with desire, and she would be
flat on her back again, with him on top of her. Unless
it was her time to be on top. Percy had scrupulously
insisted on alternating, even after she had lost count.

Victoria laced her fingers together to keep from
reaching for him. She could not possibly want to make
love with him again. She had exceeded her personal
best several times over.

Lust.

It had to be lust. That silly thought she'd had after
the first time—that she loved him—had been just that.
A silly, sex-induced illusion.

But what if it was more than lust? What if she had
fallen in love with a thirteenth-century knight?

Victoria unlaced her fingers and used one hand to
gently brush a lock of hair from his eyes. "It will never
work out, Percy. I can't take you home with me. And
I can't stay here." Assuming he would want her to,
which was highly unlikely. He would marry a woman,
a girl, really. Someone young, as young as thirteen or
fourteen. And pure. A virgin. She should not fault him
for that. Men in this century, and many centuries to
come, expected their brides to be virgins. Perceval was
a man of his times.

"Damn double standard. It isn't fair. It never was. But try to convince a man of that. Heck, modern men still wax nostalgic about the good old days, and I'm here in the middle of those days. No thirteenth-century male is going to fall in love with a nonvirgin." Which was just as well, since she did not love him. She shook him, a little more forcefully than necessary. "Wake up, Percy. It's late. We have to talk to the blacksmith today."

He groaned and turned onto his stomach. "I cannot see. You have blinded me with your insatiable demands on my poor body."

"You are not blind, you silly knight. Your eyes are closed." She used a thumb to peel back one eyelid. A green slit appeared. "See?"

"I see. The most beautiful woman in the world. Victoria . . ."

He thought she was beautiful. Victoria felt her insides go all mushy. Forcefully reminding herself that warm and fuzzy feelings were not invariably induced by love, she muttered, "I guess I'm not the only one suffering from sex-induced fantasies. Wake up, Percy. We have work to do, and not much time to do it in."

Victoria slid off the bed and reached for her gown. Holding it in front of her, she bent down and picked up Perceval's clothes. Tossing them on the bed, she said, "Get dressed."

He rolled onto his back and stretched his arms over his head. Yawning, he pulled the covers over his head. "Victoria, my delicious tyrant, using me all night, then expecting me to do your bidding this morning as well."

"I am not a tyrant. I am a strong, independent woman. Get used to it. And get up. Please."

Perceval threw back the blanket and got out of bed. He was naked, and he was aroused. "Come here, Victoria."

She stood her ground and tried to avoid looking at

his crotch. "Now who is the tyrant? We don't have time for more . . . of that."

"It will take less than a moment."

"That's nothing to brag about—Percy!" She shrieked as he picked her up and threw her back on the bed. "Good grief. Haven't you had enough?"

Percy stretched himself on top of her, crushing her into the mattress. "No. I have not had enough of you. And you have no one to blame but yourself. You started this."

"Did not. You kissed me first."

"Only a kiss. For which I contritely apologized. Then you kissed me."

"Only a kiss."

"More than a kiss. You threw yourself on me and ripped my clothes off. You pushed me onto the bed. I could not escape."

"You didn't try to escape. And you ripped my clothes off, too. My chemise is shredded."

"You did that, my sweet, not I. Happily, we do not have to waste time with clothes this time."

"No." She wriggled contentedly and wrapped her arms around his neck. "We don't. Roll over, Percy. I want to try something different."

Grinning, he complied. Victoria bent over to place kisses on his chest, his abdomen, lower. She moved over him, spreading his legs with her knees, kneeling between his thighs. Sliding her hands up his thighs, up his ribs, then down again, she watched him. Her eyes were molten gold, full of heated promises. Gareth reached for her.

She pushed his hands to his side. "Not yet. I'm not finished with you." When Victoria took his erect penis in her hands, Gareth clenched his teeth together. He would not beg her to—

She lowered her head and took him in her mouth.

Gareth climaxed almost immediately. When he opened his eyes, Victoria was sprawled on his chest, resting her chin on her hands. She smiled at him. "Did you like that?"

He could only nod.

"You will have to return the favor. Sometime. Not now. We have things to do and people to see."

"Not yet. I cannot move."

"Oh. Have I vanquished my knight, then?"

"Yes. I surrender my sword to you."

"Why, thank you, Perceval. A girl can always find a use for a good, stiff sword." With a huge yawn, she closed her eyes.

Victoria slept. After watching her for a few moments, Gareth joined her in slumber.

Gareth woke up before Victoria. She was nestled in the crook of his arm, her head on his shoulder, one small hand resting on his chest. Loath to leave her, he knew this was the opportunity he needed to question one of the survivors of Avondel alone. Carefully, he eased himself out of bed. Gareth dressed in silence and slipped out of her room.

Thomas waited for him in the room they shared, standing at the window.

"Thomas? What are you staring at? Is our friend Balen outside the inn?"

"No. Balen is downstairs, playing his lute and singing songs for a group of pilgrims who arrived last night. They are on their way from the abbey at Northumber to the friary at Donscroft." His squire turned to face him. Thomas's usually cheerful face was joyless. He appeared worried.

Gareth stripped off his clothes and began washing himself with cold water in the basin on the table next to the bed. "Is anything wrong? What have you been doing?"

"Waiting for you." The squire's voice shook, from anger or fear, Gareth could not tell. "You have been with her all night and morning."

"Yes." Gareth could not keep the satisfied grin from his face. At Thomas's shocked look, he sobered. "The time I spent with her is not your concern, Thomas."

"You said there would be no time for dalliance during this quest."

"I had not met Victoria when I said that." *Dalliance* did not begin to describe what had passed between him and Victoria. Something out of the ordinary, magical. A woman had ravished him, and instead of being outraged by her audacity, he had found her enchanting.

"She has bewitched you," said Thomas, his interruption almost mirroring Gareth's thought.

"The lady is bewitching," Gareth agreed.

"She is not mortal."

Raising his eyebrows, Gareth said gently, "Thomas, she is real."

"Aye. Your Victoria is a real enchantress. Like Morgan le Fay, the fairy who used charms and spells to ensnare Lancelot. How else can you explain your sudden fascination with her? You did not like her so much yesterday. She was to be only the means to an end, an excuse to openly question people about the amulet."

In a sterner tone, Gareth said, "She is not a fairy or a sorceress. Victoria is a woman."

"She makes herself appear to be a mortal woman. Great knights are always tested thus. Think of Galahad, or your namesake, Perceval. Think of King Arthur."

"You place me in the company of giants, Thomas. Why would an immortal bother with a humble knight like me?"

"Lord Gareth of Avondel is a great knight, heir to a magic kingdom. Do you not see that Victoria is interfering with your search, keeping you abed until noon, consuming your vital juices, leaving you weak and unable to think clearly? Wizards and sorcerers delight in such mischief. You must regain your strength, then use cunning to thwart her charms and enticements."

Gareth had no intention of thwarting Victoria, but he thought it prudent not to tell Thomas that, or that he had enjoyed being the focus of her passion. His squire had worked himself into a frenzy. Thomas would not believe him if he told him that, far from feeling weak and debilitated by Victoria, Gareth felt powerful, strong, able to accomplish anything he set his mind to. "Thomas, enough."

"Perhaps she is a descendant of Aethelwyn, come to punish you for losing the charm."

"I did not lose the charm."

"Your father did. Sorceresses often punish the son for the sins of the father."

"An interesting theory. If she is a sorceress, why did she allow Ranulf to take her lord hostage?"

Thomas gave him a pitying look. "So that you would offer to help her, of course. Have you thought that her master may not be her master at all? Walter is her pawn, the man she bewitched before you. It was Victoria who caused Ranulf to hold him hostage, leaving her free to work her magic on you. You cannot deny that magic exists—we seek the magic talisman."

"Enough, Thomas." Gareth completed dressing himself and picked up his sword. He sheathed the sword in its scabbard and prepared to leave. "I will hear no more. I am going to see Matthew. Wait a while, then have hot water sent to Victoria's room." Gareth strode from the room, leaving his squire bemoaning his fate.

As he crossed the threshold, he heard Thomas say, in a voice filled with horror, "Bewitched."

Ten

When Victoria awoke a second time, she was alone. Sighing, she said, "Men. Some things never change. Once they've had you, they leave without so much as a goodbye kiss." Her attempted pout expanded into a grin. A silly grin. She could not work up any enthusiasm for male-bashing this morning. She felt too good, and Perceval had made her feel that way.

Percy, and being as bad as she wanted to be.

Badder than bad. She had been downright wicked last night. Victoria covered her mouth with both hands. Her sexual aggression would have shocked, or at least surprised, a twenty-first-century male. What must Percy have thought?

Poor knight. He had been caught in a whirlwind of womanly passion, a cyclone of feminine power. Except for that first angry kiss, she had been the aggressor, initiating every move, every caress. She had never been so sure of what she wanted, and she had known exactly how to go about getting it. She had gotten that, and more.

Much more than she had bargained for. She loved her scruffy knight in shining armor.

Amazing, but there it was. She could see no point in denying her feelings: Sir Perceval, a thirteenth-century knight, had turned out to be the man of her dreams.

"Not fair." A more mean-spirited roll of the cosmic dice she could not imagine—sending her centuries back in time to find her own true love. To top it off, Victoria could not even hope that Perceval would return her love. No matter how much Percy had enjoyed her bad self, he would never feel anything but lust for her. She had proved to him in every way possible that she was not a "virtuous woman."

On her fingers, Victoria ticked off the days remaining before her scheduled return to the future. Less than two weeks. She could spend the time bemoaning her fate, pathetically anticipating the end of her time with Perceval. That would be a serious waste of time. She needed to squeeze every drop of happiness out of each minute she had left with Perceval.

If she were very lucky, she might find that once she was back in her own time, surrounded by familiar sights and ordinary people, her interlude with a medieval knight would fade into a pleasant dream. She would have no reason to mourn in that case, nothing to cry herself to sleep over once they were centuries apart. If she was wrong, and weeping and wailing were waiting in her future, at least she could put it off for a few hundred years.

She would treat her time with Perceval as a bonus, an unexpected fringe benefit of her trip to the past. Something to be savored and enjoyed. But she had to keep focused on her goal. She could not let her love for Perceval distract her from saving Walter.

Her lips curved in another grin. She had accomplished one goal: she had charmed her knight. And she had done it her way.

Glancing out the window, Victoria saw that the sun was high. She sat up and winced. "Uh-oh. A little sore, are we? Well, that is to be expected, you shameless hussy. The things you did last night . . . the things he did . . . oh, my."

Victoria poked her head over the side of the bed and looked at her rumpled gown. "I cannot wear that. And I cannot get dressed until I've had a nice, hot bath. How does a naked lady circa twelve seventy-four call for room service?"

A knock sounded on the door. "My lady?"

"Thomas? Is that you?"

"Yes. I bring you hot water for washing."

"Wait just one minute." Hurriedly Victoria donned her wrinkled gown, not bothering with the chemise. That garment appeared to have been torn asunder. She was pretty sure she was the one who had done the tearing—getting herself and Percy naked had been an urgent goal last night. She shoved the shredded remnants under the covers and went to the door.

Opening the door a crack, she peeked out. Thomas stood there, carrying a bucket of steaming water. "No tub?"

"Not this morning. Clement said a bath was provided only once a week."

"Oh, well. I'll make do with what you brought me. It was good of you to think of me." She opened the door wider and allowed Thomas to enter. "Thank you."

He skirted around her, head down, and mumbled, "I do not deserve your thanks. Sir Perceval thought of it. He told Clement to have me bring the water to you."

"That was nice of him. Just put the bucket down anywhere."

Thomas stared at the bed and turned as pale as the rumpled linen sheets.

"Thomas? Are you all right?" She kept forgetting that he was a teenager. A boy of sixteen, going through puberty, would naturally be curious and embarrassed by the activity that obviously had taken place on that bed last night.

Thomas jerked around, sloshing water out of the bucket. He ducked his head, refusing to look at her. He was more than embarrassed. If she didn't know better, Victoria would think he was afraid of her.

"Y-yes. I am all right."

"Where is Perceval?"

"Gone to talk to the blacksmith." Another jerky movement spilled more water on the floor.

"He went without me? How could he do that? Thomas, put the bucket down while there is still some water left in it. Why are you so jumpy this morning?"

"It is not morning," he said sulkily. "It is midday."

Victoria glanced out the window again. "So it is. Why didn't Perceval wait for me?"

"He did not say. Mayhap he wanted to speak to the blacksmith alone."

"Well, that is obvious, isn't it? I wonder why?" She thought they had reached some sort of rapport last night. Apparently it did not extend to including her in the search as an equal partner. Frowning, Victoria wondered if she had time to teach Percy a thing or two about equality of the sexes. Probably not. Time was short, and once she was gone he would have no use for the lesson. "You can go now, Thomas. I have to get dressed and go to the blacksmith's shop. Walter is depending on me. And Sir Perceval should have waited for me."

"Please, my lady, do not change him into a . . . a . . . toad. Do not harm him, I beg of you."

"Thomas, what are you talking about? Who do you think I mean to harm? Walter? The blacksmith?"

"Sir Perceval. I beg you to release him from your spell."

"Spell? What spell? Does Perceval think I've cast a spell on him?"

"Nay. I swear he voiced no accusation against you. 'Twas my idea."

"You think I am a witch?"

"A sorceress . . . a fairy . . . a . . ."

"None of the above, Thomas. I am not a witch, a sorceress, or a fairy. What on earth did Perceval tell you?" Tapping her bare foot on the floor, Victoria reconsidered playing nice with Perceval. What kind of gentleman was he? Kissing and telling was against the rules.

"He told me nothing, lady. I swear it. Nothing. Not a word did he say about what passed between you. When he remained with you last night and this morning, I guessed that you . . . that he . . . that you and he . . ."

"You guessed right. We did spend the night together. But what happened between us is personal, Thomas. Private. I'm sure you understand."

"Yes, my lady. I take your meaning." Thomas began backing toward the door, head bowed. "May I go?"

"Yes, of course." If she told him to stay, the poor boy would faint. "And thank you for bringing the hot water," she called out. The squire shut the door behind him, leaving behind half a bucket of lukewarm water. With a sigh, Victoria stripped off her robe and bathed herself as best she could.

Squire Thomas thought she was a sorceress. Victoria did not know whether to be flattered or insulted. A week ago, she would have told Thomas he was crazy, that there was no such thing as a sorceress. But since then she had met a wizard. If wizards existed, why not sorceresses?

Come to think of it, Aethelwyn must have had something of the sorceress about her. She had worked the magic of the amulet, after all. As she dressed in her gray gown and shimmery silver overtunic, Victoria thought about the Saxon lady. What a spot she had been in, that daughter of a vanquished king. Faced with death or marriage to a stranger, she had challenged, then charmed her knight. Gareth had fallen in love with Aethelwyn, and she with him.

The magic of the amulet had begun in mutual love.

Victoria rummaged in the chest of clothes until she found the silver net for her hair. *Mutual love.* She had a feeling that was important.

Gareth made his way through the village to the blacksmith's forge, set apart from the other houses because of the danger of fire. As he had anticipated, Balen followed. Gareth would have to watch him closely, to make sure he did not overhear what passed between him and the smithy.

He had good reason to visit the blacksmith alone. This was the man most likely to recognize him. As a young boy and later on his visits to Avondel when he was older, Gareth had spent time with Matthew, asking endless questions about the forging of steel and the making of knives and swords. Matthew had grumbled incessantly about being pestered by the young lord, but he had answered all Gareth's questions nevertheless.

Good reason or not, his hasty departure from the inn was not solely because he intended to visit Matthew without Victoria by his side. He was running from her again. Thomas had been half right this morning. She had charmed him, but not with magic. Victoria had entranced him with nothing more than womanly skills. The skills of an experienced woman. Victoria was not a virtuous woman.

Virtue was overrated.

With a groan, Gareth suppressed that heretical thought. Victoria had betrayed her lord. She must have a lord to whom she owed fealty; no woman could know what she knew without having received instruction from a man. Perhaps Walter was not her lord, but some man was, and that man she had betrayed.

As his mother had betrayed his father.

He could not want Victoria.

He did want her.

But that was all. He did not love her. Lust was what he felt for her, as he had lusted after other women. He knew how to deal with lust. Gareth would use Victoria until his hunger for her was sated. He felt a grin split his face. Use her, or better yet, allow himself to be used by her. Being ravished by a virago was an experience worthy of repetition.

When he arrived at the blacksmith's shop, Gareth firmly put his thoughts of Victoria aside. He would deal with her and his chaotic feelings toward her later. Glancing over his shoulder, he noted that Balen had stopped at the last house, as he had expected him to do. The troubadour was a coward and not likely to approach him openly, especially when he was armed.

Gareth pulled his sword from its sheath and approached Matthew. "Blacksmith, my sword needs an edge." He said the words loudly, so that Balen would overhear.

The blacksmith wore a leather tunic that left his muscled arms bare. He wore a perpetual sheen of sweat. At Gareth's words, Matthew looked up from the horseshoe he was shaping. His eyes widened. "Master Gareth. You have come back."

" 'Tis Lord Gareth now, Matthew. How goes it? Are you well?"

"Well enough. Your return has been the talk of the village for days now, ever since a London merchant brought word that you had come back to England. I am surprised no one told me you had arrived."

"No one knows. I have kept my identity secret because I am not ready to reveal myself to Ranulf. I am known as Sir Perceval in Darkvale."

"Perceval it is." Matthew gave the shoe another whack with his mallet. "What do you require of me? Does your sword truly need an edge?"

"Nay. I take good care of my blade, as you taught me to do. But I would have you make a pretense of sharpening it. We are being watched."

Matthew looked over Gareth's shoulder. "The minstrel. I see him." In a louder voice, he said, "Let me finish this horseshoe, then I will deal with your blade."

"Balen is spying for Ranulf. If he behaves as he did yesterday, he will leave soon to report to his lord." Gareth handed the sword to Matthew, and sat down on a crude wooden bench. "King Edward has restored the fief of Avondel to me. Ranulf is no longer lord of Darkvale and Avondel."

"He was never lord of Avondel, though King Henry named him such," said Matthew. "Ranulf did not want a cursed estate."

"Nor do I. I want Avondel as it was in my youth, before the magic left. I am seeking the amulet."

Matthew looked up from his task. "I do not know where it is. I doubt that anyone in Darkvale knows. After all, no one knew it was missing until after your father and mother . . ." He cleared his throat. "That is, until it was clear to all that Avondel no longer had the amulet's magical protection."

"I have begun to wonder if the amulet ever protected Avondel," Gareth admitted.

"Aye, it did. I am sure of that. For a time, I saw the magic shield work with my own eyes. My father told me about the magic protection it provided during his lifetime, and he repeated tales of the same magic which he had heard from his father, and his father's father. You know there was never any illness, no fevers or plague, at Avondel even when all the surrounding estates suffered. The land was always fertile, the forest filled with game, and the river with fish. Always feast, never famine for two hundred years. But it is true the magic faded away."

"When did it begin to change?"

"After your last visit, two years or so before the end. The change was gradual, you understand. It would have passed unnoticed anywhere else. A few sheep sickened and died; a field did not yield as much as it had the year before. Little things at first, then more and more until the end came."

"These changes began while the amulet was still within the castle?"

"Aye. Lady Juliana wore the amulet on feast days, as she always had done. The last time she wore it that year was at Easter."

"Tell me what you remember of the last days of Avondel."

"People were frightened. Word had reached us that a fever was killing the people of Darkvale. It seemed only a matter of time before it spread to Avondel, and the way things were going, no one expected Avondel to be spared. Guards were posted along the road, to turn back any travelers from Darkvale."

"What of my mother and father?"

Matthew looked uncomfortable, and kept his eyes on the sword edge he was honing. "They changed as well."

"Changed? In what way?"

He looked up. "My lord, I do not wish to speak of matters I did not witness."

"Tell me what you saw, then."

"I saw Lady Juliana become sadder every day. She spent much of her time in prayer."

"And my father?" asked Gareth.

"Lord William was more and more quick-tempered as the magic waned. One day I was in the castle, repairing arms. Your father came to me in a rage. He ordered me to put a keen edge on his favorite dagger, and he cuffed my ears when I did not do it fast enough to suit him."

"Why was he angry?"

"I do not know. He seemed always to be in bad humor. Some said it was because Lady Juliana—" Matthew stopped abruptly.

"I have heard. They say she betrayed my father with another man."

"That was the tale being told, but I saw nothing with my own eyes to prove the story right or wrong. Lord William's anger may just as well have been caused by the disasters befalling Avondel, calamities he could do nothing to prevent or correct. With my own ears I heard him curse the amulet and threaten to destroy it. He told me to prepare a fire in the forge, a fire hot enough to melt the stone as well as the gold setting."

Gareth's heart sank. Had his father destroyed the magic forever? "Did you?"

"No. Before your father could bring the amulet to me, word reached the castle that Ranulf was on his way with a force of men. There was panic. Many fled, including the knights who owed service to Avondel. I heard them say they would face the sword, but not the fever."

"Then Ranulf and his men arrived and the siege began."

"Yes. If you could call it a siege. It did not last long. Ranulf's men breached the square tower the second day. After that, your father challenged Ranulf. They fought. Ranulf won. The siege was over, and the curse took hold of Avondel in earnest."

"What of my mother? How did she die?"

Matthew shook his head. "I do not know. I saw her body laid to rest in the lady chapel, but I do not know how she died, though most put her death at Ranulf's feet. The last time I saw Lady Juliana alive, she was bidding Friar Bartholomew farewell at the castle gate."

"When was that?"

"The day before Ranulf arrived with his men."

"Do you know where the friar was going?" Gareth asked.

"No. He was one of the wandering mendicants, a Franciscan. They have a monastery at Donscroft. I suppose he might have been returning there, but he might just as well have been going somewhere else where he could offer comfort, perhaps to Darkvale. I spoke with the friar on several occasions, and he told me he had traveled far and wide. . . . Lord Gareth?"

"What, Matthew? Ask any question of me. I have asked enough of you."

"Will you challenge Ranulf as your father did?"

"In time. Not yet. I cannot risk my sister's life. I will meet with Ranulf once I have the amulet, and once Elwyna is safely away from Darkvale."

"Elwyna. I see her from time to time. She seems content." Matthew eyed Gareth warily. "He treats her like a daughter, you know."

"So I have heard. But I will not forgive him. I cannot forget that Lord Ranulf is the one who made Elwyna and me orphans."

"Will you forgive those who swore allegiance to him?"

Gareth slapped Matthew on the shoulder. "There is nothing to forgive, old friend. Once the curse fell on Avondel, no one could have survived there. I only hope when the amulet is restored that some of you will return with me to Avondel. Now, I must ask you to keep my secret. Do not tell Ranulf or his spy, Balen, who I am."

"I swore allegiance to your father, and I will swear it to you, Lord Gareth, whenever you ask it of me. I will keep your secret." Matthew handed the sword to Gareth.

"Thank you." Sheathing his sword, Gareth left the forge and walked back to the inn.

Victoria left the inn and almost collided with Perceval. She immediately began scolding him, but her heart was not in it. Still, she at least had to try to maintain some sort of discipline, or her knight would be impossible to live with. Shaking her finger under his nose, she said, "Sir Perceval. You did not wake me. You left me all alone while you went and talked to the blacksmith by yourself. When will you accept that I am the one who makes decisions about this? Walter is my friend, and this is my quest."

Perceval bowed his head. He tried to look contrite, but Victoria detected an unrepentant twinkle in his eyes. "Forgive me, Victoria. The blacksmith's shop is no place for a lady. 'Tis dirty and hot."

"I can take the heat." She winked at him. Saucily. Victoria was feeling saucy. Frisky, too.

He winked back. "I know. And if I had awakened you, neither of us would have gotten anything accomplished today."

Arching an eyebrow, Victoria took Perceval's hand in hers. "Is that so? Am I so irresistible, then?"

He leaned down and kissed her on the nose. "Bewitchingly irresistible."

She frowned. "Bewitching? Did Thomas—"

"Shhh. Balen approaches. He followed me to the blacksmith's. 'Tis fortunate that the smithy's is set apart from the other houses; he could not get close enough to overhear what Matthew said."

"Was the blacksmith helpful? Did he know something about the amulet?"

"Hush. Not here. Come inside and I will make a full report, my lady." Perceval took her by the hand and led her into the inn. The tavern was empty, and Clement was nowhere to be seen. "We will talk here."

"Not in my room?"

"If we retire to your bedchamber, you know it will not be to talk." He leered at her.

Victoria felt her cheeks grow warm. As well as other parts of her anatomy. Taking a seat at an empty table, she waited until Perceval sat down opposite her. "Well, what did the blacksmith say?"

"Among other things, Matthew said Lord William wanted to destroy the amulet."

"Destroy it? Why would he want to do that?"

"Mayhap because it had ceased to work its magic. The blacksmith said the curse began to take root in Avondel before the amulet was lost."

"So did the miller's wife. There *was* magic, though, for hundreds of years."

Nodding, Perceval said, "Matthew recalled how his father and his grandfather told stories of how Avondel prospered while other less fortunate estates suffered famine and plague."

Victoria placed her elbows on the table and rested her chin on her hands. "Hmmm. First there was magic; then there was a curse. There has to be more to the magic than just the amulet's disappearance."

"What more could there be?"

"You have heard the story of Aethelwyn and her Norman knight?"

Perceval nodded. "Aye. Aethelwyn is the Saxon princess who infused the amulet with magic after her husband gave it to her."

"Well, remember the part where Gareth threatened to kill her if she refused to marry him? She said if he hurt her, she would curse Avondel forever. What if the curse is part of the amulet, along with the magic?"

"I do not take your meaning."

"Several people have said the bad times began before the amulet went missing. So I wondered why that would happen, and the only thing that makes any sense is that something happened to spoil the magic before the amulet disappeared. Since Aethelwyn waited until Gareth proved his love before giving him the magic, I thought—"

"You do believe that the magic existed?"

"I do. I also believe in the curse. Anyone who has seen the ruined castle and the barren fields would believe. I think Avondel was cursed because William abused Juliana."

"If the curse began before the amulet disappeared, it was more likely because Juliana was unfaithful to her lord. Aethelwyn was a virtuous woman, loyal to Gareth."

"Really? How can you be so sure? Aethelwyn must have been a sorceress, since she is the one who took the amulet Gareth gave her and infused it with magic. Perhaps she cast a spell on her husband so that he would think she was faithful, while she fooled around with any knight she took a fancy to."

"Fooled around?"

"Seduced."

"As you seduced me? Perhaps you are an enchantress, after all."

"I am not an enchantress, or a sorceress, or a witch, no matter what Thomas thinks."

"Thomas told you he believes you have bewitched me?"

"He did. He begged me not to turn you into a toad. I promised him I would never do that. But now I'm reconsidering. You might look good in green. How can you blame Juliana for the curse? Why does everything always have to be the woman's fault?"

"You would turn me into a toad?"

Drumming her fingers on the table, Victoria pretended to give the matter serious thought. Then she grinned at Perceval, a wicked grin. "Not even if I could. I'm not done with the manly part of you just yet."

"Thomas said you wanted to drain me of my vital juices."

At that remark, her cheeks felt downright hot. "Speaking of Thomas, there he is." Victoria pointed to the door which the squire had just entered.

"Is that your desire—to drain me dry?"

"Well . . . yes." She could think of no reason to deny it. "But first things first. We cannot forget about Walter." She waved to Thomas. "Join us, please. Sir Perceval is sharing what he learned from the blacksmith."

Thomas took a seat at the table. "Did he say anything of interest?"

"Yes, he did. Tell him, Percy."

Perceval repeated what he had told Victoria, then added, "Matthew told me he saw Juliana for the last time the day before Ranulf arrived at Avondel. She was bidding farewell to a wandering friar. Friar Bartholomew."

Victoria's eyes widened. "A friar? No one has mentioned him before. Do you think . . . Could he have been her lover?"

" 'Tis possible. They could have met alone together

in her chambers or in the chapel without raising suspicion."

"Oh," she said, disappointed. "Then it could not have been him."

"Why do you exonerate the priest?" asked Thomas. "Not all of them keep their vow of chastity."

"Because suspicions *were* raised," explained Victoria. "And didn't someone say the lovers met away from the castle? Besides, if the friar had been her lover, that would have been too juicy a detail for the gossips to ignore. Still, Friar Bartholomew may know who the man was. Wouldn't Juliana have confessed her sin to him?"

"Aye," said Perceval. "We must find him. We will not learn more about the disappearance of the amulet here in Darkvale; that is certain. It is likely that Juliana confided in the friar, as you said."

"You said he was a wandering friar. How will we find him?" asked Victoria.

"Matthew said he was a Franciscan," said Perceval. "That order has a friary at Donscroft."

"Where is that? How far away?" she asked.

"Three days journey."

"Three days? Six days, there and back." Victoria frowned and chewed on her bottom lip.

"We may not return here," said Perceval. "I am beginning to think the amulet may still be at Avondel. Someone may have hidden it to keep William from destroying it. Avondel is a day's ride closer to Donscroft than Darkvale is."

That would give them a week, give or take a day or so, to find the amulet before she and Walter had to meet Tobias. If the friar was at the monastery, and if he knew where the amulet was hidden, or to whom Juliana had entrusted it . . . "What if Friar Bartholomew is not there? What if he is there but doesn't know about the amulet?"

"If he is not there, we will search for him elsewhere. If he does not know about the amulet, he will know who Juliana's lover was. She may have given him the amulet."

"We have to find the friar, convince him to reveal Juliana's secrets, then find her lover? That might take a long time."

"Yes."

"The thing is . . . Walter and I don't have much time left. Perhaps we should forget about the amulet and figure out another way to save Walter. We could bribe a guard, maybe, or find a secret passageway into the castle. Don't all castles have hidden exits? To allow the occupants to escape during a siege?"

"Not all castles are so constructed," said Thomas. "And what would we use to bribe a guard? Do you have access to Walter's chest of gold?"

"No. It's at Avondel." She did not add that she could not open the chest because it had been locked with a magic spell. Then Thomas would be positive she was a sorceress.

"It would take almost as long to go to Avondel for the gold as it will to go to Donscroft in search of the friar," said Perceval. "Do not worry about Walter. Ranulf will not harm him, not until he is sure the amulet cannot be found. If the friar knows nothing of the amulet, we can tell Ranulf we have looked everywhere for it without success. Once he knows that, Ranulf will accept another ransom for Walter—the chest of gold—rather than kill him and lose any hope of ransom."

Victoria sighed. What he said made sense. "We have to find the friar, then. Where exactly is Donscroft?"

"North of here, close to the Scottish border."

" 'Tis dangerous country," said Thomas with a shudder.

"Dangerous how?" asked Victoria.

Perceval said, "Robber knights operate on both sides of the border—Scots preying on English travelers, and vice versa." He slapped Thomas on the shoulder. "I want you to watch over Victoria while I am gone."

"Nay! You cannot go alone. You need me. And I do not want to stay with her."

"Don't worry, Thomas. I'm not staying here. I'm going with him. How many times do I have to tell you, Perceval? This is my quest."

"Victoria . . ."

"Don't Victoria me. I'm going with you, and that's final."

"If she goes, I go," said Thomas.

Perceval threw up his hands. "Cease your bickering. I yield. We will *all* go to Donscroft."

"Fine," said Victoria with a triumphant smile.

"Good," said Thomas, not looking at her.

"Now, let us discuss how this is to be managed. We must travel light and fast. We will each take only a change of clothes."

"No tent?" asked Thomas.

"Nay. But we will need food for several days."

At the mention of tents, Victoria shuddered. Staying at an inn with no electricity or indoor plumbing was roughing it as far as she was concerned. "Why are we taking food? Won't there be inns?"

"Nay. 'Tis not a well-traveled road. There may not be a road at all in places. Luckily for us, it is spring. Blankets will do in lieu of a tent."

"Your armor?" asked Thomas.

"I will wear it."

Momentarily distracted from the rigors of medieval

travel, Victoria said, "I've never seen you in your armor."

Perceval grinned at her. His expression reminded her she had seen him in nothing at all.

Victoria gave him a censorious look. "What about Balen? You know he's going to try to follow us. Do we want him tagging along or not?"

"If he follows us, he cannot report to Ranulf," said Thomas.

"He may trail after us only long enough to guess where we are going. Once he sees we have taken the road north, he may return here to tell Ranulf."

"When Ranulf finds we are all gone, what do you think he will do?" asked Victoria.

"He may do nothing but wait for our return," said Perceval. "Or he may send his knights after us."

Camping out. Being pursued by knights. Victoria wondered if perhaps she had been a little hasty in insisting on accompanying Perceval. "I hope Walter appreciates what I am doing for him," she muttered. "When are we leaving?"

Perceval said, "Tomorrow morning. Early."

Eleven

Three days. He had not seen Elwyna for three days. Walter paced the width of his cell, grumpy and impatient. And scowling fiercely. He knew Victoria made fun of his scowl, but the expression fit his mood. His food and drink had been delivered by armed guards who would not speak to him. He had asked repeatedly for an audience with Ranulf, but since the recipients of his entreaties would not talk, he could not be sure Ranulf had gotten the message.

Walter was not used to idleness or boredom, and certainly not to being confined. A man without family since he was twenty, he had gotten in the habit of thinking of himself as a loner. After only three days without company, he had ruefully concluded that his self-image needed serious revision. He was not a lone wolf. He had never really been alone. Not in his mansion—his butler, his cook, his housekeeper, his gardeners had been there. In the background, never intruding on his privacy, but *there*.

At the office there had been dozens of people, all willing to listen to him, to talk to him, to agree with him. All except Victoria. She started every conversation by disagreeing with him. She thought that was her job. And maybe it was. She would disagree with him now, and tell him he was a wimp if he couldn't amuse himself for a day or two.

He *was* a wimp. He should be able to exist without television, radio, newspapers, magazines, books, or people. It appalled Walter to know that he would welcome any one of the distractions and amusements that he had taken for granted. Walter had been alone before, but in Seattle in the twenty-first century, being alone had been his choice.

Choice had been taken from him, and now he had only himself. Walter was surprised and not a little dismayed to find that he did not much care for his own company.

He needed someone as he had never needed another person in his life. And that someone had a name. Elwyna. One short meeting with her had sealed his fate. He had found *the* woman. And he hadn't even known he was looking for her—browsing, maybe, but not seriously seeking a woman to spend the rest of his life with.

Where was she? Elwyna had promised to return when her duties allowed. Walter tried to imagine what she might be doing as de facto lady of the manor. Planning menus, overseeing the cleaning of the castle chambers, meeting with seamstresses to have gowns and tunics fitted—none of those things should have been more important that visiting him.

Wincing at his self-centered arrogance, Walter stopped pacing. If Victoria could hear him now, whining about being ignored by a woman he had met, briefly, only once before, she would call him a spoiled brat, and then she would crow with delighted laughter. Victoria knew better than anyone, because he told her so on a daily basis, that he would never marry anyone with a net worth less than his. Knowing that the high and mighty Hiram Walter Harrington IV had been brought to his knees by a thirteenth-century maid would give Victoria a great deal of pleasure. She always liked it when he was proved wrong—said it was good for him, kept him humble.

Walter reconsidered. Victoria wouldn't just laugh; she would giggle, chortle, and guffaw.

If Victoria had been there, he would have told her, using his well-known and much admired ability for financial analysis, that Elwyna most likely was not penniless. Ranulf would have provided his ward with a dowry. With several centuries of inflation looming ahead, even a modest thirteenth-century dowry, invested wisely, might well turn out to rival his twenty-first-century fortune.

Then he would have grinned sheepishly and admitted that he did not care if Elwyna had a ha'penny to her name. In his present situation, he could only hope that she felt the same way. About money, since he was without it, and about love at first sight, since he had fallen fast and hard.

With a sappy grin on his face, Walter lay down on the bed. The sun still shone brightly through his prison window, but if he slept he might dream, and his dreams would have to be more interesting than his conscious thoughts.

If he was lucky, he would dream about Elwyna.

Elwyna hurried up the steps to the tower room. Ranulf had given her permission to visit Walter, even though it had been only three days since her first meeting with him. Much sooner than she had expected, given Ranulf's intention to isolate his hostage, she would see Walter again. She had been careful not to seem too eager. Elwyna knew better than to arouse her guardian's protective instincts.

She could thank the minstrel for this visit. Balen's reports had not satisfied Ranulf's curiosity about the two strangers who had come from Avondel. The minstrel only knew that Walter's companion had found a knight to assist her, and that they had spoken with the brewer and several others who had come to Darkvale from Avondel, the miller included.

Balen also claimed the woman and her knight had become lovers on the third night they had been together, but Elwyna did not see how he could know that.

Ranulf had asked her to speak with his hostage, to see if she could discover more from Walter. He had suggested that she tell Walter of his leman's betrayal. Jealousy might loosen the man's tongue, he had said.

Elwyna had not told Ranulf that Walter had denied that Victoria was his mistress. Ranulf would have called her naive for believing him. And she did believe him. Walter's explanation of his relationship with Victoria, as he called her, intrigued her. She had never heard of a man and woman working so closely together without being related by blood or marriage.

If Walter had lied, and she had foolishly believed the lie, she still would not tell him Victoria had betrayed him. Elwyna did not want to be the one to give him the painful news. Walter was a prisoner. Surely that was all he should be required to endure.

When she reached the tower room, Elwyna tapped lightly on the door. Walter did not call out for her to enter. Motioning the guard to raise the wooden bar, she arranged the items on the tray. She had brought Walter food and ale, and her favorite book. The story, written in verse, recounted the adventures of royal lovers cruelly separated but happily reunited at the end. She would like to hear Walter read the tale out loud. She would never be so bold as to tell him that. Even if he read it only to himself, sharing the book would bring them closer somehow.

Elwyna wanted to be close to Walter, and she wanted him to feel the same way about her. Elwyna knew she was building a romantic dream on a very weak foundation. She knew nothing about Walter of Harrington. Only that he looked like an angel, his golden hair fitting his head like a halo, his clear blue eyes seeming to see into her soul.

She thought she had seen into his heart. Walter had a good heart. He had been made a prisoner through no fault of his own, and yet he had been polite—cheerful, even. He was concerned about Victoria, but he was sure she would save him. That had impressed Elwyna the most: that a man could be so confident of success when he had only a woman to fight for him. All of the men she had met before would be embarrassed to be forced to rely on a woman's ability, as well as unsure of her ability to succeed. Walter had no such qualms.

Perhaps this second visit would shatter the illusion, and her angel would prove to be only a man. She would be disappointed, of course, but then she could return to her duties without having Walter's image appear before her at the most inconvenient times. Her maidservant must think her mad, staring into space, mooning about a man she knew next to nothing about.

Elwyna motioned for the guard to open the door. "Wait outside," she ordered as she entered the chamber.

Walter was asleep. He lay on his back, one arm curved above his head, the other resting on his chest. Silently, Elwyna placed the tray on the table and approached the bed. She had never seen a man sleeping before. A soft sigh escaped her lips. Walter seemed even more angelic asleep than he did awake. He was smiling. He must be dreaming pleasant dreams.

"Mayhap he dreams of me, as I do of him," she whispered.

Walter's eyes opened, and his smile widened. "Do you dream of me, Elwyna?"

Flustered, she backed away from the bed. "No. I do not. Why would I?"

"For the same reason I dream of you, I suppose." He sat up and stretched. Rising from the bed, he bowed. "Have you brought me something?"

Elwyna glanced down at the book clutched in her hand. "Yes. A book. *Floris and Blaunchefiour.*" She pointed to the table. "And I brought food as well."

"Thank you, but I am not hungry at the moment. Not for food, anyway. I am starved for companionship. I have discovered that I do not like being alone." He took the book from her hand. "Is it a romance?"

He did not sound disapproving, but Elwyna was used to men sneering at the love stories she admired. Of course, many of those men could not read. She hastened to reassure him. "Yes, it is a romance, but there are adventures, too, before two lovers separated from each other are reunited." Shyly, she added. "It is my favorite story."

"Thank you, Elwyna. I am sure I will enjoy it very much. I promise I will take good care of it." Walter set the book on the table and pulled out the chair. "Please sit and talk with me a while."

Elwyna sat in the chair. "Have you been very lonely?"

"Very. I am not used to being alone."

"Do you miss your family? Are you . . . that is, do you have a wife and children?"

"No, I am not married, and I do not have any other family still living. My parents died in a boating accident when I was in college—when I was twenty. I miss them still."

"Oh, I am sorry."

"Thank you. You must understand how I feel, since you lost your parents at a young age, too."

Elwyna nodded. "So you have been alone for . . . many years?"

"Thirteen years, to be exact. I am thirty-three. But, even without family, I have seldom found myself alone. At my home I had servants and employees—vassals—always around. And I had friends and colleagues for company at other times, and work to keep me occupied."

"Where is your home?" Elwyna asked.

Walter considered. He did not want to lie to Elwyna, but he did not want her to think him mad, either. He quickly—Victoria would have said recklessly—decided to tell her as much of the truth as he could. "My home is west of here."

Her eyes widened. "You come from Wales? You have a strange accent, but I did not think it was Welsh."

"Not Wales. I come from farther west than Wales, from across the sea."

"Iceland?"

Shaking his head, Walter grinned at her. "I come from a land you have never heard of, Elwyna. It is called Washington. I live in a city in the land of Washington called Seattle."

"A city—like London?"

"Not quite as large, but something like London."

"How is it that I have never heard of this land?"

"Not many people have. Washington is very far from here, and few people have traveled from there to here."

"Then you and your . . . companion must have had to travel many months to get here."

"Years, Elwyna. We traveled through many years to arrive here and now at Darkvale."

"Is Washington like England?"

"We speak the same language. More or less. And our laws are similar."

Elwyna's eyes widened. "How can that be?"

"The people who originally settled Washington spoke English."

"My guardian would be interested in your land. He is something of a scholar, too. Mostly he studies books about breeding sheep and farming. But Lord Ranulf finds maps and charts fascinating as well."

"I would be happy to talk with him about my native land. Do you think you might arrange an audience for me?"

"I will ask him, but he may refuse. He is very preoccupied these days, worried about—" She stopped abruptly, looking stricken. "Forgive me, Walter. I cannot reveal what worries my guardian."

"That's all right. Asking him to grant me an audience is all I want." He shook his head. "No. That's not all. There may be something else you can do for me. Do you ever visit the village?"

"Yes."

"The next time you go to the village, would you speak with Victoria? Tell her not to worry about me. Tell her I said everything will be all right."

"Speak with her?" Elwyna seemed alarmed at the idea.

"Yes. Please. Unless you will get in trouble with your guardian. Would Ranulf object to your talking to Victoria?"

"I do not know. I had not thought of going to the village and seeking her out." She paused, her brow wrinkling in a charming frown. "I confess, I would like to see her."

"Would you? Why?"

Elwyna blushed. "I am curious about her. She must

be very brave, to travel so far from her home with a man who is not her husband or . . ."

"Lord and master?"

Elwyna nodded. "I will talk to her. As it happens, the blacksmith has made goblets for Lord Ranulf, and he sent word to me today that they will be ready for me to approve tomorrow morning. I will go to the village tomorrow, and I will stop by the inn to see Victoria while I am there." Gracefully she rose from the chair. "Now I must go."

"So soon? You only just got here. Take pity on me, Elwyna, and stay a while longer. Tell me something about yourself."

She sat down again, folding her hands in her lap. "What would you like to know?"

"Are you married?"

"Nay."

"Betrothed?"

"Nay."

"How old are you?"

"Twenty—almost twenty-one."

"Well past the age most girls marry. Why is that? I cannot believe that you lack suitors."

"A few men have asked Ranulf for my hand. My guardian allows me to decide whether or not to accept an offer of marriage. I have always declined."

"You have? Why?"

"I did not love any of them. And they did not love me. They were only interested in my dowry."

"Ah, so you do have a dowry. I thought you might. Your suitors were not all blind, were they?"

"Nay." Her brows rose inquisitively. "All of them could see."

"And seeing you, not one of them fell in love with you at first sight?"

"Not one." She admitted her suitors' failures with a rueful smile.

"Then they *were* blind and did not deserve your hand. Do you want to marry someday?

"I will not marry a man I do not love, or a man who does not love me. I promised my mother. She told me terrible things happen between a husband and wife if they do not love each other. I know that to be true." Elwyna's gray eyes misted with unshed tears.

Walter pulled her to her feet and wrapped his arms around her. "Don't cry, honey. What terrible things? Do you want to tell me about it?"

Sniffling, Elwyna shook her head and snuggled closer.

Walter held her for a moment longer, then released her. Reluctantly. He wanted to continue holding her. He wanted to kiss her, too. But Elwyna wanted comfort, nothing more. He could wait. "I am sorry my questions called painful memories to mind. Will you forgive me?"

Elwyna blinked the tears from her eyes. "There is nothing to forgive. You could not have known. And now I must go. I will tell Lord Ranulf that you wish to see him. And I will try to see Victoria."

As soon as she left, the room became a lonely cell once more. Walter began pacing, walking around the perimeter of the chamber instead of back and forth across it. His mind was going in circles; his body may as well follow suit.

Elwyna had given him something to look forward to. Several somethings. He might have an opportunity to talk to Ranulf. Hopefully, what he had told Elwyna about Seattle would intrigue the lord of Darkvale enough that he would grant his hostage an audience. Once they were face-to-face, Walter was sure he could persuade his "host" to allow him more freedom.

Elwyna might talk to Victoria and discover how the search for the amulet was progressing. The possibility of even indirect communication with Victoria cheered him up immensely. He missed her caustic remarks. He even missed her constant reminders that he was not always right. Neither was she, but Victoria had been on the mark about this trip. She had predicted disaster, and disaster had happened.

But it could be worse. They were both alive.

Victoria had never felt more alive. She had to wonder if magic mixed with new love and a soupçon of danger sensitized nerves and stirred up the blood. *Magic. Love.* Two forces, each powerful in its own way. Their combined power left her breathless. And greedy. No matter how much she had, she wanted more. Not really greedy—she wanted more only because both magic and love would disappear from her life as soon as she and Walter returned to their own time.

Snuggled next to Perceval, Victoria ran her hand across his chest, down his ribs—

Grabbing her hand, Perceval said, "No more. We need to sleep, Victoria. We begin a difficult journey tomorrow. You must rest."

"I don't want to rest. This will be our last opportunity to be together like this for several days, won't it? Riding hard by day, pursued by Balen or Ranulf's knights, sleeping in the open air at night with Thomas nearby, we won't be able to do this, will we?" Victoria sprawled on top of him and began dropping kisses on his forehead, his eyes, and finally, his mouth.

Groaning, he rolled onto his side, dumping her off of him. "We will find a way."

"Oh? Are you sure? How?"

"I will send Thomas away. To search for water. Or to hunt for game."

"He won't leave us alone. Your young squire thinks it is his duty to protect you from me."

Perceval snorted. "I do not need protection."

"Protection!" Victoria gasped, and sat straight up.

"What is wrong?"

"You and I have . . . we've been . . . often . . . without protection."

Perceval rubbed a hand down her bare back. "I will protect you, Victoria. I promised."

"I know that. That's not what I meant. . . . Never mind. Go to sleep." Victoria lay down and closed her eyes, but she did not sleep.

How could she? She and Perceval had made love a dozen times, and this was the first time the thought of protection had entered her mind. Victoria tried counting the days since her last period, but the image of a baby, a baby with sea green eyes and midnight black hair, kept popping into her mind making her lose count. After starting over three times, she gave up.

She knew better. But she had no reason to pack condoms for a trip to England. They were available at every corner chemist shop. In England, 2001, condoms were easily obtained, but not in Darkvale, 1274. This was all Walter's fault. Everything. If he hadn't tricked her into meeting him at the Any Time, Any Place travel agency . . . If he hadn't missed the right time by ten years . . . If Walter had stayed put at Avondel to wait for Tobias . . .

She would not have met Perceval.

Or worse, she would have met him when he was ten years younger—too young for her.

Victoria gave up trying to blame Walter for her predicament. The truth was, she would not have missed finding Perceval, in this place, at this time, for anything in the world.

"Walter better be prepared to give me a paid maternity leave, though. A nice, long maternity leave." Victoria propped herself up on her elbow and peered at Perceval through the darkness. His breathing was regular, and his eyes appeared to be tightly shut. "Percy? Are you awake?"

"Nay."

"Yes, you are. Have you ever thought . . . ? That is, what if . . . ? It is entirely possible, you know."

"What is possible? You are speaking in riddles tonight, Victoria."

She took a deep breath. "I may be pregnant."

"What!" He sat straight up. "How? That is, why do you think that you are with child?"

"You and I have been having unprotected sex. I could be pregnant. It is definitely possible. But I don't know if I am or not."

She felt Perceval's hand on her stomach. "A babe. Aye. 'Tis possible." He lay down next to her and took her in his arms.

"Well?" Her mouth was against his throat. "Is that all you have to say?"

"I cannot marry you," he said, his voice harsh.

"Well. Gee. You didn't even have to think about that." Victoria bit her lip. She ought to have expected that. But she hadn't, and it hurt.

"I will marry a virtuous woman."

"Yes. You have made that very clear. And since you were not the first man for me, I cannot be a virtuous woman."

"I did not seduce you, Victoria. If you are pregnant, you must share the blame. You inflamed my blood and stole my seed."

She pushed against his chest. "I'll plead guilty to

aggravated inflammation, but I did not steal anything. Any seed-spilling was done voluntarily. And enthusiastically. You like having me inflame you, and don't you try to deny it."

"I do not deny it. I will take care of you and the babe, Victoria. Do not worry."

"What does that mean—you will take care of us?" She knew what he meant. He would see that they were fed and clothed and housed. She hadn't expected him to propose, for goodness sake. But did the first words out of his mouth have to be "I cannot marry you"? She thought not. Perceval could have been slightly more tactful about the whole thing. More chivalrous. Surely the code of chivalry had a section dealing with how to handle a possibly pregnant woman—a woman a knight would not or could not marry. Perceval must not have read that section.

With a sniffle, Victoria pulled free of Perceval's embrace and turned her back to him.

"Victoria?"

"I'm asleep." Squeezing her eyes shut, Victoria felt two tears slide down her cheeks. Oh, great. Now she was going to cry over him. There was absolutely no reason for her to feel hurt. She was a modern woman. A strong, independent woman. A woman like her would never want a man to offer marriage only because she was pregnant. That kind of marriage was doomed, unless the father and mother loved each other.

And belonged in the same century.

With a sigh, Victoria let go of her disappointment. It was unfair to blame Perceval for not doing the right thing. He had made it clear from the beginning that the lady he made his wife would be a virtuous woman; Percy had never lied to her about that. He had not lied to her about anything, for which he deservedly had her admiration and gratitude.

Besides, she could not marry him even if he did ask. That would mean she would have to stay in the past, something she was not prepared to do. And she certainly could not take a thirteenth-century knight home with her. Perceval was not a souvenir.

Surreptitiously, Victoria wiped the tears from her face. She was getting emotional for no reason. It was highly unlikely that she was pregnant. Time travel could be the best contraceptive going, for all she knew. Maybe there was a rule: Thirteenth century sperm may not impregnate a twenty-first-century egg.

"Victoria, do not weep. I did not mean to hurt you. I vowed to protect you."

"Go back to sleep, Percy. I can't be pregnant. I don't know why I brought it up."

Gareth rolled onto his back and stared into the darkness. Victoria carrying his babe. That possibility had shaken him to his core. It seemed that all his long-held beliefs were being mightily tested by his quest for the magic talisman. His mother, the woman he had idealized as the model of a virtuous woman, had been an adulteress. His sworn enemy, Ranulf of Darkvale, by all accounts, was a kind and generous guardian to his sister, a just lord to his villeins. If those two revelations were not enough, the very magic of the amulet had been called into question.

And now this. He had thought that his dalliance with Victoria was just that: a pleasant way to while away the time. But having her had become much more than a dalliance. She had become necessary to him in a way no other woman, no other person, had ever been necessary. He needed her.

And if she carried his baby . . .

With a groan, Gareth turned on his side and pulled

Victoria against him. He held her, spoon-fashion, until he heard Thomas's light tap on the door. He shook Victoria. "Wake up, my lady. 'Tis time to be on our way."

Victoria turned on her stomach and pulled a pillow over her head. "Nooo. It's too early to get up. It's still dark outside."

"We planned to leave before dawn, so that Balen would not see us depart. Come, my enchantress. Wake up."

Pushing the pillow to one side, she sat up. "Oh, all right. I would not do this for just anyone, you know. Only for you and Walter would I wake up in the dark." She yawned hugely. "I am not a morning person, Percy, my love. Especially without coffee."

"Coffee? What is coffee?" asked Gareth.

"A wonderful, you might even say magical, beverage."

"A kind of ale?"

"Lord, no. It is not intoxicating. On the contrary, coffee wakes you up, gives you energy, makes you alert."

"Where do you find this drink?"

"Not here," Victoria said, her voice mournful. She threw back the covers and got out of bed. "Getting up before dawn is not my cup of tea—and don't ask me what tea is. I am not up to another explanation."

"You are a strange woman, Victoria. Are you quite sure you are not a sorceress?"

"If I had magical powers I would have changed Ranulf into a toad and freed Walter without the amulet."

"Aye. 'Tis what I told Thomas."

"And I would conjure up a cup of coffee right this minute."

They dressed quickly and crept down the stairs, through the tavern, and out the back door. When they reached the stable, Thomas was waiting with the two horses and Victoria's donkey saddled and ready to ride. They had decided against taking the packhorse, so Thomas had secured their food and clothes on the backs of the two horses.

To avoid having their departure overheard, they walked their steeds until they were away from the village, then mounted and rode north.

Twelve

The morning after Elwyna's visit, Walter was taken by two armed guards to Ranulf's chamber, located in another tower. As befitted the lord of the keep, this tower room was larger than Walter's prison. It boasted three windows and a door that led to the battlements—an arrangement that reminded Walter of the penthouse terrace outside his Seattle office. The walls of Ranulf's room were covered with tapestries expertly embroidered in rich colors, depicting scenes of hunting.

The lord of Darkvale was seated in a large chair. Several other chairs were scattered about the room, and there was a long table against one wall. The table curved like the wall of the round tower and obviously had been made especially for the room. Several large books were scattered on the table.

Walter bowed. "Good afternoon, Lord Ranulf."

Ranulf nodded his head. "Lady Elwyna said you wished to speak with me."

"Yes. Thank you for granting me this opportunity."

Motioning to a chair, Ranulf said, "Elwyna told me you come from a land far west of here, a place called Washing Town. 'Tis my belief you made that claim thinking to pique my interest so that I would speak with you."

Walter sat in the chair indicated. "I admit that was my motive. But I spoke the truth. I do come from a land far west of here."

"This place you call home is west of Greenland? Of Iceland?"

"Yes."

Resting his head on the back of his chair, Ranulf gazed at the ceiling. "There are songs sung of lands farther west, across a wide and forbidding sea. I thought these mythic lands existed only in the imagination of minstrels."

"Washington exists." Walter could say that honestly. His homeland did exist, in a rather primitive state no doubt, but the place was there, even if it was centuries before it would have a name. He did not feel it necessary to explain that Washington was across a wide sea and on the other side of a wide, undiscovered continent.

Raising his head, Ranulf directed a skeptical look at Walter. "Why should I believe you?"

Shrugging, Walter said, "I have spoken the truth, but I cannot prove what I say. Therefore, you are free to believe or not, as you see fit."

"Why did you ask for an audience? Are you ready to tell me why you came here, from so very far away, looking for Aethelwyn's amulet?"

"I have given you my reason. I am interested in the legend of Aethelwyn and her magic amulet. I saw with my own eyes the result of the amulet's loss. I want to find the amulet so that the castle and lands of Avondel will be restored to their former glory."

"Only Gareth of Avondel has that power. And you said you do not work for him."

"I do not. I was not aware that there was a Gareth, other than the Norman knight who married Aethelwyn, until you mentioned him."

"You expect me to believe that you seek the amulet for no reward, no benefit to yourself?" Ranulf's lip curled in a disbelieving sneer.

"As a matter of fact, at a loss to myself, financially. I offered a chest of gold to anyone who would help me find the amulet. So that you will not think me more of a philanthropist than I am, let me assure you that I do intend to secure a benefit from the restoration of Avon—"

"Aha! I suspected as much," said Ranulf, sitting forward in his chair.

"In the future. Not immediately, not even within a few years, you understand. I can wait. Now, as to why I begged for an audience: I wanted to ask you to give me more freedom. Being locked up without company or work to pass the time is not to my liking."

"I did not lock you in the tower to give you pleasure."

Walter smiled. "No, I didn't think so. But hostages are sometimes treated as guests, are they not?"

"Aye. And they are sometimes locked in a cell much less comfortable than the tower chamber." Ranulf spoke quietly, but Walter sensed an underlying threat. The lord of Darkvale was reminding him, none too subtly, who was in charge.

"Let me hasten to add I do not object to the accommodations, only to the loneliness. With your permission, I could entertain you and your entourage with stories of my travels. Or we might discuss some of the things I have learned in my studies. As I told you, I am a scholar. I have knowledge of many things, things which might help you manage your fiefdom." Pausing, he tried to gauge the level of Ranulf's interest. Walter found his host hard to read, and he was usually good at sizing up people. "But perhaps you do not concern yourself with such things. I understand that some lords leave mundane matters such as crops and breeding to others."

A gleam of interest appeared in Ranulf's cool, gray eyes. "I take a great interest in my lands and flocks. Any lord who does not is a fool. Crops and cattle are the source of wealth."

"I suspected as much. On my way here from Avondel, I passed tilled fields, newly planted. The cottages we passed were in good repair. I remarked to Victoria—my assistant—that the lord of Darkvale takes good care of his lands and people."

"Aye. I do. And without the aid of magic."

"I am not a magician, but I know of methods which will increase the yield of your fields and the size of your flocks."

Ranulf stared at him. "That is a bold claim. I would hear more."

"Am I correct in assuming that your villeins use only marl and manure to enrich the soil?"

"Aye."

"And, because most of the animals are slaughtered before winter sets in, there is never enough manure available in the spring when the crops are planted."

Ranulf nodded. " 'Tis true."

"I have the answer to that problem." Walter leaned forward in his chair, confident now that he had Ranulf's full attention. "Are you sure you want to hear this? Would you prefer that I explain the details of my system to your steward?"

Ranulf shook his head. "Nay. I take a personal interest in the prosperity of my lands and villeins. Let me hear what you have to say. If it sounds plausible I will call for my steward, so that he may hear you as well."

Walter launched into a thorough explanation of fodder crops, concluding with, "So you see, the cattle and sheep eat the fodder, either turnips or ryegrass or both, over the winter months. Since ample food is available to feed the flocks, you do not have to slaughter so many. Thus, more animals are alive in the spring—alive to produce large quantities of manure.

Stroking his beard, Ranulf said, "And this abundance of manure will make the fields more productive."

"Yes, but the increased amount is not the only benefit. I realize that planting crops for animals may be thought unnecessary, but the fact is the manure produced by the animals fed turnips and rye grass is richer than that produced by sheep and cattle who are fed nothing but the stubs of wheat and barley left in the fields after harvest. This manure will enrich the soil so that the next year the fields will yield twice as much grain as before. Maybe three times as much. And, of course, your herds will increase as well since more of them will live to breed from year to year."

Steepling his fingers, Ranulf gazed at him. "Where did you learn of this system? Have you seen it work?"

"I have seen it work." Walter had read about it, in a history of medieval agriculture. Reading was one way of seeing. The system did not become widespread until the late 1600s, but giving Ranulf a century or two of a head start could not hurt. "Will you try it?"

"Mayhap. It will require that additional fields be cultivated, and my villeins will not happily give me additional workdays. But if the method is successful, they will reap the benefits as well as I. I will discuss it with my steward, and if he is interested, I will have him speak with you."

"May I have the freedom of your castle? I confess, I grow bored and restless in my cell."

"Will you give me your word that you will not attempt to escape?"

Walter only hesitated for a moment. Escape would mean leaving Elwyna, and he would not do that. "Of course. I am content to wait for Victoria to bring you the amulet."

"Would you like to meet with your leman?" A crafty look appeared on Ranulf's face.

"Victoria is not my leman, Lord Ranulf. She is my employee, and my friend."

"Is that so? Then it will not cause you pain to learn that she has taken a lover." Ranulf sat back in his chair and waited for a reaction.

He got one. Walter's mouth fell open. "A lover? Victoria? I don't believe that."

"As I thought," said Ranulf, nodding sagely. "You expected her to be faithful to you, her lord and master."

"Not at all. It surprised me that she would find someone to become intimate with so soon . . . especially in this day and time. Victoria is picky when it comes to men. Too picky, in my opinion. Who is he, do you know?"

"A knight called Sir Perceval. He was at the feast the night you were brought to me. He gave you his chair."

"I remember him. Kind of scruffy-looking, wasn't he? But a knight, nevertheless. An honest-to-God knight in shining armor. Well, what do you know?" Walter grinned. "Good for Victoria. And this Perceval is a lucky man. He had better treat Victoria right, or he will have to answer to me."

"It does not anger you to know that your . . . friend dallies with her knight instead of searching for the talisman?"

"No, why should it? If Victoria is having a little fling, I say more power to her. She won't let that interfere with her job. I assure you, Lord Ranulf, Victoria will do everything in her power to pay the ransom you demand. Hey, wait a minute. How do you know about Victoria and her knight, anyway? Are you spying on her?"

"Of course."

Walter chuckled. "Then you must know what she has been doing. Besides fooling around with this Perceval, I mean. She is seeking the amulet, isn't she?"

"She and Sir Perceval are talking to those in Darkvale who came from Avondel, asking them about Aethelwyn's amulet."

"I thought as much. That is what Victoria and I had planned to do before we were brought here. Now, since we have established that the search for my ransom is ongoing, let us return to my request. Besides conversation and company, I need exercise. Perhaps I could train with your knights?"

"You would have me provide you with a sword?" Ranulf seemed surprised that Walter would even ask.

"Only for practice, I assure you."

"What need has a scholar for a knight's training?"

"A scholar needs a healthy body as well as a healthy mind. Exercise makes the body strong. I need exercise. And as a scholar, I am interested in the skills knights use in battle. I thought to learn something of these matters at your fair, but we arrived too late. I come from a country where knights and tourneys have fallen out of fashion and are seldom seen."

"Ah, yes, Washing Town. Elwyna mentioned the name of your country." Ranulf's expression made it clear he did not believe there was such a place. "A land far to the west, a land settled by people who spoke English. Who is your king?"

"George the Second," Walter said promptly, with a silent apology to George W. Bush.

"Is he Christian or Saracen?"

"He is a Christian."

Ranulf studied him for a few minutes. "Very well, Walter of Harrington. I will allow you to dine at my table at night. And you may train with my knights during the morning. But your sword will be blunted."

"Thank you, my lord." Walter rose from his chair and bowed. The meeting had gone much better than he had hoped for. Ranulf was an enigma. A lord deeply interested in his fields and flocks, a guardian zealously protecting his ward. Not the sort of man one would expect to lay siege to a neighboring castle.

Walter almost asked about the siege, but decided against it. No point in rocking the boat when things were sailing along smoothly. But he would attempt one more small request. "Is Elwyna about? I would like to speak with her."

Ranulf scowled. "You ask too much, Walter of Harrington. I have agreed to allow you out of the tower for meals. I have said that you may train with my knights. Now you ask for Elwyna. I am not so sure she should spend any more time alone with you. I suspect you may be attempting to seduce her. I have noticed my ward blushes whenever she says your name. Elwyna seems . . . taken with you."

"I hope so. I am taken with her. I assure you, my lord, seduction is not my intent. My intentions toward your ward are honorable. I respectfully request your permission to court her."

"Others have courted her without success. Elwyna does not wish to marry."

"Except for love. I know. She told me. I have every hope that she will fall in love with me, as I have with her."

"You fall in love quickly," Ranulf said with a sneer.

"Quickly, perhaps, but not easily and not often. I have never been in love before. But then, I never met Elwyna until a few days ago."

Ranulf sighed. "If she does return your love and accept your suit, I suppose you will take her from here, to this Washing Town."

"Well, yes." Walter frowned. He hadn't thought that far ahead. Walter hadn't gotten past how to persuade Elwyna to love him, a penniless scholar. Ranulf had reminded him that he would have to do more than that.

Walter would have to explain time travel and the future. Would Elwyna agree to leave the past behind? Walter had learned his lesson. He was not going to make the same mistake with Elwyna that he had with Victoria. What if Elwyna wanted to remain in her time? What would he do then? Stay? And do what? There was not much call for venture capital in a feudal society. Even if she agreed to the trip, would Tobias accept a third passenger?

Walter needed Victoria to help him answer the questions. She was very good at playing "what if." "You asked earlier if I wanted to see Victoria. Is that possible? I need to talk to her."

"Enough, Walter of Harrington. Your endless demands begin to annoy me. We will discuss your farming methods over dinner. I will think on your request to court Elwyna, and I will ask her how she feels about being courted before I make my decision. Until then, return to your chamber."

Elwyna urged her palfrey into a trot. The mare, a bit overweight and a year older than Elwyna, whinnied in protest. Usually considerate of animals as well as people, Elwyna ignored her old friend's complaints. She had to get home as fast as possible. There was much to think about, much to do.

As soon as she entered the bailey, she was met by

her maid. "Lord Ranulf has been calling for you. You are to go to his chambers right away."

Elwyna did not want to see her guardian. Not now. Not until she had thought long about what she had learned in the village. But she could not refuse him. Elwyna climbed the stairs to his tower chamber quickly, wanting the interview over so that she could retire to her room and make her plans.

Ranulf stood as she entered his chamber. "Ah, Elwyna. You have returned. I am told you visited the village this morning."

She sat down in the chair he held for her. "Yes. Matthew finished the goblets. He wanted my approval before he delivers them."

"Did you find them satisfactory?" Ranulf asked.

"Aye, I did. The blacksmith will bring the goblets, twelve of them, to the castle later today." Elwyna noticed she was drumming her fingers on the arm of the chair.

Ranulf noticed, too. "Are you all right? You seem . . . preoccupied. Is something bothering you?"

"Nay. Not bothered, puzzled. I am puzzled. I saw Balen outside the inn. He said Victoria left Darkvale early this morning. Sir Perceval and his squire are also missing."

Sitting back in his chair, Ranulf nodded. "That is true. Balen reported their departure to me moments ago. He believes they are going to Donscroft."

"Donscroft? There is nothing there but the friary. Why would they go there?"

"To find the amulet, if that is indeed where they are bound for. One of the villeins saw them go north, and the north road leads to the friary at Donscroft."

"And to Scotland." Elwyna frowned. "I do not see how the amulet could have ended up in Scotland. Perhaps the villein was mistaken. They may be going to Avondel to search for the amulet there."

Ranulf shrugged. "It does not matter where they have gone."

"You are not going to follow them?"

"Nay. That would serve no purpose. When they find Aethelwyn's talisman, they will return to Darkvale. I will wait here for them to bring me the ransom."

"Is that why you wanted to see me? To tell me that Victoria and her knight are gone from Darkvale?"

"Nay. I wanted you to know that I granted your request. I spoke with Walter this morning. You judged him well. He is an interesting man, educated, well traveled. We talked of many things. Of faraway lands, of farming methods." Ranulf paused, and gave her a searching look. "We also talked about you."

"Me? Why would you speak of me?"

"Walter told me he is courting you."

"Courting?" Elwyna's heart lifted. She could not help but smile. "He said he is courting me?"

"Sir Walter also told me he has fallen in love with you."

Something in Ranulf's tone made her smile fade away. "You do not believe him."

"Elwyna. He is a prisoner. I have threatened him with death if his leman does not deliver the amulet to me. He may seeking a way out of this trap, and—"

"Marriage to me would be better than death?" Her heart sank. Elwyna knew Ranulf would not kill his hostage, but Walter did not know that. Her guardian could be right. Walter had only seen her twice—hardly enough time for him to fall madly in love with her. A tiny voice reminded Elwyna that she had fallen in love with him in the same short time. But Walter was older, a man who had traveled all over the world. He must have met countless women more fascinating than her. She had never been outside of Darkvale.

"Elwyna. Attend to what I say. I have told Walter he may dine with me, but I want you to take your meals in your room until this matter is settled. You are not to visit him alone again; do you understand?"

She bowed her head. "Yes, my lord."

Elwyna went to her room. After sending her maid-servants away, she sat on her bed. She had to see Walter so that she could judge for herself whether what he had told Ranulf was true. Could he truly love her? If he did, then he would help her, she was certain. But even if he had lied, he would still want his freedom. She would offer to help him escape in return for his help.

She needed help. And she could not ask Ranulf or any of his retainers—not without telling them that Gareth had returned. Matthew had told her he had seen her brother, but he had begged her not to tell Ranulf. Gareth had made the blacksmith promise not to reveal his identity to the lord of Darkvale. Matthew had agreed that he would not tell Ranulf, but he had not promised he would keep the news of Gareth's return from his sister.

Elwyna had not seen her brother for twelve long years.

Matthew had said that Gareth intended to challenge Ranulf, but only after she was safe. She had time, then, to find Gareth and persuade him not to seek vengeance against Lord Ranulf. And, thanks to Balen, she now knew where Gareth and Victoria were going. Matthew had speculated that they might search for Friar Bartholomew, but he had not known they had traveled north when they left Darkvale before dawn.

The blacksmith would deliver the goblets in a few hours. She would ask him to secure horses and supplies for her. Once that was arranged, she would go to the tower where Walter was imprisoned. If he agreed to help her, she would release him from his cell. If not . . . She would worry about "if not" when it happened.

Elwyna hoped that Ranulf would not station guards outside the door to Walter's cell. She was almost sure he would not. Ranulf trusted her to obey his commands.

She was about to betray that trust.

Several hours after dark, when the castle was quiet and most of its occupants were asleep, Elwyna rose from her bed. She was alone in her chamber, having sent her attendants away before she retired. Elwyna opened the door to the hall and peered into the darkness. Satisfied that no one was about, she went to the tower room where Walter was imprisoned.

She unbarred the door and entered the room. A narrow shaft of moonlight revealed Walter asleep on the bed. A blanket covered him to his waist. His chest was bare.

Elwyna hurried to the bed and shook him. "Walter. Wake up."

His eyes opened. "Elwyna? What are you doing here?"

"We must escape. Now. Get up."

"What has happened?" Walter sat up, the blanket fell to his waist, revealing more of his bare chest.

Trying not to stare, Elwyna asked, "Where are your clothes?"

"On the chair."

Tearing her gaze from him, she looked around. "I see them." She tossed him his clothes, then turned her back. "Dress quickly. We haven't much time."

"What is going on, Elwyna? Did you see Victoria? Is she all right?"

"I did not see her. Victoria is gone from Darkvale."

"Gone? When did she leave? Where is she going?"

"She left the village this morning, before dawn. Victoria is with my brother."

"Your brother? I did not know you had a brother. Where has he been?"

"King Henry banished him years ago, but now, with the new king's permission, he has returned. My brother is looking for the amulet. And, I fear, he also seeks revenge. We have to stop him. Are you getting dressed?" A quick glance over her shoulder assured her that Walter's chest was now decently covered. She turned to face him.

"As fast as I can," said Walter, pulling on his boots. "Stop him from doing what?"

"Gareth will try to kill Ranulf to avenge our parents' deaths."

"Your parents? Gareth? Gareth of Avondel? Wait a minute. Are you telling me you are the daughter of the lord and lady of Avondel? The Lord and Lady Ranulf killed during the siege?"

"Aye. But Lord Ranulf did not murder my mother. And he met my father on the field of battle. That is why we have to stop Gareth. Ranulf does not deserve to die."

"But—"

"We do not have time to discuss this now. I will explain everything once we are away from here. Will you help me find my brother?" She wanted to ask Walter if he truly loved her, but she held her tongue. If she asked, he might say yes only to appease her.

"I will help you, Elwyna, any way I can. But are you sure Victoria is with your brother? Ranulf told me that she is with a knight called Perceval."

"Gareth *is* Perceval. He was concealing his identity so that Ranulf would not learn of his presence in

Darkvale. Matthew, the blacksmith, recognized him. Matthew was blacksmith at Avondel before coming to Darkvale. Gareth made Matthew promise not to tell Ranulf, but Matthew felt he had to tell me."

"Have they found the amulet?"

"I do not think so. Walter, when they do find it, Gareth will not hand Aethelwyn's amulet over to Ranulf. He will never pay that ransom. You must leave Darkvale now. And you must take me with you."

"I promised Ranulf I would not escape," said Walter.

"I promised him I would not see you again."

"Why? Didn't you want to see me?" asked Walter.

"Ranulf forbade it. He said you asked to court me."

"I did. I suppose he does not approve of me. Ranulf must think a penniless scholar is not good enough for you."

"Nay. He thought to protect me. He knows I have vowed never to marry a man who does not love me. Ranulf believes you would marry me to avoid death."

"That is not the reason I asked to court you, Elwyna. I am not worried about dying. Victoria will find the amulet, and Ranulf will release me. Even if your brother stops her from doing that, I do not believe Ranulf will kill me."

"Then why did you ask to court me?" she asked.

"Can't you guess? I love you, Elwyna. Please believe me. I know it happened very fast—at first sight, in fact—but I have no doubt at all that what I feel for you is love. A love that will last for all time."

Elwyna threw herself at him, making him stagger backward. "I believe you. I feel the same way. I love you, Sir Walter of Harrington." His arms closed around her in a most satisfactory manner. "Then you will help me find my brother?"

"I will. But take you where? Where are Victoria and Gareth?"

"They left Darkvale early this morning and headed north. Matthew believes they may be on the road to Donscroft. There is a monastery there, and a friar from that monastery was at Avondel when . . . in the days before Ranulf came."

"Elwyna, you were at Avondel, too. Do you know what happened to the amulet?"

"No. I swear I do not. I was a child, a frightened child. After . . . the battle began, I hid in the buttery. Lord Ranulf found me there and brought me to Darkvale."

"All right." Walter took her by the arm and led her out the open door. "Let's get out of here. Which way do we go?"

"This way. At the bottom of the stairs is a passage that leads to the forest outside the castle. Matthew is waiting there with horses and supplies."

"Is he going with us?"

"Nay. Hush, now. There are guards posted nearby."

Walter followed Elwyna. The passage she mentioned was open but unlit. "A candle? Torch?" he whispered.

"We cannot risk it. I know the way. When I was a girl, I used the passageway to sneak out of the castle when I wanted to escape my tutors. Later I used it to escape my suitors. Hold my hand, and put your other hand on the wall. Stay close behind me and I will lead you out of here."

Walter did as she asked. "The wall is wet. Are we under the moat?"

"Aye, the passage tunnels underneath the water."

As soon as they were outside, Walter blinked, his eyes adjusting from pitch darkness to the starlit night. He could see the shadow of a man and two horses. "Is that Matthew?" Walter whispered.

"Aye. Matthew, we are here."

"Lady Elwyna. Did anyone follow you?" asked the blacksmith.

"No. We will not be missed before morning."

Matthew handed over the reins of the horses. " 'Tis dangerous riding at night. Go carefully, and God be with you."

"Thank you," said Elwyna. "You take care as well, Matthew. Watch that Balen does not see you returning from the castle woods."

"He will not see me." Matthew bowed, then disappeared into the shadows.

Elwyna mounted and waited for Walter to climb aboard his horse. She took off at a canter.

"I thought we were going to go slow."

"We must catch up with my brother."

Thirteen

"That road leads to Avondel," said Perceval as they passed a road intersecting the one they were on. "We are not far from Donscroft Friary."

"Good," said Victoria. It could not be soon enough. Three days of riding from dawn until dusk, three nights of sleeping on the hard ground, eating nothing but stale bread and cheese . . . "I want a hot meal. And a hot bath."

Most of all, she wanted her knight.

"Poor lady," said Perceval, grinning. "Soft and tender—you are not suited for a long, hard ride."

"Oh, I don't know. I am very well suited for at least one kind of hard riding. As to how long that ride might last, that would depend on my mount. Some have more . . . stamina than others."

" 'Tis true," said Perceval solemnly. "I have always demanded staying power in my mounts."

"Stamina is definitely important," said Victoria. "Size, too, no matter what anyone says."

"Size?" Her knight sounded shocked. *"Size?"*

Victoria guessed that thirteenth-century women did not compare notes, at least not in the hearing of their men. "Oh, yes. The bigger the better."

"Hilary isn't very big," said Thomas, slanting a confused look at Victoria. She was riding between the squire and Perceval.

"No, but she is exactly the right size for this sort of travel," said Victoria.

After a pause, Perceval spoke up. "Your last mount—did he satisfy your expectations?" He sounded worried. "Was he . . . big enough?"

It was not kind to introduce her knight to performance anxiety, but she could not resist teasing him a little bit more. "Hmmm. Let me think. My last midnight ride was so long ago, I am not sure I can remember."

"Try," said Perceval.

Victoria thought she heard his teeth grinding together. She gave in. "All right. The word that comes to mind is . . . prodigious."

"Prodigious," Perceval repeated, relief evident in his tone. His smug grin made her heart flip over.

"And satisfying," Victoria added, feeling generous. "Very satisfying. I cannot wait to ride him again."

"Where is this mount? In Se At El?" asked Thomas.

"No," said Victoria, with a regretful sigh. "But he might as well be."

"You will ride your prodigious mount again, Victoria. Do not be sad," said Thomas.

Since Victoria hadn't worked any spells, conjured up any hot meals, or transported them to Donscroft in the blink of an eye, Thomas apparently had decided she was not a wizard or a witch after all. As a result, the young man had gone from being wary of her to being very protective. Victoria had the impression that the squire had developed a crush on her.

Time for the innuendos to stop, she decided. She did not want to embarrass Thomas. "Thank you, Thomas. I appreciate your concern. But I am not sad. I have no reason to be unhappy, not with you and Perceval by my side. I must admit, however, I will not be sorry for our journey to end."

After the short burst of talk, no one seemed inclined to say anything else. Conversation had been at a minimum for three and a half days, with everyone concentrating on the road ahead, and all three of them lost in their own thoughts.

Her thoughts had been almost exclusively about Perceval. More specifically, about making love with her knight. Victoria had become some sort of insatiable, sex-obsessed madwoman. That was not like her. Not like her at all. After her last relationship had ended, she had lost all interest in the opposite sex. Her libido had been revived—not only resuscitated but exaggerated—thanks to Sir Perceval, thirteenth-century knight.

Her new insatiable and uninhibited sex drive would have worried her more if she had been in her own time, in her own place. But here, in the company of a knight and his squire, riding on a donkey in search of a magic amulet, well, nothing was exactly normal.

Victoria squirmed in the saddle, trying to find a position that did not rub her bottom raw. She sighed. Not much talk, and not a single minute alone with Perceval. To top it all off, she was a *frustrated* sex-obsessed madwoman. Thomas stuck to her like a burr. Thomas always managed to be the one riding next to her, letting Gareth lead the way.

The road narrowed, wide enough for only two abreast. As usual, Thomas made sure that she rode by his side. Hilary trotted along at a steady pace, a few steps behind Perceval. Bringing up the rear did not bother Victoria—she had an excellent view of her knight. Perceval looked splendid in his chain mail, even if it was a bit rusty and dented in spots. He was not wearing his helm, and his black hair gleamed in the sunlight. Her fingers itched to touch it. For that matter, her whole body itched to touch and be touched.

Perceval glanced over his shoulder at her, and the look in his eyes had her squirming again. She pursed her lips and blew him a kiss. Sexy talk, hot glances, and air kisses were not very satisfying, but better than nothing. At least Perceval was thinking about her. From that last look, she knew he was growing as impatient as she was. He wanted her as much as she wanted him.

Too bad Thomas was wrong about her. If she were a sorceress, she would have put the squire into a deep but harmless sleep, so that she could have had her way with Perceval at every stop along the way.

Perceval said they were almost at their destination. Tonight they would be at the friary, and then she and Perceval could . . . Victoria frowned. No, they couldn't, not at a monastery. Surely the friars would not approve of hanky-panky on their premises. She began to feel a little panicky. Not on the way there, not at Donscroft, not on the way back. When?

The road widened again. She kicked Hilary in the side with her heel and caught up with Perceval. "I need to talk to you right now," she said. "Alone."

Perceval's eyebrows went up. "Right now? We will be at Donscroft soon enough."

"This can't wait."

"Very well." Perceval reined in his horse and dismounted. He handed the reins to Thomas and then lifted Victoria off Hilary's back.

"Why are we stopping?" asked Thomas.

"We will be a moment only. Wait here." Taking Victoria by the hand, Perceval led her into the woods. When trees blocked them from Thomas's view, Perceval stopped.

Before she realized what he intended, Victoria found

herself shoved against the broad trunk of an oak tree. "Percy? What—"

He stopped her question with a kiss. A long, hard, hot kiss. Her knight had been remembering. And wanting. Just as she had been. Victoria smiled against his mouth. "Oh, Perceval, what are we going to do? We can't make love in front of Thomas, or at the friary— I'm sure that's against the rules. We won't be alone together again for days and days."

"We are alone now."

"Not for long. Thomas—"

"Long enough. Kiss me, Victoria. Put your hands on me."

"Where?" She wailed the word against his mouth. "You're wearing armor."

"I can touch you." His hand closed over her breast. "Lift your skirts."

Before she had time to obey, Perceval did it for her, grabbing the hem of her gown and pushing it and her shift to her waist. He knelt before her.

"Percy? What are you going to—"

His hot mouth found her.

"Oh. Oh!" Closing her eyes, Victoria leaned against the tree, letting the strong trunk bear her weight. Weaving her fingers into his hair, she held Perceval's head while he used his lips and tongue to lick and suck. With one hand he held her hip, with the other he found the swollen bud eager for his touch.

Victoria exploded.

Thomas came crashing through the underbrush, dragging Hilary and Perceval's mount behind him. Perceval jerked his head up and released Victoria. She wanted to sink to the ground, but she managed to stay on her feet. Perceval stood in front of her, blocking his squire's view while she hastily straightened her clothes.

"Someone comes, Sir Perceval. I heard the creak of wagon wheels."

Victoria could hear them now, too. Perceval signaled her to remain silent. He whispered to Thomas, "Stay here with Victoria." He drew his sword.

Moving quickly and quietly, he slipped through the trees.

Heart pounding, eyes wide, Victoria reached out a hand. Thomas took it. "I'm scared, Thomas," she said, keeping her voice low. "What if the noise we hear is a Scottish knight? Worse, what if it is more than one knight? What if Perceval is outnumbered?" She pulled Thomas toward the road. "We have to help him."

"Do not worry, Lady Victoria," said Thomas, tugging his hand free. " 'Tis unlikely that robber knights would travel with a wagon."

"They might. Maybe they need a wagon to haul their loot away." Victoria started toward the road, visions of bloody battles filling her mind. "I'm going to make sure he's all right."

"There is no need. He told us to wait here. Sir Perceval will prevail against one knight or many."

"Come on, Thomas. He needs us." She was frantic, practically in tears.

The squire took her hand again and squeezed it tightly. "Do not weep, my lady. He returns."

Perceval walked toward them sheathing his sword. " 'Tis a merchant going to the friary to purchase the cheeses made by the friars. Nothing to worry about. Let us be on our way."

Victoria had a hard time staying on Hilary after their interlude in the forest. Her bones seem to have melted, and her hands could barely grasp the reins. But she held on, and soon the monastery came into view.

Built of rough-hewn stones, Donscroft Friary sat on high ground surrounded by cultivated fields. A small stream ran through the cleared acres, disappearing into the forest.

Gareth dismounted and raised the iron knocker attached to the carved wooden door. He let it fall, and the sound reverberated loudly. "That should get someone's attention."

A friar, dressed in plain brown robes, answered the knock. "Come in," he said. "Visitors are welcome here."

"We seek Friar Bartholomew," said Gareth. "Is he here?"

"Aye. I am he."

Gareth went down on one knee before the friar. "I am Gareth of Avondel."

"What?!" said Victoria, sounding shocked. "You are not. He is not, Friar Bartholomew. His name is Perceval. Percy, you shouldn't lie to a man of God."

Bartholomew's gaze shifted from Gareth to Victoria and back. "Who are you, my son? Gareth or Perceval?"

"I am Gareth of Avondel," Gareth repeated, rising to his feet. "This woman knows me as Perceval because I have been hiding my true identity."

"For what reason?"

"I did not want Lord Ranulf of Darkvale to know that I have returned to find the amulet and to reclaim Avondel."

The friar studied Gareth for a short time. Apparently satisfied, he nodded. "You have your mother's eyes. You are Lady Juliana's son."

"Aye. Matthew the blacksmith told me that you were at Avondel for a few weeks before . . . the end. And that you left the day before Ranulf and his men arrived to lay waste to my home."

" 'Tis true that I was at Avondel then, at Lady Juliana's request. She sent word to the friary that she was in need of spiritual guidance, and I was sent to her. Your mother was a kind and gentle lady, but she had a troubled soul. I hope that I may have given her some comfort when last I saw her. Come with me, Lord Gareth. We must talk in private."

When they were alone, Gareth asked the friar, "Do you know what troubled her?"

"Aye. She told me that she had broken her marriage vows. Lady Juliana said she had fallen in love with a man—"

"What man?" Gareth interrupted, impatient to know the name of the scoundrel who had been his mother's lover.

"She would not tell me his name. Lady Juliana said the man had given her love and comfort, and she would not betray him."

Gareth's lip curled. "She betrayed my father."

"That she did. She knew it, and she suffered for it. Lady Juliana was tormented by guilt and in great distress when I saw her. When she confessed her sin to her husband, hoping to win his pardon, Lord William beat her most cruelly. He refused to grant her the forgiveness she begged him for. He blamed the curse settling on Avondel on her infidelity. Lord William threatened to kill her and to destroy the amulet. When she gave me the amulet for safekeeping, Juliana told me she intended to leave Avondel and go to the abbey at Northumber."

"Not to her lover?"

"Nay. She feared that war between him and your father would be the result."

"War? The man must have been a lord, then, or a knight."

"I do not know. I do know this. Your mother told me to hold the amulet for her children, and to give it to no other but you or your sister, Elwyna. She also told me the magic of the amulet worked only when the lord and lady of Avondel truly loved one another."

"And my father's love for her died when he discovered her betrayal."

"Nay. 'Tis true Lady Juliana's love for her husband did not last, but the loss of the amulet's magic cannot be laid solely at her feet. Your mother told me that she had never had your father's love. She believed that William married her solely to win the favor of King Henry. You may recall that Lady Juliana was King Henry's ward. Your father offered for her, and he offered to take her without a dowry. He told the king that prosperous Avondel needed only a lady, not her gold. King Henry, rest his soul, was something of a miser, you know."

"Why did my father need the king's favor? Did she tell you that?"

"Aye. She said that a neighbor, Lord Ranulf of Darkvale, was a close friend of King Henry. Your father believed their friendship gave Darkvale an advantage over Avondel."

And so it did, thought Gareth, remembering his banishment. "Did they compete for my mother?"

"That I do not know, my son."

"I believe I do. I am sure now that Ranulf was her lover. He was the only lord, other than my father, that my mother saw frequently. She often went to Darkvale to shop at the village market. It must have been Ranulf who seduced my mother. I know he killed her."

"You cannot know that, Lord Gareth. You were not present at the time your mother died. And, if what you believe is true, why would Ranulf have killed her? She loved him, and she believed he loved her."

"My mother must have told Ranulf she intended to confess her sin to my father. That would explain Ranulf's attack—he wanted to strike first, before my

father came for him. He killed my father, and he killed
my mother to punish her. Do not worry, friar. I will
give Ranulf the opportunity to confess his sins before
I kill him."

"If Ranulf is guilty, our Lord will punish him, in
good time."

"I have waited ten long years to avenge my parents'
deaths. I will not be deterred. I will have my revenge."
Gareth spoke the words with determination.

"We will speak more of this later. Now, let me give
you the amulet." The friar went to chest and removed
a small wooden box. He opened it and took out the
amulet. Friar Bartholomew handed the green stone to
Gareth. "May God allow the magic to work for you
and Avondel."

"Thank you, Friar Bartholomew. I will never forget
that you kept this safe for me all these years. I swear
that from this day until the end of time, the lords of
Avondel will protect you and yours."

"God protects us all, my son. But we must be practical, especially since the friary is so close to Scotland.
Your assistance will be welcome. Now, I will show you
to your room. You and your friends must rest until
evening, then you will join us for a meal."

After she had watched the friar lead Perceval-Gareth
away, Victoria had allowed another friar to take her to
a small room, where she was provided with hot water
and a rough woolen robe. She was told to leave her
travel-stained clothes outside the door so that they
could be washed.

Victoria bathed and put on the robe and sat on the
bed, staring at the wall. She had gone numb when Perceval had told the friar who he was. "This woman
knows me as Perceval," he had said. He had called her

"this woman." Not "my lady." Not "my love." Not even Victoria. She was "this woman."

The numbness passed too soon. Victoria could feel again, and what she felt was anger. Her love, her lover, had lied to her. He was not Perceval, her knight in rusty armor. He was Gareth, lord of Avondel. Victoria was so angry, she shook with it. But she could not hold on to the anger, not for long. Soon the anger ended and the weeping began.

She cried herself to sleep.

Perceval-Gareth woke her. She opened her swollen eyes, and there he was, sitting on the narrow bed beside her as if nothing at all had happened.

"You lied to me," she said, spoiling for a fight.

"I lied to everyone. I wanted no one to know my true identity before I found the amulet. Ranulf would have killed me, had he known who I was. My plan was to find the amulet, then rescue my sister and seek revenge against the lord of Darkvale. Ranulf has caused my family much pain and sorrow. He murdered my parents, he stole my sister away, and he had me banished from England. Now I have learned that he was my mother's lover."

"Friar Bartholomew told you that?"

"Nay. But what he did tell me leads to that conclusion and no other. The last time I met Ranulf in battle, he won. I vowed to return and fight him again. Ranulf remembers that vow, and he knows that this time I will win."

She sat up and shoved her hair away from her face. "I don't care if you did have a good reason for lying to the world. You should not have lied to me. I would never have told Ranulf about you. You must have known that, at least after I . . . after we made love."

"Whether you called me Perceval or Gareth made no difference. I am the same man."

"No. You're not the man I thought you were, and that makes a huge difference to me. I thought you were honest. Truthful. Honorable. A chivalrous knight, like the ones poets write about. But you're not like that. You're just like all men. You lie to get what you want, and you don't care how much your lies hurt."

Gareth tried to take her in his arms, but she avoided his embrace. He said, "I never meant to hurt you."

"They all say that, too. You did hurt me, but don't worry about it. I will get over it. This is not the first time a man has let me down." This time the hurt was deeper, though. Bone deep. For all her brave words, Victoria feared she would never get over Gareth's betrayal. She would shrivel up and die before she let him know that, though.

"Victoria, please. Let me explain—"

"No. I do not want to talk about it anymore. What else did Friar Bartholomew tell you? Does he know where the amulet is?"

Gareth pulled on a chain he wore around his neck. A green stone hung from the chain. A green stone the size of the yolk of a chicken egg.

Awestruck, Victoria reached out a hand to touch it. "Aethelwyn's amulet? Friar Bartholomew had it?"

"Aye. My mother gave the amulet to him for safe-keeping. She knew my father intended to destroy it."

Her hand closed around the amulet. "Give it to me."

"Nay." Gareth pried her hand open and tucked the amulet inside his tunic.

Victoria saw red. "Don't you 'nay' me, you . . . you sorry excuse for a knight. I need that amulet to rescue Walter. You promised to help me find it. Well, you have found it. Now give it to me."

"I cannot. You will hand it over to Ranulf."

"Well, yes. I will. It is the ransom Ranulf demanded for Walter. You knew that when we started. . . ."

Gareth's expression turned shamefaced. "Victoria—"

"Oh, I see. You lied about that, too. You never intended to help me free Walter, did you? Some champion you are." She pointed to the door. "Go away. I never want to see you again."

As soon as he was gone, Victoria flung herself onto the bed, but she did not allow herself to waste any more time weeping over Perceval-Gareth. She had more important things to do—such as figuring out how to get the amulet away from him. She had promised to rescue Walter, and she intended to keep that promise.

How? She couldn't wrestle him for it. She could wait until he slept—no, that wouldn't work, not if he wore the thing to bed. Gareth was a very light sleeper. If only she had some sleeping pills . . .

Victoria rolled onto her stomach and hung her head over the side of the bed. Her purse was lying on the floor next to the bed. She sat up, snagged her purse, and dumped the contents onto the bed.

"Eureka," she cried, holding up a package of allergy medication. She was not allergic to anything—except lying males—but she sometimes used the antihistamine tablets as sleeping pills. Victoria counted out four tablets, and using her lipstick tube as a pestle, she ground the tablets into powder. Taking a blank page from her day planner, she emptied the powder onto the paper and folded it into a tiny, easily concealed packet.

The friars called their guests to dinner as the sun lingered on the horizon. Friar Bartholomew explained that the friars prayed, worked, and ate during the daylight hours. They retired at dusk and rose at daybreak.

At dinner Victoria, in her best subservient manner, offered to serve the wine to Gareth and Thomas. As she filled their cups, she slipped the powder into the wine. After dinner, she politely declined Gareth's offer to walk in the friary garden and returned to her room.

Victoria waited until all was quiet; then she made herself wait for an hour longer. When she was sure everyone was asleep, she slowly opened the door to her room. The hall was almost pitch black. Apparently the friars did not believe in wasting money on torches or candles.

She had learned that Gareth's room was across the hall two doors down. With her hand on the wall, Victoria crept toward her goal, feeling her way. When she reached his door, she slowly pushed it open. The hinges did not creak, for which she sent up a silent prayer of thanks.

After the blackness of the hall, the moonlight coming through the window made her blink. Gareth was on the bed, and he appeared to be sound asleep. She closed the door behind her and looked around. Where would he have put the amulet? The bed and a chair were the only furniture in the room. His monk's robe was carelessly slung on the chair. She took a step closer to the chair. Victoria ran her hands over the robe, but she felt nothing but the rough wool material.

She had hoped he would remove the amulet from around his neck before he retired. Apparently, he still wore it. She couldn't see his neck because he had the blanket pulled up to his chin. Taking hold of the edge of the blanket, Victoria tugged gently. The blanket slipped down an inch or two. At first she could not see anything, but then a beam of moonlight sparkled on the chain around his neck. He *was* wearing it.

Crouching next to the bed, Victoria slowly inched the blanket down his chest until the amulet was exposed. Picking it up, she lifted it off his chest. She almost had it over his head, when Gareth groaned softly and turned onto his stomach, jerking the chain from her fingers.

Now the amulet was underneath him.

The change in position exposed the clasp at the back of his neck. Wiping her damp palms on her robe, she reached for it. A second later, the clasp was undone, and the chain fell from around Gareth's neck. But the stone was still under him.

She had to get him to turn over again.

Leaning closer, Victoria blew in his ear. Gareth turned on his side, freeing the amulet. She had it! Before she could take it away from him, Gareth rolled onto his back, trapping her hand, the hand holding the amulet, beneath him.

Holding her breath, Victoria began slowly inching her hand from under Gareth's back. His eyes slitted open. He grinned at her, a sleepy, sexy grin. "You came to me."

"I did not. I'm not here. You're dreaming."

"I am not dreaming. I am awake." He hauled her on top of him and kissed her, a sloppy, sleepy kiss. Gareth yawned against her mouth. "I meant to come to your room after dinner to beg your forgiveness, but I fell asleep. I must have drunk too much wine."

"I should not have disturbed you," she said, trying to free her hand, trapped underneath him clutching the amulet. "Go back to sleep."

"Nay. Not with you in my bed. Not after so many nights apart." His hand went to her breast, and he nuzzled her neck. "I knew you would forgive me, sweet Victoria. 'Twas not my intent to deceive you."

"Wasn't it?" Just like a man. Catch them red-handed and they still denied everything with a smile. "What were your intentions?"

"I could not show too much interest in the amulet without raising Ranulf's suspicions. I needed you to

give me a reason to question"—he yawned again—
"everyone."

He had used her for cover, the rat. Becoming her
sex object had been a bonus he could not have counted
on. "You used me, you—"

"Aye. I did. I find you very useful, Lady Victoria.
I would use you now." He was fumbling with her robe.

Victoria opened her mouth, intending to give him a
scathing lecture. She closed it immediately. She could
not argue with him. He must still be feeling the effects
of the drug, yawning and fumbling as he was. Gareth
was not a fumbler. If she fought him, verbally or physi-
cally, he might wake up completely. And if he got too
alert, he would notice that the amulet was no longer
around his neck.

Victoria felt a draft on her bottom. Gareth had managed to pull the monk's robe to her waist. He grasped
her buttocks in both hands and squeezed. "I am still
sleepy, Victoria. You may be on top."

"Oh, you want me to do all the work." Her body
was reacting to Gareth's caresses, but Victoria was determined to resist him. She could not make love to a
man who had lied to her, a man who had—

With a tremendous effort, Gareth jerked the robe
over her head. "Aye. You will not have to work very
hard. We are naked. And you are already on top of
me." He raised his head and suckled her breast.

Victoria moaned. How had she gotten herself into this
position? Her favorite position. "Yes. Well." She leaned
back in a desperate attempt to evade his wicked mouth.
Gareth sat up, freeing her hand and the amulet. If he
looked down, he would see it. Hastily, Victoria kissed
Gareth on the mouth. At the same time, she dropped the
amulet onto the floor. It landed on the cold stone with
a thud.

Jerking his mouth free, he asked, "What was that?"

"What?"

"I heard a noise. Something fell to the floor."

"I didn't hear anything." She kissed him again, winding both arms around his neck, pressing her naked breasts against his chest.

"Ahh," said Gareth, falling onto his back and taking her with him.

Victoria made another attempt to escape. "Gareth, let me go. I'm sure making love in a friary is a sin. I should leave."

"Nay." Gareth rolled over and trapped her beneath him. "We will confess our sins tomorrow and ask for forgiveness. Do you forgive me, Victoria?"

"I have to save Walter," she said, evading the question. She would never forgive Gareth. And he would never forgive her, once he discovered she had taken his amulet.

"Ranulf will not kill Walter. When he knows I have the amulet, Ranulf will come for it. And I will kill him. Then we will return to Darkvale and free Walter and Elwyna."

"Elwyna is your sister."

"Aye. She is Ranulf's hostage, too. He has not killed her all these years. Matthew told me he treats her like a daughter." Gareth's hand slipped between her legs. "Enough talk, Victoria. Make love to me."

"Gareth, I cannot—"

He stopped her protest with a kiss. Using his teeth to nip and nibble, Gareth coaxed her reluctant mouth open. Her lips parted on a moan, and he plunged his tongue inside, to taste and torment and tempt. "Please, Victoria. Make love to me," said Gareth, his voice hoarse.

One last time, she thought. After tonight, she would never see him again.

Fourteen

Gareth woke late in the morning, alone on the narrow bed. Keeping his eyes closed, he relived the night just past. Victoria's lovemaking had been . . . different. More desperate than bold, more frantic than unrestrained. Gareth opened his eyes and stared at the ceiling. She had been reluctant to stay with him at first, although not for long. He grinned. Victoria had charmed him in every way, but he could charm her, too.

Mayhap her strange mood had been the result of learning who he really was. His stubborn damsel had not wanted to forgive him so easily. She had thought to make him suffer for misleading her, but he had persuaded her to forgive him quickly, and he had done it while half asleep. Satisfied that he had solved the mystery of Victoria's unusual behavior, Gareth sat up and stretched, letting the blanket fall from the cot to the floor. Yawning, he rubbed his chest.

The amulet was gone.

He got up and shook the blanket, thinking the amulet must have come undone during the night's activities— the narrow bed had required them to be both creative and agile. The amulet was not concealed in the folds of the blanket. With an oath, Gareth searched the room—the very small room. It did not take long to determine that the amulet was not there.

Victoria had taken it.

She had not come to his room to forgive him, or to make love with him. Victoria had come to steal the amulet. If he had not woken up . . .

Gareth clenched his teeth against a sudden and overwhelming pain deep in his gut. Victoria had lied. Her passion had been faked. Each kiss, every caress had been calculated to distract him, to keep him from discovering the loss of the talisman. Victoria had once again incited his passion and drained him of his vitality. She had made sure that, satiated, he would fall into a deep and dreamless sleep so that she could take the amulet.

Throwing back his head, Gareth howled in rage and pain. Like his namesake, he had been bested by a woman.

But not for long.

Struggling for control, Gareth willed the pain away. Gareth the First had prevailed over Aethelwyn, and he would triumph over Victoria, but he would not use soft words and gentle wooing to conquer her. He would follow Victoria and get the amulet back. Then he would leave her to her fate. No mere woman, a woman without virtue, would defeat him. He had waited too long to reclaim his heritage.

Gareth found his clothes stacked neatly outside the door to his room. He dressed quickly and immediately went to Victoria's room. The door was open and the room was empty. Her clean clothes were on the bed, and her leather pouch was on the table. His first thought was that she had not yet left the friary. Then he realized she must have left without returning to her room.

Hearing a friar passing in the hall, Gareth asked him if he had seen the lady. He had not, and a quick survey determined that she had not been seen by any of the friars that morning.

Victoria was gone.

Gareth returned to her room, opened her pouch, and shook its contents onto the bed. Thomas found him there, staring at a small, round case.

"Where is Lady Victoria?" asked Thomas. "What kind of case is that?"

"Unlike one I have ever seen." Gareth opened the case and showed Thomas. "See, the case holds powder, a soft round cloth and a mirror. The material the case is made of—shiny, hard, but not metal—is strange to me. The comb is made of the same kind of material."

Thomas looked at the other items spread on the bed. "That silver tube—"

Gareth picked it up and pulled the top off. "Some red substance is inside. But a white powder sticks to the end." He licked his finger and touched it to the powder. "Bitter. Poison, no doubt." He laid it down and picked up a folded leather case. "Look at this, Thomas. Coins, but not gold or silver. Paper rectangles, with likenesses of men on them. Cards with numbers and symbols. One of the cards has Victoria's image on it."

Tossing the leather case and its contents aside, Gareth picked up a bottle and a small box. "These hold tablets. There are other bottles, tubes, and boxes as well, but it is not clear what they are for. The written instructions on these two are difficult to read, but, the bottle directs the user to take two tablets for headache. The box holds a different kind of tablet. Writing on the box says the tablets may cause drowsiness."

Thomas's jaw dropped open. "I was right. Victoria is an enchantress."

"She is a poisoner and a thief. Last night, she poisoned the wine she gave us with these tablets." He held up the silver tube again. "She must have used this to grind the tablets into powder. That explains why sleep overcame me so suddenly."

Thomas's hand went to his throat. "What? Victoria *poisoned* us? Did she mean for us to die?"

"Nay. She meant for us to sleep soundly." Gareth did not stop to analyze why he was so certain of that. He gritted his teeth and admitted, "Thomas, Victoria stole the amulet. She intends to pay the ransom Ranulf demanded for her boss."

Gareth expected Thomas to howl in rage, as he had. Instead, the look the squire gave him held more than a hint of disapproval. "You did promise to help her rescue him," said Thomas.

His left eye began to twitch. Gareth blinked angrily. "I promised to help her find the amulet. I never told her I would hand it over to Ranulf of Darkvale. I did not lie to her."

"But . . . you let her think you meant to use the amulet to save Walter. Is that not a lie?"

"Nay, it is not."

"Why not?"

"Because it is not. And anyway, I had good reason," Gareth insisted. He had told Victoria as much of the truth as he could. If his omissions had misled her, that could not have been helped. "Walter will not die. I told her that. Once I have retrieved the amulet, I will challenge Ranulf. I *will* have my revenge. After Ranulf is defeated, I will rescue Elwyna and Walter. That was the plan. That is still the plan."

"Aye. But you made the plan before you and Victoria . . . before you and she . . . Lord Gareth, I have seen the way Victoria looks at you. She *worries* about you. I . . . I think she is in love with you."

"What?" Gareth was thunderstruck.

His squire's cheeks bloomed red as roses. "She must love you. She would not take you into her bed unless—"

"Enough," roared Gareth. He did not want to hear that Victoria loved him. That would make the small twinges of guilt he felt over the way he had lied—misled her—swell to unbearable proportions.

Thomas stuck out his chin, and for the first time in memory he ignored Gareth's order. "You instructed me in the matter of love between a woman and a man. You said a knight should love only one woman, and that woman he should treat with honor and respect. It is not honorable to lie to a woman who loves you, a woman you love."

"Your reasoning is at fault, Thomas. She may love me, but I do not l-love—" Gareth's throat closed up. He cleared his throat and tried again. "I told you about lust, the fire that sometimes burns between a woman and a man. That is all I felt for Victoria. And by her actions, she has killed any soft feelings I might have had for her."

"Mayhap she thought she had to do what she did. Her purpose was always to rescue Walter of Harrington. You told her you would help her do that."

Gareth shook his head. "I told her I would help her find the amulet."

"But she wanted the amulet to pay the—"

"Enough, Thomas. You know better than anyone that I could not turn the amulet over to Ranulf. And you are wrong about Victoria. She does not love me. And I do not love her." He could not love Victoria. She was not virtuous. And that was not her only fault. She had a sharp tongue. She was not obedient. She did not behave as a demure and modest woman should. Victoria gave orders, she made decisions, and she acted on those decisions instead of being content to allow him to do what needed to be done. He would *not* love a woman like her. "How can you defend her?" Gareth grumbled. "Victoria poisoned us. She stole the amulet."

"Mayhap she only borrowed it," said Thomas hopefully. "Are you sure she is gone? As soon as I arose, I went to the stables to see to the horses. Hilary is still in her stall."

"Victoria is not here. No one has seen her since last night. She is on her way to Darkvale."

Thomas pointed to the window. "Look at the sun. It is already high in the sky. How long since she left?"

"I do not know." Gareth had fallen asleep as soon as she had made love to him. That was hours ago. She must have left his bed as soon as she was sure he was asleep. "Since no one saw her and raised an alarm, she must have been away well before dawn. Ready the horses, Thomas. We are going after her."

Shoving the items spread on the cot into Victoria's pouch, Gareth went to find Friar Bartholomew. The friar was in the library, perusing an illuminated manuscript. When Gareth, entered, Friar Bartholomew closed the book and rose to greet him.

Bowing, Gareth said, "I must leave. Victoria has stolen the amulet and fled."

"When did she leave?"

"Early this morning, before dawn. But she is on foot and will not get far."

Victoria plodded along, putting one foot in front of the other. Walking mile after mile was getting easier, but it would never be her favored means of transportation. Her journey had started when the sun was only hinting at rising, and it was now high in the sky. Even if the sun had not told her it was lunchtime, her stomach would have. The growls, rumbles, and gurgles coming from her midsection were a constant reminder that she had not eaten since the night before.

She should have stopped by the kitchens on her way out of the friary and grabbed a loaf, or a piece of cheese. Her mouth watered at the thought. But she had relinquished food for the same reason she had left Hilary behind. The friars rose early, and some of them would have seen her depart. They probably would not have tried to stop her, but they might have wakened Perc—Gareth.

The knight's name was Gareth.

She should not have made love with him again. No two ways about it—that had been a mistake. More than a mistake, it had been a betrayal of her principles. Once she knew what kind of man he was, a lying, cheating . . . liar, she should have been strong enough to resist him.

Victoria could not excuse her behavior as expedient. Sex was not the only way to distract a man. She could have hit him over the head with the candlestick. In retrospect, that method had much to recommend it. If she had knocked him out instead of wearing him out, she would feel better about herself. She would feel stronger, more in control of her own destiny.

But she had not been able to withstand her knight in rusty armor. She had made love to him because she had no choice. She could not resist him.

"Love sucks."

It dismayed her to know that she still loved Perceval—Gareth. That had not been true of the other two men she had been involved with. When they told her it was over—the first because he wanted to find himself, the second because he had found someone else— her feelings for them had died a quick and almost painless death. She had not felt anything but stupid for falling for them in the first place.

This time, Victoria did not feel dumb. She felt betrayed, used, and horribly hurt, but she did not feel like it was her own stupid fault for once again falling for the wrong man. Percy—Gareth—whatever his name was the right man.

He just was not the right man for her.

And she was not the right woman for him. She was not virtuous. She never had been virtuous in his eyes, and he had based his opinion solely on her lack of virginity. Now she had added to her sins: she had drugged him, and she had stolen the amulet from him. If there had ever been a chance that Gareth would love her, that chance was gone. He would never, ever love her now.

She might still love him, but she would get over that in time. In a few days there would be centuries of time between them. Surely that would make it easy to forget him, especially now that his true colors had been revealed.

Victoria grimaced. Speaking of true colors, no matter how unprincipled she thought he was, he had to think she was worse. She had committed the ultimate sin. She had taken the precious talisman, the magic charm that everyone wanted.

The amulet did belong to him, her bruised and battered conscience reminded her.

But she had to have it. Gareth might be willing to bet Walter's life that Ranulf would not carry out his threat if the amulet was not forthcoming, but Victoria could not take that chance.

The sound of approaching riders ended her forlorn reverie. Victoria hurried to conceal herself behind a large oak tree at the side of the road. Holding her breath, she waited. The hoofbeats grew louder as the riders approached. Her breath sighed out of her when they grew nearer and she realized that the sound came from the south, not the north.

Ranulf must have followed them from Darkvale to Donscroft. She could hand the amulet over to him, before Gareth caught up with her. Victoria stepped from behind the tree, waving her hands at the riders. There were only two of them, a man and a woman.

"Walter!" she called out when she saw who it was.

Hauling back on the reins, Walter brought his horse to a halt. "Victoria! What are you doing here? Elwyna, stop."

Elwyna reined in her horse, and she and Walter dismounted. Laughing, Walter grabbed Victoria by the waist and swung her around. "Why are you dressed like a monk?" Putting her down, he said, "Lady Elwyna, this is Victoria Desmond, my personal assistant and good friend. Victoria, meet the woman I love, Lady Elwyna of Avondel."

"Percy—I mean Gareth's sister. How are you?" Victoria said the words a trifle stiffly. She was not sure she approved of Walter falling in love overnight. How much could he know about this woman? If Elwyna was anything like her brother, Walter had better watch out.

"Where is my brother?" Elwyna asked. "I thought you were together."

"He is hot on my trail, no doubt." Victoria reached inside the neck of her robe and pulled out the amulet. "I have Aethelwyn's amulet. I stole it from him."

"Stole it? Why?" asked Walter, fingering the green stone. "So this is the famous magic amulet. Not very impressive, is it? It looks like costume jewelry."

"Why did you take the amulet from my brother?" demanded Elwyna.

"I had to do it," Victoria replied. "He was not going to ransom Walter. Your brother intended to take the amulet to Avondel."

"That *is* where it belongs," said Elwyna, her tone unfriendly.

"Not at the cost of Walter's life," snapped Victoria.

Walter held up his hands. "Now, ladies, there is no reason to quarrel. As you can see, Victoria, I have already been rescued. Since I am no longer Ranulf's prisoner, there is no need to give him the amulet."

"I suppose not," said Victoria. She removed the necklace and handed it to Elwyna. "Here. This belongs to your family."

"Thank you," said Elwyna, her tone considerably softer than it had been. "How did Gareth—how did the two of you find the amulet?"

Victoria quickly recited the history of the search. "So Friar Bartholomew had it all along, just waiting for you or Gareth to claim it. Now it's your turn, Walter. How did you escape? What are you doing on the road to Donscroft? And do you have anything to eat? I'm starving."

Walter reached in a linen bag attached to his saddle and pulled out a round of cheese and a loaf of bread. "The bread's kind of stale by now, but the cheese is okay."

"Thanks," mumbled Victoria, chewing on the bread. "Talk. Tell me how you got away from Ranulf."

"Elwyna released me. She needed my help in finding her brother. She hopes to persuade him not to kill Ranulf."

"That won't be easy," said Victoria. "Gareth thinks Ranulf murdered his parents."

"Lord Ranulf did not murder anyone. My father killed my mother. I—I saw him do it."

"Oh, Elwyna." Walter took her into his arms. "My poor darling. Let me—"

The thunderous sound of riders coming hard and fast stopped Walter before he could say more.

"Here they come," said Victoria. She was not going to escape the past without seeing Gareth again, after all. Her heart began to beat faster, and it was difficult to breathe. Not because she was excited about seeing him again, no way. *Flight or fight.* She was experiencing an adrenaline rush; that was all. Victoria's knees felt a trifle weak, no doubt the result of so much walking. She sat down, leaning her back against the oak tree. "This should be interesting," she muttered.

Gareth and Thomas rounded a bend in the road, coming to a halt in front of Elwyna and Walter. The couple and their two horses blocked Victoria from view.

"Walter of Harrington? How did you escape?" Gareth asked.

"Your sister released me."

"My sister!" Gareth's gaze shifted to Elwyna.

Walter took Elwyna by the hand. "I believe it has been some time since you have seen each other. May I present Lady Elwyna to you?"

"Elwyna?" Gareth quickly dismounted and stood in front of her. "Is it really you?"

"Gareth, my brother." Elwyna threw herself into his arms.

His arms closed around her. "At last." Gareth buried his face in her hair. "There were times I thought I would never see you again."

"I always knew you would return. For me, and for Aethelwyn's amulet."

"The amulet! Elwyna, I had it, but it was stolen from me. I followed the thief from Donscroft, but—" Gareth stopped abruptly and looked around. "Have you seen Victoria? She was on this road, and we have not passed her. She may be lost, hurt—"

He sounded worried. Not about her, of course.

About the precious amulet. Victoria cleared her throat. "I am not lost. I'm right here."

Releasing Elwyna, Gareth strode to the oak tree. "Give me the amulet, Victoria."

She stood up. Brushing leaves from her robe so she wouldn't have to look at him, Victoria said, "I don't have it."

Gareth grabbed her by the shoulders and shook her. "Give it to me, Victoria."

"Hey!" said Walter, pushing Gareth away from Victoria. "That's no way to treat a lady."

Gareth's lip curled into a sneer. "She is not—"

"Gareth, I have it," said Elwyna, tugging on his sleeve. "See? Here is Aethelwyn's amulet. Victoria gave it to me. Walter is safe, and there is no need to pay the ransom."

Taking the amulet from Elwyna, Gareth replaced it around his neck. "You and Walter traveled from Darkvale to here together? Just the two of you?" He directed the question to Elwyna, but his gaze was on Walter.

"Aye. Matthew told me you had returned, and Balen reported to Ranulf that you had headed north. I guessed you must be going to the friary. I had to find you before you challenged Ranulf. Gareth, my brother, Lord Ranulf does not deserve to die. He—"

Gareth's attention was focused on Walter. "You spent the night—several nights—alone with my sister." His hand went to the hilt of his sword.

"Gareth!" Elwyna stepped in front of Walter. "Leave him alone. I asked him to come with me. Walter helped me find you."

Walter put his hands on Elwyna's waist and moved her to his side. "I assure you, Lord Gareth, nothing has happened between us—"

"Nothing? How can you say that?" Elwyna pushed

herself between the two men again. She faced Walter. "Much has happened between us. You kissed me, and—"

Gareth drew his sword. "Step aside, Elwyna. Walter of Harrington, prepare to defend yourself."

"Oh, for heaven's sake," said Victoria. "Knock it off, Percy. It wouldn't be a fair fight. Walter doesn't have a sword. And if he said nothing happened, then nothing happened. Unlike you, Walter does not lie." Victoria turned to Elwyna. "Elwyna, tell your brother nothing happened, except a kiss or two."

"I cannot. More than kisses passed between us—"

Gareth took a step closed to Walter. Walter raised his fists. "I may not have a sword, but I will fight you man to man."

Stamping her foot, Elwyna said, "Stop this! Gareth, Walter asked me to be his wife, and I accepted. I love him, and he loves me. That is what happened between us."

"Oh, darn," said Victoria, feeling an onslaught of envious tears threatening. Walter had fallen in love, and his love loved him back.

"You cannot marry him," said Thomas. "He is a wizard. And so is she." The squire pointed to Victoria.

"I am not!" "No, I'm not!" Walter and Victoria denied at the same time.

"The amulet will protect us from any black magic these two may use," said Gareth, sheathing his sword. "This is not the time or place to talk of marriage or wizardry. We will discuss this later. Now we must be on our way, before Ranulf and his knights arrive and take us all prisoner."

"On our way where?" asked Walter, his tone still belligerent.

"We go to Avondel," said Gareth. "Thomas, give Victoria her clothes. And her pouch."

Victoria took the bundle Thomas handed her and waited until Walter, Elwyna, Thomas and Gareth were all seated on their respective mounts. "I don't have a horse," she pointed out.

"You may ride with me," said Elwyna.

"Nay," said Gareth. "She will ride with me."

"In your dreams, Percy. Walter, give me a hand up." He did as she asked, and Victoria was soon sitting sideways on the saddle in front of Walter.

Gareth motioned for Walter to take the lead. "Since your horse is carrying a double load, we will let you set the pace."

Thomas and Elwyna followed, and Gareth brought up the rear.

They rode in silence until they reached the spot where the road forked. At Gareth's command, they took the left fork, the one that led to Avondel.

Walter said, "What's up with you and the knight? I thought you and he were an item, but things seemed a little chilly between you back there."

"An item?" said Victoria. "Who told you that?"

"Ranulf. He said you had taken a lover: Sir Perceval, a.k.a. Lord Gareth. Ranulf thought it would make me jealous. It didn't, of course. I was happy for you. Talk to me, Victoria. What's going on?"

She shrugged. "We had a little fling. It's over. No biggie." Out of the corner of her eye, Victoria saw Walter scowl.

"What did he do to you?" he asked. He sounded as if he was still spoiling for a fight. Walter did not like taking orders, and Gareth had been snapping them left and right ever since he arrived on the scene.

"Nothing. Really, Walter. There is no need for you to defend my honor or anything. Gareth did not do anything to me. I did it to myself. Again. Every time I believe in someone—"

"Victoria. Exactly what did that canned thug do to you? Tell me."

"He lied. Not just about his name. About everything. He vowed to be my champion—on his knees no less. And I fell for it, the whole knight-in-shining-armor shtick. Isn't that a hoot and a half? I should have known better. Gareth isn't a knight in shining armor. His armor isn't even sh-shiny. It's rusty; did you notice?"

"No, I didn't. I noticed that his sword was shiny. Very shiny. And sharp. That's what held my attention. What did Gareth lie about? Did the jerk tell you he loved you?"

"No. He never said anything like that. As a matter of fact, Gareth made it very clear that anything that happened between us wasn't going anywhere but the nearest horizontal surface. Or vertical. It was all about sex, Walter. Just sex and only sex. Gareth has very high standards when it comes to the woman he will love. I don't meet them."

"What do you mean, you don't meet them? You're smart as a tack, loyal to a fault, and pretty as a picture. What in hell is he looking for?"

"A virgin."

"Oh. Well . . ." Walter's cheeks reddened, momentarily distracting Victoria. She had never seen her boss blush before.

Victoria gave a nonchalant wave of her hand. "It doesn't matter. The point is, he didn't lie to get me into bed. But he did lie. Gareth said he would protect me and help me find the amulet."

"Now I'm confused. He did do that, didn't he?"

"Not for me. Or for you. Gareth found the amulet for himself. He never meant to let me use it to pay the ransom. He would have let you die, Walter."

"As to that, I'm not so sure Ranulf would have killed me. Once you get to know him, he's not so bad. He takes good care of his lands and people. And he treats Elwyna like a princess."

Victoria twisted around to look Walter squarely in the face. "Are you talking about Lord Ranulf of Darkvale? I thought he was the villain of this story."

"So did I. But Elwyna wants to save him. She thinks he's okay. She hasn't explained all her reasons—I think she wants to tell Gareth first—but her opinion's good enough for me."

Victoria sighed. "You really do love her, don't you?"

"Yeah, I do. And she loves me. Me, not my bank account. She thinks I'm a penniless scholar."

"Penniless? With a chest of gold?"

"Oh, right, the gold we left at castle Avondel. I forgot about that. But Elwyna has a dowry, so that makes us even. For what my opinion's worth, I think your knight cares about you, Victoria. When he first rode up and he didn't see you, he acted like he was really worried about you."

"He was worried about the amulet."

"Maybe. But he wanted you to ride with him."

"So he could lecture me from here to Avondel about my failings as a woman, no doubt. Are you sticking up for him? For heaven's sake, Walter, he thinks I'm a witch."

"I think I know why. They had your purse, remember? He must have looked in it. What have you got in there? Your cell phone? Makeup? Twenty-first-century money?"

"Not my cell phone. I left that in my suitcase at Avondel. But the other stuff . . . yeah. I didn't think about that. I guess lipstick and paper money would look weird to someone from this century. Walter, sooner or later, we're going to have to tell them we're from the future. And hope they believe us. We don't have much time left in the past."

"I know. I had come to that conclusion myself. But let me break it to Elwyna first. I should have told her when I proposed, but I got cold feet." Walter's hands on the reins tightened, making his knuckles white. "I'm scared she may not want to travel to the future with me."

Victoria snorted. "The way she looks at you, I think she would go forward, backward, or sideways for you."

"You do? How does she look at me?"

"Like you're the answer to a maiden's prayer. You've got the same starry-eyed look on your face. Want to borrow my mirror?"

"No, I'll take your word for it. It's odd that you and I both fell in love at first sight."

"Who said I'm in love?"

"Come on, Victoria. I know you. You love your knight in rusty armor. And you must have fallen for him pretty quick; Ranulf knew about your affair a few days after we got to Darkvale."

"Okay, I admit it. I fell in love. And now I've fallen out of love. I'm over it."

"Are you? Then why are you moping around?"

"I am not moping. Over a knight? Get real."

"Get real? This is the wrong time and place for too much reality. I think our falling in love has something to do with magic and time travel."

"I hope that means it won't survive the return trip."

"Oh, I think it will. This love is as real as time travel and as enduring as magic. When Tobias was giving me his sales pitch at the Seattle fair, he mumbled something about finding one's heart's desire. At that point, I wasn't paying too much attention, but I think he said it was a frequent by-product of a trip through time. He has a theory that only those separated by time from their soul mates are good candidates for time travel."

"That's a ridiculous theory. At his prices, good candidates for time travel are the people who have a few million lying around collecting dust. How many of his customers have fallen in love with someone in the past? Or the future? I assume he goes both ways."

"I don't know. I didn't ask. Like I said, I didn't pay too much attention to that part of Tobias's spiel. I didn't take the trip to find my heart's desire. I just wanted to be able to fix up my castle. Finding Elwyna was an amazing bonus."

"Humph," said Victoria, envious and disgruntled. "You got a bonus and I got a broken heart."

Fifteen

Elwyna was safe. He had the amulet. He would soon meet Ranulf. All the elements of his plan were coming together as he had foreseen. Gareth should have been happy, or at least content, but he was furious. No matter what he had told Thomas, the instant he had seen Victoria leaning against that tree, he had wanted her again.

As he had ridden after her, his mind had been filled with visions of what would happen when he caught up with her. Gareth had settled on a picture of Victoria falling to her knees and begging him for forgiveness—a request he had fully intended to deny.

He should have known better. Victoria would never beg for anything. She had not apologized for stealing the amulet. Why had he even imagined that she would? No doubt she thought the theft was justified merely because he had neglected to tell her the details of his plan. She had not apologized. Adding insult to injury, Victoria had compounded her sin by refusing to ride with him, denying him the opportunity to instruct her on the proper way to behave.

An enchantress would not take lessons from a mortal man, a timid voice in the back of his mind pointed out. Gareth ignored it. Knights had prevailed over sorcery before, and he would as well. His hand went to the amulet, once again hanging around his neck on its chain. Victoria had charmed him, but now he had the protection of his ancestor's talisman.

Invincible he might be, thanks to his own abilities and the magic of the amulet, but Victoria had treated him as if he were invisible. She had not even deigned to look at him. She had gone to Walter and let him take her onto his saddle. Now she was chattering away with Walter as if she did not have a care in the world, leaving him to seethe with impotent fury.

The amulet might offer him protection, but it would be a mistake to underestimate Victoria. He might know he was under her spell, but knowledge alone had not ended the enchantment. She still wielded power over him. Try as he might, Gareth could not take his eyes off Victoria, seated in front of Walter, her bottom snugly pressed against Walter's crotch, her head nestled on Walter's shoulder. Gareth did not like the familiar way Walter wrapped his arms around her, and he especially did not like the way Victoria smiled at Walter. She was *flirting* with another man. With a groan, Gareth added jealousy to the mix of emotions churning inside him.

With a prodigious effort, Gareth forced his attention away from Victoria. He made himself look at Elwyna as she rode beside Thomas. His sister was quiet and demure, as befitted a virtuous maiden. She had been solemn as a child, he recalled. Gareth smiled. He had taken great pleasure in making his little sister laugh. All their years apart, he had thought of her as a child, seeing her in his mind's eye as she had looked the last time he had seen her. Elwyna was not a little girl any longer; she was a woman grown. And she believed she was in love with Walter of Harrington.

Walter must have bewitched Elwyna, as Victoria had enchanted him.

Involuntarily, his gaze shifted from his sister to Victoria. Swallowing another groan, he looked away. He would deal with the two magicians later. Now that he had the amulet, Gareth was confident that with a little more time he could outwit Walter and Victoria and nullify their wicked spells.

There were other matters that needed to be settled first. Gareth had avoided listening to Elwyna's defense of his sworn enemy long enough. Spurring his horse, Gareth drew even with Thomas and Elwyna. "I would speak with my sister, Thomas. Fall back." When they were riding side by side, Gareth said, "Tell me about Ranulf."

Elwyna slanted a wary look at him. "Lord Ranulf is a good man, Gareth."

"He may have been good to you, but he killed our parents. I know you were a child when it happened, but how can you forgive him for that?"

Staring straight ahead, Elwyna said in a soft voice, "Ranulf did not kill our mother. Father killed Mother."

"What?" Gareth was stunned, unable to believe what she had said. "Elwyna, that cannot be true. Is that what Lord Ranulf told you?"

"Nay. I know it *is* true." She looked at him, her gray eyes filled with tears and pain. "Our father killed our mother, Gareth. I—I saw him do it." Elwyna choked a little. After a pause, she composed herself and continued, "Father killed her because she was unfaithful, and he blamed her for Avondel's loss of magic. Ranulf and Mother were lovers."

"Aye. I was told she had taken a lover. I suspected that Ranulf was the man." Lord William had taken the life of Lady Juliana? Gareth could hardly credit it, but he knew in his heart that Elwyna spoke the truth. It

was obviously painful for her to recall the terrible act
she had witnessed all those years ago.

Gently Gareth asked, "Can you tell me more?"

Taking a deep breath, Elwyna nodded. "That morning, Father discovered that the amulet was missing. He
flew into a rage, accusing Mother of destroying him
and everything that was his. Mother tried to explain,
but he would not listen. She told me to go away, but
I stayed outside the door. I was frozen with fear."

"Poor Elwyna, do not continue. Reliving that awful
day is too much for me to ask of you."

"Nay. I must tell you everything. Father said terrible
things to her, things I did not fully understand at the
time. He accused her of being unfaithful. Mother did
not deny it. She told him she loved Ranulf because he
was kind to her, because he did not beat her. Gareth,
Father *beat* Mother. I saw the bruises." Elwyna looked
at him, her eyes flashing. "If Mother was unfaithful,
she had reason to be. A husband should not treat his
wife that way."

Elwyna sounded much as Victoria had when she had
defended Juliana's actions. Gareth found himself
agreeing with them both. The code of chivalry ex-
horted knights to defend the weak against the strong.
His father had ignored that command. "You have the
right of it, sister. A husband should protect and honor
his wife." He frowned. "I do not remember Father being a cruel man, but I was very young when I was sent
to Baron Edmund. He must have changed."

"Aye, he did. As the years passed, Father became
morose and ill-tempered, especially after drinking.
Mother and I avoided him as much as possible. It was
not difficult for me. After a while, I think he forgot I
existed. M-mother was not so fortunate."

Gareth remained silent for awhile, brooding over

Elwyna's words. Finally, he asked, "Do you think that Lord Ranulf loved our mother?"

"Very much. 'Twas his misfortune to fall in love with Mother, but once Ranulf loved her, he did everything in his power to protect her from harm. He has never forgiven himself for being too late to save her from Father's wrath. And, although Ranulf did kill our father, it was not murder. They met on the field of honor."

A roaring sound filled Gareth's ears and his head began to ache. Once again his core beliefs were being challenged. Gareth had been certain that Ranulf was evil, a man bent on destroying what he could not own. Gareth had spent ten years in exile plotting his revenge against Ranulf of Darkvale. Now Elwyna was insisting that his lifelong enemy deserved not his hatred but his pity.

"Ranulf had me banished," Gareth reminded her, not yet willing to give up his goal. "His actions kept us apart for all these years."

"Aye, and that was bad of him, I agree. But Ranulf feared you then, and he fears you now. That is why he took Walter hostage and ordered Victoria to find the amulet. Ranulf thought if he had the talisman he could use it to bargain with you for his life."

"Ranulf fears me? I am one knight. He has many knights to defend his life." Gareth's protest sounded querulous to his own ears. He was whining because he could feel his justification for punishing Ranulf slipping away.

"You must not think he is without honor, Gareth. Lord Ranulf meant to face you alone, as he faced our father. Ranulf thought you deserved the right to avenge our father's death. And our mother's. Even though it was not his hand that ended her life, he has always blamed himself for her death."

"Enough, sister," said Gareth, not wanting or needing to hear more. Honor demanded that he forgive his old enemy. Lady Juliana and Lord Ranulf had been punished for loving each other—Juliana by death, Ranulf by a lifetime of regret and guilt.

With a shuddering sigh, Gareth let his need for revenge melt away. "You are right, Elwyna. Ranulf does not deserve to die."

She smiled tremulously and brushed tears from her eyes. "I knew I could make you understand. You are a true knight: honorable, brave, and wise."

Gareth grinned ruefully. "Honorable, brave, and wise? Some would argue with you."

Elwyna frowned, her expression filled with indignation. "Who? I would gladly speak out on your behalf, dear brother."

Gareth laughed out loud. Elwyna looked like a fierce kitten. He suddenly felt lighthearted and free. His thirst for revenge had burdened him for so long, he had almost forgotten how much pleasure could be found in laughter. "I have a staunch defender in my sister, it seems. Yet you do not know me."

"I know you. I remember you from our childhood together. And I heard stories about your adventures from time to time. Some of the knights and merchants who come to the Darkvale fair each year knew of you. Who slanders you, brother? Identify him, and I will flail him with my tongue."

"Not him—her. Victoria believes I lied to her."

"Victoria." Elwyna turned her gaze from Gareth to the pair riding in front of them. "Tell me about her, please. Walter had every confidence that she would save him, even though she is only a woman. He told me she was strong and brave, and I imagined her to be a woman like the warrior queens of old. Victoria is not very big, is she? I vow, I am taller than she."

"And just as fierce," said Gareth.

"Walter thinks a woman can do anything she sets her mind to. Is that not a strange belief?"

"Aye. 'Tis a belief that Victoria shares. She was determined to find the amulet and pay the ransom without anyone's help. I had to convince her she needed my assistance. Victoria is brave, as brave as a knight." Gareth sobered. "But she is dangerous. And so is Walter."

"Dangerous? In what way?"

"Walter and Victoria are sorcerers, Elwyna. Thomas was right about that. What I feel for Victoria, what you feel for Walter, may be nothing more than an illusion, a spell. They are toying with us, as Morgan le Fay toyed with Lancelot."

"Nay, I do not believe that. I love Walter, and I know he loves me. Their strange beliefs and odd way of speaking may be explained by something more mundane. They come from a different country, far to the west."

Gareth nodded. "See At El. I know that. But Victoria carries items in her pouch, curious things made of unfamiliar materials." Gareth did not add that Victoria had seduced him in an enchanting and magical but completely unmortal-like manner. He would not sully his sister's innocence with that particular confession.

"Have you asked her to explain the queer things you found in her pouch?"

"Nay. She left it behind when she fled the friary with the amulet. Victoria does not know that I looked inside."

"You said she believes you lied to her. Why would she think that?"

Suddenly uncomfortable, Gareth shifted in the saddle. "I told her my name was Perceval. And I vowed to help her find the amulet. But I did not promise her I would give the amulet to Ranulf."

"Did you tell her you would not give up the amulet?" Elwyna asked.

"Nay." Gareth blinked rapidly, to stop his eye from twitching.

"Hmmm. I understand your reluctance to reveal your true purpose to her, of course. But Victoria may be justified in believing that you lied. My tutor told me that not telling the whole truth could be the same as a lie."

Walter reined in his horse before Gareth could respond to Elwyna. "Time for a break, don't you think? There is a stream a few steps ahead. The horses could use a drink of water." Walter got off the horse and helped Victoria to the ground.

Victoria reached for the bundle tied to the back of Walter's horse. "As long as we've stopped for awhile, I would like to change clothes. This woolen robe is itchy."

Taking her clothes with her, Victoria left the road and entered the woods.

Gareth took the amulet from around his neck and handed it to his sister. "Go with her, Elwyna," said Gareth. "Watch what she does. The amulet will protect you."

Biting her tongue, Victoria just managed not to yell at Gareth. How dare he send a spy to watch over her! How could he think his sister needed protection from her? What did he imagine she was going to do to Elwyna? Turn her into a grasshopper? Tell her that knights in armor, shiny or rusty, were not the answer to a maiden's prayer? If Elwyna had fallen in love with Walter, she already knew that.

Muttering to herself, Victoria stripped off the friar's robe and put on her chemise. Shaking the wrinkles from her gray gown, she slipped it over her head and added the silver overtunic. "There," she sighed. That's better."

" 'Tis a pretty gown." Gareth's sister clutched the amulet and eyed Victoria guardedly. She looked nervous.

Gareth must have told Elwyna she was a sorceress, or worse, a nonvirtuous woman. In spite of her wariness, Elwyna glowed with the look of a woman in love. She was all dewy-eyed and dreamy. Feeling mean, Victoria was tempted to say "boo" just to watch her jump. She resisted the temptation. It would not be fair to take out her pique on Gareth's sister. With a halfhearted smile, Victoria said, "So Walter proposed to you, did he?"

"Aye. He loves me." Elwyna seemed certain to the point of smugness about that. "And I love him."

"Good. I'm very happy for you both." Victoria's chin began to tremble and her eyes filled with tears.

Elwyna rushed to her side. "Oh, Lady Victoria. You love Walter, too."

Blinking rapidly, Victoria fought for control. "Well, of course I l-love him. Walter is a very lovable person. Has he scowled at you yet? Isn't that the cutest thing? He tries so hard to look fierce, and he ends up looking like a cuddly teddy bear."

"What is a teddy bear?"

"A child's toy, a toy bear." Sniffling, she hastened to add, "I'm not crying because Walter loves you, Elwyna. I'm glad he loves you."

"You are not jealous?"

"No, I am not jealous." She might be a little envious because Elwyna and Walter were mutually besotted, but she did not want Walter. "Elwyna, you must understand. I love Walter as a friend, not the way you love him. Walter and I don't feel that way about each other—no sparks." Seeing Elwyna's confusion, she added, "We are not attracted to one another."

"Ah," said Elwyna as comprehension dawned. Elwyna grinned at Victoria. "Walter and I have sparks."

Victoria laughed. "I can see that you do."

"Tell me about Walter," said Elwyna.

"What do you want to know?"

"Everything. Nay, we do not have time for that. I know. I have learned of his virtues, but I have not seen his faults. Tell me about his faults."

"Hmmm. Well, he tends to be bossy. That is, he expects everyone to do what he says."

"All men are like that."

"But it is not our job to obey them without question. Sometimes Walter has very bad ideas. Someone has to tell him 'no' from time to time. Or else he might get worse—he might turn into a tyrant."

"Do you tell him 'no'?"

"Every chance I get. I will say that Walter is usually reasonable. If you point out the error of his ways, he takes it in good grace and rethinks his position."

"He is weak?"

"Not weak, no. It is not weakness to admit a mistake and to correct it. Walter *will* do that, even if it was a woman who pointed out he was about to go in the wrong direction. Of course, he is stubborn, too, so sometimes it takes several tries before he sees the light."

"I do not think a husband and wife should argue," said Elwyna, furrowing her brow.

"I do. As long as the arguments stay more or less civilized. I mean, I do not think a man and woman should say hurtful things to each other. But Elwyna, you cannot let Walter make all the decisions. You have an equal right to your opinion."

Elwyna appeared skeptical but interested. "I will

think on what you have told me. Women from See At El are very . . ."

"Opinionated?"

"Different. Stronger. More confident. I think I would like to be like that."

"You go, girl. You will do fine. Walter is lucky to have found you. I am very happy for Walter; I really am. I thought he would never fall in love. Walter has so much money, and he thinks everything and everyone can be bought. But he also thinks—thought—that he could never find a woman who would love him for himself and not for his wealth. I was afraid Walter would be alone all his life. He has no family, you know." Victoria reached in her purse for a tissue, pulled one out, and blew her nose.

"What is that?" asked Elwyna.

Victoria took another tissue from her purse and gave it to Elwyna. "It's a handkerchief made of paper. You use it once and throw it away."

"How clever. Did you make this with magic?" She handed the tissue back to Victoria.

"Keep it. I have more. I bought the package of tissues at the store—market. No magic. I know your brother thinks I am some kind of witch, but I'm not." She found her compact and opened it. Using the powder puff, Victoria patted powder under her eyes, trying to conceal the dark circles.

"What is that strange box?" Elwyna asked. "I have never seen the things you carry with you."

"This box is called a compact. It holds face powder." She took out her lipstick and, removing the top, screwed the lipstick out. "See this? It's lipstick. I use it like this." Victoria slid the lipstick over her lips, turning them a rich red color.

" 'Tis magic," said Elwyna, sounding awed.

" 'Tis makeup," said Victoria. "Lipstick and powder

are only a few of the things woman in my part of the world use to make themselves more beautiful. Would you like to try?"

"Nay."

"Well, I can understand why. You don't need anything to make yourself look better. You are a natural beauty." Victoria replaced her compact and lipstick in the purse and took out her comb.

"Thank you. I think you are pretty, too. Even before you used the powder and the sticklip."

"Lipstick. Thank you. I feel much better now that I've changed clothes and fixed my face. Shall we join the men?"

"Not yet, if you please. You were crying before. If you were not crying over Walter, why were you weeping?"

Victoria began fussing with her hair, not meeting Elwyna's eyes. "I've had a bad day; that's all. I've been walking for hours. I hadn't had anything to eat since yesterday, and . . . and your brother is a liar."

"I know he lied to you."

Victoria raised her eyebrows. "You do?"

"Aye. Gareth told you his name was Perceval, and he vowed to aid you in your search for the amulet. He did not tell you that he would not allow you to give the amulet to Ranulf to save Walter. Since he did not tell you the whole truth, he lied."

For some unknown reason, Victoria felt compelled to tell Elwyna Gareth's side of the story. "Well, yes. He did leave out a few pertinent facts. But he thought he had a good reason. He wanted to save you and Avondel. Gareth said Ranulf would not have killed Walter."

"He had the right of that. Ranulf is not as bad as everyone seems to think he is. Oh, I know it was wrong of him to make Walter his prisoner, but he has been very worried lately. He knew Gareth would return any day and try to kill him. That weighed on his mind." Elwyna tilted her head and gazed at Victoria, curiosity gleaming in her eyes. "Why do you defend my brother? He treated you badly."

"Not all the time," said Victoria, wincing as the comb found a particularly stubborn tangle. "Not when we made love."

"My brother made love to you?" Elwyna sounded horrified.

Dropping the comb into her purse, Victoria said, "Well, yes, he did. But I should not have told you—"

"How could he? Take advantage of a lady he swore to protect. Oh! My brother is a seducer of innocents. How awful! Wait until I tell him what I think of him." Elwyna turned on her heel and headed out of the woods.

Victoria rushed after her. "Elwyna, wait. Gareth did not seduce me. I seduced him."

Elwyna skidded to a halt. Her head whipped around, and she stared at Victoria, her eyes wide with shock. *"You* seduced *him?"*

"Yes. Actually, 'seduced' may be too mild a term. I—well, to tell you the truth, I more or less attacked him."

"You *attacked* him!" The look Elwyna gave Victoria combined wonder and disbelief. "But Gareth is so much larger than you. Did he fight back?"

"Nooo. He let me win that particular battle. Most men would. When it comes to sex, men are easy."

Elwyna sat on a stump. "I would hear more of this. Tell me exactly what you did."

"Elwyna. I'm not sure I should. I mean, you're probably a virgin."

She nodded. "Of course. I am unwed."

"Yes. Well. We don't have time for a course in sex education."

"Lady Victoria, I know what transpires between a man and a woman. At least I have been told what happens by my old nurse. And once, when I was fourteen, I came upon one of the villeins and his sweetheart in the woods. I watched—actually I heard more than I saw. There were bushes in the way, and I could not get too close without revealing my presence. But I have a pretty good idea what making love entails, but I will not know for sure until I . . . until Walter . . ." Elwyna trailed off, her cheeks reddening.

"Make love?"

"Aye. Victoria, Walter and I have spent two nights alone together. He refused to do anything more than kiss me. One kiss each night, before we slept. Walter said he will not make love to me until we are married. I do not want to wait." A twinkle appeared in her eyes, and she grinned at Victoria. "I never thought to attack him, however."

"Maybe you should wait. Something might happen to prevent your marriage." For one thing, Elwyna might not want to travel to a different time, a different place—even for love. "Travel is dangerous."

"Exactly. That is why I do not want to wait."

"But I thought . . . if you and Walter made love, and for some reason Walter could not marry you, then no other man would marry you because you would no longer be a virtuous woman."

"Who told you that? A man?"

"Actually, it was your brother."

Waving a hand airily, Elwyna said, "If I cannot marry Walter, I do not want to marry anyone else. I also do not intend to die a virgin. Can you think of any fate more horrible?"

"Now that you mention it, no."

Elwyna patted the stump next to her. "Please, Lady Victoria. Sit down and tell me in what manner you attacked my brother."

"Well, I do think Walter deserves to be attacked by someone who loves him. All right, I'll tell you." Victoria sat on the log next to Elwyna. "This is what I did. First, I kissed Percy—I mean Gareth. Do you know how to kiss with open mouth and use your tongue? How did Walter kiss you? Was his mouth open or closed?" Victoria was pretty sure she knew the answer; if Walter was trying to be noble he wouldn't risk anything more than a very chaste sort of kiss.

"Closed." said Elwyna, obviously fascinated. "Tongue? How do you kiss with your tongue?"

"The next time Walter presses his closed lips to yours, open your mouth slightly and slide your tongue along his bottom lip. He should open his mouth then, but if he resists, you can use your teeth—"

"Bite him?" Now Elwyna sounded shocked, but still fascinated.

"Not hard, just a little nip to coax his mouth open. When he does part his lips, slip your tongue inside his mouth and—"

"Elwyna! Victoria!" called Walter. They both jumped guiltily. "What are you doing? Gareth wants to get going."

"We're coming," shouted Victoria. To Elwyna she said, "I'll tell you the rest later."

When they arrived back at the road, Elwyna returned the amulet to Gareth, then insisted that Victoria take her palfrey while she rode with Walter. Walter had no objection, and Elwyna ignored the look Gareth directed at her. He thought Walter was a wizard, but she was sure he was only a man.

Once they were on their way again, Elwyna said, "I like Victoria. She is a very wise woman."

"Yes, she is. She's also a pain in the rear sometimes. That woman never does what you tell her to do. Your brother is going to have his hands full with her."

"Does she love him?"

"I think so. She won't admit it, though. They seem to be having a lovers' quarrel."

"Gareth thinks Victoria is an enchantress. And that you are a wizard."

"Does he? He's wrong."

"I know. I think Gareth is finding it hard to believe that a mere woman could . . . fill his hands. You will have your hands full with me, too, you know."

Walter chuckled, his breath tickling her ear. "You? You're nothing at all like Victoria. Don't get me wrong. I think the world of Victoria, but she definitely has shrewish tendencies. Not like you. You're sweet and—"

"Is that why you will not make love with me? Because I am *sweet?*"

"No, of course not. I was not complaining. I like sweet."

"Do you like to kiss with your tongue?"

"What did you say?" asked Walter. Elwyna was delighted to hear the surprise in his voice. She wanted to surprise him, maybe even shock him. It gave her a delicious sense of power.

"You heard. Do you?"

"W-what do you know about kissing with your— that way?" Walter sputtered.

"I know how to do it," Elwyna said smugly.

"Who taught you?"

"Victoria."

Walter choked. "Victoria *kissed* you?"

"Nay. Two women kissing? Why would we? I asked Victoria how she seduced my brother and she told me that the first thing she did was kiss him, with her mouth open and her tongue . . . But then you called, and she did not have time to explain what exactly she did with her tongue. What do you do?"

"Elwyna, how to kiss is not something I want to discuss with you at this time. Later, after we're married—"

"Is it hard to explain? Show me, then."

"Show you? You want me to kiss you now? Your brother would have me drawn and quartered."

Elwyna looked over her shoulder at Gareth, now riding side by side with Victoria while Thomas brought up the rear. Her brother appeared disgruntled and out of sorts. "I suppose you are right. Now is not a good time. Tonight will be better. When we stop to sleep. I will spread my blanket next to yours and you can—"

"No, I can't. I won't. If we kiss like that, I won't be able to—never mind what I won't be able to do."

"You are afraid kissing with your tongue will tempt you to make love with me? Victoria said that was the first step in seducing a man. She said men are easy. What did she mean?"

Walter groaned. "After we are married, Elwyna, and not before."

"I do not want to wait." She jerked her head around and glared at him.

"Tough. You will do as I say."

"Nay. Victoria does not do as my brother says. She said I have a right to my own opinion."

"You can have your opinion. You just can't have your way about this. We are going to wait for our wedding night, Elwyna, and that's final."

"But Victoria said—"

"I don't care what she said. Victoria is a modern—a woman of her time. And place. Things are different in Seattle."

"We will live in See At El, will we not?"

"Yes, but—"

"Then I must learn to behave as a See At El woman would. I would be like the women of your country, Walter. I do not want to embarrass you."

Walter's sigh tickled the nape of her neck. "You wouldn't. I like you the way you are."

"You are sweet, Walter. Loveable. But I want to be like other women you admire. You admire Victoria. You had no doubt she would be strong enough and clever enough to rescue you. And you were right to trust in her—she did find the amulet."

"Well, yes, I do admire her. And I have confidence in her. But I do not want to marry Victoria, or any woman like her. She is too prickly."

"Prickly? Because she does not always do as you say? Do you wish me to be obedient? Not to express my opinions? Never to make a decision for myself?"

"Damn it to hell. It did not take Victoria long to corrupt you, did it?"

Elwyna found her temper rising in reaction to Walter's surly mood. "Stop. I will ride with my brother. Or Thomas. No, I will ride with Victoria."

"Don't be ridiculous."

"Halt! Now!" Elwyna made as if to leap from the saddle, leaving Walter no choice but to rein the horse in.

"What now?" asked Gareth as his sister jumped to the ground and stomped away from Walter.

"I will not ride with that . . . that man," said Elwyna.

"Did he insult you?"

"Aye. He did. He thinks I am *sweet*. And *nice*. And he expects me to be obedient and . . . and . . ." Elwyna was unable to say more because a huge lump had formed in her throat.

"Walter? Is that true? You think my sister is sweet?" Gareth asked. He sounded sympathetic.

"I am no longer sure about that," said Walter. "Your sister is displaying some very unattractive traits."

"What? Elwyna isn't sweet because she wants to think for herself?" asked Victoria. "Too much sweetness can be cloying, Walter. Don't you want a little spice in your life?"

"Stay out of this, Victoria," said Walter, his brows drawn together in a scowl.

Elwyna had not seen Walter's scowl before. She did not think he looked like a toy bear. "Do not speak to her that way," she demanded.

"Enough," said Gareth in a tone that demanded obedience. "We do not have time for this. Elwyna, ride with Thomas. We must ride on as long as the sun is in the sky. With luck, we will reach Avondel tomorrow night."

"I am no longer able to think about it..." Vic-

Sixteen

That night, Gareth lay on the cold, hard ground, unable to think of anything or anyone but Victoria. Images of her naked beneath him, her long legs wrapped around his hips, arching to meet his every thrust gave way to the picture of her astraddle him, riding him hard, her lush breasts bouncing saucily until he took them in his hands. . . . Squeezing his eyes tight shut, Gareth tried to make his mind a blank.

He could not. Victoria was there, seared into his brain. Unavoidable. Inescapable.

No mortal woman could have done this to him. Victoria had to be an enchantress, a sorceress. She had used magic to enthrall him, to make him lust for her and no other. He would not have it. With the help of his ancestors' amulet, he would force her to break her spell. Then he would be free of her, once and for all.

From the way she had behaved toward Walter when they stopped for the night, Elwyna seemed to have extricated herself from his spell. His sister had said fewer words to Walter than Victoria had said to him. Walter's bewildered reaction to Elwyna's cool behavior had seemed human, not wizardly. Gareth had felt a tug of masculine sympathy, until he remembered that Walter could be dallying with Elwyna the way a cat played with a mouse.

Victoria and Walter *were* magicians, and Gareth had to find a way to control their sorcerous ways. Taking hold of the amulet, Gareth willed himself to sleep. Mayhap the solution would come to him during the night.

As soon as the sky held the first hint of gray, Gareth arose. He was smiling, because his dreams had showed him the way to end Victoria's spell, and Walter's, too. He woke the others, and after a quick meal of bread and cheese, they prepared to continue their journey.

"Who will ride double today?" Thomas asked as he saddled his mount.

"Victoria will ride with me," said Gareth firmly. "I have matters to discuss with her."

"Fine," said Victoria, surprising him by not objecting. "I have a few things to say to you, too."

The others mounted their horses, and Thomas and Elwyna started down the road. Walter hung back. "Victoria? Are you sure you don't mind riding with Lord Gareth?"

"I'm sure," she replied.

Gareth waited while Walter rode off. As soon as he was out of sight, Gareth lifted Victoria onto his horse and mounted behind her. His horse stirred beneath him, but Gareth kept the stallion reined in.

"Why are we standing still? I don't mind riding with you, but I do not want to be alone with you." Victoria tried to kick the horse in the side, but Gareth shifted his leg and blocked her.

"We will talk here, out of hearing of the others. Stop squirming, Victoria. Listen to what I have to say. You are my hostage—"

Victoria's brows flew up. Shock and outrage showed in her expressive eyes. "Hostage? Hostage! Have you gone crazy? What are you talking about? I most certainly am not your hostage." Crossing her arms over her chest, she tilted her nose in the air. "I refuse to be your hostage."

Gareth ground his teeth together. "You cannot refuse to be a hostage. I have taken you and Walter prisoner, and I intend to hold you——"

"Forget that. I don't want you holding me. Not now. Not ever."

He tightened his grasp to keep her from leaping from the saddle. "Not in my arms, Victoria. I was not referring to holding you in my arms, but in my dungeon at Castle Avondel."

She sucked in a breath. "You're going to put Walter and me in a dungeon? What about your promise to protect me? Making a person a prisoner is not protection, Percy—Gareth. Oh. I guess you were lying about that, too. I've changed my mind. I do not have one thing to say to you. Let me down, Gareth. I'll walk."

Gareth's left eyelid began twitching. "You used your magical powers to charm me into making that promise. It does not count."

"I don't have any magical powers, you dolt. If I did, believe me, I would turn you into a——"

"Toad?"

"Slug. A toad is way too high on the evolutionary scale for you."

Struggling for control, Gareth listed the evidence against her. "You *are* a sorceress. You come from a place no one has ever heard of. You carry strange items in your pouch. Your accent is not English, and you use unfamiliar words. Your magic may not allow you to change men into toads, but you have the power to arouse a man's desire and make him want no other woman but you. That is the magic you used to charm me."

"Yeah, and you loved every minute of it, Percy. Oh, excuse me. I keep forgetting that you lied about that, too. Your name is Gareth, not Perceval." She jerked her head around and stared at him. "Wait a darn minute. Did you say you looked in my pouch—purse? How dare you invade my privacy! Don't you know that a purse is a woman's most personal possession? What kind of a knight are you, anyway? Not the kind that rescues damsels in distress, obviously. You're the sort that distresses damsels."

Through clenched teeth, Gareth said, "You inflamed my passion and clouded my mind. I demand that you release me from your spell. And Walter must remove his enchantment from Elwyna, as well. That is the ransom I require to release you and Walter."

Victoria's jaw dropped open, then snapped shut. Gareth could feel her quivering with rage. His hand went to the amulet, and he held his breath, waiting for her to ensorcell him in some new and terrible way.

After a long pause, she slumped against him. Gareth could almost feel the anger draining out of her. "Fine," she said. "Consider yourself unenchanted, de-charmed, whatever. Now can we be on our way? The others will be worried about us."

Gareth let out the breath he had been holding. He waited. He took a deep breath and waited longer. He waited until he was sure before he accused her. "You did not release me from your spell. I still want you."

Wiggling her bottom against his crotch, Victoria said, "I noticed. That's your problem. I no longer want you. You have no reason to hold me hostage. Me or Walter. I am not a witch. He is not a wizard, a warlock, or a sorcerer."

"I know that Elwyna has escaped from his spell, at least temporarily. She is angry with him, and he has not punished her for her anger. But he *is* a wizard. He charmed Elwyna into helping him escape."

"Walter is charming. At least, he can be when sets his mind to it. But H. Walter would never punish anyone for being mad at him. I've made him angry lots of times, and he did not hurt me. Not ever. Walter talks mean sometimes, but it's all bluff. He's a pussycat."

"And Elwyna is his mouse. He toys with her affections, as you do with mine."

"He does not! Walter wouldn't toy with a woman's affections. He is not that kind of man. If Walter says he loves Elwyna, then he loves her. If he proposed, then you can count on it: he will marry her. Walter keeps his word. . . ." She slanted a superior look at him. ". . . unlike some people I could name."

Gareth knew his name was the one she had in mind. She had not forgiven him for lying—misleading her. He should not care if she thought him less than honorable. A sorceress was without honor. But, said a voice in the back of his mind, if Victoria was without honor, why had she done so much to rescue Walter? She had demonstrated bravery, determination, and loyalty in her quest for the ransom Ranulf had demanded.

Victoria had said Walter was her boss. She assisted him. The sorceress owed the wizard fealty. That led to only one conclusion: Walter *was* Victoria's liege lord. And Gareth was heartily tired of hearing Victoria sing Walter's praises. "I will hear no more about your lord. He is a magician. Walter has enchanted Elwyna."

"Lord? Are we back to that again? Listen, Gareth. Try to understand. Walter is not my lord. Elwyna is not enchanted, she is in love. There is a difference. The only magic Walter has, besides his charming personality, is money. But he didn't use money magic on Elwyna. He couldn't have, even if he had wanted to. Walter is broke."

"Broken." Gareth asked, confused. "Walter seemed whole to me."

"Broke, tapped out, without funds. He does not have a ducat, a florin, or a groat to his name. Elwyna fell in love with the man, not his bank account. That would be very important to Walter."

"Elwyna does not behave as if she loves him. Elwyna will not speak to him."

Victoria raised her shoulders, then lowered them. "A lovers' quarrel. She will get over it. And for your information, Elwyna is angry with Walter because he will not make love to her before they are married. She plans to use the same feminine magic on Walter that I used on you. She is going to seduce him."

"What!" Gareth was outraged. "Walter *has* enchanted her. My sister is a virtuous woman. She would not—"

"Oh, keep your chain mail on, Percy. Elwyna told me she does not want to wait until they are husband and wife to make love, and she does not want to die a virgin. You have got to stop equating virtue with virginity. You did not lose your honor the first time you had sex, did you? Of course not. You're a man, and men hold themselves to a different standard. A *lower* standard, I might point out, for all your masculine posturing about honor. Your honor is not besmirched because you have had more than one woman in your bed, is it? Why is that?"

Gareth could not answer her. Victoria had clouded his mind again, challenging another of his long-held beliefs. He concentrated on what she had said about Elwyna. After only two days together, Victoria had managed to corrupt his innocent sister. How could Victoria deny that she was a witch? He spurred his horse. He had to catch up with Elwyna before she did something rash. "I must stop her," he said. "Before she loses her honor."

Victoria clutched his arms. "Hey, what's the big hurry? They have a chaperon, remember? Thomas is with them. And Walter will not do anything to dishonor Elwyna. He loves her. He is going to marry her." In a snide tone of voice, she added, "Even if she is not a virgin when they wed."

"Elwyna will not seduce him. They will not marry," snarled Gareth. "I will not allow it."

"You should. Walter will make you a very good brother-in-law. Even though he's short of funds now, that is only temporary. Walter is filthy rich. Have you ever thought that you might need more than Aethelwyn's bauble to get Avondel up and running again?"

It took him a moment to clear his mind of the picture of his sister, his virtuous sister, seducing Walter. "More?"

Victoria sighed. "You aren't a detail man, are you? Neither is Walter. That's what he needs me for—to take care of all the little things that make his grandiose plans work."

"What details?"

"For starters, you're going to need stonemasons and carpenters to repair the castle and the villeins' cottages. Have you been there lately? It's a mess. Then you will have to buy seed and breeding animals, not to mention some new furniture for the castle. Once that's done, who is going to farm the land and tend the flocks? You will have to lure villeins away from other lords, won't you? And you will need knights, a blacksmith, a miller, a brewer, and on and on. All that costs money. How much have you got?"

"Enough," said Gareth, although he did not. He had the king's favor, and the amulet, and not much more.

"I doubt it. When it comes to remodeling, especially

remodeling castles, count on it taking three times as long and costing twice as much as you planned on. Trust me, Percy. This is one area where I have considerable experience. You will need every penny you have and every penny you can squeeze out of H. Walter. Not that he will mind giving it to you. Walter is very generous. And you will be family, after all."

Dazed, Gareth did not respond.

Nothing, *nothing* was going as he had envisioned. His plan for revenge had come to naught, his sister was in love with a wizard, he was under the spell of a sorceress, and now his ability to repair Avondel was in doubt. In all those years of plotting and planning, he had not thought beyond restoring the amulet to its rightful place in the solar at Avondel.

What had he imagined? That magic would replace the broken walls of the castle, that the amulet would somehow till the fields, fill the cottages with farmers and the garrison with knights?

Gareth had to admit to himself that he had thought that Aethelwyn's amulet would solve all his problems.

Mayhap he had been wrong about that.

Gareth had gotten awfully quiet. Victoria kept her mouth shut, too, satisfied that she had given him something to worry about besides whether or not she was going to turn him into a reptile or an amphibian. How dare he blame magic for what had happened between them! Gareth *would* think that; it would excuse his attraction to a less-than-virtuous woman.

And Gareth was still attracted to her. She could feel the evidence poking her left hip. Too bad for him. Victoria Desmond was out of the seduction business—except as an advisor. She chuckled, thinking about what Walter had in store. Elwyna seemed like a very determined young woman.

"You find me amusing?" asked Gareth, misinterpreting her giggles.

Victoria did not correct his mistake. "Extremely amusing. You think all you feel for me is lust, and not even ordinary, everyday lust. Magic, fairy-dust lust is what you think you're suffering from. All because the noble and *virtuous* Lord Gareth of Avondel would never want a woman like me, not unless I worked a spell on him. I think that is v-very f-funny." Victoria bit her lip. She was getting teary-eyed again, and damned if she would let Gareth see her cry.

"If not magic, what?" he asked, sounding disgruntled.

Love. She wanted to shout it at him, but she pressed her lips together and refused to utter one more word.

"Victoria?"

"I am not speaking to you." She forced the words through clenched teeth.

"Good. I do not want to hear you babble."

"Babble? *Babble!* I do *not* babble. I speak. Clearly and concisely. But I do not have one more thing to say to—"

A scream, faint and far away, reached their ears.

"That was Elwyna! Get down, Victoria."

Victoria found her feet on the ground before she knew what was happening. Gareth spurred his horse, racing forward after the others. "Wait there for me," he called out as he disappeared around a bend in the road.

Her heart pounding, Victoria stared after him. Wait? For what? To be attacked by wild animals? Or rogue knights? No way, José. She ran after him.

After she had run for what seemed like miles, Victoria came upon a place where the road, never exactly smooth, was churned into a stew of dust mixed with clods of dirt. The ground was covered with hoofprints, many more than would have been made by three horses.

Victoria opened her mouth to call out, then thought better of it. Their small party had been attacked; that much was obvious. But where were they? And where was Gareth? She kept running after them until a stitch in her side forced her to slacken her pace. Breathing heavily, she slowed to a walk, staying close to the side of the road so that she could take cover in the trees if necessary.

It seemed very quiet to her. Unnaturally so. No more screams, no shouts, no sounds of steel meeting steel . . .

Oh, God. What if they were all dead?

Victoria began running again.

She heard something over the pounding of her feet hitting the dirt road. Victoria stopped and listened. Clanging. Steel *was* meeting steel. There was a battle going on up ahead. Rounding a curve in the road, she saw Gareth on foot, fighting with a knight in black armor who was on horseback. Gareth's horse was nowhere in sight. The mounted knight had an advantage, and he was using it, hacking away with his sword, forcing Gareth to defend himself, but not giving him the opportunity to attack.

Victoria gave a yell and rushed forward. She must have distracted the knight, because his attention strayed from Gareth long enough for him to grab the man's sword arm and pull the knight out of his saddle. The black knight toppled off his horse, landing on his back. Gareth's sword was at his throat before he could recover.

In a short time, Gareth had bound the rogue knight with torn strips of the knight's surcoat. Only then did he turn to Victoria. "I told you to wait in the forest."

"I thought you might need help. And you did."

"Nay. I did not."

"You were on foot," she said, keeping her tone reasonable. She pointed to the other knight. "He was on a horse. He was winning."

"I would have taken him without your help."

"Sure, you would. What happened to your horse? Where are the others?"

"I was on foot, leading the horse to follow the tracks. When this knight arrived, my horse fled into the forest. There." Gareth pointed to the trees at the side of the road.

Gareth touched the knight's chest with the tip of his sword. "Where are our companions?"

The knight glared at him, but did not answer.

Pressing the edge of his sword against the man's throat, Gareth asked again, "Where are they?" A thin line of red appeared where the blade met skin.

"Gone," gasped the man, trying to move his head away from the sword's edge. "Lord Ranulf bade us find his ward and his hostage. We did find them, and the squire who traveled with them. Sir Ulrich sent me to look for you."

"Where have they gone?"

"Darkvale," said the knight, averting his gaze from Gareth.

"Nay. This road leads to Avondel, not Darkvale. Is Castle Avondel where Ranulf waits for me?" He put the tip of his sword between the knight's legs.

Now the man began to sweat heavily. "Aye, he is bound for Castle Avondel. Lord Ranulf bids you meet him there. 'Tis his wish to settle what is between you once and for all."

Gareth sheathed his sword. "Victoria, take this knight's horse and return to the friary. I will go to Avondel."

"No. I'm going with you. You cannot face Ranulf and all his knights by yourself."

"Elwyna will tell him that I have foresworn vengeance. Even if he does not believe her, he will not harm her or Walter or Thomas. He is using them to draw me out."

"If they are not in danger, then I won't be, either. Why do you want me to go to Donscroft?" When Gareth hesitated to answer, shifting his eyes away from her face, understanding dawned. "Oh, I get it. The big, bad knight is afraid to be alone with the wicked witch—me. I might inflame your passion again. You probably think you will need all your vital juices for your battle with Ranulf."

Gareth's left eyelid began to twitch. "You are wrong, Victoria. I do not fear you."

"Then there is no reason for me not to go with you. As it happens, I must go to Avondel. Walter and I have a very important engagement to keep at the castle in a day or two." Victoria felt her chin begin to quiver. How many days were left? She had lost count. Not enough to change Gareth's mind about her; of that she was sure. "I—I don't have time to go anywhere else but there."

"Do you never do as you are told?" Gareth asked, exasperated. "Do not bother to answer. I know you do not. If I do not take you with me, you will try to follow me, I suppose."

"You suppose right," said Victoria calmly. She would be cool, calm, and collected if it killed her. So she would be leaving the past in a few days, so what? She wanted to go home. She certainly could not want to remain in this benighted age, with a man who thought she was a sorceress.

"Aye, I thought so. I will take you with me. At least that way I can try to keep you from making mischief."

Gareth caught the knight's horse by its reins. "Come here."

"Please? You could try making requests instead of snapping orders, you know."

"Come here, Victoria. Please. We must be on our way."

"Oh, all right, bossy. Sometimes you remind me a lot of Walter. You both have tyrannical tendencies."

Gareth lifted her onto the saddle. Instead of remaining sideways on the horse, Victoria swung a leg over so that she straddled the horse. "I don't like riding sidesaddle," she said, hitching up her skirt. "And this horse doesn't look like a lady's mount to me. What are we going to do with him?" Victoria pointed to the trussed up knight, who was gaping at her bare leg.

"I will loosen his bonds. When he frees himself, he can walk to Darkvale or to Avondel." After Gareth had done that, he strode into the trees and returned a moment later with his horse.

They started off at a trot.

"Why aren't we going faster? Don't you want to catch up with them?"

"Nay. And we will not remain on this road much longer. When the black knight does not return, Ranulf may send others to look for us. There is another way to Avondel, a trail used by hunters. That is the way we will go."

Victoria said, "I suppose you have a plan."

"Aye."

"Are you going to tell me what it is?"

"Nay." He groaned the word.

Victoria looked at him sharply. A trickle of red was dripping from his sword hand. "Gareth, stop! You're hurt."

" 'Tis nothing. A scratch."

Victoria reined in her horse. "Stop this minute, do

you hear me? Scratches can get infected. We need to clean your wound."

Gareth stopped. At her urging, he dismounted. "Take off your armor. I want to see that cut."

He eased off his surcoat and his coat of mail, favoring his right arm. Victoria gasped when she saw his white linen shirt stained with blood. "You call that a scratch? I call it a gash." She looked around. "We need something to clean it with. Is there water nearby?"

"Nay. There is a wineskin hanging from your saddle. Use that."

"Good idea. Alcohol is an antiseptic. Sit down before you fall down, Gareth. You look pale. There is no telling how much blood you've lost." She bent over, raised her skirt and ripped a strip of linen off her chemise. Victoria folded the strip into a square pad and handed it to Gareth. "Put this on the wound and press down hard. That will stop the bleeding."

Gareth sat on the ground and leaned his back against a tree. "This is not necessary," he said, using his left hand to hold the pad firmly against the cut on his right forearm. "It could have waited until we stopped for the night."

Victoria returned to his side, the wineskin in her hand. She handed it to Gareth and took the pad from him. "Let me do that, now." She sat down next to him, facing the tree he was leaning against. Gareth closed his eyes.

Holding the pad against the wound brought her close to Gareth. Her thigh touched his hip. His forearm rested on her knee. She could feel his pulse beating beneath her fingers, could see the stubble on his chin. He smelled again, of sweat and horse. And *him*. She probably smelled, too. No one had bathed since they left Donscroft.

"We stink," she said. She did not tell him that she no longer found his smell offensive.

His eyes opened a slit. "Aye. We could both use a bath." His voice was husky. From pain, probably, but his hoarse voice reminded her of the way he sounded when they made love.

She removed the blood-soaked pad from his arm. "I think it has stopped bleeding." Victoria tore another strip from her chemise and poured wine on the cloth. Gently, she washed the blood from his arm. "Does it sting?" she asked when she noticed he was wincing.

"A trifle. 'Tis nothing."

"Hmmm," she said, not wanting to argue with him. Why did men find it so difficult to admit it when they hurt? She wanted to kiss him and make it better, but he would only think it was some kind of spell. Instead, she opened her purse and rummaged around. "I think I have a tube of antiseptic cream in here somewhere. Did you see it?"

"I saw many strange things. What is antiseptic cream?"

"Stuff to kill bacteria. Before you ask, bacteria are what cause infections. Aha! Here it is, and I have Band-Aids, too, all sizes. I always take basic first aid supplies on a trip. Walter says I overdo it, but you never know when these things will come in handy." She opened the tube and squeezed the cream onto the wound. "I don't think you need stitches. Now that the blood is cleared away, it doesn't look so bad."

"I told you. A scratch. Nothing more."

"Yes. Well. Let me put a couple of Band-Aids on it, and we're done."

After she had finished with the bandages, she stood up. She held out her hand. "Let me help you up."

Wonder of wonders, he did. Gareth took her hand

and heaved himself upright. "Thank you," he mumbled, not looking at her.

"You're very welcome," she responded, grinning. It just killed Gareth to accept help from a woman. Victoria's grin faded. He didn't think she was a woman. He thought she was some kind of paranormal being. "I guess you said thanks only because you don't want me to put a spell on you."

"Nay. I thanked you because I am grateful." He frowned. "No one has tended my wounds so gently in a very long time. Not since I left Avondel."

"Your mother must have—"

"We will not speak of her," said Gareth. All the warmth had drained from his voice.

A few miles farther on, Gareth led her off the road onto a narrow trail among the trees. The trail was overgrown and hard to follow. When the low-hanging branches threatened to unseat them, Gareth ordered her to dismount. They led the horses through the forest for what seemed to Victoria like hours.

"Are we there yet?" she asked, her feet dragging. She felt as though she had walked, run, and ridden hundreds of miles since she had left Seattle. She ought to be used to it by now. But she was tired. Tired and dirty and depressed. Every step she took brought her closer to the end of her time with her knight in rusty armor.

"We will stop for the night soon. There is a small stream up ahead. Water for the horses and us, and we can bathe."

The prospect of being clean invigorated her, and Victoria picked up her pace.

"How far are we from Avondel?"

"Not far. We will reach the castle early tomorrow. This stream feeds into the castle's river."

"What are you going to do when you get there?"

"Meet Ranulf and, as the black knight said, settle what is between us once and for all."

"He killed your parents." Victoria did not look forward to seeing another battle. Men ought to find better ways of settling their disputes. But she could not fault Gareth. That was one area where things had gotten worse, not better, as time progressed. In her day, children with guns killed other children, and they did not have motives nearly as understandable as revenge. "I suppose you will try to kill him."

"That was my plan. But I have been persuaded to forgive Ranulf."

"You have?"

"Aye. I learned from Elwyna that Ranulf did not kill my mother. He slew my father, but that was not murder. They met on the field of battle, and Ranulf defeated William."

"What happened to your mother?"

A muscle worked in Gareth's jaw. "Elwyna told me that she saw our father kill our mother because Juliana was unfaithful."

Victoria stopped in her tracks. "Oh, my God. Poor Elwyna. What an awful thing for her to witness."

"Aye. And she saw other terrible things. William beat Juliana, just as you suspected."

"Oh, Gareth. I am so sorry. I wish I had not been right about that. How sad for your mother, and for your father. He must have been in terrible pain to act so cruelly toward someone he must have loved."

"Ranulf loved my mother, too. He went to Avondel to save her, but he was too late."

"Ranulf was her lover? Oh, my. What a terrible tragedy! At least Elwyna survived, and she does not seem to bear any lasting scars from her ordeal. She is a lovely young woman, open to love."

A sad sort of smile appeared on Gareth's face.

"Elwyna told me very fiercely that a husband should never be cruel to his wife."

"Walter will not hurt her. He would die before striking a woman, any woman."

"I will never hurt my wife," said Gareth, his expression grim. "A knight must protect those weaker than he."

"I guess sorceresses don't qualify for protection since, theoretically at least, they are not weak." Victoria said sulkily. Oh, lord, now she was *sulking*. Was she going to spend her last night alone with Gareth pouting and feeling sorry for herself? She thought about that for a minute or two.

Yeah. She was.

She certainly was not going to attack him again. She had been the activist in their relationship long enough. If Gareth still wanted her, he would have to come and get her. And he would have to crawl.

"Where is this bath you promised?"

"Close. Listen, you can hear the gurgle of water running over the rocks."

Sure enough, they broke through a final stand of trees and the stream appeared. "It isn't very deep."

Pointing to his left, Gareth said, "If memory serves, there is a pool a short distance that way. You go first. I will tend to the horses."

Victoria returned from her bath, her clothes clinging provocatively to her damp body. Wet T-shirts might be a few centuries in the future, but a girl could improvise. She had promised herself she would not be the aggressor one more time, and her pride would not let her break that vow. But that did not mean she had to be completely passive.

"I'm done," she said, using what was left of her chemise to dry her hair. "It feels wonderful to be clean again. I'm only sorry I did not have fresh clothes to put on. Not even an extra chemise." She held up the tattered garment, then tossed it aside. "That is all that was left of it." In case he didn't get it, she added, "I am not wearing any underwear."

Gareth stared at her, his gaze moving slowly from her eyes down her body to her toes. Chilled from her cold bath, Victoria found herself warming up fast beneath his scrutiny. His green eyes darkened to black, the way they always did when he was aroused. Victoria held her breath. Any minute now, he would jump her.

Gareth picked up her discarded chemise and strode past her. "I will use this to dry myself."

The breath she had been holding whooshed out. Well. That hadn't worked out the way she had hoped. She was almost certain he had been turned on, but he had controlled himself. A man in love would not be able to do that, would he? Walk away from his lover without a backward glance?

Victoria felt a lump forming in her throat. She swallowed. "I will not be a victim. I will *not* be a victim. So he rejected me, so what? If all Gareth feels for me is lust, then I don't want him."

Seventeen

At the pool, Gareth stripped and entered the water in a shallow dive. The shock of the cold water had him gasping when he surfaced. He took a handful of mud from the bottom of the pool and scrubbed himself clean. Victoria had almost inflamed his passion once again. The amulet hung around his neck, and Gareth took the green stone in his hand. It felt warm to the touch, almost alive. Aethelwyn's magic must be at work, giving him the strength to resist the enchantress.

Or the strength to take her on his terms, not hers.

Tomorrow they would be at Avondel. Even though his homecoming would not be exactly as he had planned, he would be *home*. He ought to feel something. Satisfaction from reaching his goal. Relief because he would not have to shed Lord Ranulf's blood. Joy at being reunited with his sister.

Gareth felt none of those things.

Tomorrow, or soon after, Victoria would leave Avondel and him behind. The spell she had used to charm him would surely fade then. He should feel good about that, if nothing else.

Gareth felt empty and alone.

He donned his clothes and returned to where he had left Victoria. She had gotten the blanket and the monk's robe he had tied to his saddle that morning and spread them on the ground under an elm tree. Victoria was seated on the robe, her back against the trunk of the tree, her arms around her bent knees. She had a pensive look about her.

Raising her gaze to his, she asked, "Do you think Elwyna and Walter are all right? And Thomas?"

"Aye, I do. Lord Ranulf treats Elwyna as a daughter, and I believe she thinks of him as a father. Once Elwyna convinces him I have given up my quest for revenge, Ranulf will have no reason to harm any of them."

Victoria smiled, looking relieved. "Good. These past few weeks have been quite an adventure. I'm glad no one got hurt." She eyed his forearm. "Except you. I had better change the Band-Aid and put more antibiotic cream on your cut."

Gareth let her tend to his scratch. Her touch was gentle, almost a caress. He could feel his blood heating. His heart began beating in a different rhythm. He stopped breathing. Any heartbeat now, she would kiss him, overcome the magic of the amulet, and inflame his passion. He would have one last night with his enchantress. Gareth leaned his head a hair's breadth closer to hers and waited.

Victoria concentrated on applying the salve. "I had a thought about this sorcery business. Did it ever occur to you that Aethelwyn must have been a sorceress? She is the one who created the amulet. How do you suppose she did that, if not with magic powers?"

Gareth let out the breath he had been holding. "I have always known Aethelwyn was an enchantress." The knowledge had always made him uncomfortable, never more than now, when he had fallen under the spell of another sorceress. The first Gareth's gentle wooing of Aethelwyn had smacked of surrender.

Thomas had said it: the Norman knight had been bested by a maid.

With her head bent over his arm, Victoria applied the bandage to his arm. "The first Gareth did not fight against the magic, did he?"

Gareth groaned. He had been wrong. The amulet was not proof against Victoria's power over him. His whole being pleaded for her kiss, the kiss that would weaken his resolve and let loose the passion that flowed between them. "Nay," he said, forcing the words through clenched teeth.

Victoria raised her head. She was very close to him. He could see the gold flecks sparking in her light-brown eyes. "Then why do you?"

"Aethelwyn was an enchantress, but she was also virtuous." Gareth knew he was being cruel. Words would not hurt an enchantress, but they might save him from being conquered by her once again. That other Gareth had loved his enchantress. He only wanted Victoria. He did not love her. He could not love a woman like her.

Victoria's eyes filled with tears. She turned away from him. "I'm finished," she said.

Gareth was not sure if she referred to being finished with the bandage, or with him. He was certain his words had ended any chance that she might kiss him. He had won the battle.

Why did he feel defeated?

She had been close enough to kiss him. Victoria knew she would have kissed Gareth if he hadn't made that nasty crack about virtue. Well, what had she expected? That Gareth would suddenly change his attitude and admit that she was the only woman for him? That had never been a possibility. He was fixated on virtue, and virtue to him meant virginity.

His loss.

Victoria would have given up the future for her knight in rusty armor. Now she would kiss a pig before she would waste one more minute of her time on the stubborn knight. Blinking stupid, totally uncalled-for tears from her eyes, Victoria got up and moved the monk's robe several feet away from the blanket where Gareth sat. Lying down, she closed her eyes and willed herself to sleep.

And not to dream.

The next morning, Victoria and Gareth rose with the sun and began the last leg of their journey. It was not long before Castle Avondel rose out of the mist. "Is it always misty?" she asked, breaking the silence for the first time that day.

"Nay. In the past, the mist went away when the sun appeared. This perpetual fog must be part of the curse."

"Along with the barren fields and the overgrown forest?"

"Aye."

"You will end the curse today," said Victoria. "That must make you proud. And happy."

"Aye."

Gareth didn't sound happy. As they drew closer, Victoria could make out several tents standing in the field opposite the drawbridge. "Ranulf and his knights?"

"Aye."

Gareth, never garrulous, was being downright taciturn this morning. Victoria felt the minutes slipping away—time they should be using to communicate, to share their thoughts. If he would show the slightest spark of warmth, she would tell him she loved him. Not to change his mind about her, but only to let him know she cared for him. Knowing he had been loved by her might bring him comfort someday when he needed it.

If she could not tell him that she loved him when

he was in such a surly mood, she at least ought to try to explain about time travel. When Tobias appeared to whisk her and Walter back to the future, Gareth would be in for a big shock unless she prepared him for it.

Victoria had tried several times to start a meaningful conversation, only to be met with the medieval equivalent of "yep" and "nope." She would try one more time. "Is that all your have to say? Aye, this. Nay, that. What are you thinking? What are you feeling? This is a momentous occasion. Your homecoming, the return of the amulet. Aren't you excited?"

"Aye," said Gareth, reining in his steed.

Three knights in armor suddenly appeared in front of them. Victoria quickly halted before she collided with them. She had been looking at Gareth and not paying attention to what was ahead.

"Lord Gareth?" asked one of the knights.

Victoria recognized him. He was the one who had dragged her from the inn.

"Aye," said Gareth. "I am lord of Avondel."

"Lord Ranulf awaits you. Will you come with us?"

Gareth nodded. In a matter of minutes, they were in front of the tents. Lord Ranulf stood in front of the largest tent. Standing behind him were Elwyna, Walter and Thomas.

Gareth dismounted. "Lord Ranulf," he said by way of greeting. He bowed.

"Lord Gareth." Ranulf bowed in return. "Elwyna has told me a tale I cannot credit. She said you will not want to joust with me on the field where I defeated your father."

"My sister spoke the truth. Elwyna told me what happened here. You loved my mother and tried to save her. I am certain her loss was more punishment than you deserved. I have no need for revenge."

Ranulf sank to his knees in front of Gareth. "I had

thought today would be my last. If not my life, I owe you my allegiance. Hence forth, you are my lord."

"Rise, Lord Ranulf. You honor me, but I cannot accept your pledge. You must continue to serve our king. Edward would not forgive me if I stole away one of his lords." He looked over Ranulf's shoulder. "Elwyna?"

Elwyna flung herself into Gareth's arms. Thomas went to Gareth's side, grinning from ear to ear. Victoria found herself enveloped in a bear hug, courtesy of Walter. Walter released her and slapped Gareth on the back. "Isn't this great? We're all together again."

Elwyna went from Gareth's embrace to Walter's arms. With his arm around her waist, Elwyna said, "Walter has been giving Lord Ranulf advice about increasing the yield of the fields at Darkvale. You should listen to Walter's counsel, too, Gareth."

"Later," said Gareth. "We have more pressing matters to take care of first. I want to return the amulet to its rightful place."

"I have its box," said Elwyna. "I have kept it safe all these years. Lord Ranulf brought it with him from Darkvale. Let me get it."

Elwyna disappeared into the tent and reappeared moments later with a small silver box, inlaid with mother of pearl.

Drawing in a deep breath, Gareth said, "Let us proceed, then."

Gareth and Elwyna led the way into the castle, up a flight of stone stairs to the chamber reserved for the lord and lady of Avondel. The door creaked open, and the party entered.

"The box was kept there, remember?" Elwyna pointed to an arched niche recessed into the wall.

"Aye. I remember well," said Gareth. He took the amulet from around his neck and placed it inside the silver box Elwyna held open. He closed the box, and together they took it to the niche and placed it there. " 'Tis done."

Nothing happened.

Victoria, conditioned by years of motion-picture special effects, had expected *something* to happen—a flash of light, a crash of thunder, perhaps a snatch of majestic music. Magic ought to make itself known in some dramatic way.

"The curse is ended," said Elwyna, but she sounded doubtful. She must have been expecting a sign of some sort, too.

Looking grim, Gareth said, "I did not expect the amulet to work its magic immediately. The curse took hold of Avondel gradually. It makes sense that it would not end in the blink of an eye."

"I'm not sure there is anything sensible about magic," said Walter, looking around the room. "There ought to be some way to tell if the curse is gone."

"The mist should fade," suggested Thomas. He went to the window and looked out. " 'Tis foggy still." His shoulders drooped in disappointment.

Victoria felt her heart constrict. Gareth had waited years for this moment, and nothing had happened. Her knight looked discouraged, defeated. She wanted to rush to his side, to take him in her arms and comfort him. She took one step in his direction. He pinned her with a gaze full of . . . some emotion she could not identify. Dismay? Regret?

Victoria stayed put. She looked at the others. No one looked happy. Walter was scowling. Ranulf frowned. Elwyna had tears in her eyes.

Elwyna broke the gloomy silence. "Mayhap we must help dispel the curse. We can begin by cleaning the castle from the parapets to the cellars."

"Magic helps those who help themselves?" Victoria murmured.

At the same time Walter said, "That's a good idea. Where shall we begin?"

"I will explore the castle and make notes of what needs to be done. Then we can send to Darkvale for helpers and supplies." Elwyna bustled from the solar, calling over her shoulder, "Squire Thomas, come with me, please."

"I would speak with you, my lord," Ranulf said to Gareth. "There are several families in Darkvale who have sons in need of land to farm. You will need villeins. Perhaps we can come to some sort of agreement."

Gareth and Ranulf strode from the room deep in conversation with each other, leaving Victoria and Walter behind in the solar.

Walter began pacing. "Brother Thomas has a lot to answer for. He got the date wrong, there was no siege by Scots or by anyone else." He stopped in front of the niche and scowled at the box. "And, after all we've been through, the damn amulet doesn't work."

"You don't know that, not for sure." Victoria righted an overturned chair and sat down. "Not everything turned out badly. It looks to me like you and Elwyna have made up."

Walter's scowl disappeared and he beamed at her. "Yeah. We have. I apologized—"

"For what?"

"I'm not sure, but it worked. Elwyna forgave me, and I"—Walter's cheeks took on a rosy hue—"I taught her how to French kiss. She liked it."

"What's not to like? So the engagement is on?"

"Yes. I asked Lord Ranulf for her hand, and he granted his permission, although he said his blessing might not be enough. He is her guardian, but, as her brother, Gareth apparently has the final say."

"Elwyna has the final say," Victoria reminded him.

Walter walked to the window and looked out. "I know that. But I want to do this right, in accordance with the customs of the time."

"Speaking of time, you haven't told them yet, have you? That we are from the future?"

Turning around, Walter faced her. "No. Did you tell Lord Gareth?"

Victoria shook her head. "No. I was going to, but he wasn't in a talkative mood this morning. Why didn't you tell them?"

Walter shoved his fingers through his hair. "It's not an easy subject to bring up. What if they don't believe us?"

"You said everyone in this age believed in magic."

"They do, or did. Now that the amulet is a bust, they may not be so willing to believe in another kind of magic."

"Just because the castle was not magically restored in a split second does not mean the amulet isn't magic. Everyone agrees it worked for hundreds of years. Gareth may be right."

"About it being a slow-acting curse remover?" Walter shook his head. "I don't think so."

"Well, then, maybe there is more to it. Maybe something else has to happen before the amulet can do its thing."

"Like what? Say a few magic words, for instance? I don't think so. There is nothing in the legend of Avondel about any magic except the amulet," Walter said peevishly. He turned around and looked at Victoria, his trademark scowl on his face once more. "If I hadn't met Elwyna, this whole trip would have been a waste of time and money."

"Walter—"

"The castle is not going to be any more repairable

next week than it was before we came here. As soon as I get back to Seattle, I'm going to sell it. If no one will buy it, I'll give it away. No sense in throwing good money after bad."

"Walter, stop worrying about the damn castle. I know what you're doing: you're fixating on Avondel because you don't want to do what needs to be done. You have to tell Elwyna where and when you're from, and you have to do it today. You can't just whisk her eight hundred years into the future without warning her. Elwyna is entitled to a choice."

Walter's scowl faded, replaced by a look of terror. His face turned the same gray shade as the wall he leaned against. Victoria raised her brows. She had never seen Walter afraid before, not even when Ranulf had threatened him with death. "Walter? Are you all right?"

"No, I am not all right. I'm scared spitless. What if Elwyna chooses to stay behind? I know I could stay with her, but I don't want to stay in the past. I can't. I'm nobody here, and I'm too old to start over. Knight training starts when a boy is eight years old. I'm thirty-three, Victoria. I can't make it in this time. If I stay, I'll be a poor relation, and, after a year or two, Elwyna will loose all respect for me."

"Oh, I don't think—"

"Yes. She will. And I will lose respect for myself. I don't want to be poor. I *like* being rich and powerful, Victoria." Walter had the decency to look ashamed of himself.

"I know you do," said Victoria, giving him a pat on the shoulder. "But I thought you loved the Middle Ages."

"I do . . . as long as they are eight hundred years in the past. This is not my time, Victoria. I am a modern man, and I want to live in my time. I will still sponsor the Medieval Fair every year, of course—think what a help Elwyna will be with that."

"Walter. Tell her."

"Oh, all right. I will. You have to tell Gareth. We might as well do it together."

"He won't care. Gareth does not want anything more to do with me. He still thinks I'm a witch, and that I am the wrong witch for him."

"I think you're wrong about that. I've seen the way he looks at you."

She had, too. That look he had given her minutes ago probably meant he was sorry they had ever met. "I'm not going to argue with you, Walter. Come on, let's find the others and get this over with."

It took some time for them to locate everyone, but eventually Gareth, Ranulf, Elwyna, and Thomas were all seated at tables in the great hall. Victoria had retrieved her suitcase from the lady chapel. It was on the table in front of her, along with her purse.

"Well," said Walter, wiping the palms of his hands on his tunic. "Victoria and I have something to tell you."

"You are wizards," said Gareth, folding his arms across his chest.

"No," said Walter. "We are not wizards. However, we are acquainted with a wizard, one Tobias Thistlewaite by name. Tobias brought us here to Avondel. We come from a different place and . . . we are from a different time."

Four pairs of eyes stared at Walter.

"Walter is trying to tell you that we traveled through time to get here," said Victoria. "We came from the future. From the year two thousand one, to be exact."

"That cannot be true!" Thomas blurted.

Walter smiled at him. "Victoria didn't believe in time travel either, not until she was on the way here."

"Not even then, Thomas," said Victoria. "Not until we got here. But it really happened."

"Travelers from the future?" said Ranulf. "How is that possible?"

"A wizard . . . magic . . . 'tis possible," said Gareth.

"The things you found in my purse, Gareth—those are things that do not exist in this time but do exist in my time." Victoria looked from Gareth to Ranulf. "So are my suitcase and the things in it."

"Show them your clothes, Victoria," Walter suggested. "And your cell phone."

Victoria opened her suitcase, took out her skirt suit and held it up. "In my time, women wear short skirts, like this."

Elwyna reached for the skirt. Victoria handed it over, then picked up her cell phone. "And we talk to one another at great distances with telephones, like this." She held up a pair of Levis. "Women and men both wear pants like these. They are called blue jeans."

Ranulf remained silent, staring blankly at the items Victoria pulled from her suitcase. Elwyna began rummaging through Victoria's suitcase, pulling out other items of clothing and holding them up to her body. Thomas picked up the cell phone and began punching the numbers. No sound came from the phone to startle him; Victoria knew the battery must have run down days ago.

"Why did you come here?" asked Gareth, his voice cool. "To this time, and this place?"

"Walter owns Castle Avondel," said Victoria. "He bought it two years ago."

"Two years before we came here, that is," said Walter. "I bought the castle intending to restore it. But I couldn't fix it up. The stones would not stay on top of one another; the mortar crumbled as soon as it was set. No matter how we tried to repair Avondel, nothing worked. The castle was cursed."

Frowning, Thomas put the phone down. "You mean the curse lasts for eight hundred years? But how can that be? Gareth has recovered the magic amulet and restored it to the solar. The curse should end, if not today, then soon."

"Yes, that is a puzzle," said Walter. "Maybe the amulet disappears again, sometime between now and two thousand one. Or maybe Gareth would not have found the amulet if Victoria and I had not come along."

"That must be it," agreed Thomas. "Remember, my lord? Your plan to locate the amulet had a weakness. We needed Victoria so that we could question the people of Darkvale about the amulet without raising suspicion."

Victoria glanced at Gareth. He looked her in the eye, a look that dared her to accuse him of using her. She shrugged and kept silent.

Walter continued. "We cannot know what happens between now and . . . later. When we return to Castle Avondel in two thousand one, if the hole in the tower is fixed, I will know the curse is over. But if the castle is the same way I left it . . . I don't know what that will mean. I confess I am not clear on how magic and time travel and curses work. In our time, we have forgotten about magic."

"There is no magic in the future?" Thomas was shocked. "Then I, for one, would not want to go there. I want there to be fairies, and elves, aye, even dragons and witches. Life is more interesting with magic."

"You may be right, Thomas," said Walter. "But we do have compensations. Medicine that cures most diseases. Wagons that travel without the need of horses . . ."

"We fly like birds from place to place in carriages with wings. And women are men's equals, not their chattel," added Victoria. "A wife is her husband's partner, not his servant. Remember that, Elwyna."

Elwyna dropped the green silk teddy she was examining. "Partner?" she asked, her eyes wide. "Walter, is that true?"

"Yes." He shot a fulminating look at Victoria. "I had planned to tell her that. Later."

"I'll bet. Fifty or sixty years later," muttered Victoria.

Elwyna looked from Walter to Gareth. "Brother, Walter has asked me to be his wife, and I have accepted. But I did not know that would mean I would never see you again." She appeared to be on the verge of tears.

Walter put his arms around her shoulders. "Don't think about that now, darling. Let me finish telling you about the wizard. I met Tobias at my annual Medieval Fair, and—"

"What is a medieval fair?" asked Elwyna, sniffling.

"People in our time are fascinated by this time, which we call the Middle Ages, or the medieval age. I sponsor a fair each year which honors your time and traditions. We dress in clothes like the ones you wear; we prepare food like the food you eat; and we have jousts. With wooden swords, you understand. No one gets hurt."

Victoria chimed in. "At the fair Walter met Tobias Thistlewaite, the wizard with the time travel agency."

"Yes. Tobias convinced me that he could take me back in time—for a price. I wanted to come to this time because I knew about the amulet. Victoria had given me a book that told the story of Aethelwyn's amulet and the siege of Avondel."

"There was not a siege," Ranulf objected. "I did not besiege Avondel."

Walter nodded. "There were several errors in the book as it turned out. But I thought if I could come back before the amulet disappeared, I could make sure it stayed put. As long as the amulet was at Avondel, the siege would fail, and the castle would be saved. But we miscalculated the time, thanks to another error in the book, and we arrived too late."

"Since we were here and had to stay until Tobias came to get us, Walter decided we should spend the time looking for the amulet." Victoria turned to Ranulf. "That is why we came to Darkvale and began asking questions about it."

"Now Aethelwyn's amulet is back where it belongs. I hope that means I will be able to restore the castle when I return to my own time," said Walter.

"How can you babble on about your castle? You are leaving me!" wailed Elwyna, obviously at the end of her patience.

"Elwyna, dearest, you know I want you to go with me."

"I am not certain I want to go with you. I will be a stranger. I will not know your customs."

"You can learn. I will help you adjust, and so will Victoria. Won't you?" Walter shot a pleading look in her direction.

Victoria hesitated, until she realized she was waiting for Gareth to ask her to stay. Fat chance. She smiled at Elwyna. "Of course I will," she said. "You'll like the future, Elwyna; it's a much better time for women. As Walter says, everything will be all right."

The stormy look on Elwyna's face told Victoria Walter had some more convincing to do. Sure enough, Elwyna rounded on Walter. "What if I want to stay here? With my brother. I have not seen him for twelve years, and now that we are reunited, you want me to leave him? To never see him or my home ever again?"

Sobbing, Elwyna ran from the hall. Walter started after her, but Gareth grabbed his arm. "Let her go. You have told us an incredible story. She—we all need time to think about what you have said."

"Oh, yeah," said Walter. "I guess you're right."

Gareth followed Elwyna, motioning Thomas and Ranulf to go with him.

When they were alone, Victoria looked at Walter. "Well. That didn't go very well, did it?"

"That was a lot for them to take in. I never thought about taking Elwyna away from her family. What do you think she will do? What would you do if you were in her place?"

"I would want to be with the man I love," Victoria said decisively.

Walter breathed a huge sigh. "Thank God. I only hope Elwyna feels the same way. Are you really going to stay in the past? We had better think up a story to tell Aunt Crystal."

"I was speaking hypothetically."

"Bull. I know you, Victoria. You are in love with Gareth."

"Yes. But he is not in love with me. Gareth is not about to ask me to stay."

Elwyna paced back and forth in the solar. Thomas and Ranulf had left, and now Gareth and his sister were alone. "Walter will not stay in this time. He wants me to go with him to Se At El. To the year two thousand one."

"Aye," said Gareth.

"But I do not want to leave you. We have been apart for so long, and now that we have found each other again . . . Oh, Gareth, what should I do?"

"I cannot tell you, Elwyna. You must follow your heart."

"But my heart wants to stay with you, and it wants to go with him. I cannot choose between you." Elwyna burst into tears.

"Dear sister, we have been apart for years, and yet you were always in my thoughts and in my heart."

" 'Twas the same for me," she said, hiccuping.

"Then it will be the same if we are parted again. We will always have each other here." Gareth touched his heart.

"Oh, Gareth, thank you. I love you. And I love Walter."

"Go to him. He will want to know you are going with him."

When she had gone, Gareth climbed the stone stairs to the top of the round tower. When he reached the parapet, he stood and looked over the barren fields and the encroaching forest. Victoria had been right. There was much work to be done.

He had hoped that once the amulet was returned, magic alone would restore the castle and lands of Avondel.

Magic. Had it ever existed? But for the strange tale told by Walter, Gareth would have had no trouble denying the very existence of magic. He had never seen a fairy or an elf, or a fire-breathing dragon. Gareth grinned ruefully, remembering that he had told Victoria he had slain two dragons. That was one lie Victoria had never called him on. If he had not been faced with proof of travel through time, Gareth could have convinced himself that luck was the only thing that had kept Avondel safe from harm.

But then he would have to admit that Victoria had not used magic to charm him. He would have to acknowledge that what he felt for her was not lust, not a temporary passion induced by a witch's spell.

Gareth would have to admit that he loved Victoria.

The amulet only works its magic if the lord and lady of Avondel love one another.

Eighteen

That night, after a meal provided by Ranulf and cooked over open fires in front of the tents, Elwyna and Victoria retired to the castle. They had spent the afternoon cleaning a chamber to sleep in, and finding the linens and other items to make it comfortable. Since there had not been a siege, most of the castle furnishings remained, not necessarily clean, or whole, or where they were supposed to be, but there. There were chests filled with clothes and blankets—a bit musty, but still serviceable.

The men remained outside the curtain wall, preparing to spend the night in the tents.

"I want a bath," said Victoria. "Preferably a hot one. Is that possible?"

"Aye. Thomas and I found the copper tub yesterday, and the cauldron used to heat water. They are in the kitchen."

Pulling her suitcase behind her, Victoria followed Elwyna through the castle to a chamber almost as large as the great hall. The kitchen boasted two huge fireplaces on opposite ends of the room. Various pots and utensils were scattered about. Victoria headed for the oval tub sitting in front of one of the fireplaces.

"The fire is banked but not out, and Thomas and

Ulrich brought in plenty of wood yesterday." Elwyna poked the embers with a metal rod until they glowed, then began adding sticks of wood. A cauldron hung from a hook on the end of a moveable iron arm attached to the interior wall of the fireplace.

"Where do you get water?"

"There is a cistern on the roof of the kitchen wing," said Elwyna. "Water is piped through the walls, and comes out there." She pointed to a copper pipe protruding from the wall. "Turn the spigot and the water will flow."

Victoria picked up a pot and filled it with water. She carried it to the cauldron and poured it in. It took several trips before the cauldron was full. When she was finally soaking in the tub, she sighed with pleasure. "This is wonderful. A hot meal and a hot bath, both on the same day. What more could anyone want?"

"You want Gareth," said Elwyna, bluntly. "Walter told me you are in love with my brother. That is why you seduced him."

"Walter has a big mouth," Victoria muttered. She did not feel like discussing her disastrous affair with a happily engaged woman.

"Did he speak true?"

Victoria didn't answer her. She couldn't speak around the lump in her throat. She nodded.

"Oh, Victoria. I am sorry. You are weeping again because of my brother."

Clearing her throat, Victoria said, "No, I'm not. I got soap in my eyes, that's all."

"What are you going to do?" asked Elwyna.

"About what?"

"Gareth. You cannot leave him here. Alone. With no one to love him."

"He does not love me, Elwyna. Gareth has made that very clear."

"But he must love you. He made love with you."

"That was lust. Lust. Love. Two different, although sometimes overlapping emotions, Elwyna. In Gareth's case, pure lust. No overlap."

Elwyna looked doubtful. "Are you sure?"

Victoria shrugged. "He is. And in this situation, his opinion is the only one that counts. You mustn't worry about him being alone, Elwyna. I'm sure he will find a woman to love, a virtuous woman who will love him." Her rendition of the word "virtuous" might have been a trifle waspish, but all in all, Victoria thought she was handling Elwyna's painful questions with dignity and grace.

"But what about you? Will you find someone else to love?"

"Sure. That won't be a problem," Victoria gave up on dignity in favor of an out-and-out lie. She stood up and reached for one of the linen towels Elwyna had found in a chest in the solar. "Hand me my nightshirt, will you please? It's right on top in my suitcase."

Elwyna opened the suitcase and took out the cotton-knit nightshirt. " 'Tis soft," she said. "Will I sleep in something like this when we are in Sea At El?"

"Oh, there are even softer things than this," said Victoria, dropping the shirt over her head. "When we get home we'll go shopping, first thing. You will need a complete new wardrobe. Not to mention a wedding dress."

"Walter said we would get married right away. He said there is a place—Lass Gave Us?"

"Las Vegas." Walter *was* in a hurry. She almost told Elwyna to hold out for a less tacky wedding, but Elwyna would be so dazzled by all the wonders of her future world, she probably wouldn't notice. And she was eager to be bedded. "The place he told you about is called Las Vegas. I'm ready for bed. Are you?"

Elwyna nodded, and they climbed the stairs together.

The next morning when Victoria awoke, her first thought was "two more days." Tobias would be arriving the day after tomorrow to take them to April 21, 2001.

She did not want to go.

She had to go. She did not have a choice.

Victoria waited all that day and the next for Gareth to say something to her, anything at all. If he was consciously avoiding her, he was doing a very good job of it. Gareth had managed not to say one word to her in two days.

Gareth, Ranulf, and Walter had spent hours tramping over the fields, still blanketed in mist. Elwyna said they were talking about fodder and manure. Elwyna was passing the time trying to make the castle more comfortable for Gareth before they left him behind.

Thomas was helping Ranulf's knights pack up their tents and equipment in preparation for a return to Darkvale. It had been decided that the squire would go with Ranulf, armed with a list of items and servants that Elwyna had decided were needed to make the castle livable for Gareth. Ranulf's party would leave tomorrow, after seeing the time travelers off.

Everyone seemed intent on keeping busy, using whatever activity presented itself to avoid thinking about what would happen with the next sunrise. It seemed that all of them had tacitly agreed tomorrow would be a sad day, a day of farewell.

Tobias would arrive early in the morning. Around the same time they had left Seattle, Walter had said.

Victoria sat on the floor in the solar, opposite the niche where the amulet rested. She was wearing her favorite pair of jeans and a yellow cotton sweater. And her Reeboks. Wearing her own twenty-first-century clothes today had been an attempt to leave the past behind—a way to anticipate tomorrow.

If Victoria had thought clothes would change her back into the woman she had been three weeks ago, she had miscalculated. She was changed forever, and she could not change herself back.

Unlike the others, who went from one activity to the next with hardly a break, Victoria could not muster the energy to do anything but think. She would have avoided thinking if she could have figured out a way to do that. Staring at the niche, she wondered for the zillionth time: Why wasn't the magic working? She would feel better about leaving Gareth if she knew Aethelwyn intended to protect him as she had all his ancestors.

Up until his father.

Why had Lord William wanted to destroy the talisman? Because the amulet had lost its magic? Or because he had lost his mind? Or had the magic fled when Juliana gave the amulet to Friar Bartholomew for safekeeping?

Leaning her back against the cold stone wall, Victoria hugged her knees close to her chest and rested her chin on her knees. Three weeks. It seemed a lifetime ago that she had left her condo for a taxi ride to Pioneer Square.

A lifetime, or a nanosecond. Time was a strange thing. It could move as slowly as molasses in winter or as fast as a rocket blasting off for the moon.

Now that it was almost time to go, the way time passed was alternating wildly—one minute whizzed by; the next dragged. Victoria was torn between wanting time to pass quickly, and needing it to wait for her to do . . . something.

Tomorrow she would go back to her condo, back to her job as Walter's personal assistant. She would fuss over Aunt Crystal until her aunt found another husband. Then she would go to the animal shelter and get herself a cat. Or two. She would have a pleasant life, a good life. A life without love, but that would be okay. Better than okay. Love hurt.

Home. In less than twenty-four hours she would be back home. That was what she wanted. No, she ought to be honest with herself. She wanted to stay right where she was, at Castle Avondel. But only if the lord of Avondel loved her enough to make her his wife.

Victoria had thought about proposing to him: *Lord Gareth, I am not a sorceress. I am a woman in love. With you. Will you marry me?* She had taken the initiative in everything else, after all. But as much as she wanted to do something—anything—but sit around and wait to see Gareth for the very last time, Victoria could not bring herself to do that.

One part of her—the reckless part—thought she was a coward, but her sensible side reasoned nothing would be gained by asking the question when she knew the answer would be a resounding "No!" Gareth had rejected her. She would have to be a masochistic idiot to give him the opportunity to do it again.

Victoria had also thought about telling Gareth what a stupid jerk he was, but she did not want that to be his last memory of her. She wanted to be a ghost in his memory, the ghost of a woman who had loved him with all the passion in her heart. Gareth had to know she loved him. There was no need for her to humiliate herself by telling him.

After two days of thinking about it, Victoria had settled on a polite good-bye. That much she owed Gareth, and that much she could give him. She stood up and brushed off the seat of her jeans. She might as well get it over with.

Victoria found Gareth on the parapet, staring at the

forest. "Tobias is coming for us tomorrow morning. Early."

"I know," he said, not bothering to turn around.

So that was the way he was going to be. No problem. She could say good-bye to his back. That might actually make it easier. "Well. I came to find you because I wanted to tell you . . . that is, I came to say . . ."

Victoria took a deep breath and started over. "I wanted to thank you for being my champion and helping me find the amulet. Even if you had your own reasons, I could not have found it without you. And I wanted to tell you that I . . . I had a very nice time."

Gareth spun around. He looked incredulous. "You what?"

"I had a nice time," she said primly. "With you, I mean."

"A *nice* time?" He sounded insulted.

She might have known. Tell a man he was anything less than spectacular, and his ego got all bent out of shape. "Oh, all right. Better than nice. Stupendous, in fact. I had the best time of my life. I will never forget you. I only wish that . . ."

Victoria threw up her hands. "That's it. I can't do this. Not this way. That was not me talking just now. That was the wimpy wuss I've turned into, thanks to you. Nothing I said is true. I did *not* have a nice time. I had a perfectly rotten time. I fell in love with you, and you did not fall back. You thought I was a witch, that I inflamed your passion with magic." She poked him on his chest, aiming for his heart but not sure she hit the target since she was blinded by tears. "For the last time, I'm not, and I didn't. All I used was love. I know—my love isn't good enough for you, you jerk, all because I was not a virgin. I am not a virtuous woman, and now I have to leave, and I'll be dreaming of knights in rusty armor for the rest of my life, and

I will always, always love you." She stopped to take a breath.

Gareth was staring at her, his eyes wide, his mouth hanging open. He looked stupid. For some reason, that made her feel a whole lot better. She wiped away the tears streaming down her face. "Well, that's it. That's what I had to say. Now I've said it, so I'll be going." Victoria took a step backward. "I'm leaving now, Gareth." She took another step away from him. "You will never see me again."

Gareth did not move.

"Okay. Bye. I hope you will be very h-happy." Her voice cracked. Victoria turned and fled down the stairs.

"Victoria, wait!"

Victoria pretended she hadn't heard him and ran faster. Gareth caught up with her, but not until she had reached the door to the bailey. Before he could say anything, the door opened, and Walter ushered Friar Bartholomew into the hall.

"Look who is here, you guys. Friar Bartholomew. He's come to see how things are going with you, Lord Gareth."

Gareth came to a halt immediately behind Victoria. She could feel his hot breath on the back of her neck. "Hi," she said inanely. "Nice to see you again."

"I see you found her," the friar said to Gareth. Friar Bartholomew was looking Victoria up and down. After he completed his perusal, he did not mention her clothes but smiled and said, "Lady Victoria, I rode your donkey here from Donscroft."

"Hilary? Thank you, but I . . . I won't be needing her anymore. You may keep her."

The friar's face fell. "You are leaving Avondel?"

"Yes. Tomorrow morning. Walter and I are going home. Elwyna is going with us." Victoria tried to look as if she were thrilled at the prospect, but her trembling chin probably gave her away. It wasn't easy to lie to a friar.

"Elwyna and I are getting married," said Walter.

"Congratulations," said Friar Bartholomew. Turning to Gareth, he asked, "Has the amulet been placed in the solar?"

"Aye," said Gareth.

"And yet the curse is not lifted. The mist still enshrouds the castle and environs." The friar looked from Gareth to Victoria. Something on their faces must have alerted him. "Have we interrupted something?"

"Oh, no," said Victoria. "I was telling Lord Gareth good-bye and thanking him for his help, but I was all done."

"Yes, you did interrupt us," said Gareth. "If you will excuse us, I have something to say to Victoria." Grabbing her hand, he hauled her up the stairs, moving so fast her feet barely touched the steps.

Only when they reached the solar did he let her go. He pulled her inside the chamber, closing the door behind him. "I told you to wait for me."

Victoria backed away from him. "I heard you. I chose to ignore you."

He came after her, striding across the room until he was only inches away from her. "What did you mean, you love me?"

"I mean I *love* you, you dolt. I don't think that statement needs further explanation. I. Love. You. That's pretty darn clear, in my opinion. What do you think I mean?" Victoria could hear her voice rising. Shrill, shriller, shrillest. She was on the verge of hysteria; she knew it, but she couldn't seem to do anything about it. He must think she was crazy, babbling on about love. No, Gareth was the crazy one. Why did he want to torture her? Hurt, Victoria could not bear to look at him. She let her head fall forward, to rest on his broad chest.

Gareth took her by the shoulders. He gave her a little shake. "Victoria. Listen to me. Do you want to be my wife?"

Her head came up fast, almost clipping him on the chin. "What kind of question is that? Do I want to be your wife? Is that a hypothetical question? Or do I mean rhetorical? It certainly is not a proposal." She narrowed her eyes. "You aren't proposing, are you?"

"Aye. I am." Taking both of her hands in his, Lord Gareth of Avondel sank to his knees before her. "I love you, Victoria. I want you to be my wife."

This cannot be real, she thought. "I'm dreaming," said Victoria.

"Not a dream, Victoria. But it will be my dream come true if you say yes."

Her heart was beating so hard and fast, Victoria knew it could not be broken any longer. "Are you sure you love me? What about all that virtuous woman sh— stuff?"

Gareth rose to his feet and took her in his arms. "You are wise, courageous, and loyal. You have every virtue I admire, every virtue a noble woman could have. You honor me with your love, Victoria. Please stay with me. If you leave me, there will be no magic at Avondel. Now, or ever."

"No magic?" said Victoria dreamily, feeling as if she might levitate. Of course there was magic. Gareth *loved* her.

"Not without you. When we were at Donscroft, Friar Bartholomew told me that the magic amulet does not work unless the lord and lady of Avondel love each other. If you go, Avondel will never be restored, because I will never love another."

"Oh, Gareth. I will never love another, either. I will marry you." She stood on tiptoe to reach his mouth.

Gareth met her halfway and their lips joined in a gentle, forgiving kiss, a sweet, soft kiss that lasted only long enough for Victoria to use her teeth and tongue to coax Gareth into making the kiss deeper, hotter, more arousing.

When the kiss ended, Gareth gasped, "You are inflaming my passion."

"That was my intent. You inflamed me first, when you told me you loved me and asked me to marry you. That brings up a question: how do we do that? Get married, I mean."

"We will—"

There was a pounding on the door. "Victoria! Gareth! Are you in there? What's going on? Is everything all right?"

Gareth strode to the door, keeping Victoria bound to his side. He opened the door. Walter and Elwyna stood outside the solar with identical worried looks on their faces. "Everything is perfect," Gareth told them. "Victoria has agreed to be my wife."

"Well, I'll be . . . Congratulations! Elwyna, did you hear that? There's going to be a wedding at Avondel." Walter snatched Victoria away from Gareth and whirled her around.

"I heard," said Elwyna, her voice gleeful. "Can there not be two weddings? Friar Bartholomew can hear our vows. We will not have to wait one more night, Walter."

"Where is the friar? We will say our vows now, today before one more moment passes," said Gareth with flattering eagerness.

"Now?" said Victoria, looking down at her blue jeans. "I can't get married now. I don't have anything to wear."

* * *

As it happened, Ranulf had brought a chest filled with Elwyna's clothes, and the two brides were suitably and beautifully gowned when they spoke their vows.

Walter offered to give Victoria away. When the blank looks made him understand that custom was not yet part of the ceremony, he settled on giving Gareth and Victoria the chest of gold as a wedding present. "I was going to use it to pay Elwyna's fare, but now I won't need it. Mrs. Harrington can use Victoria's ticket."

A wedding supper followed the brief ceremony, attended by the newlyweds, Lord Ranulf, Thomas, the friar, and the knights from Darkvale.

At the table, Victoria told Walter, "Tell Aunt Crystal not to worry about me, will you? And see that she gets my condo and my four-oh-one-K. Oh, my goodness, I just had a terrible thought. If I don't come home, Crystal may think you did something to me."

"No, she won't. You can write Crystal a note and explain all about—"

"Time travel? Magic?" Victoria asked.

"Yeah. Why not? Your aunt is a firm believer in magic. One of the few in the twenty-first century. Why else would she keep getting married? Don't worry about Crystal, I'll take care of her."

After dinner, Walter and Elwyna went to the chamber Victoria and Elwyna had shared the night before. Victoria followed her husband to the solar. She and Gareth undressed slowly, savoring each heated glance, each touch, not hurrying.

"Time, Gareth, my love. We have all the time in the world now." Victoria kissed him, slowly, tenderly, satisfied to be in his arms now and for thousands of nights to come.

* * *

Time moved slowly all through the night, as the two lovers joined together time and time again. When at last they were content to lie entwined in each other's arms, Gareth spoke.

"The men—all those men you made love to in See At El—"

Victoria raised her head from his shoulder and looked at him. *"All?* Two, Gareth, my love. There were only two."

"Those two men have not yet been born."

"True," Victoria agreed, her brows coming together in a puzzled frown. "They won't be born for another eight hundred years."

Gareth smiled complacently, then pulled her head back to his shoulder. "Then I am the first man in your bed."

Shaking with laughter, Victoria said, "More importantly, my noble knight, you will be the last."

The next morning, Gareth shook Victoria awake. "Tobias is here, my darling wife. Dress quickly. We must go and say good-bye to Elwyna and Walter."

When they reached the bailey, they found the time-travel agency nestled between the lady chapel and the curtain wall, looking as if it had always been there. Elwyna and Walter were talking to Tobias. Walter caught sight of them. "I've been explaining to Tobias that Elwyna is taking Victoria's place on the return trip."

"No substitutions," said Tobias, his ginger mustache quivering. "And no postponements."

"We are ready to go, my good man. I paid for two, and you will be carrying two. I do not see the problem here. This woman is my wife. Victoria has married the lord of Avondel. Victoria stays. Elwyna goes with me. You would not separate married couples, would you?"

Tobias looked from Walter to Victoria and back. "You each found your heart's desire?"

"We did."

"Well, why didn't you say so?" Beaming, Tobias opened the door to the agency. "Come right in, Mr. and Mrs. Harrington."

"Wait, we haven't said good-bye," said Elwyna, throwing her arms around Gareth's neck and kissing him on the cheek. She released her brother and grabbed Victoria. "Good-bye, sister. Be happy!" She entered the shop.

"I will be," said Victoria, laughing. "Haven't any of you noticed?"

"Noticed what?" said Walter, stopping on the threshold of Any Time, Any Place, and looking around.

"No time," said Tobias. "Time to go." The door closed, and the travel agency disappeared.

Gareth blinked. "That happened fast," he said. "They are really gone. Gone to the future."

"Are you sad?" asked Victoria, winding her arm through his.

"Nay. I will miss Elwyna, but I have you. With you by my side, I will never be sad again." Gareth led Victoria toward the castle. "Now, 'tis early yet. Too early for a lord and his lady to be up. Let us return to bed."

"Gareth. Stop leering at me and look around. Don't you see?"

"See what?" he said, not taking his gaze away from her. "I have eyes only for my lady love."

"Look at the sunshine, Gareth. There is glorious sunshine everywhere. The mist is gone. Aethelwyn's magic has returned to Avondel. Gareth, we must take very good care of the amulet."

"Aye, we will," said the lord of Avondel to his virtuous lady as he led her back to their chamber. "But you and I will have magic even without the talisman. We have love, Victoria, and you have taught me that love is the best magic of all."

ABOUT THE AUTHOR

Linda Kay lives in Louisiana. She loves to hear from readers and you may write to her c/o Zebra Books. Please include a self-addressed stamped envelope if you wish a response.